PRAISE FOR

PRAISE FOR FATE AND FURY

This romantasy is going to take readers by storm.
  –@readingwithsammy

A thrilling and darkly seductive entry into the world of Slavic-inspired romantasy.
  —@bookcandlelight

I am destroyed! I am not okay! I LOVED this book! ... An excellent blend of romance and plot with conflict brewing all over the place...a really sexy, haunting, forbidden romance.
  —@sarahs_reading_books

One of my BEST reads of the year! Fast-paced with incredible world-building and storytelling, this book is a fantasy lover's dream. 10/10. A masterpiece. Highly recommend to everyone—don't sleep on this one!"
  @chaptersandcomfort

This book is an absolute masterpiece of dark fantasy and forbidden romance, and it's one of those rare stories that grabs hold of your heart and refuses to let go... I am OBSESSED.
  –Rebecca Young, Goodreads Reviewer

PRAISE FOR THE SEVEN SINS SERIES

- WINNER, 2022 Gold Moonbeam Award for Best Book Series
- WINNER, 2022 Silver IPPY Award for Young Adult Fiction
- WINNER, 2021 North Carolina Indie Author Award in YA Fiction
- FINALIST, 2021 & 2022 Foreword INDIES Award in YA Fiction
- SHORTLISTED, The Manly Wade Wellman Award for Science Fiction and Fantasy

This book is absolutely unputdownable. It's all my favorite things about high-stakes fantasy and dystopian... Badass, rebellious characters. DEEPLY forbidden love. Swords, hand to hand combat fight scenes. Secret societies, escapes, withstanding torture... I didn't even realize how much I'd missed books like this until I fell into this one.

— MICHELLE HAZEN, AUTHOR OF *BREATHE THE SKY*

A beautifully crafted story with so many intense moments I couldn't stop reading. This is the best book I've read in a long time.

— YA BOOKS CENTRAL

Thrilling, heart-wrenching, and blood-pumping.

— KARISSA LAUREL, AUTHOR OF *THE*
STORMBOURNE CHRONICLES

A romantic dystopian with a fantastic—and unexpected —twist ... *Seven Sins* is powerful, sexy, hopeful, and unsettling.

— HEIDI AYARBE, AWARD-WINNING AUTHOR
OF *FREEZE FRAME*

An absolutely mind-blowing, spine-tingling, action-packed extravaganza ... an electrifying, imaginative, phenomenally well written book. The tension, banter and angst blazes.

— EMERALD BOOK REVIEWS

With an intriguing world, an impossible love story, and characters I both loved and loved to hate, the stakes are high. What if love was a death sentence? ... A series everyone should know about.

— M. LYNN, USA TODAY BESTSELLING AUTHOR
OF *THE QUEENS OF THE FAE* SERIES

ISBN (Pbk.) 978-1-961469-10-5
(Ebook) 978-1-961469-09-9

BLACK ORCHID
BOOKS

Published by Black Orchid Books
Wilmington, NC
Cover Design by Lisa Amowitz

One for the fire. Two for the storm.

Fate and Fury

Fate and Fury

BOOK ONE IN
THE BONE MOON DUOLOGY

Emily Colin

BLACK ORCHID
BOOKS

One for the fire
Two for the storm
Three for the black dog that guards against harm
Four for the silence that follows the dark
Five for the cold one whose path is stark
Six for the dream that brings secrets to light
Seven for the curse that spreads blight through the night
Eight for the loss that cuts beyond price
Nine for the heart carved wholly from ice
Ten for his tears
The rest for her fears
Eleven for the blood that has tasted the blade
Twelve for the one who breaks yet is bold
Thirteen for the story that remains untold

—SHADOW AND DIMI BONDING VOW

Vila to Shadows, as dawn slips to dusk
Never Shadow to Dimi, betrayal of trust
In the slow slide to hate, so come secrets to light
Fuel for the war, for the unnatural fight
So will they forfeit what they love the most:
Lost demon. Witchfire. Wandering ghost.
So shall she burn as she brings his demise
The Dark will fall. The shadow will rise.

—PROPHECY FROM THE BOOK OF THE LIGHT
MAGIYA LIBRARY

AUTHOR'S NOTE

This is a book that jumps right into the story and builds the world around you. I've included a Glossary and Pronunciation Guide at the end, so please feel free to check it out!

Happy reading. I can't wait for you to meet Niko and Katerina!

I

KATERINA

In Katerina Ivanova's twenty-one years, she had been many things.

A witch, certainly. The strongest Dimi that the dukedom of Iriska had known in three centuries, able to command all four elements rather than just fire, wind, water, or earth.

A protector, sworn alongside her blood-bonded Shadow to defend Iriska from Grigori demons, hungry to devour their souls.

A secret-keeper, along with everyone else in her village of Kalach. For if the Kniaz—the duke who ruled Iriska and its Seven Villages—discovered what Katerina could do, he would covet her beyond measure. Damn the Trials; he would have Reaped her years ago for his own, and left Kalach without its best defender.

And above all, a liar and a traitor. For if Baba Petrova, the Elder Council, and—Saints forbid—the Kniaz himself knew the truth of what her heart harbored, her death would be swift.

But never, except for once, long ago, had she been weak. Her mother had died because of it, and Katerina had never forgiven herself. Now here she was, preparing to let Baba bind her magic. Hobbling herself on purpose, and risking the death of the man she loved most.

She watched as Baba knelt in front of the fireplace, dipping her fingertips into a bowl of ash. The ancient Dimi traced a circle on her cottage's wooden floorboards, just large enough to hold Katerina and her Shadow. Above her, from the ceiling's blackened crossbeams, swayed thin-skinned braids of garlic, for healing, and ropes of gray-green sage, for purification.

There would be no healing what Baba was about to do to her, not until the old Dimi decided to break the binding. As for purification, as far as Katerina was concerned, it was far too late. She'd lost her heart to a man who was off-limits long ago, and every time she looked at him, she was reminded of how much she craved his body. Good luck purifying *that* with a handful of dried herbs and a prayer to the long-dead Saints.

Unable to help herself, she glanced across the hearth at her Shadow. Eight years ago, she and Niko had stood in this very room, beside a cauldron seething with ink and blood, sealing their vows as Shadow and Dimi. Then, he had regarded her with barely tempered eagerness; now, his expression was guarded, his face carefully blank. He didn't like this any better than she did, but he would endure it, for the sake of the village. Of the two of them, he had far more to lose by rebelling.

Baba's knobbly finger completed the circle, and the power within it snapped into place: a low hum that set Katerina's teeth on edge.

Next would come the rune. Then the binding spell.

She was running out of time.

Katerina drew a deep breath, letting the layered air fill her lungs: the burn of herbs, the bite of the oil Niko used to cure his blades, the smoke of the rowan-fire as it curled upward. "There has to be another way," she said for the umpteenth time since

Baba and the Elders had demanded she do the unthinkable. "I can control myself. If you trust me to fight for Iriska, then surely you believe I can command my gifts."

The words emerged haughty, a challenge rather than an entreaty, and Niko arched one dark eyebrow in warning. Along with the Elders, Baba's word was law. Arguing would get Katerina exactly nowhere. And yet she couldn't help herself.

Baba Petrova was a small, gnarled woman who had long fought on the front lines of their war against the Grigori. Her back was bent now, her face wrinkled, and she spent more time training Dimis and Shadows than patrolling the village's borders. Still, her air of authority was formidable. It rolled off her in waves as she straightened and glared at Katerina.

"You are wasting time," she said.

Irritation bubbled through Katerina's veins, and, as if to disprove her point, the fire in the hearth leapt high in response. Now, it was Baba's turn to raise an eyebrow.

Katerina ignored her. "With the rise in attacks, how is it wise to send us to Rivki hobbled, with me only having the use of my fire? What if we encounter demons on the road? Why cripple us like this?"

Next to her, Niko made a disgruntled noise low in his throat, perilously close to his black dog's growl. "Are you insinuating that I can't protect you, Katerina?"

For a Shadow, blood-sworn to fight beside his Dimi and stand between her and evil in his human form or the form of his black dog, there was no greater insult. And Niko was the alpha of the village's Shadow pack. Such an accusation pierced his pride, Katerina knew. And yet—

"We protect each other," she said, meeting his storm-gray eyes. "We fight *together*."

As they would in the Bone Trials at Rivki Island, the seat of

Iriska's dukedom. As they had been commanded by the Kniaz to do.

Baba didn't reply. Instead, she knelt to draw the rune. Freed from her scrutiny, Niko took the moment to mouth, *What are you doing?* at Katerina.

She hazarded a glance at him, then wished she hadn't. He'd tied his hair back with a piece of rawhide, baring the scar that ran from his chiseled jaw to his temple, earned in a fight to protect their village from Grigori invasion. Above it, his eyes gleamed silver in the sunlight, piercing through her defenses as they always did. She couldn't afford for him to look at her like that. Not now, when she had so much to hide.

What I must, she mouthed back, and looked away.

Putting the finishing touch on the rune's complicated angles, Baba stood. "It's because of the rise in Grigori attacks that I must do this," she said. "You know as well as I do that the two of you are Kalach's best defense. We need you here, not at the Kniaz's right hand, great as the honor may be. Perhaps if you didn't want to be summoned to the Trials, you would have endeavored to make yourself less appealing to the Kniaz the last time you delivered the tithe."

Her voice was mild, but Katerina bristled just the same. Held every other year, the Trials pitted a powerful Dimi and Shadow pairing from each of the Seven Villages against each other. Two victorious pairs would advance to the second round the following year, taking the interim twelve months to train. The winning pair would be selected to expand the Druzhina—Iriska's elite warriors and the Kniaz's personal guard against the demons who threatened their borders. And in so doing, leave their village behind.

She had tried so hard to be ordinary each time she and Niko went to Rivki. To avoid drawing undue attention. But the Kniaz had noticed her, anyway. And now here she was, about to submit to a barbaric rite, just because Baba and the Elders didn't believe she had the self-possession to suppress her magic under duress.

Infuriated, Katerina called the wind to lift a spoon from Baba's wooden table, coaxing it to scoop up a bit of sugar and then delicately stir the cup of tea that sat, cooling, in its saucer. The porcelain cup rose, floating through the air until it prodded, insistent, at Baba's hand.

"Not a drop spilled," she said as Baba snatched the teacup from the air with a huff and stomped back to the table to set it down again. "I can more than control my magic. See?"

"That is not the point—" Baba began, but Katerina was out of patience. She called the wind again, this time to send the china in the cabinet rattling and the earth to ripple the floorboards beneath their feet. The flames leapt and churned, threatening to breach the hearth.

"Whether with precision or brute force, I can wield my power as I will. But I had no wish to impress a tyrant." The words were frigid as they left her mouth, ice-tipped. "I did nothing. Niko, tell her."

Her Shadow sighed, broad shoulders heaving beneath the fabric of his linen shirt. "We delivered the grain as promised. And Katerina acted only as a firewitch, nothing more."

Impatiently, Baba motioned for the two of them to step into the circle, atop the rune. "Well, it doesn't matter what he saw in you. He asked for you by name, Katerina. And by extension, your Shadow."

It was one thing for her and Niko to travel to Rivki with the tithe. It was quite another for them to enter into battle, where Katerina's magic would be challenged and tested. Katerina understood the risks, especially now, when Kalach needed her more than ever. Her gifts were the village's best-kept secret; this was the worst possible time for the Kniaz to discover them, with demonic attacks on the rise, when Kalach was under its greatest threat. Not to mention, the consequences of having hidden something this extraordinary for so many years would no doubt be dire.

But that didn't mean she had to be forcibly bound. The idea sent horror curdling through her, as if anticipating a brutal amputation. No matter how many times Niko reminded her it was temporary, nothing more than a safeguard, she couldn't resign herself to it. She'd been lobbying against it for weeks, ever since Baba had come to her with the Elders' decision.

"Please," she said now, a last resort. Tears pricked her eyes, and she fought them back. Being at the mercy of those who wished to bind her magic, torn between her loyalty to Kalach and her autonomy, was bad enough; she'd be damned if she'd let Baba see her cry.

"I'm sorry." Finality marked Baba's voice. "Come, now. The Vila await their Shadows by the river, and the two of you must get on the road if you are to reach shelter before dark."

The kohannya ceremony was the very last thing Katerina wanted to think about right now. Her muscles tensed, and Niko's eyes met hers. *He* probably couldn't wait to get to the river, where his lovely Vila had crafted a paper boat just for him, sealed in red wax and inscribed with runes for romance and fertility, promises of a thousand kisses and caresses. The thought made Katerina want to vomit. And *that,* she definitely couldn't show.

Holding Niko's gaze, she strode to the center of the rune. A moment later, her Shadow followed. He stood facing her, close enough that his leathers brushed her pants.

"Take her hands," Baba instructed.

His eyes never leaving hers, Niko obeyed. His calloused fingers wove through Katerina's, their touch achingly familiar.

As vicious as he could be with a blade, he was gentle with her, as if he held something priceless. As if she were breakable.

Katerina squeezed his fingers hard enough to hurt, but Niko only smiled at her, his full lips rising. How could he smile at a time like this? She wanted to hit him, bite him, send her magic through him like a sharpened arrow—anything to break that perfect composure, meant to reassure her. She wanted to press her lips to his and devour him, and let the world burn.

But that was beyond forbidden. Even thinking about it was a betrayal. Acting on it would have horrific consequences.

It was fortunate Katerina was good at keeping secrets.

"Sant Antoniya, patron saint of Dimis, hear me," Baba intoned. "Sant Andrei, patron saint of Shadows, be with your child now."

Beneath their feet, the rune shuddered. The aftereffects rippled through Katerina's body, and Niko gripped her hands harder, holding her steady. *It will be all right,* he mouthed.

Katerina pressed her lips together and shook her head. How could she allow this, no matter what Baba and the Elders had decreed? Panic gnawed at her bones. She had to leave this circle, she had to stop this—

"Before you stands Katerina Ivanova, your loyal servant." Baba's voice resonated throughout the room, echoing off walls and floor and ceiling. "You have gifted her with powers beyond reckoning, and we are grateful. But now, for the sake of the village she is sworn to protect, we ask your permission to bind all her gifts but one. We ask this in the name of the trifold Saints, as penitents to your grace."

As if in response, Katerina's magic surged. The fire shot upward in the hearth, the water in the kettle bubbling, the shutters rattling as the wind outside began to rage. Niko winced as the force of it hit him, his breath hissing between gritted teeth. *Easy,* he mouthed.

Did he think she was his stallion, Troitze, to be soothed with a command and the gift of an apple? Katerina bared her own teeth at him, dread coiling in her gut as Baba spoke again.

"With salt, we bind Dimi Ivanova's waterwitch." She pulled a pinch of white crystals from the pocket of her dress, scattering them on the rune at Katerina's feet. "With vervain, we bind her windwitch." The dried purple petals fell atop the salt, and a terrible choking sensation seized Katerina, as if a thousand zlydini spirits had hold of her lungs and were clenching their tiny, malevolent fists. She gagged, and Niko's eyes widened in horror. He was speaking now, his voice low and urgent, but Katerina couldn't make out a word. Her ears roared with the beat of her own blood, her mouth filled with the taste of salt-water. She spat, and spat again, but it made no difference. Air, she needed air, she needed—

"With roots of cypress, we bind her earthwitch." Baba's voice was inside Katerina's head somehow, inescapable, threading through bone and sinew. The lemon-spice scent of cypress shavings filled the air as Baba opened her hand and let them fall. "May all three rest, and wake no more until I free them."

The rune flared with heat, the floorboards shuddering. Pain shot through the soles of Katerina's feet and arrowed upward, sharper than anything she'd ever known: the loss of her mother, the slice of a poisoned Grigori blade, the desperate, doomed desire she felt for her Shadow. She shrieked, unable to contain it, and the cypress shavings caught fire before they hit the ground. Somewhere inside the inferno, Niko was shouting: *Stop* and *you're hurting her* and then a fusillade of incomprehensible syllables that ended in her name. Through the falling embers, his face loomed up and then disappeared again, pupils blown wide so that only a rim of silver iris remained. The roar of his black dog filled the air, ripped from his human throat.

It was unthinkable for a Shadow to interfere with Baba Petrova's magic this way, to stand between her and the ceremony she and the Elders had deemed must be done. Baba was their leader, owed deference and respect. But Niko growled louder and louder, the vibration echoing through his body and into his hands where they still gripped Katerina's. His body flickered with the first hints of his Change, a moment before his hands fell away. And then he was moving her, pushing her off the rune and out of the consecrated circle. In the world beyond the agony that tore through every inch of Katerina, as if someone were trying to rip her magic out by the roots, porcelain clattered and smashed. Someone was screaming. She thought it might be her.

Her back hit the wall, knocking the remaining air out of her lungs. Niko pressed against her from head to toe, his body hot and insistent and trembling with a rage she could taste, copperbright on her tongue. But she could taste something else, too: fear, tart and dark as the blackcurrants that grew by handfuls beside the village gates. Fear for *her*.

Niko was suffering. And no one hurt her Shadow and lived.

In the hollow of her throat, the silver amulet that held a drop of Niko's blood throbbed, reminding her of what mattered most. Her deepest fear was losing him. Failing him and watching him fall to the Dark. And yet here she stood, on the verge of surrendering the very gifts she relied upon to defend him.

You are a Dimi, Katerina told herself grimly. *Born into war. So, fight.*

The pain was everywhere, woven into the very fabric of her being. It pierced her heart and throat and belly, as if her magic had shattered into shards of glass that wounded her from the inside out. But she could think past it. She must.

She shut her eyes and sank down, down into the depths of

herself. Past the pain and the heat of the flaming cypress, past Niko's roars of fury and Baba Petrova's commands. In the quiet, she envisioned the roots of her magic, anchored deep in the soil of her soul: red for flame, brown for earth, blue for water, white for wind. In her mind's eye, she fell to her knees and dug her fingers into the soil. *You are mine,* she whispered to her power. *Mine to keep. Mine to command. My gifts from the Saints, and I will not let you go.*

The force that had hold of her magic pulled, insistent, fighting to rip the roots free. But Katerina held fast, with every ounce of strength she possessed. Inch by inch, bit by painful bit, she gained ground, until, with a bellow of fury at being deprived of its prize, the spell let go. The pain retreated with it, her magic anchoring firmly within her once more, until Katerina was alone in her skin again, shaken but whole.

Her eyes flickered open, and she peered over her Shadow's shoulder, blinking. The air still burned, shot through with flecks of fiery cypress. The table had been overturned. And Niko's body was pressed against hers, his back against her front, both of them crowded against the far wall. His arms spread wide, hands touching the plaster on either side of her in a clear gesture of protection. At their feet lay splintered china—Niko's doing, perhaps, in his haste to break the circle and get her away from the rune that fueled the spell.

He was still growling, one long, unbroken burr that would doubtless fill most people with terror. The sound comforted Katerina, as familiar and soothing as a lullaby.

"Let her go," Baba was saying, with the exaggerated patience of someone who had been repeating themselves for quite some time. "This had to be done. And I mean her no harm."

Her Shadow merely snarled, body shaking with the effort to hold his human shape.

Enough was enough. Katerina cleared her throat, which ached as if she'd swallowed ground glass. "I'm all right, Niko," she said. "Stand down."

The growl ebbed, and Niko spun, grabbing her by the shoulders. His eyes were wild, his black hair half-loose from its tie. "Thank the Saints. Are you hurt, Katerina? Are you—"

"I'm all right," she repeated, though she wasn't sure if it was true. Her body still ached with the after-effects of the spell, a fine tremor running through every limb. But Niko didn't need to know that, did he? Not when he was looking at her like she might go to pieces under his hands, crumbling to the floor in a heap of tears and ashes.

Her Shadow's gray eyes narrowed, gaze sweeping over her from head to toe. "Are you," he said again, a statement this time rather than a question.

Inside her, magic stirred: fire, earth, wind, and water, all there to call to her hand. Could he feel it, bound to her as he was?

If so, he didn't say a word. Jaw set, he turned to face Baba. "Is it done?"

Baba gave a curt nod. "I am sorry," she told them both, with a wry glance at the wreckage. "It was never my intention to hurt you. The moment you come home, I will undo the binding. And even with only one of your gifts at your command, you are powerful, Katerina. Trust in that."

Katerina would have to. She had no intention of abandoning her village by unleashing her other gifts in the Trials. But neither did she have any intention of telling Baba the truth: that the spell had failed. That she would ride out to Rivki in possession of her full powers.

There might be demons on the road, after all.

And a Trial of her own to conquer, here in Kalach, before she could ride to meet them.

2

KATERINA

Katerina had always thought the kohannya ceremony was sweet, if silly. For a Dimi like herself, who had the freedom to choose whoever she wished to marry, there was no need to cast a tiny boat into the river that bordered Kalach and wait to see who scooped it up downstream. But for Vila, raised to marry Shadows and perpetuate the Vila and Shadow lines, there was an undeniable romanticism to the tradition. Vila spent weeks crafting their miniature boats, sealing them with wax dyed from red madder, then hand-painting them with runes for love, loyalty to Sant Viktoriya, and steadfast hearts.

The whole village turned out for the annual ceremony, where the Vila launched their boats and waited with bated breath to see which Shadows would pluck them from the water. For while Baba Petrova and the Elders had final authority when it came to marriage pacts, Vila and Shadows' wishes held considerable weight. Kohannya was a time of crushes revealed, of discovering whether love was requited. It was, Katerina thought dryly as she strode down the path to the river, one hand knotted around her horse's reins, a Vila's dream come true.

And today, it was Katerina's nightmare.

"Are you all right?" Next to her, her best friend, Ana, poked Katerina in the side. Never one to sit still, Ana was always in motion—whether it be her hands, her body, or her magic. When the two of them were children, she was always getting in trouble for touching things she shouldn't. Today, apparently that thing was Katerina.

"Ouch!" Rubbing her side resentfully, Katerina tore her gaze from the gathering in the distance, just visible through the copse of trees. "Why does everyone keep asking me that?"

"Oh, I don't know." Ana rolled her eyes. "Let's pick a reason, shall we? Maybe because I've called your name at least three times. Maybe because you're staring straight ahead with a death glare on your face, as if you'd like to light the whole lot of them aflame." She gestured at the crowd clustered on the riverbank, the rays of the early-spring sun breaking through the canopy of evergreens to illuminate her olive skin and the blue-black highlights in her hair.

"Or maybe it's because you just endured a binding ceremony the likes of which hasn't been attempted in our lifetime," she went on, her tone deliberately innocent. "Maybe it's because we could hear your Shadow raising a commotion all the way in the village square. Maybe it's because you look like you're about to fall over, or because when Niko came to collect Alexei for the ceremony, he snapped at my Shadow like he was about to murder someone—"

"Okay, okay." Katerina held up a quelling hand. "I get it. Enough."

Ana was a firewitch, and a powerful one at that. She held up her own hands, a small flame burning above each palm. "You don't get to tell *me* what to do, Katerina Ivanova. And you can pretend to everyone else that you're just fine, but you don't have to put on an act with me."

Sighing, Katerina guided her mare, Mika, around a log that had fallen across the path. The worst of it was, she *did* have to pretend with Ana. There was no way she was going to burden her friend with the knowledge that the spell hadn't worked, and that she had no intention of letting Baba try again. If the truth came out somehow and Baba discovered Ana had known all along, it wouldn't be pretty. "It was awful," she admitted. That much, she could share. "I felt like I was dying. Like an essential part of me was being torn right out of my body. The pain—that's why Niko got so angry. He couldn't stand that it was hurting me."

Ana nodded in sympathy, stepping to the side to make way for a small group of Dimis and Shadows hustling down the path. "I've never heard anyone shout at Baba, much less threaten her like that," she said when they passed, her voice hushed. "It was all we could do to restrain the other Shadows from going to his aid. Can you imagine? They would have ripped that cottage apart."

"We did enough damage on our own." Katerina knotted her hands in Mika's reins, and the mare whickered, sensing her tension. "I suppose destroying Baba's cottage and setting the entire pack of Shadows on a rampage would have been a poor beginning to kohannya."

Her voice was light, but Ana's gaze sharpened, nonetheless. "Is *that* what's gotten you so out of sorts? This silly ceremony?"

They were on dangerous ground now. Katerina shrugged, as if the answer were simple, obvious. "It just seems so frivolous, knowing what's out there. We're ten days from the full Bone Moon. Every day until then, the veil between the living and the dead thins, and the demons find it easier to break through. And the increasing attacks that travelers between villages have reported—the raid on Povorino..." She snorted. "It's like none of that matters to the Vila. Like none of it's *real*. All they have to worry about is tending the children and looking pretty, while we..."

She let her voice trail off, afraid of saying too much. Sounding too bitter, because although everything she'd said held a grain of truth, the real reason that this particular kohannya ceremony made her stomach churn was something she could never, ever speak aloud. Not even to Ana. Not to anyone.

"While we fight on the front lines." Ana finished her sentence. "It's their role, Katerina. They take pride in it. Just as we take pride in protecting Iriska and the world beyond our borders. You can't begrudge them that."

Neither Katerina nor Ana had ever left Iriska. The realm was protected, hidden. Still, though she'd never set foot beyond Iriska's wards, she knew well what lay beyond: a world filled with innocent humans, unaware of the demonic threat that lurked beneath their feet. As a Dimi, it was her job to make sure they *never* knew—to stop the Grigori from overrunning Iriska and spilling, hungry, into the world beyond, where no one had the tools to defend themselves.

It was a heavy burden, but one she was used to carrying. One the Vila would never have to bear. Though the latent gifts that simmered in their blood empowered them to bear Shadowchildren and Vila, they possessed no magic of their own. They were nurturers, not defenders.

"I suppose I can't." Katerina ducked to avoid an overhanging branch. "Maybe I'm just restless. The sooner we go, the sooner I can fail to impress the Kniaz at the Trials and the sooner we can come home." She forced her voice to sound neutral, not to reveal the fact that she was dreading and looking forward to returning to Kalach in equal measure. Because when they returned, the night of the full Bone Moon, Niko would be betrothed to his Vila.

Chosen for him for her beauty and piety, Elena Lisova was everything Niko needed and deserved. She would be loyal to him, faithful.

She would break Katerina's heart.

Romantic love between a Dimi and her Shadow was beyond forbidden. The prophecy in the Book of the Light said so, the one every Shadow, Dimi, and Vila learned from the cradle: if a Dimi and Shadow lay together, demon-infested Darkness would fall upon Iriska and overtake the realm. Dictated by the three Saints to their scribes centuries before, the prophecy was sacred. Defying it was unthinkable.

So Niko could never be Katerina's, not in the way she sometimes dreamed, in the depths of her most secret heart. If he knew she looked at him with the slightest hint of desire, anything beyond the holy bond that tied a Dimi to her Shadow, he would be horrified. And if anyone suspected how Katerina felt about him, the punishment would be swift. She and Niko would be separated, their bond severed, or worse. It would destroy them both.

This was the real reason she was dreading this ceremony. Because today, her Shadow would stand downriver and wait for Elena's boat to sail into his outstretched hands. And the moment he rescued it from the waters and held it high, he'd be acknowledging that he wanted Elena just as much as she wanted him. That their bond wasn't simply dictated by Baba and the Elders, a match made for an alpha Shadow to perpetuate the strength of his bloodline—it was something Niko chose, a future he was proudly claiming as his own.

Katerina wanted him to be happy, more than anything. If marrying Elena and giving her Shadowchildren and little Vila was what he dreamed of, she should support him. But how could she, when the thought hurt more than having her magic nearly torn out of her body by the roots?

Her agony must have shown on her face, because Ana squeezed her free hand in solidarity. "You will come home," she said fiercely. "You will come home, and Baba will unbind your magic, and together we will stand against the Grigori, just like we always have. Whatever threat is rising, we will face it with our Shadows at our side."

Ana didn't voice the unthinkable—that Katerina and Niko would die in the arena. It happened, more often than the Kniaz acknowledged. The purpose of the Trials was to single out the strongest among them. If that meant crippling or even killing their rivals, so be it. A Dimi and Shadow pairing that could not stand against their own, or against whatever horrors lurked in the arena to test them, was unworthy of defending Iriska.

Katerina was spared a response, because as Ana finished speaking, they stepped off the path and into the clearing that bordered the river. It buzzed with activity, crowded with Dimis, Vila, Shadows, and villagers alike. Clouds had gathered, heralding a coming storm, and the air was thick with brine, overlaid with the spicy scent of the rowan-fires that burned by Kalach's borders, to keep the demons away.

Elder Balandin gave an approving nod when she caught sight of Katerina, as if relieved that robbing her of her gifts hadn't reduced her to a sniveling heap. Baba had no doubt reported the havoc they had wreaked on her cottage, and if Ana spoke true, the Elders had heard Niko's vociferous objections for themselves. They had no reason to believe the spell had failed, and Katerina intended to keep it that way.

All of the Elders were looking at her now, their gazes heavy with expectation. Elder Mikhailova gazed up at her from his wheeled chair, hands clasped atop the blanket draped over his withered legs and eyes narrowed as if taking her measure.

Offering him a small smile that she hoped conveyed both resignation and resilience, Katerina tied Mika up and gave the mare a carrot from the saddlebag to keep her happy. Then she and Ana crossed the clearing, joining their fellow Dimis. They stood some way back from the riverbank, in between the cluster of giggling, wide-eyed Vila and the leather-clad, blade-wielding Shadows. Instinctively, she scanned the clearing, looking for Niko, but didn't see him among his brethren.

As their alpha, it was unusual for him to be separated from his pack in a gathering like this. She opened her mouth to ask Ana where Niko had gone after he'd come to collect Alexei, his second in command—but the words died on her lips as her Shadow emerged from the trees, leading Troitze, his ornery, midnight-black stallion. Alexei strode by his alpha's side, head tilted as he took in Niko's last-minute instructions to hold the village in his absence.

Ana had been right: Niko's jaw was tight, his muscles tensed, as if he were striding into battle rather than about to collect a love token made by his soon-to-be-betrothed. Her friend elbowed her, perilously close to the same spot where she'd poked Katerina earlier. "What did I tell you?" she muttered. "Braced for murder."

It was true that, unlike the Shadows who stood downriver, loose-limbed and smiling, Niko looked far less at ease. His gaze roved over the crowd, settling first on his pack, who straightened and came to attention under his scrutiny. It flicked over Katerina, lingering long enough to make sure that she was, indeed, unharmed. Guilt flashed through her at not telling Niko the spell hadn't held—that she was whole. But how could she make him complicit in her deception? Why should they both be punished for her refusal to surrender?

She already kept one secret from her Shadow, after all. What was another?

A hum of excitement arose from the cluster of Vila, and Niko's eyes left her, seeking its source. Elena stood in their midst, her buttercup-yellow gown and matching tresses gleaming, as if the sunbeams that broke through the clouds had done so for her benefit alone. She separated from her sisters and walked toward Niko, her face lit with joy.

Katerina forced herself to watch as her Shadow handed Troitze's reins to Alexei and met Elena in the middle of the clearing. The Vila was as lovely as a storybook princess, with her long, flaxen hair and eyes as blue as the hyacinths that bloomed, defying the lingering touch of winter, on the riverbank at their feet. The perfect disciple of Sant Viktoriya, she was everything Katerina wasn't: demure, soft, willing to bend to please others. Coming to a halt in front of Niko, she lifted her gaze, dimpling prettily, and held her ornate, gold-painted boat up for his inspection. The wind ruffled the loose tendrils of hair around her face, and she brushed it back, twining the strands around one finger before letting them go.

Niko said something to her, but Katerina couldn't make it out. Was he telling the Vila how beautiful she looked? How he'd miss her dearly when he was gone? Maybe, Katerina thought, throat tight with misery, he was confessing how he couldn't wait to be the one to cradle the golden boat in his hands at the end of its maiden voyage—the same hands that had clung to Katerina as if she were something precious in Baba's cottage not two hours before.

Suppressing the jealousy that clawed at her, Katerina looked away. Her gaze swept over the assembled Vila, Shadows, and Dimis, then shifted right, toward the villagers crowded behind the ribbons Baba's acolytes had strung up between the trees.

The kohannya ceremony was much-anticipated throughout Kalach; for weeks, children had traded bets on which Shadows would pluck each Vila's boat from the waters. The little ones jostled for position, clutching boats of their own making: crude hunks of wood that were as likely to sink as swim, painted brightly with the pigments of crushed flowers. Behind them stood tradespeople and teachers, seamstresses and black-smiths, all of whom it was Katerina's job to protect. Farther down the riverbank stood the small Shadows, Vila, and Dimis, watched over by the married Vila whose kohannya days were behind them.

This was what she was fighting for. These people, who trusted her.

She fought for them, and for the Light. For her sacred mission, handed down to her by the Saints: to guard the borders of her village and the realm from demonic incursion. To be a force against the Darkness, with her Shadow's aid.

She had faced demons many times, since childhood, and though she had faith in her ability to vanquish them, they never failed to strike a chord of terror in her heart. She had seen too much for it to be otherwise. What did it say about her, then, that, more than the threat of dying beneath the blades or teeth of the Grigori, she feared watching her Shadow take another as his wife?

A distraction, that was what she needed. Something that would take her mind off the kohannya ceremony and keep her from betraying the traitorous contents of her heart.

Crossing to where Mika grazed amongst the trees, Katerina made a show of sorting through the contents of her saddlebags. Antivenin, bandages, and salves, in case she and Niko encoun-tered a demon on the road. Smoked sausages, cold vareniki dumplings. Bits of cheese. A full flask of water. A sheathed knife, though fighting with a blade was more Niko's province than hers. She hardly needed an edged weapon to do damage.

Unfortunately, this position put her closer to the very

people she was trying to ignore. Elena held up the boat, chattering about how much time she'd put into it, then hiding it playfully behind her back when Niko tried to examine it more closely. "You'll see it when you brave the river to catch it," she said, trilling a silvery laugh. "You must earn your prize, my Shadow." She batted her lashes at him, the implication clear: the true prize in this scenario was *her*.

"As you wish," Niko said, stepping backward with his palms raised, and Elena beamed.

"Don't worry, my Shadow," she said, sidling up to him once more. "You don't have long to wait."

My Shadow. Was that all he was to Elena—a possession, proof that her maniacal dedication to Sant Viktoriya had paid off? For Katerina, he was so much more: her best friend, her conscience, the other half of her soul. How could he be someone else's Shadow, when all her life, even before the blood vow that bound them, he had only belonged to her?

She ducked her head, terrified that the white-hot misery that scorched every inch of her being would show on her face. Inside her, power stirred, desperate for an outlet. The river was *right there,* the Vila clustered on the bank in their rune-embroidered gowns, cradling their wax-coated paper boats as if cupping treasure in their hands. One gust was all it would take to send them flapping over the river like a flock of beautiful, shocked birds, their boats scattered to the four winds. One thought, and the river would crest its banks and swallow all of them whole, sucking Katerina and her humiliation into its depths.

She'd assured Baba that she had control of her magic. She had trained for years to channel it with the same focused precision with which Niko wielded his blades. Wasn't her ability to resist Baba's spell proof of her strength? She refused to be undone here, now, when to do so would mean exposure as a liar, not to mention the surety that Baba and the Elders would insist on performing the spell all over again. The thought of undergoing that agony a second time chilled her to her soul.

How could it be a bad thing to be in possession of all her powers, just a few short moonrises away from the full Bone Moon, with Grigori attacks increasing by the day? She couldn't travel all the way to and from Rivki weakened, a fraction of her true self. She *wouldn't.*

But she couldn't stay here another moment, either. Not like this. Every instant she lingered meant risking discovery—and devastation.

Maybe she was a coward, not to be able to watch her Shadow claim Elena's boat—and, by extension, the Vila—for his own. Or maybe she was only looking out for the village she'd dedicated herself to protecting since her mother fell at the demons' feet, throat torn open, a broken and bloodied doll.

Maybe both.

An idea came to Katerina then—a wonderful, terrible idea, destruction and deliverance in equal measure.

To reach Rivki, she and Niko would have to cross a bridge that spanned the river a half-mile to the north. A spring storm two weeks ago had left it in less-than-ideal shape. Katerina had seen the state of it, when she'd ridden upriver to gather medicinal herbs for their journey: the railing was loose and some of the spokes and slats were gone, leaving gaps like missing teeth. She and Niko had debated taking a different, longer route, concerned the bridge wouldn't hold their horses, but Gabiska, Kalach's head carpenter, had tested it and declared it fit for one last crossing. If it fell, though...

They would have to ride farther upriver, into the rolling hills that licked the base of the mountains, then through one of the lower passes. The trip would add hours to their journey. Time they couldn't afford to waste, if they wanted to arrive on schedule for the feast that preceded the Trials and pay the Kniaz the respect he believed was his due.

A storm was on its way, telegraphed in the low-hanging clouds that darkened the horizon and the humid air, sparking with latent electricity. Half a mile upriver, who could say whether it had already begun to rain?

One hand on Mika's back, she pictured the bridge: flaking, white-painted slats; struts rising from the riverbanks on either side of rushing water. Oaks and rowans curved overhead, their leaves stirring in alarm, speckled with the first drops that fell from a blackening sky.

Careful not to disturb the surface of the soil, she sent her magic out, snaking beneath the riverbank. It curled around the voles that crept through their tunnels. Wove between the knobbly roots of the great oaks. Tasted the thorny sweetness of guelder roses, slumbering until the warmer temperatures beckoned them to bloom.

The earth was *hers*. Hers to embrace, to protect, to command.

She reached farther, carving her way, until her magic tasted something solid, rich with river-silt. Sending out another tendril, she found its companion, anchored deep within the earth: the clay footers of the bridge.

No one was looking at her, beneath the trees with Mika, pretending to forage through the saddlebags. The weather was poor; the bridge was in disrepair, a half-mile away; Katerina's earth-magic was bound. If she went through with this, no one would suspect.

She closed her eyes and rested her forehead against her mare's warm flank. Mika stood steady, her slow, even breath centering Katerina as she wrapped her magic around the footers: tight and tighter, until they creaked beneath the strain.

Yield to me, she commanded silently.

The earth heaved, struggling against her. The footers had stood for fifty years, since a storm had washed that section of riverbank away and Kalach had had to rebuild. The ground didn't want to give them up. Its grip on the clay was strong, but Katerina's was stronger.

Yield, she demanded again, drawing harder on her magic. *Now.*

Perhaps Sant Antoniya was with her, because though she had not called on her water-magic, the river stirred, its gentle lap-lap-lap against the shore becoming louder, more demanding. The sky opened, drops of cold rain spattering Katerina's shoulders. Above her, the leaves of the low-hanging oaks whispered, disturbed from their rest. And upriver, two of the bridge's footers broke loose at last, sending the dilapidated structure plunging into the water with a deafening roar and an impact that shook the forest.

Katerina opened her eyes to chaos.

3
KATERINA

The good news was, no one was paying any attention to Katerina whatsoever. The bad news was, she had created mayhem: a frothing river, a flood of debris, a shrieking crowd, who feared an attack of Grigori until Baba and the Elders assured them otherwise.

Though the kohannya gathering was downstream from the collapse, the river's banks were wide. No one was hurt; the waterwitches had made sure of it, fighting together to tame the flow, even as the earthwitches, led by Baba, shored up the soil on either side. Gabiska and his crew had ridden upriver through the hard-driving rain to confirm the bridge's demise, though the chunks of wood that the current carried past them were evidence enough. The carpenter had shaken his head on his return, saying it had only been a matter of time—and how fortunate they were that Dimi Ivanova and her Shadow hadn't been crossing the structure when it fell.

Katerina had held her breath, scrutinizing Baba for any hint of suspicion, but found none. The elder Dimi had focused first on ensuring everyone's safety, then on determining the extent of the damage. Bits of wood littered the riverbanks on both sides, tangling in the reeds that flanked the shore, and despite the earthwitches' best efforts, the surging debris had gouged chunks of clay from the banks. It would be hours before the site was fit for kohannya—hours that Katerina and Niko didn't have, if they were to make it to Rivki on time.

The storm had passed as quickly as it came, the heavy rain slowing to a trickle that fell, improbably, from a sun-streaked sky. Now, in the still-sodden clearing, Baba clapped her hands, and the riverbank fell silent. All eyes sought the elder Dimi in her cobalt robes, her salt-white braids coiled atop her head. Even the children ceased clamoring and stood still, bright-eyed and attentive as hawks.

"Today, a great disaster was averted," Baba announced. "The Saints are truly with us, for had Dimi Ivanova and Shadow Alekhin been atop the bridge when it crumbled, Kalach would have lost their greatest champions."

Katerina spared a glance for Niko, standing once again by Elena's side. The Vila clung to his arm, eyes wide with the terror of what could have been, but he wasn't looking down at her. He was staring straight ahead, his eyes locked on Katerina's face.

"Thanks to the efforts of our own, the collapse of the bridge caused us no lasting harm." Baba's thin lips pressed together. "In gratitude to the protection of Sant Andrei and Sant Viktoriya, the kohannya ceremony will go on, though later than we planned." She gestured at the river, where the water still foamed, agitated by the bridge's collapse and the passing storm.

A cheer arose from the crowd, the children lifting their makeshift boats high, and Baba lifted a hand to quell it. "Alas," she said, her gaze roving between Katerina and Niko, "Dimi Ivanova and her Shadow cannot stay. For with the bridge down, they must take the long way to Rivki, and they cannot afford to tarry."

Even across the clearing, Elena's gasp of disappointment was audible. But Katerina was still looking at Niko, and in the depths of his gray eyes she saw the most peculiar of expressions, there and then gone so quickly she might have imagined it: relief.

"Worry not," Baba said, bestowing a smile on Elena. "For Shadow Alekhin and his Vila, the ceremony is a mere formality, as their union has already been assured. You will still cast your boat upon the waters, Vila Lisova, so it may follow your Shadow on his journey and give him luck."

Elena gave a small, trembling smile in return. "Of course, I will."

Raindrops spangled Baba's braids, darkening them, as she nodded in approval. "Now we must bid goodbye and good fortune to our champions," she said. "May they do their duty at the Trials and return to us once more."

Murmurs rose from the crowd, some of assent and some of disagreement. The whole village was sworn to secrecy about Katerina's abilities, but they knew well what she could do. While the more strategic among them understood that excelling at the Trials might well mean losing her to Iriska in twelve months' time, others were less sanguine. Becoming one of the chosen pairs to advance to the second round of the Trials was an honor; failing to do so, a mark of shame. She'd heard rumors in the taverns that some people thought binding her magic was blasphemy, a perversion of the gifts given to her by the Saints.

If they only knew… Would they revile her, for clinging to her gifts despite Baba and the Elders' demands? Or praise her, for doing what she must to protect Kalach and her Shadow?

She held her head high until the murmurs died to silence once again, and Baba spoke. "They have their duty, and we have ours. Go with our blessing and the blessing of the Saints, Dimi

Ivanova and Shadow Alekhin. May you walk always in the Light."

There was a beat of silence. Then the crowd exploded with applause. As it quieted, the Vila drifted back to the riverbank—all except Elena, who stood by Niko's side, her brow furrowed with worry.

"I know you need to go. But I wish you could stay for the ceremony." She peered up at Niko, her eyes wide and blue and guileless. "It...it's tradition."

"I'm sorry, Elena." Niko's voice was a low rumble. "I know how much this means to you."

Elena tilted her head upward, her lower lip protruding in what could only be described as a pout. As Katerina watched, she extended her free hand toward Niko, doubtless expecting him to intertwine her fingers with his. But her Shadow didn't move. His hands were shoved in the pockets of his leathers, his body leaned slightly back and away from the Vila. Her touch skirted the sleeve of his jacket, and then her hand fell back to her side once more.

Was it her imagination, or was her Shadow avoiding Elena's touch?

Surely not. That would be absurd. It was coincidence, that was all, seeing what Katerina wanted to see. What she *wished*, in the depths of her wicked witch's heart: that the Vila's touch repulsed him. That he longed to share Katerina's bed, and claim her heart as well as her soul.

Saints, how long was she meant to stand here, waiting, as her Shadow flirted with his betrothed? How much could her heart take?

"Niko!" she snapped, the word a whip. "Come."

Her Shadow's gaze flicked to hers. Was she imagining things once again, or *was* it relief that showed in its depths?

"Calling me like a dog now, I see," he said, tone laced with faux annoyance.

Katerina forced a smirk onto her face. "If the shoe fits..."

He made a low, amused sound, then bent his head toward Elena's. Saints, was she going to have to watch him kiss the Vila goodbye?

Katerina braced herself, unable to look away. To pay the penance of watching Niko's lips brush Elena's, if she must. But her Shadow was nodding to the Vila, stepping back. Obeying Katerina, as he was sworn to do. Joining her under the trees.

As she untied Mika, Niko did the same with Troitze, avoiding the testy stallion's bite as he tossed his head. "Katerina," her Shadow said, low-voiced. "The bridge. Did you—"

By the Saints. What had he seen? Had he felt it, when she wrenched the footers free?

"Of course not." Her voice was sharp as she swung up into the saddle. "How could I? My earthwitch is bound, remember? *Why* would I, besides?"

Niko snorted, sounding for an instant like his stallion. "Whatever you say."

He cast her a final suspicious glance as he mounted Troitze. Eager to escape his scrutiny, Katerina dug in her heels and Mika moved out, past Ana, who mouthed, *See you soon* with an imperious wink that suggested she'd accept nothing less. Troitze, never one to follow, pushed forward to take the lead.

Sunlight striped the banks and sparkled on the rippling water, the great oaks sighing overhead in a wind that was not of her making, as Katerina and her Shadow breached the edge of the forest, leaving Kalach behind.

4

KATERINA

It was a beautiful night to burn, and a ridiculous one to die.

Standing shoulder-to-shoulder with her competitors in the pit beneath the Bone Trials arena, Katerina inhaled the mingled scents of sweat, damp earth, and rowan-fire, and pleaded with her magic not to betray her. Next to her, Niko rested his palm against the small of her back, offering comfort. The heat of his touch radiated even through her fighting leathers, and Katerina jerked away.

Her Shadow looked down at her, puzzlement warring with battle-eagerness on his face.

"All right?" he said, voice pitched low so the other Dimis and their Shadows wouldn't hear.

"Never better," Katerina bit out, straightening her spine. The roar of the crowd seeped through the bars, ebbing and flowing like the waves that lapped Rivki Island's shores, and she swallowed, her throat thick with disgust.

The ride from Kalach had been uneventful, other than poor weather that had spooked the horses and forced them to arrive in Rivki looking like they'd been dragged backward through a blackberry hedge. They'd broken their ride in Drezna, as they usually did when delivering the tithe, then ridden hellbent through the rain to make it in time for the Trials' opening feast. Now they were here, crammed into a space so small that Katerina's skin crawled with the spillover of her fellow Dimis' magic, about to turn against each other for the benefit of a dictator.

Six nights before the Bone Moon, when the veil between humanity and the Underworld grew thinnest, the Seven Villages' most powerful Dimis and Shadows should be home, defending Iriska against soul-devouring Grigori demons. Not doing...this.

At least Katerina had been able to keep the retention of her abilities a secret. There had hardly been cause to use them on the road, what with the lashing wind and the downpour. The only one they'd needed was her fire, to dry out wood for kindling and set it aflame. She'd come so close to telling Niko the truth again and again—she *hated* lying to him, any more than she had to—but in the end, she'd decided against it. With luck, she wouldn't need to call on her water, earth, or wind to defend them, and they'd be back in Kalach before anyone was the wiser.

A horn blew in the arena above, putting an end to her musings. Amplified by witchwind, it jarred small pebbles loose from the walls. They spattered against Katerina's leathers, and beside her, a fellow Dimi—Trina Samarin, of Povorino—gave a grunt of disgust as the pebbles struck the side of her face, drawing blood. Katerina could smell it, iron-rich in the damp air.

"Pleasant accommodations, no?" Katerina said, cocking her head at the confines of the pit. "You'd think they'd treat us better if we're meant to be Iriska's best hope of survival."

Trina sneered at her, as if making idle conversation were tantamount to admitting weakness. The light filtering through the bars fell in stripes across the umber skin that marked her as hailing from Povorino, and her green eyes shone, bright with malice.

"There's no *we* about it," she hissed, her voice surprisingly girlish to be filled with so much venom. "Think of me when you're lying in the dirt of the arena, choking on dust." She lifted a hand, summoning the wind to command the pebbles at her feet. They peppered Katerina's leathers in a fusillade before falling to the stone floor once more.

Trina had been nasty to Katerina since they'd met at the previous night's feast, as if sensing a threat to her victory in the arena. At first, Katerina had ignored her, which only seemed to spur the other woman on. By now, moments before they were about to fight for their lives, Katerina's patience had worn thin.

"If one of us is about to be lying in the dirt," she said sweetly, "I hardly think it's me." Fire flared in her palms and she let it rise, heat forming a wall between them. Trina took a startled step back. Beside her, her Shadow bared his teeth, but instead of responding in kind, Niko chuckled.

"Watch yourself, Fyodor," he said. "My Dimi doesn't make idle threats." He refrained from saying the rest of it: that if anyone here knew what Katerina was capable of, they'd think twice before pelting her with pebbles.

The horn blew once more, drowning out Fyodor's retort, as Katerina called her witchfire to heel. "Dimis and Shadows of Iriska. Citizens of Rivki." The Kniaz's voice boomed over the receding blare of the horn, echoing throughout the arena and into the chamber below. "We are gathered here today to determine the strongest among us, so that they may one day fight alongside my Druzhina." Through the bars, Katerina could make out the proprietary sweep of his hand, gesturing left and right at the entourage that flanked him.

The Druzhina Guard were the strongest Dimis and Shadows

Iriska had to offer. Yet Kniaz Sergey spoke as if he owned them, as if their power were his to command, rather than their own. Who cared if he had inherited his throne, his bloodline anointed to rule Iriska by the Saints? His hubris infuriated Katerina.

Dimis—*women*—held the power of the elements in their hands. So why did Iriska cling so tightly to tradition, ceding its governance to an entitled, overindulged man?

"Tonight, we will see displays of strength that dazzle us," the Kniaz announced. "But we will also watch as the weaker among us fall, dishonoring the villages they call home."

The crowd howled in approbation. In the dimness of the pit, Katerina rolled her eyes.

"Only the two most powerful pairs will be chosen to advance to next year's Trials and compete for a chance to join the Druzhina." Kniaz Sergey's voice vibrated with satisfaction. "And if the Saints smile upon us, perhaps we will witness a third pair of such strength that at the Reaping, they will displace one of our own."

There was another roar, this one of protest. Every so often, Kniaz Sergey would choose an additional pair of victors, ousting a bonded pair of the Druzhina. It was his way of culling the herd, keeping his Guard on their toes—and it worked. Whenever Katerina came to Rivki to deliver the tithe, she could sense their gazes on her and Niko, assessing the competition.

Everything about this was wrong. Dimis and Shadows fought together, on the side of the Light. They should be allies, not enemies. Yet here the Kniaz was, seeding dissent where there should be unity. She glanced around; other than Trina, whose eyes shone with excitement, her companions in the pit looked grim. Sofi, Drezna's Dimi champion, turned her back to speak to her Shadow; her hands carved the air in a series of intricate gestures, but with Sofi facing away, the words were unintelligible. Mute since birth, Sofi communicated primarily through sign; Katerina and Niko had both learned the language so they could converse with her whenever they visited Drezna. Whatever she had to say now must be both private and unnerving, because her Shadow shook his head, clapping a reassuring hand on her shoulder.

Watching them, Dimi Roksana, who hailed from Satvala-by-the-Sea, lifted her chin. "Good luck," she said. "May the best of us rise to defend Iriska."

"Good luck," they all echoed—except Trina and her Shadow, who smirked as if nothing would make them happier than to watch their fellows fall one by one, and trample on the remains. What was *wrong* with the two of them?

Kniaz Sergey's voice broke through the howls of the crowd and the mutterings of the Dimis and Shadows in the pit. "Let the Bone Trials begin!"

Katerina turned toward the stairs that led up to the arena, Niko stalking beside her and leveling a menacing glare at anyone who attempted to push past them. At twenty-two, he was the youngest alpha Shadow in Iriska. He couldn't afford to show weakness by letting anyone else take the lead. Not for the first time, he reminded her of Troitze—an observation she wisely kept to herself.

"This will be over soon," he muttered as they climbed the narrow steps, the crowd's roars growing louder the closer they got to the surface. "On your weakest day, you're stronger than the rest of them, no matter what Baba did to you."

"Shhh," Katerina demanded, cutting her eyes at him in warning, but her heart clenched. Neither of them had families left to protect. Still, the thought of Iriska's so-called nobleman finding out that an entire village had been keeping her secret and punishing Kalach's vulnerable citizens in her name sent bile surging up her throat.

Niko inhaled, his nostrils flaring in disgust at the dank scent of the moldering stairway. His voice dropped, skirting the edge of the black dog that lived inside him. "I know I told you this was for the best. But now—maybe I was wrong, Katerina. Maybe I should have fought harder for you when you protested the binding. And maybe in the arena...you shouldn't have to hide what you're capable of, and damn the consequences."

Katerina's heart twisted. The two of them were joined; her inability to show her true strength was a reflection on him, as well. Above and beyond his pride, Niko had good reason to seek victory in the Trials. Every day, her Shadow fought to reclaim his family's good name, and nothing could bring him more honor than being chosen to fight in the Druzhina. She hated to let him down. But how could she do otherwise?

"Niko," she said, low-voiced.

He arched a dark eyebrow at her. "Hmmm?"

She couldn't tell him what was in her heart—how she thought of him in a way a Dimi was forbidden to regard her Shadow, how she crumbled inside every time she thought about what awaited them when they got back to Kalach. How things would change for the two of them, forever. But before they set foot in the arena, she could tell him the truth about the binding ceremony, so he didn't stride into battle believing he'd failed her.

If it hadn't been for him, who knew if she would have found the strength to resist the spell? She could be splintered now, a fraction of herself.

As usual, she owed him everything.

"I—" She paused mid-step, and a huff of annoyance split the air behind her.

"Having second thoughts, Dimi Ivanova?" Trina said, her tone mocking.

Niko's shoulders tensed beneath his black leathers as he

turned, fixing his storm-gray eyes on the Shadow and Dimi who stood on the steps below them. A growl rumbled in his chest, and Fyodor growled back, the sound dripping with menace.

Katerina's desire to confide in her Shadow fled, replaced by irritation. "I flee from no one," she said, lifting her chin. "Can you say the same, Dimi Samarin? I heard the last time Grigori attacked a group of travelers outside Povorino, witchwind failed to drive them back. A firewitch had to step in to save them." She opened her hand, a small flame licking above her palm. "Tell me, was it weakness that almost killed those people? Pure cowardice? Or both?"

Her lips rose in a smirk, and the flame rose with it, illuminating the other Dimi's furious expression. Katerina didn't wait to hear what she had to say. She turned away, clenching her fist to extinguish the flame, letting her fury spur her onward.

Three more steps to the top. Two. One.

Trina's witchwind shoved at Katerina's back, sending her stumbling across the uneven stone threshold and onto the sand of the arena. She gritted her teeth as her own power rose in response, itching beneath her skin, eager to be used.

Today, you are a firewitch, she told herself fiercely. *Nothing more. If you need to set this whole damned arena alight to save yourself and your Shadow, so be it. But you will keep tight hold of the rest of your gifts, or pay the price.*

Her fellow Dimis and their Shadows spilled from the doorway behind her as Katerina blinked, her eyes adjusting to the moonlight. The Trials were always held at night, simulating the conditions of a Grigori attack as closely as possible, though the exact nature of the threat varied from year to year, a closely-kept secret. She'd half-expected to be set on the moment she crossed the threshold, but the floor of the arena was empty. Tiered seating rose all around it, so high it nearly obscured the gilded domes of the Kniaz's palace atop the tallest peak on the island. In the distance, she could see the gleam of the lake that surrounded Rivki, filled with Vodyanoy water-spirits to keep the demons away.

The seats were packed; the Trials were the most notorious event in Iriska, with tickets at a premium and a lucrative betting ring on the winners. But it was impossible to miss the Kniaz. He sat front and center, three rows from the pit, surrounded on all sides by the Druzhina. Next to him reclined a dark-haired woman draped in blue velvet—Dimi Zakharova, his consort. She glared at Katerina, which made no sense at all. The very last thing Katerina wanted was to take her place.

Ah, well. Katerina wasn't here to make friends. If no one in Rivki could stand her, so much the better.

She turned her head, inspecting the arena. But there was nothing to see, save for the rowan-fires that burned to the left and right of a small door, carved into the opposite side. Smoke curled into the air, silhouetted against the star-speckled sky and the harsh, cratered face of the waxing Bone Moon. The stormy weather that had dogged them all the way to Rivki had passed; the night was still. Even the crowd had gone quiet.

Katerina regarded the fires, her mind churning. Rowan-smoke was toxic to Grigori. The trees' fire granted the demons a true death, as did Shadows' blessed blades and their bite, in the form of the black dogs they could take at will. But there could be no demons here, not inside the most powerfully warded spot in all of Iriska. Rivki was protected by the Druzhina and surrounded by a moat where the Vodyanoy lurked, poised to devour any Grigori foolish enough to try to cross the bridge. So why the fire? Was it merely a symbol, or did it portend something more?

The arena was too silent, too empty. If a threat lurked here, it was invisible. How was she meant to defend herself against something she couldn't see?

The other six Dimi and Shadow pairings spread out, giving themselves room to fight. Katerina kept a careful eye on Trina and Fyodor, thirty feet away. On their right stood Sofi and Damien, her Shadow. As Katerina's gaze swept over them, Sofi gave her a small, tense smile. Outside the arena, the two were her friends, sworn to fight beside her and Niko. But now, the Kniaz had made adversaries out of them. For while they wouldn't be fighting each other hand-to-hand, there was plenty of room for subversive tactics and sabotage.

Katerina wished she could tell Sofi the truth about what she could do. She wished she could explain that she'd rather be eaten by the Vodyanoy than serve in the Druzhina. But instead she just smiled back, her gaze narrowing as the door on the other side of the arena creaked open.

Sand crunched beneath Niko's boots as he shifted his weight, his right hand falling to the blade he favored. "There's something unnatural inside there," he whispered. "Not human, not demon. Katerina, I don't know—"

His voice disappeared beneath the roar of the crowd as the door eased the rest of the way open and a man strolled through, hands open at his sides. His dark hair was cropped short, his face clean-shaven. He wore a forest-green tunic and slim black pants, the picture of a fashionable gentleman. Katerina had seen many just like him in Rivki's Perun District, dining at establishments far fancier than any to be found in Kalach.

The direction of the wind changed, blowing the sharp-edged, resinous fumes of the rowan-fires toward the man. He coughed, the sound carrying across the arena, and Katerina stiffened. On either side of her, the other Dimis and Shadows did the same.

"Demon," she said, watching in horror as the doorway behind him filled with more and more of his kind—twenty men and women clad in richly dyed fabric. Grigori were shapeshifters, able to take on the forms of whoever they chose; it was part of what made them so lethal. But if they'd penetrated the capital, surely the Druzhina wouldn't just let them loose in the arena for the sake of the Trials. Would they?

Her power rose, buzzing in her fingertips, as the demons fanned out behind their leader, with him as the tip of their arrow. "Niko," she said, her voice urgent.

Her Shadow drew a deep breath as the wind changed again, sampling the creatures' scents. "Not true demons," he said grimly. "Illusions of some kind. But," he finished as all twenty of the false Grigori drew blades, "dangerous nonetheless."

There was no time for Katerina to wonder what sort of strange magic this was, or whether the blades the illusions carried had been bathed with the Grigori venom that was fatal to a Shadow in human form. Because as the crowd bellowed in anticipation, the demons' leader raised a hand, beckoning, and all of the creatures charged.

5

KATERINA

The familiar coldness of battle settled over Katerina, the world coming to her in fragments: A yellow-haired illusion-demon barreling toward her, teeth bared and blade clenched. The rumbling growl of her Shadow as he braced himself in front of her, palming two of his knives. The sizzle of her magic beneath her skin, begging to be used.

She could see the colored threads that connected her to each of her gifts so clearly. It would be easy for her to collapse the ground as the illusion-woman arrowed toward her Shadow, to summon the wind and send her hurtling backward. But no. *You are a firewitch*, she thought grimly, and prepared herself to burn.

The woman neared and Niko pinched one of his blades by the tip, arm poised to hurl it. Another step and he let it fly, the silver gleaming in the light of the Bone Moon as it winnowed straight for her. But the moment before it struck, a gust blasted from the left, where Trina stood. It sent Niko's blade tumbling end over end, embedding uselessly in the sand. Never breaking her stride, the illusion-woman snatched it up, lips rising in a mirthless smile. And behind her came five more of her kind, eyes lit with a sick avidity.

By the Saints, how had Rivki's Dimis done this? They were all taught basic charms from the cradle: how to summon shadow to conceal themselves, how to make a small light bloom and cup it in their hands. But this magic—conjuring illusion-demons—was unlike anything Katerina had ever seen. It must have taken the scholars at the Magiya Library months to discover the trick behind such a thing.

A howl rose from Katerina's right, where Roksana Gaidar and her Shadow battled two of the creatures at once. Dimi Gaidar was a waterwitch, a skill that did her little good in this arena filled with sand and rowan-fire. She would have to rely on her Shadow to fight, and he was falling, two of the illusion-creatures wrestling him to the ground. His body shimmered as he struggled to shift into the form of his black dog, but it was too late: One of them drew back its lips and sank its teeth into his neck, just as the other plunged a blade into his side. He let out a roar that shook the arena's walls, and Roksana shrieked, the sound so full of fear and rage that it momentarily froze the illusions charging at Niko and Katerina. As one, they turned their heads toward the melee, just in time to see the fallen Shadow cough up a horrifying amount of foamy blood. His eyes glazed over, staring sightless up at the moon-bleached sky.

Venom, Katerina sent to Niko along their bond, horror clear in her mind-voice, the way they were only able to communicate in battle. *Its teeth—the blade—*

I know. He pinched another knife by the tip. *We will not die in this arena, Katerina. Firewitch or no, we will not die tonight.*

The conviction in his voice galvanized Katerina. She moved to his side and raised her hands, concentrating on the center of the horde that had unfrozen and was sprinting toward them at inhuman speed. *If they bite and stab like Grigori, then they can die like them,* she told Niko, and let her witchfire free. It might not be able to kill them, but it should wound them long enough for Katerina to get her hands on a limb from one of the rowan-fires. Saints, how she wished she could harness the wind right now.

Her witchfire streaked from her palms in a focused stream, hitting the yellow-haired illusion at the tip of the horde just as Niko's blade found its home in the heart of the one behind her. A ululating cry ripped from Katerina's throat as she concentrated on splitting the stream, turning each strand into a flame-tipped missile. The illusions bellowed in agony as they caught fire, their forms flickering within the blaze until, with a crack that shook the ground, they exploded, sparks scattering in all directions. A complex rune shone where they had been, as if burnt into the very air of the night. Then it, too, vanished. Their blades clattered to the ground, and Niko dove for them, holstering them before another one of the illusions could use them against a Shadow. *Not entirely like Grigori, then,* he said.

The six that had come after her and Niko were dead. But a few feet away, Roksana was sobbing, kneeling in the sand next to her fallen Shadow, her palm pressed to the Mark on his upper arm as she begged him over and over to come back to her. Sunk in grief, she didn't so much as lift her head as two of the four creatures that Sofi and Damien were battling broke away from them and scuttled straight for Roksana, each gripping a venom-soaked blade.

Katerina spared a glance for Niko, but he had spun to battle another one of the illusions. If she wanted to save her fellow Dimi, she was on her own. And so she did the only thing she could think of: she screamed.

"Hey!" Waving her hands above her head, she made herself as large of a target as possible, desperate to focus the illusions' attention on her rather than Roksana. "I'm right here. Don't you want me?"

She let a hint of flame seep from her fingertips, tracing a thin stream of fire along the sand—a path guiding them straight to where she stood. "Imagine how much more there is where this came from," she taunted, just as she would if they were fighting a true demon horde. "Think how much you'll enjoy absorbing all of this power, how much stronger you'll be. How delicious I'll taste. Wouldn't you rather feed on my fire than her fear?"

She wasn't sure if the illusions were sentient enough to understand her, but sure enough, their heads cocked an instant before they changed trajectory, skirting Roksana and coming straight towards Katerina. She gathered her power, feeling it pulse in her palms. It took more effort than she liked to separate the strand that controlled her witchfire from the rest, but she managed it. *Not yet,* she told herself. *Wait for it...wait...*

Behind her, she heard a grunt and then a tearing sound as a blade sank deep into flesh. Her heart sped in terror. But when she dared to test her bond with Niko, she felt not pain, thank the Saints, but satisfaction at his kill, colored with anger that she'd put herself in harm's way. *This is not a rescue mission,* he snarled at her.

Trust me, she sent along their bond, but didn't pause to hear his reply. The two illusion-demons charged, and she waited until they were a foot away before igniting them, close enough that a hint of her own witchfire caressed her skin. The demons howled as they burned, fragmenting just as their counterparts had, the same rune burnt into the fabric of the night.

But as they dissipated, yet another one of the damnable illusions charged for Roksana. The other Dimi was on her feet now, yanking one of her Shadow's blades out of its holster. Unlike in Kalach, where Dimis trained hand-to-hand alongside their Shadows, in Satvala they had no such practice. Roksana's blade went wide, thunking into the sand far to the left of its mark. The illusion-demon came for her, and before Katerina could stop it, the creature let its own blade fly.

A venom-soaked blade was not inherently fatal to a Dimi, the way it was to a Shadow in human form. But when plunged into a Dimi's heart, it could kill just the same. Roksana's eyes flared wide, her mouth a soundless o of agony. Katerina watched in horror as the other Dimi's lifeless body toppled, landing across her Shadow's so that he broke her fall, even in death. The illusion wrenched its blade free with as much indifference as if it had stabbed a hunk of beef and then came for Katerina, laughing.

One instant, the two of them faced each other, fire sparking from Katerina's fingertips. The next, a massive black dog hurtled between them, sharp canines bared. Clamping his powerful jaws on his prey's neck, Niko shook the illusion-demon, muscles rippling beneath his glossy fur. The creature shrieked, writhing, as the scent of demon blood filled the air—then evaporated. Niko's razor-sharp canines grazed the tip of the rune that had powered the illusion a moment before it, too, vanished. He howled in victory, turning his head to make sure Katerina was unharmed even though she knew he could feel as much through their bond.

She shot him a reassuring glance, then shoved her sweat-matted hair back from her forehead and surveyed the arena. She and Niko had slain half of the illusion-demons. Sofi and Damien were battling two more. Halfway across the arena, Fyodor lunged in front of Trina and sank his black dog's teeth into the belly of one of the illusions. Blood and flesh sprayed onto the sand, and the creature shrieked, the awful rending of metal on metal.

Four of their fellow warriors had fallen. The Dimis and Shadows of Liski, Voronezh, and Bobrov were on their feet but fighting for their lives, the Shadows engaged in close combat with all six of the remaining illusion-demons as the Dimis' magic flared, gusts of wind driving the rowan-fires skyward, tongues of flame licking at the illusions' skin.

Dimi Nevolin of Bobrov was an earthwitch—for the love of the Saints, why did she not open a pit in the arena and dump these forsaken creatures in? Maybe the woman was frightened. Maybe she just wasn't used to fighting without her fellow Dimis and their Shadows by her side. Either way, Katerina's heart sank as Nevolin toppled beneath one of the illusions' blades, her Shadow leaping for her in time only to have three of the creatures fall upon him. The crowd caterwauled, and money changed hands, as if this were no more than a horse race. Bastards.

Niko prowled to her side, leaving bloody pawprints on the sand, as Trina raised her hands and sent witchwind hurtling at four of the illusions. They stumbled backward, snarling—and then sailed across the arena, skidding to a halt mere feet from Katerina. Across the expanse of sand, Trina met her eyes and smirked. She carved a hand through the air, evoking a second blast of wind that sent Niko flying.

The illusion-demons found their feet and crouched, assessing Katerina. She stared back at them, power brewing within her, a gathering storm. Niko roared with rage, struggling against Trina's witchwind as he fought to get to her, but the other Dimi held him back, gale-force winds whipping the sand into a maelstrom that obscured Katerina's vision. She scrubbed at her stinging eyes, forcing them open enough to see the illusions advancing, venom-soaked blades gripped in their hands. They surrounded her, a circle of knives and teeth and vitriol.

I'll kill her. Niko's mind-voice came, ice-cold with wrath. *Her corpse will lie at your feet.*

Promises, promises, Katerina told him. And then she struck.

Drawing on the well of her power, she hauled the strand of

fire up, up, up, pouring her energy into it until it curled around the charging illusion-demons, forging flaming vines that wrapped ever-closer, binding them. The yells of the crowd grew louder, competing with the crackle of the conflagration she'd ignited, but Katerina had no time to listen. All her attention was fixed on the flame-vines tightening around the illusions, choking the life out of them.

Beyond the burning demons and the swirling sand, she could just make out Trina's face. The other Dimi's eyes widened with disbelief an instant before they narrowed in calculation. And then her mouth lifted in a smile so malicious, it could only mean one thing.

Its outline visible through the haze of sand and flame, a black-clad form streaked straight for Niko, clutching a blade in each hand. These were the demons' knives, the hilts a dull, uniform maroon rather than the rune-engraved onyx that topped Shadows' blades. And yet, Katerina realized as bone-deep rage broke over her, it was a Shadow who wielded them.

Fyodor, in human form once more.

Trina had not only separated Katerina from her Shadow to weaken her. She had done it to isolate Niko while the other illusion-demons sought their quarry. Sofi and Damien couldn't break free to help him, and the pairings from Liski and Voronezh were too far away to help, even if they would. The two remaining illusions had seized upon them as the weakest of the survivors, crowding them against the wall of the arena even as the Dimis and Shadows, half in human form and half in the form of their black dogs, sought to bring them down.

Don't shift, she cried out to Niko. *He has their knives—*

But it was too late. Her Shadow had already shifted back into human form, the better to fight from a distance. He'd managed to reclaim his blades—and his leathers, minimizing his exposed skin—but if Fyodor so much as nicked him, here in the arena without antivenin...

By the Saints. Trina could do what she liked to Katerina, but she would never touch Niko, with her Shadow's hands or her own. Katerina would see her dead first.

She drew one burning breath, then another. The world slowed to a series of images once more: The illusions screaming as they burned. Damien snapping his prey's neck and running to Niko's aid, all four of his midnight-black paws pounding the ground, sand skidding in his wake and blood spraying from his jaws. The crowd on their feet, stomping and hollering. Trina laughing, Saints damn her, head thrown back and dark hair flying in the wake of her witchwind. Her own power, gathering inexorably in her chest and forking through every vein like lightning.

This wasn't just her witchfire. It was everything: her four gifts offering themselves up, desperate to be channeled in the service of saving her Shadow. To use them would mean putting herself on display, stepping into the full strength of her power in front of the Kniaz, the Druzhina, and all of Rivki. If she were caught, everyone who'd known what she was capable of and kept her secret would be accused of committing treason against the realm. It was wrong, and rash, and dangerous.

But Katerina would do far worse, if it meant Niko lived.

She inhaled. Exhaled. And set her power free.

Her gifts snaked beneath the earth, seeking Fyodor, spreading fire as they went. Imbued by her power, the sand heated degree by degree, as incandescent as her fury. She fed her rage into the earth and the earth answered, rising and shaking and shimmering and fusing as Katerina's witchfire transformed it at last to glass. It shattered beneath the illusion-demons, leaving them writhing aflame in midair, then splintered under Fyodor's feet.

He tried to leap away, to dodge, but she wrapped her witch-wind around him and propelled him toward her, straight through the flame-broiling demons. They winked out of existence, leaving fire-edged runes behind, just as he slid to a stop at her feet, bleeding and burning, his venom-laced blades still clutched in his hands and a look of incredulous hatred on his face.

"Surprise," Katerina said sweetly, and bent down to pluck the blades free.

ABJECT MISERY WARRED with dizzying relief as she and Niko sought their place in line with the surviving Shadows and Dimis.

This was exactly what Baba had feared. With Niko's life on the line, Katerina had done what she'd sworn she wouldn't: lose control. Her love for him had already made a liar out of her; now it had made her break her word and betray her home into the bargain.

She wasn't sorry. And yet, she shouldn't have done it.

True, the burning demons had formed a wall of flame between Fyodor and the Kniaz, hopefully blocking the nobleman's view. And with luck, Fyodor's burns could be attributed to the wrath of a firewitch whose Shadow was in mortal danger. The cracking earth could be blamed on heat alone, the wind on Trina Samarin. But in the moment, Katerina had been thinking of none of that. All that had mattered was that she save her Shadow, Kalach and her vow to Baba Petrova be damned.

Regret forged a lump in her throat. "Niko," she whispered, "I'm sorry. I should have told you. I shouldn't have—"

He tilted his head to look down at her, his gaze impenetrable. Try as she might, she couldn't make out what was going on behind his slate-gray eyes. "Not now, Katerina."

She wanted to demand to know what he was thinking. To have the same access to his thoughts as she did when they fought side by side. But all she could do was nod in tacit agreement as they strode across the bloodied sand of the arena, side-stepping the bodies of the fallen Dimis and Shadows. It was better that they both lived, was it not, no matter the price? They could fight later. At least they would be alive to argue.

The crowd was eerily silent as Dimi Novikova, head of the Druzhina, stood from her place at the Kniaz's right hand. "Ten survive," she declared, her witchwind carrying her voice across the arena. "Four have fallen. We commend their souls to the Saints and pray for their deliverance to the Light."

A murmur of acceptance rose from the crowd, quieting as Dimi Novikova spoke again. "Come forward, Dimis and Shadows of Iriska's villages. Stand before us and face your verdict."

Terror flashed through Katerina's body, as potent and lethal as her magic. There was no coming back from this. One by one, Dimi Novikova would call their names. And then, when they all stood in front of the Kniaz, he would make his choice.

She glanced left and right, at the other Shadows and Dimis. Their bodies were taut with anticipation, their gazes fixed on Dimi Novikova. All of them would do anything, sacrifice anything, to be chosen today. And Katerina would do anything to be passed over.

Her hands shook, and she balled them into fists to hide their trembling. She had made her decision, the moment she prioritized saving Niko above all else. Now she would have to live with the consequences, no matter how grave they might be.

Dimi Novikova pointed at the furrowed stretch of sand in front of the cordoned-off area where the Kniaz and the

Druzhina sat. "First, I call Dimi Oglievich of Drezna and her Shadow."

Head held high, Sofi limped forward, Damien at her side, in human form. The left leg of her fighting leathers was dark with blood, but her expression revealed no pain.

"I call Dimi Samarin of Povorino and her Shadow!" Novikova pointed at the spot to Damien's right, and Trina marched forward, her despicable excuse for a Shadow at her side.

"I call Dimi Ivanova of Kalach and her Shadow!"

Katerina followed the line of Dimi Novikova's finger. She was pointing at the spot right next to Fyodor, because...of course she was. Was this a further test, to see if Katerina could stand at his right without either getting stabbed or burning him to ashes?

Either way, she had no choice. Niko at her side, she walked forward, taking her place. Fyodor stared straight ahead, not sparing her a glance, burns marking every visible inch of his bronze skin. Good: let him suffer. He lived, which was more than he'd intended for her Shadow.

"Dimi Fenenko of Liski and her Shadow!" Novikova called. "Dimi Essen and her Shadow, of Voronezh!"

When they all stood for inspection, some in worse shape than others, the Kniaz rose to his feet, smiling. "Citizens of Rivki!" He raised both hands to the sky, as if embracing the waxing Bone Moon. "Tonight, we have indeed witnessed marvelous things. Yes, some have fallen, but better now than when Iriska's existence depends on it. And those who have risen to the occasion have done so with great aplomb."

He paused, and Katerina suppressed a shudder. Surely it was her imagination that his gaze lingered on her...unless, of course, he'd seen the truth of what she'd done. A tremor ran through her, and she steeled her spine, refusing to show fear.

"It is my great pleasure to announce the victors of this year's Bone Trials!" the Kniaz bellowed, and the crowd erupted, stomping their feet and rattling the shell-shakers they'd bought from the street-vendors outside the arena's walls.

"Silence!" Dimi Novikova's voice boomed, amplified by her witchwind. The arena fell quiet, and Katerina held her breath, praying as she had never prayed before.

"The first victors of this year's Bone Trials, bound to return for next year's competition and a chance to join the ranks of the Druzhina, are"—the Kniaz paused for effect—"Dimi Oglievich and Shadow Tikhomirov, of Drezna!"

Sofi's face paled, going white as the face of the moon with excitement, before she seized Damien's hand. She stepped forward, lifting their joined hands high in triumph, and the crowd roared. As Sofi and Damien stepped back into line, Katerina shot them a small smile. It felt false, dredged from the depths of her being, but—this was what Sofi wanted. They'd talked about it often enough, when Katerina and Niko stopped in Drezna to break their ride to and from Kalach.

Besides, the Trials only called for two victors. Maybe three, if the Kniaz felt taken enough with a third pairing, but that was rare. Sofi's triumph was Katerina's, as well.

The Kniaz cleared his throat. "I am proud to announce the second victors of this year's Bone Trials. May I present to you" —he swept his hand wide—"Dimi Samarin and Shadow Makarov, of Povorino!"

Trina stepped forward, gripping Fyodor's hand, her Shadow flinching as her fingers closed around his burned flesh. It was a small gesture, squelched as quickly as it appeared, but Katerina saw it nonetheless, and hid her smile.

That was two, she thought as Trina and Fyodor stepped back into line. The other Dimi aimed a gloating look at Katerina, but she was too dizzy with relief to care. Maybe the burning demons had been enough of a distraction from the way the earth had buckled and the wind had shifted, sending Fyodor hurtling into the flames. Maybe she had pulled it off, just another Dimi from a border village who was strong enough to survive but not good enough to warrant anything more.

She waited for the Kniaz to dismiss the rest of them, for the crowd to boo and hiss as they filed out of the arena. It would be an insult to her pride and Niko's, but there were worse things. Her Shadow could yell at her all he wanted later, for keeping secrets and compromising their village to save his life. All that mattered was that they go home, returning only to deliver the tithe.

Iriska's ruler regarded the line of Dimis and Shadows, his dark brows lowered and his expression grave. One by one, his gaze lingered on each of them. And then he spoke.

"As the third victors of this year's Bone Trials, I name Dimi Ivanova and Shadow Alekhin, of Kalach."

6

KATERINA

The blood drained from Katerina's face. Next to her, Niko gave a low growl, so quiet that if Katerina hadn't felt its vibration, she might not have noticed it at all. It was his warning growl, meant to herald impending danger.

Every eye on the crowd was on her, including the Kniaz's and the Druzhina's. This was supposed to be an honor, not a nightmare. She had to act like it.

She straightened her spine, letting a small smile lift her lips, as if this were no more than her due. On her left, Trina gave an angry, disbelieving snort, and Katerina cut her eyes at the other Dimi. "So much for choking on your dust," she said, just loud enough for Trina to hear.

The look Trina leveled her with was murderous, but Katerina ignored it, fixing her gaze firmly on the Kniaz. Trina Samarin was the least of her problems.

She had let Baba Petrova down. Regardless of whether the Kniaz had seen the extent of what she'd done, she had performed too well. She'd lied, failed to be the mediocre Dimi she'd promised to be, and with it, she'd endangered Kalach. Who knew how bad the growing Grigori threat might be a year from now, by the time of the second round of Trials and the Reaping? Katerina and her Shadow were Kalach's best hope of protection, and now her carelessness might have doomed them all.

Shame flushed her face, and Niko growled again, this time responding to the upward tick of her heartbeat. His hand closed around hers, the fingertips rough from years of bladework, and he pulled her forward, raising their joined hands in a gesture of triumph.

The crowd rose to their feet, roaring in approval, but the Druzhina didn't cheer. Flanking the Kniaz, they regarded Niko and Katerina with identical grim expressions. Katerina couldn't blame them: if she and Niko succeeded at the Trials next year, they would be Reaped, unseating one of the Druzhina pairings. Katerina was just making enemies left and right today.

Niko lowered their joined hands, tugging Katerina back into line. He relinquished his grip, and she missed his touch. He grounded her, and she needed that right now, badly.

If anyone had seen through to the truth of what she'd done, it would be the Druzhina. And now, she had to face them. What would they do to her? Reap her and Niko on the spot? Haul them both away? Send riders to Kalach to punish Baba and the rest?

Nausea swept Katerina at the thought, and she had to fight to keep a poker face as the two pairings who had failed the Trials were dismissed. They filed out of the arena, heads lowered. The hunch of their shoulders and the slant of their backs broadcasted shame, and a part of Katerina was grateful not to be among their ranks, even though she mourned the loss of control that had led her here. How could she regret it, though, if it meant Niko lived?

How could she not?

The crowd began to filter down through the amphitheater,

streaming toward the doors carved into the stone. The victors would have to wait until the arena had emptied, then pay their respects to the Druzhina and the Kniaz. Baba Petrova had drilled the protocol into Katerina, just in case. She knew the names of each of the Guard and their abilities, who saw eye contact as an insult and who demanded to be the first to initiate a handshake. She knew that she had to curtsy to the Kniaz, whereas Niko had to bow. What she *didn't* know was how to reconcile her failure with Kalach's survival. What would she do if the Druzhina saw right through her?

Katerina stood, her stomach churning, as she watched the crowd file out. The Kniaz rose, making his way down onto the floor of the arena with his consort, and the Druzhina followed. They formed a receiving line, each of the fifty Shadow and Dimi pairs facing each other. Trina and Fyodor turned, the closest and thus the first to make their way toward the waiting Guard, and Katerina and Niko followed, Sofi and Damien on their heels.

When it was their turn, Katerina stepped forward to greet the head of the Druzhina, holding her breath. "Dimi Novikova," she said, inclining her head in a gesture of respect.

After a long, tense moment, the older Dimi nodded back at her, the slightest brush of her witchwind brushing Katerina's hand in greeting. Katerina let a hint of her witchfire rise in response, the other Dimi's wind feeding it. Then she closed her hand around the flame, extinguishing it as Baba had taught her.

Dimi Novikova didn't smile at Katerina, or welcome her to Rivki. But she didn't demand to know why Katerina possessed the ability to buckle the earth or call the wind, either. Katerina's chest expanded with a deep, relieved breath. Had she gotten away with it, after all?

Turning from the older Dimi, she moved through the receiving line, Niko behind her. None of them spoke to her beyond what politeness required, but to her chagrin, Shadow Berezin began interrogating Niko about a particular bit of clever bladework. She had no choice but to leave him and move forward, fearing exposure with each step and craving the security of having her Shadow at her back, until at last she cleared the gauntlet and felt her pulse slow.

But her relief was short-lived as she came face-to-face with Kniaz Sergey, eyeing her like he'd like to undress her right here on the sand; and his consort, glaring as if she'd take great pleasure in stabbing Katerina through the heart.

7

KATERINA

"Your Grace," Katerina said, sinking low into a curtsy, just as Baba had instructed her. "Dimi Zakharova."

She'd seen the Kniaz many times before, of course, when she'd taken her turn delivering the tithe. But then, he'd always been seated on his throne, giving her no more than an imperious nod as she and Niko knelt and placed a ceremonial bushel of wheat at his feet. Katerina hated that the nobleman demanded such a thing from them, just as he did from the other six villages in Iriska: oil from one, firewood from another, potatoes from a third. She hated *him*.

Now here he was, right in front of her, close enough to incinerate with a thought. And instead, she had to act as if he'd just bestowed the greatest honor imaginable upon her.

She fixed her eyes on his silver-buckled shoes, engraved with runes of safety and protection, waiting for permission to stand. As much as it galled her to bend to him, it was a thousand times better than being hauled away for treason to the realm.

"Rise, Dimi Ivanova." The Kniaz's voice was as imperious as

always, laced with Rivki's distinctive accent: clipped vowels, a slight roll to the letter 'r.'

Katerina obeyed, taking him in: white stockings, woven with silver runes; black breeches; a fine, brocade cobalt coat; jeweled rings winking from every finger. She met his eyes at last, onyx, deep-set orbs that contrasted with the pale skin of his face, like ink spilled on bone china. They sparkled in the light of the Bone Moon, bright with cunning.

"You know my esteemed consort by name, I see," Kniaz Sergey said, waving an indolent hand at Dimi Zakharova. "But have you two had the pleasure of meeting?"

"We have not," Katerina said, glancing sideways at the woman who stood by the Kniaz's side. She was an earthwitch, everyone knew that. It was beyond Katerina why she would allow the Kniaz to leash her, to dress her in blue velvet to match his waistcoat and parade her about like a pet. But the last thing she wished to do was offend either of them, not when she had so much to lose. "It is my pleasure."

"Is it?" Dimi Zakharova said, her nostrils flaring as if she smelled something foul. Perhaps she did, come to think of it; Katerina probably stank of ashes and sweat. Well, that was nothing to be ashamed of. She squared her shoulders and met the other Dimi's gaze head-on.

"You tell me," she said, giving her most innocuous smile. "I certainly hope so."

The Kniaz waved his bejeweled hand again, dispelling the rising tension between them. "Now, now. The battle is over, and it's time for more enjoyable things. I must say, you performed admirably today, Dimi Ivanova. Should you do the same at the second round of the Trials next year, I'll look forward to the moment when you call our fair city home." He tilted his head, a sparrow eyeing the first juicy worm of spring. "Tell me, will you be bringing an entourage, or will it merely be you and your Shadow?"

"I beg your pardon? Your Grace," she added hurriedly as Dimi Zakharova frowned.

"Are you...attached?" His gaze flickered over her, lingering on hips and waist and breasts, and Katerina swallowed back the retort that rose to her lips.

"If you mean, am I promised to another, Your Grace, then the answer is no." Unlike a Shadow, she had the right to choose her own mate: a strong man who would share her bed, get her with child, and continue the Dimi line. Konstantin, maybe. Or Maksim. Both citizens of Kalach were tall and handsome, with land to their name. Though she didn't love them—had barely spoken to either of them—the time was coming when she'd have to decide.

Katerina had no interest in Konstantin or Maxim. Her heart belonged to another. But right now, she'd rather be wed to either of them than endure the insolent way the Kniaz's gaze slid over her, as if he were touching her with his hands rather than his eyes. Next to him, Dimi Zakharova stiffened, the hostility in her expression intensifying.

"Excellent, excellent." Kniaz Sergey rubbed his palms together with glee. "And your Shadow?" He nodded at Niko, who had freed himself from Shadow Berezin but was still paying his respects to the remaining Druzhina in turn. "Does he have a lovely Vila back home? For if not, the selection in Rivki is grand indeed. He'd have his pick of the litter." He gestured to the second level of the amphitheater, where a group of women fluttered like butterflies, adorned with jewels and arrayed in brightly colored, ornate gowns.

Katerina had no particular affinity for Vila in general, and Elena in particular. Beyond her obsession with Niko, Elena's fanaticism about following the will of the Saints to the letter drove Katerina mad. Still, her chest tightened at the indifferent way the Kniaz spoke of the Vila, as if they were chattel rather than individuals with thoughts and opinions of their own. She didn't trust herself to speak, but luckily, he mistook her indignant silence for awe.

"They may be mere broodmares, but they're lovely to look at, are they not?" he said. "They'll be lining up for a handsome, powerful Shadow like yours. Unless he has another?"

The only thing she wanted to think less about than being the Kniaz's plaything was this. It was bad enough that Niko was to marry Elena. But watching her bear his children? That might actually kill Katerina.

"My Shadow will be betrothed to his Vila when the Bone Moon is full, three nights hence," she said, raising her chin. "Alas, the Vila of Rivki Island will be safe from his advances, long may they weep."

Kniaz Sergey stared at her for a long moment, as if he'd never seen anything quite like her. Then he began to laugh. He chuckled until his eyes ran with water and he had to wipe them with his brocade sleeve. The harder he guffawed, the more Dimi Zakharova's glare intensified, and Katerina shot her a hard look. What was her Saints-damned *problem*?

"I like you, Dimi Ivanova," he said at last. "You surprise me, which is a rare thing. As for your talented Shadow, here he comes now."

"And not a moment too soon," Katerina muttered under her breath, a smile plastered on her face as Niko bowed to the last of the Druzhina and strode toward her.

He came to a halt by her side, flashing her a quizzical look before he bowed to the Kniaz and his consort in turn. "Your Grace," he said with impeccable politeness. "Dimi Zakharova."

As they exchanged pleasantries, Katerina caught the other Dimi's gaze, flicking back and forth between her and Niko.

Under other circumstances, she'd demand that the woman speak. But here and now, she was afraid she didn't want to hear what Dimi Zakharova had to say. Fear gripped her heart, its tendrils wrapping ever-tighter. What had the woman seen?

There were secrets, and then there were *secrets*. And some were never meant to be told.

Next to her, Niko cleared his throat, and she forced herself to focus. Sofi and Damien had come to the end of the receiving line and were waiting for their audience with the Kniaz. The other Dimi signed to her Shadow, hands flying as she communicated whatever she wanted to say, in case Kniaz Sergey or Dimi Zakharova couldn't understand. Katerina stood at the wrong angle to catch every word, but she could see *grateful* and *proud to fight for Iriska* clearly enough.

Katerina was the grateful one. Because thank the Saints, with Sofi and Damien right there, it was time for her and Niko to go.

"I look forward to seeing your performance in next year's Trials," Kniaz Sergey said, clapping Niko on the back as if they were old friends. "In the meantime, make the most of our hospitality, won't you? You're not betrothed yet, after all." He winked at Niko, letting his gaze wander to the flock of twittering Vila.

To his credit, Niko managed to keep his expression stoic—although for all Katerina knew, he was planning to end the evening with a Vila-themed bacchanalia. After a battle, Shadows were well known to seek release in a bed or a bottle... not that she and Niko ever discussed such things.

And we won't start now, she told herself sternly. *What he does when he's not fighting by your side is none of your business, Katerina. Pull yourself together.*

That would be a lot easier if adrenaline weren't still whipping through her body, demanding release. Back in Kalach, she'd seek peace in her favorite elderflower clearing or else light something on fire. But here, no such option was open to her. Maybe *she* was the one who should find solace in someone's bed tonight. If only she could stomach the thought.

Niko was her Shadow, sworn to stand by her side, the other half of her soul. But in private, she'd always called him her Lightbringer—her best friend, the boy who knew her better than anyone else, who could always make her laugh and lead her out of her own personal darkness. It was a lethal combination, and she couldn't imagine anyone would ever measure up.

She stole a sideways glance at him as they walked from the arena, but he was looking straight ahead, his expression impassive. They stepped onto the path that cut beneath the seating area, paved with red stones forged in Povorino's lava fields and shipped to Rivki at great expense, and still he said not a word. Stubbornly, neither did she.

The path widened, connecting with Maripol Avenue. The street was abuzz: vendors hawking their wares, children waving orange streamers meant to simulate witchfire, gamblers' money changing hands. Katerina drew a deep breath, taking in the welcoming scent of vareniki dumplings, her favorite. She didn't have any coins on her, but perhaps she could charm one of the people who'd bet on her into buying her some. Tilting her head, she scanned the crowd.

"There will be plenty to eat at the feast," Niko said, breaking his silence at last.

Her gaze snapped to his, vareniki forgotten. "Oh, so now you can talk?"

"What do you want me to say, Katerina?" His voice was laced with a weariness that tore at her heart. "What *can* I say, that's not going to start a fight?"

"How about what you're thinking? That would be a start!" She kept her voice low, so as not to be overheard despite the chaos of the crowd. "Tell me you're angry with me. That I might have ruined everything. That I lost control of my magic. That you're ashamed of me—"

He took hold of her upper arms, spinning her to face him. "Never say that again. I am not, nor will I ever be, ashamed of you, my Dimi. I am honored to fight at your side."

She peered up at him, biting her lip. "Then—"

His head lowered, the words a whisper against the shell of her ear. The heat of his breath sent a shiver through her entire body. "You didn't lose control. You fought for me, as your instincts demanded. But..." He drew back to look at her face. "You kept the truth from me, Katerina. Baba never bound your magic at all, did she? What happened with the bridge at kohannya—that was you."

Katerina drew a deep, shaky breath. Then, she nodded.

Her Shadow's eyes widened, the moonlight falling full on his face. He ran an absent-minded fingertip over his scar, the way he did when truly troubled. "But...why?"

This close to him, with his black dog able to pick up every shift in her scent and fluctuation in her heartbeat, she couldn't lie. So instead, she settled for a partial truth. "The longer we stayed, the more scared I was that Baba would figure out the spell hadn't worked. When she tried to bind me..." She shuddered all over at the memory. "It was like I was being torn apart. I couldn't go through that again."

His eyes scanned her face, as if trying to figure out what she'd left unsaid. She couldn't help it; her pulse sped in response, imagining what he would say if she shared the rest: *It was breaking me to watch you with Elena. A minute longer, and I would've shattered.*

"I understand that part," he said at last. "Watching you suffer—I couldn't do that twice, either. But Katerina...after we left, why did you not tell me?"

63

The hurt in his voice pierced her. "I wanted to, Niko. I did. But I didn't want to ask you to keep that kind of secret." Her voice broke. "And if something went wrong—like it did tonight —I wanted you to be able to say you didn't know."

Niko's hands slid up to her shoulders, gripping them like he had in Baba's cottage. This time, though, he shook her, hard enough that her head came up and she glared at him. "I trust you with my life, Katerina. You trust me with yours. But you don't think I'm worthy of being trusted with the truth?"

A sarcastic retort bubbled up, but she bit it back when she saw the pain in his eyes. "You're right," she said, making an effort to sound humble. "I'm sorry."

His gaze softened. "I know what you were doing. Trying to protect me, like you always do. Like you did in the arena. But we're meant to be partners, Katerina. And of the two of us, I'm the one who vowed to stand between you and the Darkness, to lay my life at your feet."

Katerina swallowed hard. "I tried to keep my powers leashed," she said, her voice a whisper. "If Fyodor hadn't come for you, I could have done it, Niko. I swear I could have. I didn't mean to be thoughtless, or to endanger Kalach—"

"Hush." His grip on her shoulders loosened. "What Baba tried to force on you was unnatural. Your magic is as much a part of you as your hair"—his fingers ghosted over her red waves, freed from their braid and matted with dust—"or your incorrigible attitude. Binding ceremony aside, it's no surprise it broke free when you thought my life was threatened."

"So you're not mad," she said, raising an eyebrow.

He tucked a rogue curl behind her ear, shaking his head in exasperation when it sprang free again. "Not in the way you mean. What I care about is *you*, do you understand? You thought you had to bear this secret alone. Now you've added your guilt for what happened in the arena to the bargain. And that's what I can't stand."

Katerina's eyes burned, and she sought some way—any way—to lighten the mood, before he saw too much. "Really," she said, struggling to keep her voice light. "That's all?"

His lips rose in the half-teasing smile she'd always loved. "Well, that, and the idea that you thought that you needed to intervene on my behalf. Seriously, Katerina. You don't think I could've taken that joke of a Shadow on my own? In this form or the form of my black dog, he's nothing more than an inconvenient snack." He snapped his teeth near her ear, and she smiled, as she knew he'd intended her to do.

"There," he said softly, taking a step back. "That's more like it. Now, let's go get changed for the feast, my Dimi. You can eat vareniki to your heart's content. Maybe even hurl some at the Kniaz's head, if he says something that tests the limits of your patience."

"As if I would do such a thing," Katerina said, but she was still smiling.

He took her by the shoulders again, turning her and then carving a path for both of them through the crowd, which parted for him like butter before a knife. They fell silent once again as they made their way to the grandiose inn where the visiting Shadows and Dimis were staying, but this time it was companionable rather than strained.

Inside the high-ceilinged hallway of the inn's foyer, Niko paused at the foot of the winding staircase. His room was on the first floor, whereas Katerina's was on the second. At home, he slept on a quilt in front of the hearth of their shared cottage. She wasn't used to having him so far away, but perhaps this was good practice. Three months from now, when Niko and Elena were married, he would no longer sleep in front of her fire.

And here she was, thinking about Elena again. The warmth that her conversation with Niko had kindled in her chest faded to ashes, and she fought not to let her misery show on her face. If Niko was happy about his betrothal, she should be, too—and he had given her no indication that he objected. Besides, other than Shadows whose preference was for men, it was expected of them to marry a Vila. Otherwise, the Shadow and Vila lines would die out. This was the way it needed to be, so why could she not resign herself to it?

The foyer was quiet, most of the others doubtless still among the revelers. Katerina heard only the sound of her own breath and Niko's as he scanned her face, his head tilted. She braced for him to ask what was troubling her. But all he said was, "Do try not to incinerate anyone in the few minutes you'll be out of my sight, won't you? It might put a damper on the festivities."

"I make no promises," Katerina said, her tone deliberately haughty. His low laugh echoed as she climbed the stairs, the polished wooden railing smooth and cold beneath her palm.

It was a good thing she hadn't given him her word. Because when she pushed open the double doors that led to her bedchamber's hallway, she found an unexpected—and unwelcome—guest waiting for her.

8

KATERINA

"Dimi Zakharova," Katerina said in wary greeting.

By all the Saints and demons, how had the woman gotten here so quickly? And why?

As the Kniaz's consort, she traveled with a retinue. Yet here she was, a glass of kvass in each hand, clad in her dusky blue velvet gown, her hair spangled with tiny diamonds. Next to her, wearing blood-and-dirt-spattered battle leathers, Katerina felt nasty to the nth degree.

"Why are you here?" It came out less than polite, but she'd used up the last of her good manners when she'd refrained from ripping off Fyodor's head and sending it flying at his murderous bitch of a Dimi. Not to mention playing nice with the Kniaz.

"Perhaps I'm just here to offer you a drink," the other woman said, her voice saccharine as she extended one of the tumblers of kvass to Katerina. "You must be thirsty, after... extending yourself in the arena tonight."

There was the slightest pause before 'extending,' but it was enough to tell Katerina all she needed to know. The woman *had* seen, damn her. The question was, how much?

She gathered her magic, feeling it tingle in her fingertips

and sizzle beneath her skin. "I'm fine, thank you," she said curtly. "Now, if you'll excuse me, I need to get changed for the feast." She took a step forward, but Dimi Zakharova didn't retreat.

"I know what you're doing," the woman hissed, her gaze raking over Katerina. "You intend to worm your way into the Druzhina, and then to take my place."

Katerina snorted. "Is that what this is about? Believe me when I tell you that's the last thing I want." *On every count.* "Now, step aside. I won't ask again."

"*Believe you?*" The marble statue of Sant Antoniya in the alcove by Katerina's door tipped, then righted itself, as Dimi Zakharova's earth-magic rose. "Because you're so truthful, Katerina Ivanova. The Magiya's records say you're a firewitch, like your mother before you. But you're not, are you?" She took a step closer, until the skirts of her gown brushed Katerina's legs. "Who has lied for you, Dimi Ivanova? If the truth came out, what price would they pay?"

The woman had sent for copies of Katerina's genealogy and bonding ceremony from Iriska's largest repository of knowledge, halfway across the realm from Rivki. Did that mean she'd suspected Katerina long before the incident in the arena today?

Maybe it meant nothing. Perhaps this type of surveillance was done on all of the candidates for the Trials. Still, fear iced the blood in Katerina's veins.

Steady, she told herself. *Hold the line.*

"I am a firewitch," she said, each word dropping like a stone into the still air of the hallway. "If you've troubled yourself to look that deeply into my origins, you know every woman in my mother's line since the Saints conferred their blessings on Iriska has been a firewielder. What else would I be?"

She let her lips rise in a mirthless smile, the one that usually preceded stabbing a demon through the heart and sending it hurtling into the Void. "I'm sorry to waste your time. But I *am* flattered you've concerned yourself with me, Dimi Zakharova. Why, I don't know the slightest thing about you, save that you're happy to warm the bed of a tyrant and a fool."

The other woman's eyes narrowed, rage heating their depths. A muscle in her jaw twitched, and the ground beneath Katerina's feet shook, forcing her to fight to keep her balance. "You dare to speak so of the Kniaz? Perhaps I was wrong. Perhaps you truly don't want to share his bed." Her voice lowered to a hiss, laden with suspicion. "I saw the way you looked at your Shadow, when you thought he couldn't see. Is that where your heart lies, Dimi Ivanova? For if so, you're a threat of an entirely different kind."

Katerina's pulse kicked up, pounding so hard, she swore she could taste it. A quarter-hour in the arena and five minutes in a hallway, and Dimi Zakharova had seen deeper into her heart than anyone ever had. It was insufferable...and dangerous.

"How dare you suggest such a thing?" she said, her voice ice-cold. "My Shadow will be betrothed to his Vila before all of Kalach the night of the Bone Moon. He is a man of honor."

"One can be betrothed, and even marry, and still betray one's vows." The other woman was so close, her breath brushed Katerina's cheek. "So many lies, Dimi Ivanova. So many lives you hold in your hand. For surely everyone in your village knows you are not merely a firewitch. Keeping a secret that could mean so much to the realm...the price for such a thing would be steep beyond measure."

By all the Saints and demons, she refused to make twenty-one years of sacrifice and silence be for nothing. "What is *wrong* with you?" she snapped. Better to put the other woman on the defensive than to be constantly caught wrong-footed like this. "Are you so desperate to keep your place in that bastard's bed that you're willing to betray a fellow Dimi to have what you want, inventing threats where none exist?"

She dropped her voice, letting a full measure of viciousness fill it. "Or is that he's grown tired of you, Dimi Zakharova? Does he not reach for you as often; do you sense his gaze roving, as he seeks a wife to give him heirs? I feel sorry for you. Such petty insecurity is beneath a Dimi. The world bends to our will, not the other way around."

The woman sucked in a sharp breath. She stepped back, scanning every inch of Katerina, her lip curling in scorn. "I don't know what you are, little Dimi," she said. "But I intend to find out. Because you might not wish to be the Kniaz's consort, but he covets pretty things. He covets power. The choice might not be yours. And I have no intention of being displaced at all, much less by a liar and a traitor."

The marble floor beneath them cracked with the force of her outrage, the movement jostling the glasses in her hands. As liquid sloshed over the rims, Katerina smelled what she hadn't before: bitter cascara, a potent laxative.

If she'd accepted the kvass, she wouldn't have died, no. But she would have spent a very uncomfortable evening, away from the covetous gaze of the Kniaz, just like Dimi Zakharova wanted. And next time, her drink might be laced with something worse.

Her gaze flicked to Zakharova's face. The other woman was watching her, dark eyes glittering with malice. A satisfied smile lifted her painted lips.

For the love of the Saints. This was what happened when a greedy tyrant pinned a beautiful, powerful woman under his thumb: insecurity and jealousy. In another world, Katerina and Dimi Zakharova would be allies. Katerina might even look to her as a mentor; the woman was politically savvy, able to navigate the treacherous waters of this despicable place without so much as turning a hair. But instead, the other Dimi hated and feared Katerina, not because of her power but because she inspired the Kniaz's unholy lust.

It was just one more reason to despise the man. But right now, he wasn't the threat. Dimi Zakharova was, and though Katerina would never have started this fight, there was no way to turn from it now.

She couldn't light a fire inside the Kniaz's palace. Nor could she use her other magic, without confirming Dimi Zakharova's suspicions and endangering everyone in Kalach. She was trapped, Saints curse it. Hatred burned inside her, desperate for an outlet, as she bared her teeth. "Count yourself lucky I don't yet call Rivki home. You may not know what I am, but trust me when I say I am powerful enough to end you. For your insinuation that something improper exists between myself and my Shadow alone, I should make you pay."

The other woman lifted one shoulder in an elegant, disdainful shrug. "Watch what you eat and drink tonight, Dimi Ivanova. For I have taken on far more worthy opponents than you. And the Kniaz can't Reap you if you're dead."

Giving Katerina one last, weighted look, she turned and strode through the carved wooden doors at the opposite end of the hallway, the earth trembling in her wake.

9

KATERINA

Katerina knocked so hard on the door to Niko's room, it threatened to bruise her knuckles. She wanted to pound on it, but that would draw attention. Already, the other Dimis and Shadows were streaming in, some of them obviously the worse for drink, with Sofi and Damien bringing up the rear.

Sofi slid Katerina a grin, which Katerina did her best to return. She was pretty sure she did a terrible job, because the other Dimi rolled her eyes in response. She didn't stop to question Katerina, though, thank the Saints, just signed, "Later," and headed up the stairs. Behind her, Damien raised his tumbler of kvass to Katerina in salute, then padded down the hallway toward his room, leaving a trail of bloodied sand in his wake.

By all the Saints and demons, what could be keeping her Shadow? She knocked again, more insistently still. "Niko, I don't care if you have a bevy of Vila beauties in your bed," she snapped, though it was a blatant lie. "Open the door this instant, or—"

The words died on her lips as the door swung inward, the

firelight within illuminating the form of her Shadow. He was bare from the waist up, clad only in his leather fighting pants. On the bicep of his left arm gleamed Katerina's Mark: three interlocking circles, the black pigment of the dye mixed with her blood. He'd taken the rawhide tie out of his dark hair, and it fell loose to his shoulders. The tips dripped water onto his muscled chest, crisscrossed by scars that she knew as well as the lines of her own palm: A thin, long-healed souvenir from his first sparring match. The silvered track of another Shadow's teeth, which would never heal completely. An etched, jagged line from a blade soaked in Grigori venom.

As if taunting her, the firelight flickered over the white streak in his dark hair that had come after Baba Petrova inked Katerina's Mark on his skin. Every Shadow had a distinguishing feature, something besides their Mark that showed how they'd been changed by the bond. It was just Katerina's luck that Niko's was so visible. Each time she looked at it, she was reminded how he was hers and yet not, all at the same time.

Why did he have to be so Saints-damned beautiful? Speech-less, she tried to stop staring but only succeeded in glancing downward, to the V of muscles that disappeared beneath the waistband of his fighting leathers, which didn't help. At all.

"You called?" Niko said, his voice wry. "For someone who wanted my attention, Katya, you don't seem to have a lot to say."

Her childhood nickname, the one only he was allowed to use, did the trick. Lifting her head, Katerina found his eyes locked on hers, glittering with amusement and an emotion she couldn't quite decipher. She opened her mouth, shut it again, then mastered herself with an effort. "Sorry to pull you away from whatever orgy kept you from answering the door, but we have a situation."

At the word 'orgy,' Niko snorted, swinging the door wide.

His room was empty, the bed neatly made, his clothes for the evening's feast laid out across the foot. "I can't decide whether to be gratified that you think I'm capable of satisfying a host of women after the night we've just had, or insulted that you think I'd betray Elena that way," he said, motioning for her to enter. "I was getting dressed, Katerina. And attempting to bathe. I see you had no such concerns."

Elena's name was like a bucket of cold water dashed right into Katerina's face. She stalked into his room and stood in the middle of his hearth rug, letting the fire warm her. He followed, shutting the door and then leaning back against it, regarding her with that same indecipherable look. "What's the matter, Katya?" he said, his voice soft.

The gentleness in it almost broke her. But she couldn't afford to break, not now. She had to be strong. "We need to leave," she said, her tone clipped. "For the love of the Saints, dry your hair and put on a shirt, would you? You're dripping everywhere."

Niko arched a quizzical eyebrow but obeyed, turning away from her to grab a towel from the armoire. "Please tell me there wasn't an assassin waiting in your bedchamber." His voice was light, but with a distinct edge.

"Replace 'assassin' with 'woman who wanted me to have the shits all night' and 'bedchamber' with 'hallway,' and you'll be right on the nose," she said, doing her best to ignore the way the muscles in his back shifted as he straightened.

Niko spun, using the preternatural speed he usually only reserved for battle. "Explain yourself," he said, his tone clipped, all amusement drained away.

So Katerina did, leaving out only Dimi Zakharova's insinuation that an inappropriate relationship existed between her and Niko. She was *not* going there, not now. Not ever.

With each word she spoke, Niko's gray eyes darkened. He

ran a hand through his damp hair as she finished, ending with, "We need to go now, Niko. Tonight. If she tells the Kniaz what she suspects... We need to get back to Kalach. To warn Baba."

He paced in front of her, the firelight playing over his face. Thank the Saints, he'd put on a shirt—not the ruffled one that lay at the foot of his bed, but the fitted one he normally wore beneath his fighting leathers. "Do you want me to kill her?"

She peered at him, trying to ascertain if he was serious. He stared back at her, giving her nothing, and she threw up her hands in exasperation. "No, Niko, I don't. If I wanted her dead, I would've done it myself. You don't think murdering the Kniaz's pet would draw even more unwanted attention to us, if anyone connected the dots?"

Niko sank down onto the edge of the bed, his shoulders heaving in a sigh. "You're right. But we can't just leave, Katerina."

"Why not?" she challenged.

He shot her an incredulous look. "For one thing, we're expected at the feast tonight. If two of the six victors don't show up, you don't think *that* will draw unwanted attention? For another, what with the increased attacks, riding through the night, this close to the full Bone Moon, is tempting fate. I vote we keep an eye on her and leave first thing in the morning."

Now Katerina was the one pacing. "Saints only knows what harm she could do in a single evening. We have to go. We can make our excuses to the Kniaz, tell him we're needed at home."

He snorted. "We're needed at home so badly that we can't spend a night eating food the likes of which we'll never see in Kalach, being honored before Iriska's royalty, then drinking until we can't stand up? No one leaves before the feast, Katya. Even the Shadows and Dimis who failed today will stay until the morning. We'll be hard-pressed to explain this away."

Desperate, she drew her trump card. Niko was sworn to protect her. Maybe this would work, if nothing else did. "As despicable as I find Dimi Zakharova, she was right about one thing. Kniaz Sergey doesn't just crave my power. He wants *me*."

Niko stared up at her, his jaw working. He didn't say a word.

"My *body*," she clarified, in case he didn't understand.

"How do you know this?" The words were a growl.

"He all but came out and said it." Power prickled at her fingertips at the memory, and Niko shifted his weight as the spillover pulsed through their bond.

"Did he touch you?" Her Shadow's fists clenched the coverlet so tightly the fabric protested, the seams giving way under his grip.

"He did not." She came to a stop in front of Niko, endeavoring to pry his fingers loose. "Quit destroying the bedclothes, would you, or we'll have yet another crime to answer for."

He turned his furious gaze on hers. "Did you want him to, Katya?"

Katerina stopped trying to rescue the coverlet from Niko and stared at him instead. "Now I'm the one who can't decide whether to be insulted or... No, I'm just insulted," she said, each word a cube of ice. "Did I want a man I can't stand, who uses his power to manipulate those who have no choice but to obey, to put his hands all over me? I can't believe I have to dignify this with a response, but no, Niko, I did not. I'd break his fingers first and sell his Saints-cursed rings to feed all of Kalach."

Her Shadow dropped his head, staring at the rug beneath his feet. His shoulders were rigid beneath the thin material of his shirt, but when he spoke, his voice was laced with a plea. "I apologize for the insinuation. Forgive me, Katya."

She took a deep breath, inhaling his familiar scent: leather and blood, sweat and mint. No matter where she was, he was home.

But the two of them didn't belong here, and the sooner they left, the better. "On one condition," she said. "We ride for Kalach tonight."

Niko's head came up, his eyes dark with fury, his jaw granite-hard with resolve. He unhinged the latter long enough to utter a single syllable.

"Done," he said.

IO

KATERINA

The trees edged close on either side, hemming them in, as Katerina and her Shadow rode hard through the darkening woods.

"Maybe we should have waited until morning to leave Rivki, after all," Niko said as they rounded a bend in the path and were forced to slow, his shoulders tensing beneath his black leather gear. Above, the waxing Bone Moon hung low, glinting against the star-pocked vault of the sky, and Niko gave it an uneasy glance. "Kniaz or no Kniaz, this doesn't bode well."

They'd made their excuses to Kniaz Sergey, claiming Niko was needed at home to prepare for his betrothal. It was a poor explanation, but the Kniaz had accepted it reluctantly, saying only that he regretted seeing them go and extracting a promise that they'd come to deliver the tithe next month. Next to him, Dimi Zakharova had given a small, self-satisfied smile, which Katerina had wanted to smack right off her face. Instead, they'd packed, retrieved their horses, and ridden over the bridge that separated the island from the mainland. Now here they were, picking their way along a moonlit path that cut through

Cherkasy Forest, with Niko insisting he could sense Grigori lurking in the woods.

"Enough," Katerina snapped. "We'll make it to Drezna tonight, and tomorrow we'll go home."

But she wasn't so sure. Maybe it was just Niko's nagging, but she could swear she felt the weight of the demons' eyes peering at her from the treeline, forming a cold spot between her shoulder blades.

Damn her Shadow. And damn her overactive imagination. They *were* going home; she willed it to be true. They would reach it in one piece, make their confession to Baba Petrova, and deal with the consequences. Anything was better than staying in Rivki for one more second.

Niko sighed, glancing over his shoulder back the way they'd come. "I'd defend your virtue, my Dimi. The Kniaz would never lay a finger on you unwanted, nor would that bitch of a Dimi speak a word. You have it on my honor. It's not too late to go back."

"Yes, it is." They'd been riding for hours. What was the point of turning around now?

"It's not." The blades at his waist clinked, and he put a hand down to settle them in their holster. "Better to face the devil we know than to be alone in the woods with Saints knows what, still miles from Drezna."

Katerina made a low sound of disagreement, but Niko didn't give up. "Blini with caviar," he coaxed, his voice honey-smooth. "Borscht with sour cream, all you can eat."

She coaxed her mare, Mika, next to his stallion as the path widened. "Naming my favorite foods won't help. We have to get back to warn Baba. And whatever might be in these woods, together the two of us are more dangerous than it could dream of being."

"There *is* something in the woods," Niko said, raising his

face to the wind. He breathed deep, tasting the air. There was a wildness to the gesture, and for a moment Katerina saw not the man who had been her friend since childhood, before he'd taken a blood vow to stand by her side, but the black dog that lived inside him. "I know you feel it."

Indeed, Katerina could. The air trembled, heavy with the portent of things to come. An edge of hunger rode the breeze, sentient and waiting.

Beneath her, Mika whickered uneasily, and Katerina gripped the reins, peering ahead. They were picking their way carefully now, the light of the moon all that illuminated their path. "Whatever's here," she said, raising her voice, "it will not dare cross us. The spirits of the forest should take heed, for they seek to wound us at their peril." Bracing herself, she sent her gift out through the earth and into the trees, seeking, but found nothing in return.

Next to her, Niko shivered as a tendril of her magic ran through him. "Katya," he said quietly. "I see that look on your face. But be reasonable. We can go back to the island, wait until morning."

Katerina was *not* trotting back to Rivki with her tail between her legs, especially if Dimi Zakharova had opened her big mouth. Edging her horse closer to Niko's, she grinned up at him —her razor-sharp grin, the one she wore before crumbling a demon to dust—and leveraged the one subject she was sure would distract him, no matter how little she herself cared for it.

"Surely you're eager to get back to Elena," she said, batting her lashes. "Wouldn't you rather be with her than penned up on an island with me, a water spirit, and a tyrant? We'll reach Drezna, and you'll be that much closer to having her in your arms."

He shot her an aggravated look out of the corner of his eye. "Leave Elena out of this."

"How can I?" Katerina said, her voice as insouciant as she could make it. "She's soon to be your betrothed, my Shadow. To bear your children. That's something to look forward to, is it not?" She winked at him, as if the answer didn't have the potential to break her heart.

Niko growled, a low sound more at home in the throat of the black dog than the man. "I'm looking forward to a warm bed without the evil that roams this forest breathing down my neck, Katerina. At this rate, I won't live long enough to have a Shadowchild with Elena. I'm telling you, something's not right."

As if it had heard him speak, the darkness deepened; the trees loomed taller. The silence that fell was absolute, even the small creatures of the forest growing quiet.

Katerina ignored the roiling sensation inside her, her magic rising to the call of whatever lurked in the woods, that told her he was likely right. Instead, she kicked her mare up to a canter, heedless of the darkness and the narrow path.

"I am *not* going to ride back over that bridge," she told him over her shoulder. "I'm not going to hide and cower. If there is a threat out here, we should face it, before it poses harm to the people of Drezna."

"Certainly," Niko said from behind her, his voice dry. "It has nothing to do with the fact that you'll bow for no one. Saints forbid you ask for help, or that you show caution—"

"Caution is for people who are weaker than we, Niko Alekhin. We are the ones that the creatures of the Dark should fear."

Katerina never heard his reply, if he made one at all. Because that was when a deafening crack split the air, her Shadow was ripped from her side, and the world was swallowed by an unrelenting black.

II

KATERINA

Her mare reared, letting out an unearthly cry. She struggled to hold on to the reins, but it was no use. Mika bolted from beneath her, fleeing, and Katerina fell to the ground with a thud that rattled her bones.

Her Shadow. Where was Niko?

She couldn't hear him. She couldn't see him. In fact, she couldn't see anything. This wasn't normal darkness, but rather *Darkness*—the sense that all Light had gone from the world. It was the pitch-black of the abyss.

She reached for her bond with her Shadow, and felt...nothing. There was a gaping hole where Niko should be. A bolt of horror ripped through her, and she fought to gain her feet. "Niko!" she howled. "To me!"

He didn't answer her.

She opened her mouth to call for him again, but agonizing pain doubled her over, searing through every nerve ending. It was like being stabbed with a million blades, spiked with lightning...except the lightning was ice-cold.

Katerina clutched her chest. Had someone—something— severed their bond? Such a thing shouldn't be possible, unless...

Was he dead? Had someone killed her Shadow, before she'd ever had the chance to tell him what was in her heart?

Her agony retreated into numbness. A sense of utter terror and hopelessness consumed her, weighing her down. Nothing was right, nothing would ever be right again...

Once, when Katerina was very small, she'd fallen into a snowbank. The snow had closed over her head, surrounding her. When she'd opened her mouth to scream, it had found its way inside, taking the place of her words. It had pressed her down, squeezing her lungs, stealing her breath, freezing her magic. Her Dimi mother had found her less than a minute later, melting the snow and setting Katerina free, but Katerina had never forgotten what it had been like to be trapped that way, inside an icy fortress that wanted only to keep her for its own.

This was like that: an ice-cold weight, pinning her to the ground, invading every part of her. She couldn't see. Couldn't move. Couldn't think. When she reached for her magic, there was only...emptiness.

For an instant, an eternity, she lay crumpled on the path in the dark. And then a gleam appeared in the gloom—a tiny light, growing stronger the longer she looked.

The amulet at her neck that held Niko's blood seared red-hot, scorching her. Her Shadow bond sparked to life just as a blaze illuminated the darkened woods.

Niko stood on the path, burning like the Lightbringer she'd always teasingly called him. A glow encased him, emanating from the blessed blade he held in his hand. She had never seen him look like that—a living embodiment of the Light to which he and Katerina were consecrated. For years, she'd thought of him as bringing her out of the metaphorical darkness that had lurked inside her ever since her mother's death, but in this moment, she wondered if her assessment had been more accurate than she'd ever realized. The illumination spread from him in ever-increasing circles, until at last it touched the place where Katerina lay.

That awful sensation of being encased in ice retreated, taking the unbearable hopelessness with it. She ran for Niko, claiming her place by his side, as his Light chased the last of the unnatural gloom away and then faded, her Shadow assuming his normal form once more.

The world was as it had been before the Darkness had descended upon them: road and moon and forest. But both of their horses had fled. And emerging from the woods on all sides, surrounding Niko and Katerina, was the biggest horde of Grigori demons she had ever seen. Normally, they wandered as rogues or attacked in packs, commanded by one of their filthy brethren, but this was no pack. This was an army.

They looked like people; they always did. Only their characteristic rosemary-and-clove scent, meant to entice humans to them, gave them away—and with them en masse like this, it poured off them, permeating the air. Next to her, Niko choked on it.

In human form, her Shadow could meet his death at the hands of a blade bathed in Grigori venom or from a demon's venom-coated bite. And there were so many of them here, encroaching nearer, closing the circle. Clad all in black, poisoned blades and bared teeth glinting under the light of the waxing moon.

Niko was right: they should have turned back. Damn her stupid pride, her insistence that they press onward. They were alone here, without the aid of a rowan-fire or the fellow Shadows and Dimis who always fought alongside them. It was just the two of them, and a host of demons determined to see them die.

There was no time to wonder why the Grigori were here in such force, on a lonely road far from Drezna. Whether she and

Niko were their deliberate prey, or whether encountering the two of them was coincidence, en route to whatever the Grigori were really after. There was nothing to do but fight. To defeat the demons, or die trying.

Katerina prayed to Sant Antoniya, Sant Andrei, and Sant Viktoriya for strength. She called her magic, feeling it rise from the earth, filling her like she were a vessel and it a thick, syrupy liquid. "Stand by my side, my Shadow," she said.

"Always," he answered her.

And then the demons were on them.

Niko stood his ground, blessed blades in hand, spinning like a whirl of light, slicing through one Grigori after another before they could reach her. The Grigori howled as they fell, the sickly-sweet scent of their blood scorching her lungs and soaking the air. But there were always more.

Desperately, Katerina sent her sixth sense out, searching the woods. Her magic curled around one rowan after another, uprooting them and sending them hurtling into the fray, piercing the demons' hearts. A thought, and she set the trees aflame. The fires consumed the Grigori's corpses, and as others charged toward her, their flesh and clothing caught as well. They melted before her eyes, and their voices filled her mind, fraught with agony: *Vengeance upon you, cursed Dimi. May Gadreel seek his revenge on your body and your soul.*

Gadreel. The Fallen Angel of War himself, a king among Grigori and one of the first of the Fallen Watchers. The demon who had schooled humankind in the art of weaponry and killing blows. Helper of God, before he and the rest of the Grigori had fallen to the Dark.

Katerina had no time to consider why Gadreel's army was loose upon this road, nor what it might mean to be the target of his vengeance. She stood, feet planted, hands outstretched, and called the wind. It rose to her bidding, driving the Grigori back.

But there were so many of them, and they bent themselves against it and just kept coming. One of them broke ranks and charged Niko, a blade in each hand. They flashed in the moonlight as the demon raised an arm high, meaning to take him through the heart.

She screamed, a howl so loud it scraped her throat. Magic exploded from her, harnessing the wind and blasting the demon backward. It flew through the air and tumbled into the flames. But there were five more right behind it.

They came for her, ignoring Niko this time. She pulled on the earth itself, tearing it up in front of them, tree roots catching at their legs, entangling them. One fell. Two. But the rest—

Beside her, Niko's body shimmered. A moment later, his blades clattered to the ground and a growl shook the forest. In the form of his black dog, he leapt, knocking the demons away from her. Snarling, he ripped out the throat of the closest one, coughing in disgust as blood poured from his mouth and drenched the ground.

You will never touch her. His voice echoed inside her head, the way it always did when he was in the shape of his black dog. *She belongs to the Light, Grigori filth.*

Another demon fell beneath his teeth and claws. Blood spattered Katerina as she ripped tree after tree from the ground, impaling the Grigori and lighting them aflame. She spun in a circle, igniting the rowans at the treeline, burning the demons who snarled in pain as they fought to get through. She incinerated them where they stood, but there were still more and more—

And then one of them was on her, slicing at her with its blades. She twisted, fighting to escape, but it was no use. A knife sank deep into her thigh, and the demon howled in triumph. Its fellows echoed it, and Niko raised his head, eyes catching hers in horror.

He ran for her, dropping the demon in his jaws to the ground like a ragdoll, but there were more of them now, descending on her, and she could barely see him—

No, his mind-voice said, tight with terror. *No! Katerina, fight!*

She thrashed and struggled, heating her body with witch-fire from within as the demons tore at her clothes. They wailed in pain as it scorched them, but didn't let go. The Darkness sucked at her, as eager to devour her soul as the demons were to pierce her body, to claim her for their own. They were servants of the Dark, and the Dark was hungry.

Katerina rolled left, then right, dragging the demons with her. She couldn't light them aflame, not when they were on top of her. But if she could drive them backward, into the fire...

Bit by painful bit, she pulled herself toward the flames. Out of the corner of her eye, she could see Niko battling two Grigori, still in the form of his dog. He tore the entrails from one of them, but the other sliced at him, and no matter how he dodged and weaved, he couldn't get free.

Katerina!

The fear in Niko's voice almost undid her. Not for himself, she knew. For her.

She refused to die here. Not like this, and have him believe he'd failed her.

Katerina reached deep, deep into the well of her magic. She had never reached so far before, didn't know what cost she would pay. But whatever it was, she would pay it, and gladly.

Sant Antoniya, help me now, she prayed. *Give me your strength, lend me your Light.*

Power burst from her, buckling the very earth. A flash of illumination turned the road and forest bright as day as the wind rose still higher, driving every Grigori back, ripping those who had hold of her away. The demons shrieked, an ear-split-ting sound that made the air quake.

And then, every single one of them burst into flame.

~

KATERINA PROPPED herself on her elbows, panting, as the demons burned, taking the forest with them. Her leg ached where the Grigori had stabbed her. Their venom wouldn't affect her as it did Niko—just as a Shadow's bite could take down a Grigori, so a demon's venom could fell a Shadow—but even still, it hurt like hell. She pressed her palm against the wound, staunching the flow of blood, as Niko knelt by her side, half-clad and in human form once more.

Dirt and blood streaked his face. His eyes were wide with shock and...something else. Wonder, maybe. "Katya," he said, his voice hoarse. Taking his shirt from the ground where it had fallen when he shifted, he tore a piece of fabric from the bottom and set to binding her wound. She grunted as he pulled the tourniquet tight. "Talk to me. Is this the only place—are you hurt—"

He fumbled at her shirt, trying to lift it, and she shoved his hands away. "I'm all right. But Niko, did they stab you?"

She didn't know what she would do if he said yes. They were alone here, stranded between Rivki and Drezna, and Grigori venom was fast-acting. Katerina was trained in the art of healing, as all Dimis were, but the antivenin was in her saddlebag, and the horses had run off—

But he shook his head. "Grazes while I was in the form of my dog, nothing more. See." He raised his arms, showing her the defensive wounds there, doubtless acquired as he fought to protect his muzzle. "But you...Katerina, what did you do...?"

Together, they regarded the destruction she'd wrought. The road was buckled and broken, littered with the corpses of charred Grigori and burning tree limbs. Though they sat, untouched, in Katerina's circle, all around them, the woods burned.

"Protected you," she said, simply. "Saved myself."

That look of wonder was still there in his eyes, and something else, too. Fear, perhaps. "You've never done anything like this before, against so many. I didn't know you could."

The idea that Niko might fear her sent a spike of dismay through Katerina's heart. It made her voice tight as she said, struggling to sit all the way up, "Says the one who blazed with more Light than I've ever seen. Desperate times, my Shadow. Would you rather we died here, on a lonely road, at the hands of demons?"

He regarded her, his expression cross. "Of course not. And quit that, you'll make it worse. Here, lean on me." He pulled her back against his chest, his long legs encircling hers, careful not to touch the wounded one. "I just—what if you hadn't been able to do that, Katya? I couldn't reach you, I couldn't get to you..."

The pain in his voice pierced her. She twisted, looking up at him. His eyes were haunted as he gazed at the ruins of the path to Drezna. "You didn't have to. You shoulder too much, Niko."

His arms wrapped around her, holding her close. She knew it was the simple protective instinct that a Shadow held for his Dimi, especially given the terrible danger they'd just faced. It was her fault, her flaw that she couldn't help but wish for more.

Niko had wanted them to turn around. He'd warned her, again and again, and she'd been too stubborn and headstrong to listen. Too convinced that she could handle whatever came.

Because of Katerina's arrogance, her Shadow could have been killed.

Guilt festering inside her, she peeled his arms away. "Help me up. Enough wallowing. They're dead, but who knows if there are more? I'm not waiting on this cursed road like a sitting duck for them to find me."

Without comment, Niko lifted her, setting her upright. He inspected her, assessing the wince she couldn't suppress when her injured leg took her weight.

"You need a healer," he said. "Don't try to argue. And don't try to walk. Maybe you can ride home like that, Katya, but you're not stumbling on that leg all the way to Drezna. I can't believe I let the bastards close enough to touch you. Grigori scum," he growled, and spat on the body that lay at their feet.

Katerina forced a smile. "What's the alternative? Our horses are gone. And I don't intend to camp on the road amongst the corpses of our enemies."

Niko didn't smile back. He glared at her, scanning every inch of her body, and she fought not to quail beneath the uncharacteristic wrath in his gaze. "I don't intend for that to happen either, Katya. I'm going to pick you up. Tell me if I hurt you."

"I'm fine," Katerina insisted, gritting her teeth against the pain in her leg. "Really, Niko, I'm okay. There's no need for—"

Ignoring her protests, he swept her up and carried her down the path toward Drezna, his arms tight around her. Despite her discomfort, Katerina couldn't help but notice how warm his body was, how right it felt to have him hold her this way. Surrendering, she rested her head against his shoulder. She breathed in his familiar scent of mint and the oil he used to feed his blades, blended now with the sickly-sweet aroma of Grigori blood. It was better than the reek of the rowan-fires and the nasty stench of roasting demon.

An overpowering sense of dread at what they might find when they arrived on Drezna's doorstep simmered inside her. What if the demons had somehow penetrated its defenses? What if they'd hurt the people who called the village home?

She had never seen anything like this army of demons, three nights before the Bone Moon grew full. Why had the Fallen Angel of War, more of a myth than a true threat, set his sights on Drezna? Could Katerina's feelings for her Shadow have set the prophecy in motion? Could this somehow be her fault?

Niko's expression was grim, his jaw tight as he strode down the road. His heart thumped against her, as steady as his footfalls on the packed dirt. Closing her eyes, she imagined arriving in Drezna: the warm welcome they'd receive from Baba Volkova, the comforting knowledge that their friends were safe —especially Tanya and Alexandr, who they often spent time with on the way home from delivering the tithe. Soon the apple trees would be blooming in Kalach; farther to the west, Drezna's trees bloomed even sooner. She imagined wandering in the village orchard as she and Niko had done in Kalach when they were children, picking the red-blushed fruit to make the cinnamon-apple pies that were her Shadow's favorite.

A decade ago, Katerina had brought Niko a basket of those pies as he sat by his mother's grave, and kept him company as he ate them one by one, mechanically, as if they were made of sawdust. When he finished, he lay down with his head in her lap, watching the sun set over the stones of Kalach's small cemetery. "I wish I'd been enough," he'd said, as she'd run her fingers through his hair. "Enough to make her stay."

Katerina had lost her mother and father years before, in a demon raid. She knew, better than most, what it was like to feel alone and adrift. The idea of Niko feeling that way had broken her heart.

"You are enough," she'd told him fiercely. "You will always be enough for me."

He was enough, still. He had saved them both, tonight. That awful moment when she thought she'd lost him forever...her first thought had not been worry for herself, or fear of what might come boiling out of the woods to attack her in the Dark. But terror of losing him—not because he was her Shadow, but because of all he meant to her.

In almost every memory she had, Niko was by her side. It was a wondrous and terrible thing.

"Katerina," her Shadow said, breaking the silence. "Look."

She lifted her head from his shoulder and opened her eyes. And then she sucked in her breath.

So close to the spring solstice, they wouldn't see another frost until the coming year. Yet the earth was blanched. The tender shoots of grass that grew along the path and the leaves of the evergreens that flanked it were lined with crystals of ice. It shone in the glow of the moon, reflecting the light with an eerie, unnatural glint.

But that wasn't the worst of it. As far as they could see, the bodies of deer and wolves and squirrels were strewn across the road toward Drezna. Blood seeped from them, frozen into icy pools.

Katerina had seen a lot of things in her twenty-one years. But she'd never seen anything like this.

She looked for their horses among the fallen—Mika, who'd carried her uncomplainingly for miles, and Troitze, as fierce and wild as Niko himself. She didn't see them, thank the Saints. They had escaped whatever scourge came this way.

But the corpses were fresh, not even stiffening.

A chill ran through Katerina, and she looked back the way they'd come. In one direction, the fallen Grigori lined the road. In the other, these beasts lay dead.

The frost, on this part of the road only. The road that led to Drezna.

The dead animals.

The demons, more powerful and numerous than any she'd seen before, emerging from the woods.

A sudden, awful thought struck her. "Niko," she said, "I don't smell the fires." Normally, at this distance, the scent of the omnipresent rowan-fires that burned at the perimeter of every village would fill the air. But there was nothing here other than the lingering scent of Grigori venom and the faint hint of animal blood.

He raised his face, inhaling. "Nor do I. But I smell Grigori, Katerina."

"That's us," she said, trying to strike a desperate bargain with the Fates. "We were just surrounded by a horde of them."

"No." Niko's nostrils flared as he breathed deeply once again, making sure there could be no mistake. "This is airborne scent, not the scent we carry. They were here before us. They came this way."

His words echoed her worst fears. "Then—"

"We didn't outpace the demons," he said, horror clear in each syllable. "We're retracing their steps."

Then he was running, Katerina clutched tight in his arms, leaping over the bodies of the fallen beasts as only a trained Shadow could. The path widened, the way it always did when they arrived in Drezna. But the warmth of the fires didn't burn to greet them, nor did a Shadow stand sentinel at the gates. Here, all was quiet and dark.

"Niko," Katerina said, her voice breaking.

"I know." He shifted her weight, lifting a hand to smooth her hair back from her face. "Something bad happened here, Katya."

Dizziness swept Katerina as they followed the road that led to the heart of the village. The gardens that hugged it were bled by that same frost, their nascent plants lying limp and dead. She caught sight of the apple orchard, the tree limbs blackened and peeling beneath a layer of ice. Nothing moved on the path or in the fields.

"Hello?" she called out. "Is anyone here?"

But no one answered her call. Not so much as a dog came trotting out to meet them.

A village would never leave itself unprotected this way. Shadows rotated on constant patrol each night, especially so close to the Bone Moon. No one could simply walk into Drezna, not in these times.

They passed Baba Volkova's cottage. The door hung open, a gaping maw. When Niko peered inside, the place was empty. But in the hearth, a fire still blazed.

A chill ran through Katerina again. With him holding her like this, they were vulnerable. "Put me down," she said. "I may not be able to fight, but I can still use my magic."

Without a word, he set her on her feet and put an arm around her, supporting her. She limped by his side as they made their way toward the heart of Drezna, where the market-place and the artisans' shops hugged the town square. At night, they'd be locked up tight, but most merchants slept above their places of business. Surely someone would come out if Niko and Katerina called.

"They must be hiding," she said, unable to conceal the note of hope in her voice. "Maybe they're afraid. They'll see we're here to help them, and they'll—"

Her Shadow had never lied to her. He didn't start now. Instead, he took more of her weight as they walked the last few steps, emerging from the path that wound past the field where children had played the last time they visited, chasing each other in an age-old game of catch-the-demon. Now, it was deserted and sheathed in ice, the blades of grass shriveled and the stems of the yellow-wreathed preteska snapped.

Clouds scudded over the face of the moon as they left the field behind and stepped onto the cobblestones. She took one step, two. And then Niko jerked her back with such force that she almost tumbled to the ground. A growl rumbled from his throat, low and threatening.

"What—" she began indignantly. But then she saw for herself what his keener Shadow vision had noticed at once.

The two of them stood at the verge of a precipice. Another step, and Katerina would have tumbled into it. Where the bustling village center used to be, there was nothing but a crater—as if everything that once stood there had been sucked into the earth.

It was impossible. It was also true.

The village of Drezna was gone.

12

KATERINA

In shock, she and Niko walked the length and breadth of Drezna, unable to believe it had vanished. They stared into the depths of the crater, and the Darkness stared back at them. It whispered to Katerina, hissing her name.

For all she knew, she was staring into the Void, the vacuum from which the Darkness originated. A shard of it lived within each of the Grigori, its evil powering them. She had never seen it like this before: ink-black smoke, swirling free, a residue of demonic assault.

By the time they were done, Katerina's leg ached so badly she could hardly stand. They had found no survivors. It was as if that awful crater had swallowed the village whole.

"The portal to the demon realms lies outside the village limits," Katerina said at last, as they stood again at the precipice. "But somehow, the Grigori must have come out of the earth here. That sound we heard before they attacked us...I'm sure it was the destruction of Drezna. What other explanation can there be?"

Niko shrugged. It was an odd, uncomfortable movement, as if his shirt had suddenly become too tight. "I don't know," he said. "I'll tell you what I do know, though." He raised a hand, ticking off his points one by one. "You're injured. Night is falling. We're alone, without our horses. Trouble is here, and in our road. We need shelter. And to heal you as best we can."

Katerina nodded, the movement jerky. "But not here, Niko. I don't care if Baba Volkova's house is still standing. I can't...I can't stay here."

"Agreed." His mouth set in a grim line, and his jaw clenched as he gazed down into the pit. "The healers' cottage may be gone, but Baba will have medicinals. We'll patch you up and take what we need, and then we'll leave this place."

PREDICTABLY, Niko wouldn't let her enter Baba Volkova's cottage until he'd gone over every inch of it for threats. She waited, leaning against the wooden siding to take the weight off her leg, her eyes roving over the silvered runes painted on the eaves, the trim around the windows and doors. They were meant to be a defensive layer against demonic invasion, and they had held; Baba's house stood, when so many had been lost. But Baba herself was nowhere to be found. She must have run for the center of the conflict, despite her advanced age. She'd fought for Drezna, and died defending it.

At least Sofi and Damien had survived, safe in Rivki—though 'safe' was a relative term. Katerina had never been grateful for the existence of the Bone Trials before—but because of them, her friends lived, when so many others had fallen. Their home was destroyed, though, their families gone. What if she and Niko returned to Kalach, only to find it had met the same fate? Pressing her hand against the strength rune that twined around the doorframe, Katerina suppressed a shudder.

At last, Niko loomed up in the doorway. "No Grigori have

been inside," he said, his dark brows knitted. "I found Baba's medicines and some food to replace what we lost in the saddlebags. Come in, Katerina, and let's be done with this."

Katerina followed him inside and instructed him as to what she needed. Then she lit a taper and sat on one of Baba's high-backed chairs, trying to hold back the wave of sadness that threatened to swamp her. "Niko," she said as he set willowbark to brewing on the stove and mashed garlic, ginger, and echinacea into a paste under her direction, "so many of our friends. Tanya, Alexandr, Sasha, Leonid...gone. How can this be?"

"I don't know." His face was white to the lips as he knelt in front of her and undid the tourniquet, taking the candle from the table so he could get a better look at the wound. "A clean gash," he said, and she could tell he was fighting to keep his voice dispassionate. "It doesn't smell of infection, Katya. And the bleeding's stopped. Tell me what I need to do."

A quarter-hour later, she was freshly bandaged and full of willowbark tea, to fortify her against the pain. She'd insisted on spreading the healing herbs along the cuts on Niko's arms, too, and though he'd argued with her that it was unnecessary, he allowed it. Katerina thought he could see that she needed desperately to find some way—any way—to be of use.

Biting her lip, she limped to Baba Volkova's bedroom and lifted an armband bearing the elder Dimi's sigil from the dresser. "For Baba Petrova," she said to Niko, who was leaning against the doorframe, arms folded and one dark eyebrow quirked. "For remembrance. And for proof."

"You think we're going to need to *prove* what happened?" There was a quiet fury in his voice as he put an arm around her and guided her to the door. "I think the giant crater with Darkness swirling at the bottom of it, along with the trail of animal and demon corpses, speak for themselves."

I want proof that my feelings for you didn't cause this, Katerina

wanted to say. *Proof that something*–anything—*else is to blame.*
But voicing such a thought would be unthinkable, and so she
made no reply.

~

THEY CAMPED that night in a grove of rowan trees, as far from
Drezna as Niko deemed Katerina fit to walk. She wanted to
protest, but it was pointless: she'd refused to let him carry her
again, knowing that compromised their defenses, and each step
sent a bolt of pain shooting through her leg. By the time she
sank onto the bed of ferns that Niko had hacked from the plants
that grew at the base of the rowan trees, she was trembling all
over.

He regarded her with concern. "Should I cut some of these
limbs for the fires, Katya? Or can you—"

Katerina drew herself up, trying to summon her usual confidence. Seeing her compromised like this was troubling her
Shadow, and that simply wouldn't do. "I'm injured, not
broken," she said, her tone haughty. "Stand by me, out of the
way."

He came to her side as she said a brief prayer to the spirits of
the trees: *For your life, that we may live, we are thankful.* Then she
closed her eyes and called the wind. It rose to her hand, and the
limbs of the rowans splintered and fell. Niko gathered them,
stacking them in piles that formed a wide circle with Katerina
at its epicenter. Then he stood back and she set them aflame.

Niko dug in the leather satchel he'd brought from Baba
Volkova's cottage, coming up with the potatoes he'd found in
her pantry. Once he'd gotten them roasting, he dug a silver flask
out of the satchel and extended it to Katerina. "Drink."

"What is it?" she said, eyeing the flask suspiciously. She
wouldn't put it past him to have crumbled some sleeping herbs

into it; he could recognize those easily enough, and she knew he wanted her to rest.

"Kvass," he said. "You need it."

Her leg throbbed, and her body trembled with exhaustion. "Fine," she said, snatching the flask from him and taking a gulp. The liquor scorched her throat and settled, warm, in her belly. Tossing back her hair, she took another sip. Then a third.

She might've drained the whole thing, had Niko not wrested it from her hands. "Don't be greedy, Katya," he said, tilting the flask back to his own lips. "I've had a hard day."

By the flickering light of the fires, she could see the long line of his throat move as he swallowed. It was a thing of beauty, and she had to look away so he wouldn't catch her staring.

He thrust the flask into her hand, and they took turns drinking until he pulled the potatoes out of the fire. Katerina stifled a giggle as he bit into one and let out a stifled cry of pain. "My tongue," he muttered, glaring at the potato like it had done something to offend him. "Those are hot, Katya. Watch out."

"Duly noted," she said, amused that his need to protect her extended even to potatoes. "Here." She sent a small wind out, blowing over the surface of the root vegetables, cooling them. "Try it now."

Niko obliged, and let out a small sound of appreciation. "Much better. Don't let Baba Petrova know your talents extend to the culinary, Dimi mine. She'll have you in the kitchen before you know what's happened to you. I can hear her now: *Develop stronger discipline for the things you believe are beneath you, Katerina.*"

Katerina smiled, as he'd clearly meant her to do. But she couldn't help but think of what they would tell Baba Petrova when they finally made it back to Kalach. Unless riders passed them on the road, she and Niko would likely be the first to bring the news of what had happened to Drezna. Unless they should—

She fidgeted, and Niko, who'd finished eating and was leaning back on his hands, glanced over at her. "Are you all right?"

"I just—you don't think we should go back to Rivki, do you? And tell the Kniaz what's happened? Not to mention poor Sofi and Damien?"

Niko considered this, tilting his head to gaze up at the moon. Finally he said, "No. I want to go home. Besides, the Kniaz will find out soon enough. And you know what they say about shooting the messenger." He ran a hand through his hair, his brow furrowing. "As for Sofi and Damien, there's nothing they can do. Let them have a few final moments of peace, before they have to reckon with the loss of everything and everyone they love."

Relief permeated every fiber of Katerina's body. "Agreed," she said.

"Good."

Silence fell between them, broken only by the crackle of the fires' blaze. Katerina forced herself to eat, stuffing bits of potato into her mouth. She'd rarely felt less hungry, but she'd used a lot of her magic today and needed to replenish her energy stores. If she didn't, she'd risk draining Niko too. Her body would pull energy from his to sustain itself, and he would give it, until there was nothing left.

She gulped down the final bite, and he busied himself with pulling a blanket out of the satchel and setting their small campsite to rights. "Niko," she said to his back, "what in the name of all the Saints do you think happened? There were so many of them. And the Darkness—it was like it had gotten loose from inside the Grigori somehow. As if it had taken on a life of its own."

The night was mild, with just a slight bite to it, but still she wrapped her arms around herself, remembering her hopelessness when she'd been lying there, before Niko had blazed up with Light and saved them both. "I felt so cold," she said. "As if I would never be warm again. As if I'd lost you forever."

He was poking up one of the rowan-fires, but at this, he turned and made his way back to her. He knelt beside her, crushing the ferns. Their sharp green scent drifted up to her as he held her eyes with his own.

"You could never lose me, Katya. Do you understand? I'm yours. Always."

She struggled to contain the shiver that rolled through her. "The cold...the Darkness... Did you feel it too?"

Slowly, as if it cost him to make the admission, he nodded. "Our bond—it was like it had been cut in half. I've never felt pain like that. I feared you were dead. I couldn't see you, Katya. I couldn't see anything. And then the Light burst from me. I thought for an instant it was your fire, that you'd called it, but it didn't taste of your magic. I think...I think it was because there were so many of them. I stood there and I burned and then—they came."

This time, when the shiver took her, she didn't fight it, and Niko's eyes narrowed. "Are you cold?"

"No," she said automatically, but he was already picking up the blanket and tucking it around her. When she shuddered again, he lay down next to her, curving his body around hers. Cocooning her.

"Let it go, Katya," he said into her hair. "Let it out."

All her fear, all her rage, rolled through her body, shaking her from head to toe. He simply held her, murmuring into her hair that he had her, that she was safe, that for now at least, it was over.

Niko had never held her like this. She had dreamed of it for so long, imagined how all of his coiled strength, his focused intensity, would translate in a touch, a kiss. She longed to feel what it would be like for him to lose all of his control in her arms, to send her witchfire licking along his skin until he came apart.

But that...that might be the end of everything.

She shook harder, and Niko's arms tightened around her. "I have you, Katya." His voice was gravelly, rough. "I will protect you to my last breath."

Speaking of breath, she could feel his on the nape of her neck, a warm, tickling sensation that sent a hot flush trickling through her. Her heartbeat quickened, her body quaking along the length of his, and behind her, Niko went stock-still. He shifted, creating a small space between their bodies, and Katerina was glad he couldn't see the blush that heated her cheeks. Surely he would be horrified if he knew what she was thinking right now, when his only intention was to keep her safe. If he knew that just maybe, her feelings for him were responsible for what had happened in Drezna.

"I know you will," she managed. There was nothing she could do about how husky her voice sounded; with luck, he would attribute that to the smoke from the fires.

"You fought with honor today, Katya. You fought with valor." His fingers touched her hair, brushing it away from her face. They trembled, and Katerina worried that he was more undone by what had happened than he was letting on. She tried to turn to face him, but he held her still. "You have leaves and twigs here. If I may...?"

Wordless, she nodded, and his fingers combed through her tangled waves, his touch deft despite the slight tremor. To her shame, the sensation was relaxing and sensual all at once. She couldn't suppress the purr that moved through her, and Niko froze, startled. His fingers paused in her hair. "Do...do you want me to stop?" he said, his voice a hint unsteady.

Surely it was Katerina's imagination that his words seemed heavier than they should be, weighted with meaning. As if he felt the same desire she did, and feared they walked a razor's edge.

That was ridiculous. All he was doing was keeping her warm. Removing bark and dirt from her hair.

"No," she said, struggling to keep her voice level. "Not unless you want to, that is. Don't feel...obligated."

Niko made a sound that hovered somewhere between a growl and a bitter laugh. He muttered something, but even close as they were, she couldn't make it out. Just as she was about to sit up, to put an end to whatever this was, his fingers took up their slow, tortuous sifting through her hair once again.

Her shaking stilled, but Niko didn't let go. He lay behind her, a bulwark against the night. After a bit, he rolled onto his back, doubtless so he could have a better view of their surroundings, but kept his free arm wrapped tight around her, pulling her with him, careful not to jar her wounded leg.

Katerina should move—Saints, she knew she should—but instead she lay with her head on Niko's chest, listening to the steady, comforting thump of his heart. He'd removed all the debris from her hair, but he was still stroking it, calm and easy now, the way he petted Troitze when the stallion, who was high-strung, threatened to spook.

The way he *had* petted Troitze, anyway. Where were their horses? Were they dead, somewhere in the woods? She thought of Mika, who always took carrots from her hand and then nudged Katerina's shoulder in thanks. Such a sweet horse. She didn't deserve what had happened to her today. And now she was lost.

Tears filled her eyes, and her breath thickened. Niko pulled her closer. His lips ghosted over her hair when he spoke. "Shhh. We're together. It will be all right."

She wanted to ask him what he thought had happened to Mika and Troitze. If they would ever see the horses again. How they would get home, with her leg like this. What they would do if they encountered another horde on the road. How the Darkness had boiled out of the Void and devoured a village whole, then threatened to consume their souls before the Grigori attacked. But she knew he had no answers, and she was afraid that if she started talking, the magic of the moment would shatter. That she might blurt out the truth: when he held her this way, all she could think about was the feel of his body against hers. That what had happened to their friends, to their horses, to Niko himself, might be all her fault.

So she said nothing, just lay still, trying not to cry as she thought of all they had lost in the destruction of Drezna. Hoping the villagers hadn't suffered. That it had been quick.

She wished, more than anything, that she could have saved them.

Niko was quiet, and she was sure he was wishing the same. He had been especially close with Alexandr and Leonid. Together with Damien, they'd often drunk kvass around the fire when she and Niko were the ones to deliver the tithe, and Niko had joined them on patrol. All Shadows were brothers, packs that fought together. She knew he must be mourning them, though he hadn't said a word about it. Nor would he; a Shadow's job was to protect, not to grieve for what had been lost. Maybe that was what was troubling him: he had no outlet for his sorrow.

She cried for them both, silent tears running down her face, until she had none left to shed. Around them, the fires blazed high, the wind stirring the branches of the trees. Overhead, the stars shone brightly, as if nothing terrible had happened at all.

Katerina's chest tightened at the sight of the Firebird constellation, beak dipping low to drink in the night and wings spread wide above the disk of the moon.

Her father had called her mother his Firebird, because of the color of her hair and the flavor of her magic. When Katerina was born, he'd called her Little Firebird, well before they knew she could call not just flame, but earth, wind, and water to her hand. Even now, fifteen years after her parents had been taken from her, whenever Katerina saw the Firebird in the night sky, she couldn't help but think of them.

Katerina had been there when the demon ripped out her mother's throat. She'd called her magic, meaning to incinerate the Grigori filth where he stood. But she'd only been six then, and her gifts, though powerful, were unpredictable. The demon had laughed while her mother bled to death, and Katerina's Vila minder had fled, with Katerina howling in her arms.

Katerina would never forget the look of determination on her mother's face when she flung herself between Katerina and the demon, nor the helplessness when her own magic failed to rise. Her mother had died saving Katerina's life, and Katerina had dedicated herself to never feeling that helpless again. She'd vowed never again to fail those she cared for, let alone those she was sworn to protect. Now, not only had she put Kalach in danger with her stunt at the Trials, but an entire village had fallen to the Dark on her watch. Guilt and regret swirled in her stomach, a bitter brew.

She forced herself to stop thinking of such terrible things. Surely she was not responsible for what had happened tonight, for the attacks that were rising all over Iriska. It didn't matter what she felt, after all. It only mattered what she *did*. And she had done nothing before the demons attacked, other than being too contrary and over-confident to turn back.

She hadn't lost Niko, no matter her mistakes. He was still here, still hers.

Closing her eyes, she tried to memorize him: his hard chest, the carved muscle of his upper arm as it encircled her, the silken brush of his hair against her cheek. His familiar mint-and-blade-oil scent, undergirded with the garlic-and-ginger paste she'd dabbed on the scratches from the Grigori blades. He smelled, she thought, like a meal that might arise and stab you through the heart if you looked at it the wrong way. A smile lifted her lips at the thought.

Beneath her, her vicious meal of a Shadow shifted his weight. His muscles tensed, ready to spring into action, but his fingers in her hair were gentle, his touch soothing. Despite the worries that plagued her mind and the desire that heated her body, she drifted off to sleep at last, safe in her Shadow's arms.

13

KATERINA

When Katerina woke up, the sun had crested the trees and Niko was no longer beside her. The rowan-fires were still burning, though lower now, and Niko stood next to one of them, talking in soothing tones to—

"Mika!" She leapt up, wincing as her injured leg took her weight. Hobbling over to the mare, she threw her arms around her horse's neck. "Niko, where did you find her?"

She could hear the smile in her Shadow's voice. "She found us. I dozed off for a bit before sunrise and woke to her nosing at my face. I suppose she thought I wasn't doing my duty."

Katerina drew back, still hugging Mika, and shot him a glare. "Did you sleep at all?"

He waved a dirt-smudged hand. "I slept enough. Don't worry about me. Worry about your horse. She looks..." His voice trailed off, but the concern in it had gotten Katerina's attention. Reluctantly, she stepped away from Mika, giving her mare the once-over.

Mika's mane was singed, her sides heaving. There were shallow gouges along her flanks, as if she'd shoved her way through branches and undergrowth. Her eyes were wide, the whites showing all around the irises. But she stood steady under Katerina's touch, and when Niko offered her some dried apples from Baba's satchel, she took them eagerly enough.

"Troitze?" Katerina said, hardly daring to look at Niko.

He shook his head, his shoulders slumping. Katerina knew how much he loved the big, stubborn stallion. "No sign of him. Which is too bad, because he could've carried us both. But Mika will carry you, and I'll walk beside her. It's better than what I'd expected."

"She can carry us both for a short way," Katerina argued. "I know her. She's strong."

"Maybe," Niko said, sounding doubtful.

"Where do you expect she's been all night?"

He looked the mare up and down and then sighed. "Nowhere good. Come on, Katya. It's time to leave."

THE TRIP back to Kalach felt as if it took a thousand years. True to Katerina's word, Mika was able to carry them both for some time, but Niko didn't want to risk tiring her, and so he walked next to the mare for a good deal of the way, his hand on her reins.

Katerina feared another Grigori attack, especially with the Bone Moon getting ever closer, but none befell them. There were no villages between Drezna and Kalach, just the road that wound through the woods and mountain passes. It was a wary journey, and Katerina's decimation of the bridge required them to take the long way home. When at last they smelled the rowan-fires that signaled the approach to Kalach, a weight slid off her shoulders.

Their village still stood. Whatever plague had been loosed upon Iriska, it hadn't reached Kalach...at least, not yet.

It was late afternoon, the day before the Bone Moon was set to rise, and Oriel and Galdrich were patrolling, one on either side of the iron gates that marked the main entrance to the village. The two Shadows came to attention as Katerina and Niko approached, her on the mare's back, him holding Mika's bridle. They dipped their heads in recognition of their alpha's return, then lifted them again in greeting. Dismay dawned on their faces as they noted Troitze's absence and Katerina's wounded leg. But when they asked about the Trials, Niko shook his head. "You'll hear soon enough," he said. "Katerina and I need to speak with Baba."

Katerina led Mika to the stables and gave the horse an apple and a grateful pat before turning to Niko. "There isn't time to clean up, is there?" she said, her tone rueful.

He wiped a smudge of dirt from her cheek. "I wish there were. But no. Come on."

They made their way past the farrier's and the blacksmith shop, then onto the cobblestone path that took them past the orchard and toward the small cottage where Baba Petrova lived. Without discussion, they'd chosen the most out–of-the-way route, the better to avoid questions about their battered appearance, Katerina's limp, and the results of the Trials. But luck wasn't with them today, because children played alongside the path, tended by Vila—including Elena. Even from a distance, the golden gleam of her hair was unmistakable, as was the joy that broke across her face when Niko and Katerina approached.

She hurried toward them, her green-and-white dress swishing against her legs. "You're back—both of you!" she said, skidding to a halt in front of them. "Oh, I've been so worried. You're strong, of course, but anything could happen at the

Trials. I burned incense at my shrine, asking for your safe return. And my prayers were answered. Thank the Saints, you're here!"

She stepped forward to embrace Niko, and Katerina braced herself for the inevitable twist in her gut. But Niko caught Elena by the wrists and held her still. "I'm filthy," he said as puzzlement knitted her blond brows. "We've come straight from the road."

The Vila's smile dimmed, but she nodded in understanding as Niko let her go. "Of course." Her cornflower-blue gaze slid sideways, taking Katerina in for the first time. It darkened with concern, and Katerina felt like a terrible person. "Here I am, chattering away, and...are you *injured?* Could Rivki's healers not at least patch you up before you got on the road home, or did something happen on the way? Niko, are you hurt?"

Behind her, the children Elena was meant to be tending were staring at Niko and Katerina, eyes wide, no doubt imagining that the two had returned from a glorious mission. When Katerina was small, she'd envisioned Rivki as a place of incredible riches, with its gold-domed churches and noblefolk dressed in fine fabrics. Only later had she come to understand it was a prison for the likes of her.

She cleared her throat, not wanting to frighten them. "We're fine. But we need to see Baba, Elena. Something's happened, and she needs to know about it at once."

"But..." Elena said doubtfully, her gaze flicking between the two of them. "Your *leg,* Katerina. And Niko...your arms..."

"Just defensive wounds." He offered her a conciliatory smile. "I'm whole. Katerina's right, though; we need to talk to Baba. And," he said, gesturing behind her, "I think your charges are getting restless."

The Shadowchildren and young Vila and Dimis had come up behind Elena, peering shyly around her skirts. One little

Dimi girl in particular, Esther, stared at Katerina with awe. She whispered to the young Vila next to her, whose face took on a similarly worshipful expression. Blind from birth, Halya negotiated Kalach with confidence using a cane that her Shadow father had carved for her from rowanwood. She and Esther were often together, and Katerina had overheard the Dimichild, a gifted artist, painting the world for Halya with words. Surely, she was doing the same thing for the Vila now, describing Katerina and Niko's glorious return.

Normally, this would have amused Katerina. But now, it terrified her. What if she couldn't keep Esther or Halya—keep any of them—safe?

As Elena stroked the braids of the children who clung to her, admonishing them to go back to playing in the garden, a chill ran through Katerina. She imagined all of Kalach vanishing into that awful crater, everyone she knew and loved gone. She'd been so worried about being Reaped, but this was far worse.

She swayed, and Niko touched her arm, steadying her. "Baba will feed us," he said, mistaking her unsteadiness for hunger. "We'll tell her everything. Then we can go home, wash, and rest."

Katerina forced a smile. "Okay," she said. "Let's get this over with."

She glanced back once as they walked away, Katerina favoring her injured leg. Elena stood on the path, watching them go, her gilded hair shining like sheaves of wheat in the bright sunlight, her expression troubled. A pang of guilt shot through Katerina. As Niko was meant to protect her, so she was meant to protect the Vila. She pushed her uncharitable feelings down, down, down into the depths of her soul, and went to do what must be done.

~

THE ONLY POSITIVE thing to come out of the destruction of Drezna and the demon-battle on the road was that Katerina's misstep at the Trials paled in comparison. She and Niko had agreed to spin the truth, saying that when his life was in danger, Katerina's magic had somehow burst through the constraints of the binding. It had taken her by surprise, she said, so she hadn't been prepared to guard against it. She'd never meant for this to happen.

Baba Petrova's initial anger at her lack of control had faded into the background with each word Katerina spoke. By the time she and Niko finished, unspooling the whole ugly story, the Kniaz's decision to have the two of them advance to the next round of the Trials was the least of Baba's concerns.

"This bodes no good," she said, pacing the length of her parlor after they'd told her everything and handed over Baba Volkova's sigil. The old Dimi had been pacing for so long, it was a wonder she hadn't worn a hole straight through the floorboards.

Katerina couldn't take it anymore. She couldn't risk mentioning the prophecy; to do so would be to implicate herself, and Niko along with her. And he had done nothing, other than protect her as a Shadow should protect his Dimi. He was innocent in all of this. Not to mention, he'd worked so hard to reclaim his family's name. How could she drag him into the muck, based on her unforgivable one-sided feelings? But if there was a chance that something else was to blame, a force that could alleviate the awful weight on her chest that threatened to suffocate her, she had to know. "We've told you everything," she said, impatiently. "What can it mean?"

Baba Petrova's face was as shriveled as a wizened apple. Somehow, the lines in her cheeks managed to carve themselves even more deeply when she said, "I don't know, Katerina. First, the rise of your powers, in all their complexity and immensity.

Now, this. There must be balance in the world, you know that as well as I. You are a great force for the Light; but your power has called, and the Dark has answered."

What if the ancient Dimi was right that Katerina was the cause of this madness...but for reasons that she would never dream of? Katerina wished desperately that she could talk with Baba in private, to confide in her, but that would be madness. Instead, she hid her horror, pulling sarcasm around her like a shield. "What are you saying? That perhaps I should have done us all a favor and died on that road?"

Baba stopped her pacing and took a gulp of the cooling tea from the porcelain cup on her kitchen table, as if for strength. "Don't be ridiculous. I'm only speaking what's in front of all our faces. Besides, your ceasing to exist now would do no good at all. The damage has been done."

Indignation flushed through Katerina's body, heating her cheeks. Her magic stirred inside her, uneasy, and the air in the cottage stirred along with it, rustling the curtains, feeding the hearth's flames. The silver samovar that hung from its ring above the fire rattled, the water inside sloshing, and Baba shot her a warning glance.

"I'm not the damage," Katerina snapped, worry sharpening each syllable. "The *damage* is what we did to those Grigori scum who now line the road to Drezna. The *damage* is what they did to an entire village of innocents, not to mention our fellow Dimis and Shadows!"

"Yes," Baba said, dismissing Katerina's temper. "We must grieve for them properly. Mourn them. It's a terrible blow. But we also need to know more, for our own safety and the safety of Iriska. I'd like you to share everything you've told me with the Elder Council; I'll call a meeting. I'm sure they'll recommend sending someone to the Magiya. But not the two of you," she said, before Katerina could speak. "We need you here. And you've been through enough."

Neither Niko nor Katerina had ever been to the Magiya. It was a week's travel on horseback, in the heart of Volshetska, a mountain fortress, surrounded by the strongest wards imaginable and run by elder Shadows and Dimis who had devoted their lives to scholarship. If the answers to what had happened lay anywhere, it was there.

"If not us, then who?" Niko said, dropping their empty borscht bowls into the washbasin with a clank. Katerina eyed him with surprise; it wasn't like him to be so argumentative, let alone so careless with Baba's china—the destruction that he'd wreaked the morning of the failed binding ceremony aside. But he wasn't looking at her. His gaze flitted between Baba's face and her front door, as if he suspected a threat might be lurking right outside.

"Nadia and Oriel, probably. It'll be up to the Council to decide. But the scholars at the Magiya need to know what's happening. Perhaps they can stop this evil before it spreads." Baba sank into a chair, downing the dregs of her tea. "And we need to inform the Kniaz. Doubtless he'll send someone to investigate; the road will have to be cleared for safe passage, and the crater consecrated and sealed. Rivki is on the way to the Magiya; if the Council approves, I'll have Nadia and Oriel take word. But not tonight, and not tomorrow, either." She cast her gaze outside, toward the darkening sky. "The dead won't rest easy in their graves until the Bone Moon passes, and even as we speak, the barrier to the Underworld grows thin."

Fear seized Katerina at the thought of Nadia and Oriel on that road, alone. "What if something happens to them?"

"We can't spare anyone else. My hope is that the Kniaz will send them to the Magiya with reinforcements, once he hears what they have to say." Baba peered down at her sodden tea leaves, as if their pattern might reveal the future. "You did what you had to in the woods, Katerina. I don't begrudge it, and thank the Saints your magic was no longer bound. Make no mistake, though: People might have overlooked what happened at the Trials. They see what they want to see. But after this, there will be no hiding what you're capable of."

"I shouldn't have to hide it," Katerina protested. "Niko's Light and my magic saved us. It saved anyone else that demon horde would have encountered. How can that be a bad thing?"

Sadness swam in the depths of Baba's faded eyes. "Because you've made yourself a target, Katerina, for *Gadreel,* no less. And with you, all of us. You must be cautious where you go now, what you do. For strange things are afoot. I know that without hearing back from the Magiya, and so do you."

"Wait for it..." Niko muttered, almost to himself.

Katerina glared at him, then lifted her chin. "I'm not afraid."

Niko sighed. "And there it is."

Baba Petrova regarded her with an expression that bore a suspicious resemblance to pity. "You should be, Katerina. You should be very frightened indeed. Because now, Gadreel knows that you exist. What you can do. And mark my words...he will come for you."

EXHAUSTION PERMEATED every fiber of Katerina's body as she and Niko limped up to the front door of the cottage they shared. It was a blessedly familiar sight, the door painted a vibrant blue to ward off evil and the shingles freshly whitewashed, the trim that adorned the roof inscribed with protective runes: safety, strength, Light. Elderflowers bloomed in the planters flanking the doors, and the glass chime that hung from the rowan in the front yard sang softly in the breeze.

She pushed the door open and stepped inside. Everything was just as they had left it: the small wooden table with its white porcelain pitcher; the red rag rug in the center of their living space, with two comfortable chairs weighing it down; the hearth, with its fire banked by one of Baba's young herbalist apprentices. The pallet where Niko slept was neatly rolled up in one corner, his blue quilt folded next to it. Through an arched doorway, Katerina could see her four-poster bed with its white quilt, a dried spray of lavender hanging above her headboard so nothing would trouble her dreams.

Niko had put it there, after she'd woken screaming from a nightmare of the demon's teeth sinking into her mother's throat. *To protect you in your sleep,* he'd said. *Where I cannot.*

It had been the sweetest thing anyone had ever done for Katerina. But she'd seen the way her Shadow's gaze couldn't hold hers, the way he fiddled with his blades rather than meet her eyes, and knew he'd felt self-conscious. So she'd let it go... but every night, when she slid into bed, she knew he was watching over her.

"Home at last," he said, coming in behind her now. "And not a moment too soon."

It was the first thing he'd said since Baba had done her best to heal Katerina's leg, using a combination of herbs and charms, and they'd departed her cottage. The whole way down the winding streets that led through the village square and past the pastures where the horses grazed, he'd walked in silence, only grunting in response to Katerina's attempts to make conversation. His head swiveled, like he expected demons to come creeping out of the trees or between the small cottages the Vila shared, near the red-roofed, wood-sided building where they cared for small Dimi, Vila, and Shadowchildren. His eyes had lingered on the runes inscribed on the window trim and the shutters, as if to see if they'd been tampered with.

The silence was unlike him. Katerina was usually the one to brood, and he the one to jolly her out of it. But there was no jollying Niko out of anything. Whatever strange mood had settled upon him in the clearing last night had returned full-force. He'd glared at Elena's cottage as they passed it, the shadows beginning to slip from the trees to lick their way up the path that led to the Vila's door. He'd glared at the birds who had the audacity to cross their path. And he was glaring at their cottage now, stalking the length of the front room and then into Katerina's bedroom, where he peered under the bed as if checking for evil spirits or monsters.

She came up behind him, and he whirled, only relaxing a hair when he saw it was her. "Kikimora usually live in the cellar or behind the stove, you know," she told him, endeavoring to lighten the mood. "And we haven't got a cellar. If there's a house spirit behind the stove, perhaps I can persuade it to make us a cup of tea."

"Everything is a joke to you, Katya," he said, stomping past her as if he actually intended to inspect the stove for demonic invasion. But no; he grabbed the fireplace poker and thrust it into the chimney, looking satisfied when he skewered nothing but air. He made sure the door was locked, then pulled his spare blades from the rune-carved cabinet, undid the velvet cloth that held them, and began grimly sharpening them one by one.

When Katerina was upset, she usually set something on fire. Niko, on the other hand...well, he didn't get upset, not like this. He faced whatever was bothering him head-on and then got over it; she supposed it was the only way he was able to deal with her volatility, to strike the balance that made them the perfect warrior pairing. She had no idea how to handle this new version of her Shadow, who glowered at his blades as if he would like to put them through the eye of the next creature that was unfortunate enough to cross his path.

Well, the only creature here was Katerina, and she had no intention of getting eye-skewered. She stayed out of his way, tidying their cottage—sweeping the floor, setting a pot full of sweet-smelling herbs on the wood-burning stove, boiling water for chamomile tea and then crumbling bits of lavender, valerian, and lemon balm into it. She set a cup next to Niko, hoping the soothing aroma would help, but he didn't so much as acknowledge it. Instead, he finished sharpening his blades, lay two of them on the table as if he expected a demon to come calling, and then stalked to the cabinet and put the rest carefully away.

Katerina thought that now, surely, he would speak. But no: he paced to the windows, peered out, then grabbed his pallet and unrolled it in front of the hearth. His aura was a stormcloud, so dark that for a terrible instant, she wondered if holding off the Grigori on the road had infected him somehow.

She couldn't take it anymore. "What is it? What's troubling you?"

"Nothing."

This was so obviously untrue, she didn't dignify entertaining it. "Is it because I insisted we stay on the road? Or do you miss Elena?" The Vila's name tore at Katerina's throat, and she forced a smile. "Maybe you wish to seek solace with her, after what we've been through. That's understandable; I wouldn't resent it if you wanted to abandon my hearth for hers."

Lie, a voice whispered inside her head. *Lie, lie, lie.*

"I don't want to go see Elena." His voice was gruff as he unfolded his quilt, set it to the side of the fireplace, checked the windows for intruders. Checked them again.

Relief flooded Katerina, and she fought to squelch it. "No? Then for the love of all the Saints, can you stop fidgeting and look at me?"

At that, Niko turned. The look on his face was like nothing she'd ever seen before: a cold black fury, turning his gray eyes to chips of mica and setting his face in lines of granite. She took an involuntary step backward as he stalked toward her.

"Are you that oblivious, Katerina? Do you really not see?"

"See what?" It was an effort to keep her voice level as he advanced on her. She stepped backward, once, then again, until he caged her against the wall by her bed. "What are you talking about?"

"Elena is *fine.*" He spat the words, an inch from her face. Rage rolled off him, staining his aura with a near-tangible red tint. "You, on the other hand... How do you think it made me feel to hear Baba say you are the cause of what happened on the road to Drezna?"

This close to him, it was hard for Katerina to breathe, let alone think. She stared up into those storm-dark eyes and gave it her best effort. "Angry with me?"

He growled, the sound rumbling up from his chest and shaking them both. His hands were braced on either side of her head, his body tense as if for battle. "You are impossible!"

Katerina had never seen him like this. Teeth bared and blade bloody in defense of her and of Kalach, sure. Filled with unspoken fury and grief at what had befallen the citizens of Drezna, without question. Irritated with the risks she took, definitely. But never had the slow-burning, controlled rage that simmered within him been directed at her. "I'm sorry," she managed. "I should have listened to you. We never should have left the island—"

"You think that's what I'm upset about?" His voice was low, dangerous. "We've been over this. If we hadn't been there, on that road, who knows where that horde would've gone next? We couldn't save Drezna, but we saved others, Dimi mine. You were right to face the danger, rather than to run from it."

Puzzlement creased Katerina's brow. "But then what—"

He slammed a fist into the plaster beside her head. Dust rose, sifting through the air. She flinched, and he swore, shaking his head so that his dark hair, loose from its tie, spilled into his eyes. "Saints, Katerina, don't you see? This evil...the attacks across Iriska...it's coming from too many places at once. None of those demons survived, true, but they were minions. Whoever sent them will have long since discovered what befell his soldiers, and will be on the hunt for the cause. You heard Baba: Gadreel himself will want you. To take you, to destroy you, to use you. How am I supposed to protect you now?"

Pain lanced through Katerina, so sharp it made her gasp for breath. She looked up into her Shadow's furious eyes and realized, to her horror, that the pain wasn't her own. It was his.

She could bear anything but that.

"Niko." She brushed her fingertips across his face, rough with stubble. "Don't do this to yourself. This burden isn't yours to bear."

He stared down at her, his eyes darkening further still. And then his hand came up, wrapping around hers, their fingers intertwining. His eyes held hers, and Katerina's magic rose. It knew him. It wanted him.

Slowly, so slowly, his head lowered, his lips a breath from hers. He froze there, her claiming his breath for her own, him taking it back again. Katerina's heart pounded, her skin tingling. Her magic spiked, wanting out, and air hissed between Niko's teeth.

What was happening?

She forced herself to think of the men in the village who she might wed. Of Konstantin or Maksim. Katerina didn't have to love them. But they were the ones she should want to kiss. To bed. Not Niko.

It was no use. Despite herself, she pictured him pressing his lips to hers. Touching her. Tasting her. And what would become of them then? Already, the demon horde had destroyed Drezna. What if her love for her Shadow burned down their entire world?

"Katerina," Niko said, low-voiced. She could see him trembling.

A hint of witchfire escaped her—not enough to burn, just enough to caress. It curled around Niko, tendrils of heat slipping down the column of his neck, twining down his arm. Seeking his Mark, and finding it.

The moment her magic met her own blood, infused into the tattoo Baba had given him at their bonding ceremony, the spark became a flame. She felt the sear of his brand as if it marked her own skin a moment before he leapt back from her. She caught a glimpse of his face—pale and shocked, with blotches of high color staining his cheekbones. His eyes were wide and dark, the pupils blown wide, consuming the irises.

They stared at each other for a long moment. Niko's chest heaved, and he pressed his palm to his Mark, teeth bared. Around Katerina's neck, her amulet throbbed. She reached for him, but he took one shaky step back from her, then another.

She opened her mouth to speak, but Niko shook his head, turning away. Without another word, he lay down on his pallet by the fire and pulled the quilt over himself, leaving Katerina standing there, cold and alone, her back against the wall.

Shame coiled through her. What had she done?

Niko lay still and silent, eyes fixed on the flames. The six feet between them might as well have been a gaping crevasse. She didn't know how to cross it. Didn't know if she should.

Drawing a deep, shuddering breath, Katerina straightened her spine. She wasn't some helpless girl, a Vila destined to vie for Niko's attention or a villager who dreamed of one day bedding a Shadow. She was a Dimi, and the world bent to her will, not the other way around. If he was going to ignore her, then Saints be damned. She wasn't going to beg him.

She made herself move, scrubbing her teeth with a willow twig, then walking down the path to the necessary. Back inside, she stepped behind the screen in her bedroom and changed into the thin white shift she wore for sleeping. She washed her face and brushed out her long red hair as she always did, sitting at the vanity by her bedside. A hundred strokes; she counted them, trying to time her breathing with each passage of the brush through her hair. It was no use: her heart pounded like a wild thing, and her breath came short, no matter how she tried to calm it. In the living room in front of the fire, Niko didn't move. Didn't joke with her, or greet her with a smile, or chastise her for walking to the necessary without him.

Had she broken things between them? Had she ruined everything?

For a moment, she could have sworn he wanted the same thing she did. But of course, he hadn't. What had she been thinking?

Grimly, she stood and went to her bed, slipping between the crisp white sheets, beneath the spray of lavender Niko had hung for her. She tried to tamp her magic down, but it roiled inside her. The wind picked up, sending a loose shutter banging against the cottage.

Katerina stared at the white plaster ceiling, watching the shadows of the rowan's branches play across it, listening to the thud of the shutter. Her stomach churned.

She'd touched him with her magic, when he hadn't asked for it. She'd let her witchfire twine around his body, committing an act that was intended only between a Dimi and her lover, and then, only in the marriage bed. How horrified by her he must be now. No wonder he wouldn't speak to her.

Then again, he'd slammed a fist into the wall next to her head. Perhaps they were even.

No, she told herself. They would never be even, not when she felt this way for him. And tomorrow night, he would be formally betrothed to Elena, in front of the entire village.

It was bad enough that she'd lied and betrayed Kalach, that the Kniaz had chosen the two of them to advance to the next round of the Trials, all because she couldn't stand to see Niko hurt. Now, she'd disgraced herself. She had compromised her bond with her Shadow, while hordes of Grigori were afoot. If she had indeed loosed the demons on the world because of her feelings for her Shadow, then surely she had just made things ten times worse. She had ruined everything with—

"Niko," she said, before she could stop herself.

Through the gap in the door, she saw him stir, though he didn't turn. "Go to sleep, Katya."

"But—"

"Sleep," he said again. "I'll keep you safe."

Katerina lay still. She closed her eyes, feigning unconsciousness. But sleep didn't find her that night.

14

KATERINA

The Bone Moon rose, pitiless and all-seeing, the night Katerina Ivanova's Shadow pledged his life to another. It was a holy ceremony, the promise of a Vila to a Shadow. The entire village of Kalach had turned out for the occasion: the farmers and the artisans, the shopkeepers and the scholars. The other Vila, of course, to witness the moment Elena had dreamed of since she was a child. Niko's fellow Shadows, to stand in solidarity with him. Katerina and her fellow Dimis. The five Elders, who governed Kalach. And Baba Petrova, who presided over it all.

Clad in their ceremonial blue robes, emblazoned with runes for wisdom, knowledge, and justice, the village Elders took their places behind Baba Petrova. They fanned out in a line, with Elder Mikhailova all the way on the right, to give him the best angle of sight from his chair.

The five of them—Elders Dykstrova, Gamayun, Balandin, Dobrow, and Mikhailova—had governed Kalach for as long as Katerina could remember. With their lined faces, intricate, silver-white braids, and long beards, the three women and two men seemed both ancient and ageless.

Elders Gamayun and Balandin hailed from Povorino, far to the south, where volcanoes lurked within mountains and lava fell like rain. Their skin was darker than the others', a beautiful, burnished brown. Elders Dykstrova, Dobrow, and Mikhailova had been raised in Kalach, and their parents had governed the village before them. The Elder Council was the village's mind; Baba was its heart and soul. Together, they honored Kalach's traditions and kept the peace.

Moonlight filtered through the arched, stained glass windows of the chapel, illuminating the forms of Sant Andrei, Sant Antoniya, and Sant Viktoriya. Elena was resplendent in her mauve dress, its sleeves embroidered with vynohrad vines and fruit, signifying domestic happiness, and diamond-shaped rhombs, for fertility. Velvet-petaled guelder roses wove through her blond hair, their plump crimson berries representing the passion of the marriage bed.

Elena's eyes shone, her expression transported. All Vila were descended from Sant Viktoriya, but Katerina was hard-pressed to think of any who worshiped the ancient saint as ardently as she did. Since they were small, Elena had wanted nothing more than to follow in Sant Viktoriya's footsteps, to wed and give birth to Vila and Shadowchildren to defend the glory of Iriska. Sometimes, Katerina wondered if Elena truly loved Niko, or whether she loved what he represented. What he could offer her.

Her Shadow stood across from Elena, clad in gold. The lapels of his jacket were embroidered with oak charms, their thick trunks and sprawling branches symbolizing strength and commitment. With his dark hair tamed into submission and his gray eyes gleaming like the silver surface of wishing-fountain coins, he was too much for Katerina to look at, altogether.

She was here to support his engagement to Elena. But every

second she stood by his side and pretended this was anything but agony made a liar out of her.

She swallowed hard, averting her gaze to Baba's apprentices, who were lighting a circle of candles around Elena and Niko. Though the girls didn't possess magic, they'd been chosen for their gifts for healing and their dedication to the village's ways. They had lit the candles on Katerina's thirteenth Bone Moon, when she and Niko were sworn to each other as Shadow and Dimi. Niko had vowed that night to fight for her in his mortal form and in the form of his black dog, to protect her from supernatural forces and mortal threats alike. And she had vowed to stand with him, to bind her soul to his, to fight only for the Light.

The two of them had been so young then, battles with Grigori nothing but imagined glory, and the Kniaz's claim a far-off threat. Now, they had the deaths of innumerable demons to their names, and there was just a year until the second round of the Trials, when Kniaz Sergey might well Reap them and force them to leave everyone they loved.

Now, Niko was about to pledge himself to Elena.

The apprentices lit the last candle, blew out their matches, and stepped back, looking to Baba for approval. It was a foolish element of the ceremony, Katerina thought; she herself could have lit the candles with no more than a passing whim. But Baba was a believer in conserving magic, in only using it when the situation demanded. *Every spell has its cost,* she was fond of saying. *If you don't pay it now, you'll pay later. Watch out, or you'll pay in blood.*

Baba inclined her head at the apprentices, in their diaphanous white gowns, and then turned to face the villagers, Dimis, Shadows, and Vila, crowded into the wooden pews. She raised her gnarled hands, and the candles' flames flared higher. "People of Kalach," she said, her cracked voice resonant. "We are gathered here today to witness the pledging of alpha Niko Alekhin, the Shadow of Dimi Ivanova, and Elena Lisova, blessed among the Vila. In three months' time, the two will marry. And our covenant with the Saints will remain an unbreakable chain, binding us to them, protecting us from the Dark."

Katerina gritted her teeth and stiffened her spine. She was a powerful Dimi and spellcaster, the strongest in centuries. She could master this.

Niko had never been meant to be only hers, forever. She could find a way to let him go.

One of Baba's apprentices came forward, bearing a precious copy of the Book of the Light. Facing the congregation, the ancient Dimi took it and began to read.

"In the beginning, there was the Dark," she intoned. "It hungered. It waited. It *wanted*. But it was not alone."

Katerina had heard this story a hundred times—as a child at Baba's knee, during her training as a Dimi, at every marriage and bonding ceremony. Still, she forced herself to listen.

"From the heavens, the Grigori Watchers fell one by one, cast out for disobeying the will of the Light. The fallen angels descended into Darkness, and the Darkness welcomed their fall. It crept inside them, a pitch-black tendril that twined around their souls. It lived within them, and fueled them, and still it hungered for more. For the Darkness is never satisfied."

As one, the villagers shuddered. Across from Katerina, Elena shuddered, too, as if the words pained her. It was all Katerina could do not to roll her eyes.

"The Grigori carved out territory in the Underworld," Baba said, turning the page. "But soon, they craved more human souls to fuel their empire and preyed on the world above ground, nearly claiming it for the Dark. All might have been lost, if not for those who would become Saints: Sant Antoniya, Sant Viktoriya, Sant Andrei." She let her eyes linger on Katerina, Elena, and Niko, in turn. "Across the world they fled, hunted by the Grigori, until they reached the village of Kalach. When they could run no more, they built a chapel in the woods and prayed to the Light for strength. And the Light answered."

She turned to Katerina, inclining her head in a gesture of respect. "To Sant Antoniya, it gave the holy gift of the Dimi: to command the wind and move the trunks of the trees; to call storms to her will and spur fire." Her gaze shifted to Niko. "To Sant Andrei, it gave the gift of the Shadow: to transform into a guardian that would stand between humanity and evil, cleaving unto his Dimi, a Light to help her battle the Dark." Her eyes settled, finally, on Elena. "And to Sant Viktoriya, it gave the gift of the Vila: to bear Shadowchildren and young Vila, to safeguard the Light that would vanquish the Darkness of this world and the next."

The congregation murmured in approbation, then fell silent as Baba cleared her throat once more. "And so the Seven Villages of Iriska—Kalach, Drezna, Satvala, Liski, Povorino, Voronezh, Bobrov—became a realm within a realm, home of the portals to the Underworld, warded to protect the world beyond. The Saints founded a dynasty, and together, Shadows, Dimis, and Vila rose against the Grigori, keeping the covenant of the Light."

Six villages now, Katerina thought. And who knew which would be the next to fall? But Baba's face was calm, betraying no hint of what had befallen Drezna, when she spoke again. "The battle for our souls still rages, as it will while the Grigori demons walk the path between this world and the next. Shadow or Dimi, Vila or villager, it is our responsibility to fight." Her gaze fell now on the congregation, and her voice rose, deep and cracked. "It is our sacred duty to keep the Dark at bay and defend the Light."

"It is our duty," the villagers chorused. And, "It is our duty," the assembled Dimis, Shadows, and Vila echoed in turn.

"May we honor the Saints," Baba said, eyes rising to the stained glass windows. "May we pray for their protection; may we tread always on the side of the Light."

Two of her apprentices broke ranks, materializing by Baba's side. One took the Book of the Light with careful, reverent hands. The other handed Baba a ceremonial goblet of wine.

"In the words of our holy Saints," Baba said, raising it high, "by the gleam of the Bone Moon, may we lift a glass in honor of those who have perished so we might live: One for the fire, two for the storm."

She closed her eyes and drank, her wrinkled throat moving as she swallowed. When she finished, the apprentice reclaimed the goblet, then took up her place once more.

Baba's dark eyes flickered open, arms raised, as if to welcome the arrival of the Light. "There is a rhythm to Kalach. As there is to all of Iriska."

"Blessed be Iriska," the villagers intoned, as one.

At Baba's signal, the apprentices lifted their treshchotkas from the table next to the altar. They had carved these instruments for the occasion, sanding the boards, threading them carefully with a blessed string until they fanned out evenly. Their hands moved in a blur, flickering in the flames from the candles and the wall-mounted sconces, as the boards of the treshchotkas clacked together, a hypnotic backdrop for Baba's words.

"First we sow," Baba said. "And then we reap. As it is meant to be."

"As it has ever been," the villagers echoed.

"Blessed be the union of this Shadow and his Vila, so that the spirits may look favorably upon our fields. Blessed be the Saints, by whose grace we live and thrive."

"Blessed be the Saints."

"Blessed be the Kniaz, the Saint-anointed protector of our realm. Blessed be the harvest, so that we may have enough grain to gift him our tithe."

"Blessed be the Kniaz," the villagers chanted.

Fighting to keep her expression blank, Katerina let her gaze drift over the faces of the crowd that filled the pews. There was Dmitri, the blacksmith, who forged the Shadows' blades. Elyosha, who had crafted Katerina's amulet, carving the sigil of the Dimi into the precious metal of its surface. And Trinika, who baked the cinnamon-spiced apple pies that were Niko's favorite.

Behind them sat Konstantin and Maksim, a few seats apart. They looked like negative images of each other; Konstantin was dark-haired and dark-eyed, serious, whereas Maksim was yellow-haired and green-eyed, his lips always on the verge of a smile. Despite his lighthearted demeanor, Maksim was the more observant of the two. He caught Katerina's eye and winked.

He was charming. Good-looking. Hard-working. There was nothing wrong with him at all, except that he wasn't the one she wanted.

Embarrassed, she glanced away, her gaze falling on the children in the front row. Their lips formed the words of the response, their faces transported, lulled into complacency by the steady thud-thud-thud of the treshchotkas and the confidence in Baba's voice.

"We tithe, and in return, the Kniaz offers us protection," Baba said. "Should there be a war, he will defend us. Should there be a famine, he will share what we have given, to be sure we eat. For his line was chosen by the Saints to protect us."

Katerina didn't believe this for a second. The Kniaz took

what he would, and cared not for Kalach or anywhere else. But to say so aloud was treason—not to mention blasphemy.

"Blessed be the Dimis and their Shadows." Baba turned, looking at Katerina and Niko, then at the Dimis that stood by the altar, flanked by their Shadows. "For they defend our souls from descent into the demon realms, where they would be used as fuel for the Grigori's fire."

The stronger the Dimi, the greater her ability to fend off demonic invasion, with her black dog at her side. But the stronger the Dimi, the more alluring she was to the Grigori, who sought to harness her power to fuel their own. It was the greatest of ironies: the better able to defend Kalach Katerina became, the more she drew the demons to its doors. And if Baba Petrova were to be believed, the very gift that had allowed Katerina to defeat the Grigori on the road to Drezna was tied to the reason the demons had been there at all.

Katerina didn't know which was worse: to believe that her very essence had caused the destruction of Drezna, or that her feelings for her Shadow had summoned the demons. Either way, she was to blame.

"In a year comes the Reaping." Baba's eyes were bright now, lit from within. A stranger might mistake this for fervor, but Katerina knew what it truly was: fury for what Kalach must lose, mixed with a healthy dose of fear. "It comes as no surprise that Dimi Ivanova and Shadow Alekhin shone at the first round of the Trials, despite the binding of their power. At the next Bone Moon, a year hence, they will compete again for the right to serve in the Druzhina. In so doing, they will serve the Saints, as well."

Rage coursed through Katerina's veins at the thought of leaving the village to fend for itself during these dark times, and she tamped it down with an effort. This was her own fault, after all. If her love for her Shadow hadn't superseded her commitment to their village, she wouldn't be in this position. But that didn't mean she had to like it.

As if divining her thoughts, Baba gave Katerina a sad, acknowledging smile. "If and when they depart," she said, "their brethren will remain behind, to defend us from the hungry, greedy Grigori. And where a Dimi and Shadow go, so shall the Shadow's Vila."

"Blessed be the Vila," the villagers intoned. "For they continue the Shadow line."

Elena's ruby-stained lips lifted in a euphoric smile, as if she were picturing the moment such a thing would occur. Katerina fought the urge not to throw up.

"Niko Alekhin," Baba said, and the treshchotkas stilled. "Shadow of Kalach. Black dog of Katerina Ivanova. Do you accept the Vila Elena Lisova as your betrothed?"

Silence hung in the air, and Katerina's hopes hung with it. She didn't know what she was hoping for, exactly—that Niko would tell Baba no? That he would refuse?

He couldn't do such a thing. For one, this betrothal was a sacred covenant, owed to the Saints. For another, he of all people had to honor this union, after the way his father had tainted the family name. What had almost happened last night —he was right to have turned from her, for so many reasons.

She knew he had to answer Baba. But still—

Next to her, Niko drew one deep breath, then another. "I do," he said.

"Do you vow to protect your Vila with the last drop of your blood after you are wed? To consummate your union, and be blessed with a new generation of Shadowchildren and Vila?"

Katerina fixed her gaze on the dust motes that drifted through the air. She inhaled, letting the musky scent of incense fill her lungs, and pretended Niko's answer wouldn't break her heart.

"I do," he said.

"Elena Lisova of the Vila." Baba's voice was grave. "Do you accept the Shadow Niko Alekhin as your betrothed?"

Katerina forced herself to look at the woman she'd grown up playing hide-and-seek and hunt-the-demon with. Elena was glowing, her pale cheeks rosy and her blue eyes bright. "I do," she said, and behind her, the other Vila let out a murmur of approval.

"Do you vow to be a soft place for him after battle, to welcome him at your hearth and with your body, so that he may sire on you the next generation of Shadowchildren and Vila?"

"I do," Elena said without hesitation. "I will."

"Then take his hands," Baba told her.

A beatific smile lighting her face, Elena reached for Niko. Her expression was one of elation and absolute trust, as if she never doubted he would receive her. But Niko wasn't looking at her. He had turned his head, and his gaze fell full on Katerina.

What did he want from her? Acceptance? Approval? Neither of those things were hers to give. She looked back at him, head held high, and fought not to light the chapel aflame.

Niko's gaze dropped from her face to the amulet around her neck, the one that marked him as hers. It throbbed against her collarbone once, twice. And then he turned back to Elena, squared his shoulders, and extended his hands to her.

The apprentices approached from the four corners of the chapel in their flowing white dresses. Each of them held a ribbon that represented one of the four elements: red for fire, blue for water, white for air, brown for earth. And then came a fifth, clad in black, weaving her way between the candles. Once. Twice. Seven times, for luck. She held another ribbon: yellow, for the light a Shadow brought to shatter the dark.

The fifth apprentice had been born with a deformed foot

and one leg shorter than the other; Pietyr, one of Kalach's cobblers, had crafted her an ingenious shoe that evened her gait. The wooden heel thumped, hollow, as Feya traced her path between the flames, clutching her yellow ribbon. The sound echoed throughout the chapel, an ominous thud-thud-thud that reflected the anxious beat of Katerina's heart.

Baba lifted her hands, and one by one the apprentices in the circle brought their ribbons to her, laying them across her palm. They gleamed in the torchlight, dyed with madder root and wild blueberries, with saffron and walnut hulls. And one by one, Baba took the ribbons and twined them around Elena and Niko's hands, binding them together.

"Blessed by the elements," she intoned. "Blessed by the Saints."

Katerina had always thought that when a Dimi's heart broke, it would be a sound as loud as the shattering of a thousand glasses. That it would have the power of a hundred Dimis, drowning entire villages in a tidal wave, lighting the world aflame.

But her heart broke in silence, and the only person who drowned in its aftermath was Katerina herself.

15
KATERINA

"Tell me what you're thinking," Niko whispered. "Please."

Katerina spared him a glance, even though it hurt her to look at him. He was stretched out in front of the fire atop his blue quilt, chin propped on his hands, dark eyes fixed on her face. She'd dyed and sewn the quilt herself, a Dimi's gift to her Shadow. In return, he'd given her the Mark that burned on his arm and the gift of his soul. Outdoing her, as usual.

He'd changed out of his finery, clad in the rough white linen he wore for sleep. His shirtsleeve was pushed up, and Katerina's Mark glowed in the firelight, blue-black and gleaming, as if lit from within.

Her heart ached to look at it. It ached worse when she thought of Elena running her hands through Niko's dark, unruly waves, even though she knew she herself had no right to touch him that way. He was hers, but not like that. *Never* like that.

"Katya," Niko said, pleading. His voice broke on her name.

"I'm not thinking," Katerina lied. "Just cleaning. See?" She straightened the ribbon at the neck of her shift, then tidied her bedclothes, pulling the quilt tight.

Niko's lips twitched. "Making your bed before you get into it? I see."

The Kniaz damn him. "I like a neat bed." *I like a neat bed?* What in the name of all the demons was wrong with her?

Her Shadow's gaze flickered. He took a sip of the ginger tea she'd brewed when they got back to their cottage: for purification, for healing, for strength. And then he met her eyes head-on. "I had to do it, Katya."

Katerina's pulse quickened. There was no point pretending she didn't know what he was talking about, so she didn't try. "Of course you did," she said, occupying herself with straightening the spray of lavender above her headboard. "Why are you saying this to me?"

"You know why." His voice was deeper now, skirting his black dog's growl. "Last night... You must know how I—"

"No!" Katerina's fingers tightened on the flowers. They crumbled, bits of sweet-smelling petals falling onto her pillows. *Blue for melancholy and blue for the lost,* Baba's voice echoed in her head, one of the elder Dimi's many proverbs. *Blue for the protection of the storm-tossed.*

"I have to say it, Katerina." Porcelain clinked as he set the cup down, and the air shifted as he rose. She didn't have to look to know he was standing now, moving toward her, his feet soundless on the cottage's floorboards. "Saints help me, but I do."

"You *don't.*" Her heart beat in an uneven shudder as she turned her back to him. What was the point of confessing something he could never take back, something that only stood to ruin them both?

She felt him behind her now, through the thin material of her shift, his big body a line of heat that trickled along her spine. When they were fighting, his presence meant both safety and power. But now...now it terrified her.

"Turn around, Katya." The words were a demand, but the tone...it was a plea. "Turn around and look at me."

She shook her head, but he just waited. One moment. Two. And then, as if his words had the power to compel her rather than the other way around, she turned.

The fire limned Niko's body, outlining him in crimson. "I see how you watch me," he said, each word dropping slow as honey. "I know, because I watch you the same way."

"I don't watch you!"

He stepped closer still. "Just once, Katerina," he said, his breath warm on her skin. "For just a minute, forget the prophecy and the vow I made today. Just once, let us see what it could be like between us."

She should say no. She should flee, never mind the prowling demons and the fact that she only wore her shift. She should remember Konstantin and Maksim. And Elena.

But instead, she lifted a trembling hand to touch Niko's face. His skin was warm, the plush of his stubble prickling her fingertips. He closed his eyes, breath hissing through his teeth, as if her touch caused him equal pleasure and pain. Desire bloomed inside her, as lush as the velvety petals of the flowers that unfurled from their tight buds only at night.

She opened her mouth, intending to tell him what he asked was impossible. That it was a terrible idea. The worst imaginable. But instead—"Just once, my Shadow," she said.

Niko's eyes opened, shock clear in their depths. "Just once," he promised, and then his head bent and his mouth found hers.

He tasted of ginger tea and broken promises, of a hint of Katerina's magic and of the Light that could drive Grigori demons into the Dark. His calloused hands threaded into Katerina's hair and his tongue traced her lips, urging her to open for him. Against the hollow of her throat, the amulet that held his blood beat like a second heart. She gasped, and the flames in the hearth leapt higher, casting strange, dancing shadows on the wall.

Katerina knotted her fingers in the rough linen of his shirt, desperation searing through her body. If this kiss was all they would ever have, then she would make the most of it. She would show him how a Dimi and her Shadow could burn. Her hands roamed his body, igniting heat everywhere they touched, and her witchfire followed, caressing places her hands could not. Niko moaned as he felt it, gripping her tighter.

The wind picked up, mirroring the growing storm inside her, whipping the trees against the cottage. He cursed, a mumbled string of words that ended in her name. And then they were on the floor in front of the fire, her long red hair streaming down around him, and he was looking up at her, his lips parted, his eyes wide and dark and fixed on her like she was all he could see.

"You're the one I want, Katya." The words caught in his throat, but his gaze was steady on hers. "I will always belong to you."

Katerina felt him everywhere: the restraint of his hands, digging tight into her hips; the leashed strength of his warrior's body beneath hers; the pulse of their Shadow bond, deep in her witch's heart. She had to bite her tongue to keep from speaking: *I want you, too.* Saying it would make what was happening between them real, would give it shape and form. There would be no taking it back, then.

Outside, the wind rose from a murmur to a roar. The trees bent, their limbs lashing the cottage harder than ever, twigs scraping glass and wood in a discordant complaint. And Katerina bent, too, pinning her Shadow's wrists above his head, her lips inches from his. She held him there like an offering. He could have had her on her back in an instant. But he held still, letting her do with him what she would.

Which was...what? What were they doing? How had it gotten so out of hand?

Niko gazed up at her, his eyes wide. The tips of her breasts brushed against his chest, sending electricity prickling through her body, and he drew a ragged breath, shifting beneath her. "God, Katya," he whispered. "Please."

She could feel how much he wanted her, and wanted him the same way. Not just his body, but his heart. But how could she tell him so? It would bring about their undoing. The undoing of everything and everyone they loved. Everything they fought to protect.

She let go of his wrists, struggling to catch her breath. "Niko, we can't."

He sat up, reaching for her, and Katerina drew back. If he touched her now, she wouldn't be able to resist. And then what would become of them?

But all he did was stroke her cheek, his expression filled with unutterable sadness. "I'm not sorry," he whispered. "Saints help me, Katerina, but I don't regret this. I never will."

The tenderness in his touch galvanized her. Katerina leapt to her feet, knocking over what remained of his tea. She snatched a shawl from the hook beside the door and fled into the storm that had arisen outside—*her* storm—dumping rain onto the cobblestones and sending the shutters banging against the windows.

Niko didn't follow.

16

KATERINA

Clad in her thin white shift and the scarlet shawl she'd dyed from madder root, Katerina fled through the deserted apple orchard, the sodden grass squelching beneath her feet. The farther she got from Niko, the more the storm died down, until finally the trees stilled and the wind fell to a murmur. The orchard was silent, lit by the all-seeing eye of the Bone Moon.

A branch cracked behind her and she spun, panicked—but there was no one there. Just the skeletal trees, reaching toward the vault of the sky. Still, a Dimi on her own could never be too cautious, especially in times like these.

"*Noch,*" she whispered, and the night detached itself from the edges of things, curling around her body like a satisfied cat, concealing her. She glanced behind her, but the orchard had fallen silent once more. Nothing moved in the dark.

Clutching the shawl at her throat, Katerina passed through the orchard and into the forest, relieved when the gnarled oaks and scrub pines hid her from view. Baba Petrova had warned her often enough that she was never to go into the forest at night on her own, much less this close to the slippage between worlds, when everything threatened to come undone. She was supposed to take Niko, to always have him at her side.

But tonight, he was the thing she was running from.

Katerina came to a halt in the elderflower clearing where she often foraged and shook her head with frustration, letting her long hair fall loose around her. She hadn't wanted Niko to follow her—had she? But then why did part of her wish he had? Gazing into the trees, she half-hoped, half-feared he'd materialize in their midst. Maybe it was her imagination, but she could swear she felt his gaze resting on her.

Or maybe it was just her guilt.

Well, better Niko than packs of prowling Grigori who were hungry for her soul. Although at this point, perhaps her soul was compromised beyond repair.

Pushing her thoughts aside with an effort, she rummaged inside a hollowed-out tree for the straw basket and knife she'd stashed in the clearing. Kneeling in the grass, the basket beside her, she began gathering the small blue flowers, always more potent for healing when picked by starlight. As their roots came free of the soil, she whispered the same age-old prayer of gratitude she'd given the rowan trees near Drezna: *For your life, that we may live, we are thankful.*

Drezna...which might have fallen because of Katerina. She wondered where Sofi and Damien were right now, whether Nadia had gotten word to Rivki before Sofi had come home to find her village naught but ashes. Grief rose in her throat at the thought, threatening to choke her.

"That we may live," said a familiar voice from the treeline. "Well, one of us, anyway. Is my presence that distasteful, then, Dimi mine?"

Katerina startled, falling backward. She landed in the patch of flowers as Niko strode into the clearing, his dark hair rumpled and his spine rod-straight with offense.

So she hadn't been imagining his presence after all. But the fact that she hadn't heard him coming— Well, he was a Shadow, after all, trained to move like a piece of the night. And she had been more than a bit distracted.

She scrambled to her feet, gripping the knife and brushing crumpled flowers from her shift. Despite their circumstances, Niko's mouth twitched.

"If that's an invitation to leave, I'm not taking it," he said.

The moon bathed his face, accentuating the ridged scar that ran from temple to jaw. Her fingers ached to touch it, and she clenched her free hand into a fist. "Why did you follow me?"

He took a step toward her, hands shoved deep in his pockets. "Why did you run?" His words came dangerously close to a growl, all humor vanished. "The dark of night. The heart of the forest. And me, left behind. One might imagine you are seeking trouble."

"I seek nothing but healing remedies," she snapped, gesturing to the basket at her feet. "And the only trouble I seem to have found is you. Again."

He stepped closer still, his jaw set hard as granite. "Why did you run from me, Katerina, no matter what happened between us? What were you thinking?"

She clutched her knife tighter—as if it would do her any good against him. "I was thinking that I needed to pick elder-flower," she said, fighting to keep the tremor from her voice. "The plant secretes its nectar late at night, when the moon is full. This is the time to harvest it."

"Right." Niko rolled his eyes. "And you couldn't be troubled to tell me that, before you fled into the forest, half-dressed? Or to take me with you?"

"You're not my keeper!"

EMILY COLIN

"Am I not?" He was a foot from her now, his expression the inscrutable mask he wore to hide strong feelings and his hair so tousled, it fell into his eyes. It was tousled like that because of *her,* she thought, and had to suppress a shiver. "Have I not sworn to stand between you and evil? Do I not wear your Mark on my arm—and do you not wear mine around your neck?"

"It's an amulet, Niko," she said, her voice steady, and for a moment felt the throb of his pulse where the necklace rested above her breasts. "Not a collar."

He shoved his sleeve up, bearing his tattoo. "*This* is a brand, and well you know it. When you ran, I felt it burn. For all you know, there could be a horde of demons creeping closer by the moment. If something were to happen to you—"

A wind woven from Katerina's magic stirred the trees above them. It whispered through the grass and lifted the tendrils of her hair to brush her face, a light touch that was both promise and warning. "Is that all you care about, then? Your obligation to me? Your bloody pride? God forbid you should fail as your father did—"

His voice came low and furious. "I told you what I care about, Katya. Run from it all you like. And I am not my father!"

Katerina had been ten when Niko's father was exiled from the village for betraying his Dimi. During a demon attack, he'd chosen to save his Vila wife rather than stand by his Dimi's side. In the eyes of the village, there was no greater crime. She would never forget the look on Niko's face as he watched his father leave: shame and grief and fury, all warring for position. A year later, his mother died of heartbreak, and Niko was alone—until he became hers.

Six years after that, he'd risen above the legacy of scandal his father had left behind to become alpha of his Shadow pack. Baba had bestowed the honor after Niko had distinguished himself in battle, risking his life for his fellow Shadows, putting their well-being before his own. His pack respected him for his kill count despite his youth, and the former alpha, who had grown old, had given his approval. Niko's pack was everything to him—the family he'd lost, the proof that he was worthy of his title and his role. Everything, that was, except Katerina.

Mirroring her mood, the wind picked up, bringing with it the scent of the rowan-fires from Kalach, where the flames burned all night to keep the demons away. Niko inhaled, shaking his head. "I'm not afraid of you, Katerina. I'm not afraid of this."

That made one of them. Katerina thought of the look on Elena's face when Niko had pledged to marry her, of how hurt Elena would be if she could see them now. Of how furious Baba Petrova and the Elders would be if they knew she and Niko had violated the natural order of things. *Unto another each must cleave,* Baba had said after their bond was forged. *Strength will feed strength. Together you fight. Together you fall.*

Well, she was falling now.

She looked away, scooping the basket from the ground. The wind slowed to a breeze, rifling through his hair and flattening the rough cotton of his shirt. He closed his eyes, as if feeling her touch on his skin.

"You are promised to another. And you are my Shadow, Niko. What can we ever be to each other but that?"

Niko's eyes flickered open, their gaze wary. "You tell me. Unless...is there someone else, Katya? Someone who you—"

Katerina pictured Maksim and Konstantin's faces. She should say yes. But instead she swallowed hard and shook her head. "No. But what happened between us was a mistake. You know that as well as I."

His jaw clenched. "It doesn't have to be."

"You've lost your mind," Katerina said, ignoring the way her traitorous heart leapt at his words. "And for once, I'm sure Elena would agree with me."

"Well," Niko said, offering a rueful half-smile, "that would be a first."

"Is it my fault I want more from life than to be a broodmare?"

Niko sighed. "You have an obligation to bear Dimichildren, too. And you know she doesn't think of it that way. For her, it's an honor."

Katerina was silent, remembering what Elena had once said to her. *The greatest strength of all runs through my veins—for without Vila, there would be no more of my kind and no Shadows, and without Shadows, evil would triumph.* She might be a zealot, but she wasn't wrong. And she had centuries of tradition on her side.

She'd never thought to find herself being jealous of a *Vila*, of all people, but at the thought of Niko abandoning her hearth for Elena's bed, envy gnawed at her. It was humiliating.

Niko cleared his throat. "Katya, what I saw in your eyes today when Baba promised me to Elena—it slayed me. And tonight, when—when we... You cannot tell me you felt nothing."

She swallowed hard, remembering how he had knotted his hands in her hair and kissed her until neither of them could breathe. How he'd groaned when her witchfire had licked at his skin. She'd fled into the storm, hoping it would wash her clean of her desire for him. But it was her storm—a reflection of the turbulence inside her—and even though the wind had died down, the war inside Katerina still raged.

"The prophecy—" she said, but Niko didn't let her finish.

"Damn the prophecy. Old wives' tales and trickery. This is between us, not some words inscribed in a dusty book. I don't believe for a moment that that's what called up the demons on the road near Drezna. Because when they came—nothing had happened, Katya, other than the feelings I held for you in my heart."

"Maybe," she said, staring down at the severed elderflower stems, "that was enough."

"If that's all it takes, then I'm already damned. When you told me that the Kniaz wanted you, it took every bit of my restraint not to hunt him down, nobleman or no. And that night, when we lay together in the rowan grove, it was all I could do to keep from..." His voice cracked. "You were so warm. So beautiful. I lay awake for hours, memorizing the way you felt in my arms. I never dreamed you felt the same way, until last night."

Shock broke over Katerina. Niko's decision to leave Rivki, the way he'd held her in the woods...none of it had been for the reasons she'd thought. The whole time she'd been agonizing over her desire for him, he'd been doing the same.

It should have changed nothing. But yet—

"Do you want me?" His voice was low, desperate. "Because if you do...then the prophecy be damned, Katerina. For the Grigori are already loose upon the world. And I already burn for you in the Light."

Katerina dropped her head, teeth worrying at her lower lip. Maybe he was right, and the prophecy was no more than superstition. Still—what about Elena? And what if they were discovered? Where could this possibly end?

She hadn't seen Niko move, but somehow he was in front of her, his big hands light on her upper arms. "Look at me," he said, his voice hoarse, "and tell me you don't want me. Tell me that, and I'll never speak of it again."

Slowly, Katerina lifted her head. His gray eyes filled her line of vision, the precise shade of the sky before a winter storm. She shook her head, unable to say the words. The wind spoke for her instead, lashing through the trees, bending the tender saplings to the ground.

His grip tightened, and the basket fell from her hand, spilling the delicate blue flowers. "Say it, Katya." The words were a growl, his form flickering as his other nature rose perilously close to the surface. As a Shadow, he was taught exquisite control. Katerina had never seen him look like this—the black dog barely leashed, threatening to break his hold. "Say it and set us both free. Or don't, and I'll do as you wish. In all things, as I always have. As I am sworn to do."

The wind was a gale of her own making, the leaves and needles whipping around their feet, rising higher to swirl around their bodies. She reached up and locked her hands around his neck, twining her fingers through the rough silk of his hair. He smelled of ink and soap and sweat—and beneath that, the wildness of the forest itself.

When he spoke, his mouth brushed hers, sending shivers through her. "Say it."

"And you'll do as I wish?" she whispered against his lips.

"On my oath as a Shadow. No matter what it costs me."

"Then kiss me," she said, hands fisted in his hair.

He took a sharp, startled breath. Then his mouth closed over hers and his tongue traced the seam of her lips, tasting of mint and night and Niko.

His fingers caught her hips, tugging her closer. He outlined her eyebrows in the darkness, then ran a fingertip down the column of her neck. His palm came to rest above her heart, just below the amulet that held a drop of his blood. "Ah, Katya. I have loved you since we were children, playing, long before I took my oath. And when Baba Marked me, I thought first not of the honor—but that wherever I went, I would bear your touch on my skin."

With his free hand, he pressed her palm to the tattoo on his arm that marked him as hers. A Shadow's Mark was his bond, a promise made and a vow kept. To lay your hands on it was more intimate than a lover's caress. Battles had been fought over the ignominy of such a touch. Even Elena would have no right to it when she and Niko married. It was Katerina's claim, and hers alone.

She ran her nails over it, following the lines of the circles by the light of the Bone Moon. "One for the fire," she whispered as the Mark burned beneath her fingers and the wind raged. "Two for the storm."

At the words of their bonding ritual, Niko's hand fell from hers, clenching into a fist at his side. He drew himself up, the way he had eight years ago, when they'd stood in Baba's cottage and sworn their vows in blood. "Three for the black dog that guards against harm." His voice was a rasp.

Emboldened, she pressed her lips to the Mark, and Niko gasped. She ran the tip of her tongue along the interlocking circles, tasting salt, and he shook against her.

He cupped her face, tilting her head back. His eyes had gone ink-dark, the gray swallowed by the black of his pupils. She had seen him look this way before—in the heat of a fight, before he struck the blow that brought his opponent to their knees. It had filled her with an odd, unspoken thrill then. It did the same now, vibrating through her bones and settling low in her belly.

Niko inhaled, taking in the shift in her scent. He nipped at her lower lip with sharp, white teeth, his hands weaving their way into her hair.

Katerina thought of other things she had seen those teeth do—in human and canine form—and knew a sensible person would be afraid. But fearing Niko was an impossibility. Far more reasonable that he should fear her. Or what Baba would do to the both of them should she come into the clearing and find them this way.

If Dimi Zakharova saw this, she would use it to end Katerina. To the Saints with exiling her from the Kniaz's bed; this would be ammunition enough to destroy her. But the consort was miles away, her threat toothless. Right now, all that mattered was Niko, here in Katerina's arms.

She lifted her chin and nipped him back, a challenge. A faint coppery taste filled her mouth and he growled in warning, pulling her hard against him. Like called to like, as Baba had always said: Her body recognized his blood and called to it, wanting more. The amulet throbbed like a second heart, a throbbing that ran through her veins, a question that demanded an answer.

Niko's hands tightened on her hips. He lifted her, walking them backward toward the flat stone that stood in the clearing, where they had picnicked when they were children. Then he lowered her down, as carefully as if she couldn't destroy the forest around them with a single thought. The stone still held the heat of the day; she drew against it with her magic and a circle of rowan-fire sprang up around them, holding the rest of the world at bay.

He held himself still above her, his weight on his elbows, searching her face. "I swear on all we hold holy, Katya, you are the other half of me. You are my blood. You are my blade."

The blaze raged higher still. At his sharp intake of breath, she looked down: its red glow outlined both their shapes, as if they had truly caught aflame. The light was a live thing between their bodies, twining, casting shadows. When he bent his head to kiss her, she tasted blood and fire.

Her hand rose, red in the firelight. It slipped under his shirt, tracing the length of the scars she knew as well as the lines of her palm, as Niko's leg slid between hers. His dark hair came loose from its rawhide tie and fell forward, tickling her cheeks. The pressure of his hard body against hers felt both as natural as spellcasting and unbearably new. It felt too big for Katerina's body to contain, spreading outward into the flames and the wind that swept through the forest.

She drew on the wind, letting a tendril of it creep through the circle. The breeze licked at Niko, brushing over every inch it could reach.

"Saints, Katya." His voice was hoarse. "How could I want another woman, when everywhere I go, I feel your touch on my skin?"

"Do you give yourself to me, then?" The words were a caress, her lips tracing the line of his throat as he reared over her.

He closed his eyes, leaning into her touch. "Only if you want me," he whispered. "Only if you want this."

She flattened her hand on the small of his back, pressing him down to her. He came, letting her bear his weight. His eyes flickered open, meeting hers, the question in them clear.

He'd promised to throw himself into the face of danger if it meant she would survive. When they'd taken their vows, she had accepted his sacrifice as her due. But now—was his life worth so little, and hers so much? What would be left to her, if she lost him?

What would be left of him, if he failed? And what if they were caught? What then?

She thought, then, of the final lines of the prophecy: *So will they forfeit what they love the most: Lost demon. Witchfire. Wandering ghost. So shall she burn as she brings his demise: The Dark will fall. The shadow will rise.*

Niko seemed so sure it was an old wives' tale. But what if it wasn't? Could she really put him at risk for the sake of her selfish desires?

What if it meant Katerina would lose her magic, and her final act would be to bring about Niko's death? That the Dark would be destroyed, but at the expense of his life? That he would ascend to the Saints and leave her behind, powerless to help?

She wouldn't bear that. She *couldn't.*

Hands braced on the rock, he drew back to see her face. "Katya?" There was doubt in his voice, uncertainty. Her heart broke at hearing him sound that way—Niko, whose bravado was as much a part of him as his grace with a blade or his need to protect anything defenseless.

She loved him. She wanted him. He was everything to her.

And this would have to end, wouldn't it—when he married Elena, prophecy or no prophecy? For he would never walk back his engagement to the Vila. Say what he would; his father's betrayal had marked Niko deeply. Every day, Niko fought to reclaim his good name. To atone for what had been done to his mother. This was temporary, and so she would savor it while it was hers to have.

She would give herself to him this one time, then. Once only. A single betrayal that surely wouldn't be enough to bring the prophecy down upon them—for she still believed in it, even if Niko didn't. She would keep the memory of this moment close, a precious thing, no matter who came between them.

She ran her fingertips over the silvered line that ran from his temple to his jaw. "A blade cuts deep, and leaves a scar. So, too, may what lives between us. Do you still want me, then?"

His lips rose in a fierce smile, tempered by sadness at what his words might cost them both. "More than my next breath."

"I'm yours, then," she said, and, lifting her shift above her head, let it fall. "But just this once, my Shadow. We can't risk more."

His eyes on hers were hot and hungry as he mirrored her, slipping free of his clothes. Under the Bone Moon, his Mark glowed, and around her neck, her amulet pulsed. She felt the echo of it everywhere, throbbing in her body, passing through her into him. He shook as he arched above her, as her witchfire lapped at his skin. "Just this once," he vowed, and made of their bodies one twining, yearning thing.

Beneath him, Katerina burned. And deep in the woods, unseen by all but the owls roosting in the trees, the Darkness bared its teeth and uncoiled, feasting on the chaos to come.

17
GADREEL

The demon Gadreel didn't know whether to curse his Darkforsaken luck or raise a glass to the Dimi witch who might be his salvation.

He stood on the road to Drezna among his slaughtered people, the single lieutenant who'd managed to survive by his side. The demon was babbling, like he'd been ever since he'd fled the devastation that the Dimi and her accursed black dog had wreaked on Gadreel's army. He'd arrived back in the Underworld smelling unpleasantly of rowan-fire, with a tale of fleeing through the forest and flinging himself through the crater in the middle of Drezna—the last of which Gadreel could attest to, as the demon had landed at his feet.

"You see, sir," he blathered now, pointing a finger at the charred corpses of his brethren. "She...she incinerated them. We had a hundred foot soldiers, set to do your bidding. Drezna should have been a delectable feast, but that...that..." He gestured in the direction of the crater. "It took them all! When the animals fled the forest, it froze them where they stood. We regrouped, pleased to find a Dimi and Shadow on the road, but then the...thing...swept onward, until the witch and her black dog did the impossible. And now...now your loyal soldiers..."

"Shut up," Gadreel said absently, and snapped his fingers. The demon—what was his name? Azagrel? Benatroyd?—fell mercifully silent, his lips sewn together by the force of Gadreel's will. Honestly, the creature was useless. Why couldn't it have been Gremory by his side—a grand duke of Hell, commanding twenty-six legions? But no. Gremory was under Sammael's dominion, and Gadreel was forced to deal with this fool, who was no more than an expendable minion. Unfortunately, Azagrel/Benatroyd was also the only witness to one of the few fascinating events that Gadreel had encountered in thousands of years, since he had been cast out of the skies and sentenced to roam the earth and rule in the Underworld.

Well, that blind human scribe Milton, who'd lived and died in a world far beyond Iriska's borders, had been correct. It was, indeed, better to reign in Hell than to serve in Heaven. Sammael aside, Gadreel had a huge territory in the Underworld, far more than he'd ever been granted back when he had wings of white and was expected to kowtow to the Almighty. *Don't think for yourself. Don't fornicate with human women. Don't teach humankind how to defend themselves from threats.* Truly, Gadreel had had enough. He was far more of a doer than a Watcher, after all. When he'd fallen, along with the rest of the Grigori, it had not been long before he'd realized his good fortune.

But he hadn't been the only one. Happy to serve whoever would provide enough hedonism and bloodshed to keep them satisfied, demons weren't leaders by nature. As long as there was a steady flow of souls to devour, pain to inflict, and bodies to debauch, they did just fine. The exception was Gadreel's archrival: the fallen Archangel Sammael, Venom of God.

The demon was an annoyance, especially because he had his eye set on Gadreel's corner of the Underworld. In the beginning, they'd divided Hell up neatly, with a minimum of battles to the death. Everyone had been pleased. Even the minor Watchers, who didn't want the responsibility that came with managing a large realm, had ceased complaining.

Then came Sammael, with his protestations that he needed more land, more demons to command, more souls to devour. More, more, more, that was Sammael. No matter how many minions and commanders Gadreel won over, no matter how many souls fell beneath his foot soldiers' swords, Sammael was always there: a thorn in his side, a threat to his realm.

The Dark Angel of War Gadreel, Scourge of Humankind, Slayer of Dimi and Devourer of Souls, would not be lesser than the Venom of God. It was insupportable.

Gadreel had spent centuries seething. And then, at last, it came to him.

The Underworld was fueled by human souls; the more that perished at the hands of Gadreel's Grigori, the stronger his territory became. The same was true of Sammael, as well as the lesser demon lords—but those hardly counted. Brooding on this, Gadreel had concluded that if he could command the source of the Darkness, he would be stronger than Sammael had ever dreamed of. With this unshakable conviction in mind, he had unleashed the Darkness, known to Dimis and demons alike by the same name.

Once the idea had entered his mind, it had become, Gadreel was not embarrassed to admit, an obsession. He began to brood, reading all he could in the demonic scrolls, hunting out forgotten, half-faded spirits in the corners of realms that did not belong to him. It was not like he had much else to do, other than defend his realm against Sammael's insistent onslaught. It was getting, quite frankly, rather boring.

Then came the moment when Gadreel had found the answers he'd sought for so long. He'd made the necessary sacrifices, laying souls aplenty and even his own body at the feet of the Darkness. He'd had intimate congress with all sorts of creatures over the years, including Sammael's Lilith—ah, cuckolding his nemesis had been so sweet—but he'd never experienced anything like that before: an icy greed that devoured him from the inside out, always seeking, never satisfied. It had been most unpleasant, and coming from Gadreel, who had once shared a tent with a hydra that hadn't brushed its nine sets of teeth in three centuries, that was really saying something.

But what he'd freed in return was far more than he'd bargained for: a conscienceless, unadulterated hunger for human souls, with no thought for moderation or consequence. He'd thought he could contain it or command it, but he'd been terribly wrong.

Much as it pained Gadreel to admit, he'd lost control over the thing that he'd let loose on the world. It had chewed its way straight through the center of Drezna, sucking humans, Dimis, Shadows, and Vila alike into the Underworld, along with the village itself. Splintered wood and frozen fruit, human and animal corpses, half-forged Shadow blades and half-eaten meals…it had all come thundering straight into Gadreel's throne room, when he was in the middle of dinner. To say it had been unappetizing was the understatement of the millennium.

He'd ordered his minions to clean up the wreckage, threatening to remove their limbs should they so much as question how it had appeared. It had been pure luck that he'd dispatched a small detachment to perform reconnaissance on the path to Rivki, staging an attack on Drezna in an effort to keep the Darkness fed. They'd arrived mere moments before the Darkness had grown impatient and decided to show Gadreel up by boring a hole into the center of the town itself, devouring all of the living souls within. His army had fled—some soldiers they were

—whereupon they'd encountered the Dimi and her Shadow on the road to Drezna. And now look at this mess. Corpses everywhere, a hundred ten soldiers wasted, and a witch who could stand against an army of minor demons, flanked only by a single Shadow.

Well, one thing was certain. Gadreel had to lay claim to what had happened, to use it to bolster his power. Sammael and the minor Grigori had to believe it had been his army that had blasted a hole in the middle of Drezna—for there was no way to contain an event of that magnitude, any more than there was a way to contain what the Dimi and her Shadow had done.

Neither should have been possible. Yet here he stood, in the aftermath of both.

There was only one witness to what had transpired in the village that day, and to what had happened afterward, on the road. That was a loose end, and Gadreel hated loose ends.

"I regret this," he said, and snapped his fingers again. The unfortunate minion who stood beside him—Azatroyd, that was it—fell to the ground, his throat pouring blood. A glance, and he burst into flame.

Gadreel gazed down at his soldier's sizzling body, satisfied that at least he would no longer have to listen to the demon's babbling. He would lie here, indistinguishable from the rest. But next time, Gadreel might not be so lucky.

He had to get control of the Darkness. If he could not, it would destroy all of humanity. He personally had no fondness for the creatures, but human souls fueled the Underworld. If the Darkness ate all of them, his realm would collapse and so would the others. His millennia of battles against Sammael would amount to nothing, a mere footnote in history. He would disintegrate into the Void—the nameless, shapeless, lightless space from which new demons originated and into which demons went when they were slaughtered—taking all of his people with him. Sammael would follow, and there they would be, at each other's throats for all of eternity.

It was a nightmare.

He needed an ally in his battle against the Darkness, someone with enough power to put the Dark back where it belonged. But there was no way he could tell Sammael how, in plotting against him, Gadreel had fatally overshot. That would be the end of thousands of years of work; the bastard would finally have the ammunition he needed to unite the minor realms against Gadreel and rise up against him. And *still* the Darkness would rage uncontained.

No, there was only one thing to do. He would have to ally himself with the Light, repellent as the notion might be. Together they could drive the Darkness back into the Void. He would have to get his hands on this terrifyingly powerful Dimi, for she and she alone might have the power to aid him.

But if what his minion had told him was true, her black dog was no ordinary Shadow. The man had blazed up with a Light that had illuminated the entire road, driving the Darkness back. And when he and his Dimi had fought side by side, they had defeated Gadreel's army, which was an impressive inconvenience. His soldiers were replaceable, but still.

He would have to capture the Dimi and bend her will to his own—for she would never believe they were on the same side of this fight—but to get to her, he would have to kill her Shadow. Then he would force her to help him re-quarantine the Darkness. After that...well, perhaps he would keep her by his side, as entertainment. Why not? Surely she would be amusing, and he did so hate being bored.

It was no small series of events to put in motion. But if there was one thing he loved, it was a challenge.

18

ELENA

The sun streamed through the window of Kalach's nursery, making the little ones giggle and lie on their backs, pretending to be kittens luxuriating in its warmth. Elena Lisova reached out and tickled Dominika, the child closest to her. In response, Domi wound herself around Elena's ankles and did her best to purr.

Stroking the little girl's hair, Elena looked through the nursery's window, following the path of the sun. Niko stood next to Katerina at the edge of Kalach's huge vegetable garden, his dark hair gleaming in the light like a crow's wing. Katerina was telling him something, gesticulating at the garden. Whatever it was, it made Niko smile, and Elena couldn't help but do the same.

Soon, they would be wed. Soon, she would be waking up to that smile each morning.

"You really love him, don't you?"

Elena turned her head to look at Alyona, her fellow Vila and closest friend. In addition to sharing a cottage in the Vila's quarter of the village, they worked together in the nursery, preparing for the time they would hold their own children in their arms.

Physically, the two of them were as unalike as you could imagine—Elena was tall and slim, with long, straight blond hair and wide blue eyes, whereas Alyona was short and curvy, with green eyes that tilted up at the corners like a cat's, mahogany skin, and wavy auburn hair that escaped her every attempt to tame it. They'd been inseparable since they could walk, though, drawn together first by a common sensibility and later by their shared belief that bearing Vila and Shadowchildren was a higher, holy calling.

"You love him," Alyona said again.

The note of envy in Aly's voice spurred Elena to touch her friend's arm in comfort. Alyona was prone to bouts of anxiety, especially when thinking about the future, and the last thing Elena wanted to do was make things worse. "I do. But don't worry. Whoever Baba Petrova chooses for you to wed will be wonderful. I know it."

"Maybe," Alyona said, picking up a rag doll that one of the children had dropped and handing it back. "But it won't be someone I've adored for years, like you and Niko."

Elena had fallen in love with Niko Alekhin when she was eleven years old and he had rescued her from the back of a bee-stung horse. The horse had lost its mind, tossing its head, rearing, threatening to throw her. Niko had ridden alongside, leaned out of his stirrup, grabbed her around the waist, and somehow dragged her from her horse to his. He'd wrapped his arms around her waist, holding her close, and asked her if she was all right.

Somewhere between his question and her answer, Elena had given her heart to him. Their love was written in the stars; they were destined for each other. He was the fulfillment of the vow she had sworn to Sant Viktoriya, whose ancient blood ran in her veins. Every day since childhood, she'd knelt at her bedroom shrine and prayed to embody the beauty, purity, and fertility of the Vila line. Her marriage to Niko, a handsome, kind, and alpha Shadow bonded to the strongest Dimi in centuries, was the culmination of all she'd prayed for. All she deserved.

"Do you ever think—" Alyona began, her eyes on Niko and Katerina. They'd turned away from the garden and were standing side by side, deep in conversation.

"What?" Elena said when Aly didn't continue. "No, Dominika—don't throw that! We don't hurt other people. It isn't kind." She wrested the rag doll from Domi's hands. "Go on, Aly. What did you mean to say?"

"Nothing," Alyona said, bending to scoop Dominika into her arms. "Come here, kotik. You've got milk all over your face."

Kotik meant 'pussycat,' and the little girl giggled. She was an adorable sight, but Elena wouldn't be dissuaded. "Tell me, Aly."

Alyona dabbed milk from Domi's face, then set the child on the floor again. "It's just—do you think he feels the same way? That he loves you as much as you love him?"

A pang shot through Elena's chest. "Why would you ask that?"

"Has he said he loves you?" Alyona pressed.

"No," Elena said, "but I wouldn't expect him to. We aren't married yet. It wouldn't be proper. I haven't told him, either." A tinge of anger crept into her voice, born of fear. Of course Niko loved her...didn't he? "What are you trying to say?"

"It's just—" Alyona said again, her voice faltering, "people talk, you know. And I've heard rumors—that is, I sometimes wonder—do you think all that exists between Niko and Katerina is friendship?"

Elena's eyes snapped wide. "What rumors?"

"Never mind." Alyona fidgeted, toying with the hem of her

dress. "I shouldn't have said anything. Niko is a good servant of the Light, and he will stand by you regardless of where his heart lives." She gave Elena a shy smile. "You are lucky to love him yourself. Who knows what Shadow Baba will match me with? It could be Mischa, for all I know. He smells like garlic, no matter how often he washes."

Elena stared at her friend, speechless. She had never considered that Niko might not love her in return. They were sworn to each other; though they had never so much as exchanged a kiss, she had always known he was destined for her. It went without saying that Niko was dedicated to the Light—but surely his heart would be dedicated to her as well.

She glanced out the window again, at the spot where her Shadow and his Dimi stood. They had turned and were walking down the path that led from the courtyard. Katerina's face was tilted up toward Niko's, and Elena caught the flash of her mischievous grin, a moment before Niko lifted his hand to brush away a leaf that had landed in Katerina's hair. The touch was brief, as casual as the way she herself might wipe a smudge of dirt from a child's cheek.

Elena watched them go, trying to understand what Alyona saw that she herself did not.

"They're close, that's all," she said. "They've been best friends, always, the way you and I have. It's a tremendous gift to have that sort of friendship between Shadow and Dimi. It makes them stronger."

Alyona knelt, straightening little Vadim's shirt, scooping up the carved wooden dog that his Shadow father had made for him. "You're right, Elena. Of course there's nothing between them. I shouldn't have spoken."

Elena regarded her friend with narrowed eyes. Alyona wasn't a gossip. If she'd seen fit to bring this up, she had a reason—and Aly wasn't coy. Once she found the courage to

EMILY COLIN

broach a difficult subject, she didn't shy from seeing the conversation through.

Maybe this was different, though. Elena had loved Niko for the past ten years—almost half her life. Marrying him was her birthright. The idea that Niko and his Dimi were engaging in some kind of illicit flirtation—that they had feelings for each other, Saints forbid—had the power to break Elena's heart.

Elena wasn't a fool. She'd known Niko and Katerina were closer than the average Shadow and Dimi. She'd grown up with them, always on the outside of their private jokes and bizarre antics, the long talks that left the two of them sitting at the outskirts of the village, in burning distance of the rowan-fires, tempting fate long after the sun sank below the fringe of the trees. Once or twice, she'd caught Niko's eyes on Katerina in an unguarded moment, when he hadn't known Elena was watching, and thought maybe—

The thought had fled as quickly as it had come. They were bonded, a warrior union until death sundered one of them from the other's side. Such closeness would only serve to strengthen their connection. Elena had been ashamed of herself, suspecting anything more existed.

When Baba Petrova had placed her hand in Niko's, announcing their betrothal, she'd thought her heart would burst with joy. Now, she thought, Niko would look at her the way he'd regarded Katerina: As if Elena were a miracle, a treasure he couldn't believe he got to keep. As if she were *his*.

And when he hadn't, when he'd gazed at her the way he had the day before and the day before that—with a brotherly tenderness that verged on forbearance—she'd convinced herself he only needed time.

Maybe that's what Aly meant. Maybe she too had seen the way Niko looked at Katerina, with the awe and reverence he

164

only reserved for his Dimi—and then the way he looked at Elena, like she was a little sister or a trusted friend.

Maybe everyone in the village had seen, and was laughing at her. Or worse, pitying her. Elena Lisova, prized among Vila, blessed by Sant Viktoriya, cuckolded by the man she loved. Robbed of her rightful destiny. The thought of it sent a sick chill down her spine.

"It's not true," Elena said, her voice too loud in the quiet nursery. "Niko is loyal. We will be happy together."

"Of course you will," Aly said, but the words fell flat.

Elena watched her Shadow and his Dimi as they walked down the path that led to the cottage they shared, and tried to banish the doubt from her heart. But it had taken root, and began to grow.

19

KATERINA

The morning that would change Katerina's life yet again began like any other: with her averting her eyes from Niko as the two of them readied themselves for the day. She did her best to ignore the broad stretch of his shoulders beneath his linen shirt and the grace with which he slid his blades into their holster before striding out the door. And then she braided her hair in preparation for training and stomped after him, sticking her tongue out at his back. He had no business looking so irresistible. Nor being so cool and collected when she was burning up inside.

Her leg was healed now; Baba Petrova's herbs and charms had worked their magic. Still, she felt undone, off-kilter. It was Niko's fault, Saints damn him. He was right there, but she *missed* him. Missed having him the way they'd been together in the elderflower clearing three nights ago, hearing him whisper that he wanted her more than his next breath.

She'd said, *Just this once,* and by honoring it, he'd only done what she'd asked. But then why did she want to shake him, right before she pinned him to the wall of her cottage and took his stupid mouth with hers?

Ana was waiting at the bottom of the walkway, Alexei beside her. Niko fell into step with him as her friend looked Katerina up and down, her wide mouth rising in a sardonic grin. "In a good mood this morning, I see."

Raising an eyebrow, Katerina summoned a hint of wind and pushed Ana back a step. "Does it show?"

Ana shoved a warning hint of heat back in Katerina's direction, making Katerina give a genuine smile. It was good to be among other Dimis, to remind herself of who she was and where her priorities lay.

"Just a tad," Ana said, holding her fingers apart an inch or so. "I mean, you seem a little more annoyed with the world than usual. As for your Shadow"—she gestured at Niko—"you'd think he'd be a bit more cheerful after his engagement to Sant Viktoriya herself. But there he is, looking as uptight as he's been since you came home from the Trials."

Katerina and Niko hadn't so much as exchanged an inappropriate glance since the night of the Bone Moon. They'd never even spoken of what had transpired between them. Still, hearing Ana mention her Shadow's engagement to the Vila cut like a knife.

"He's not *uptight,*" she snapped. "You weren't there when the Grigori swarmed out of the woods. You didn't see the crater that devoured Drezna. What if whatever it is comes for us next?"

Ana shot her an apologetic look as they stepped onto the path that led to the outdoor arena by the river where the Shadows and Dimis trained together—the easier to summon water and put out fires. "You're right, Katerina. I was just... joking. Trying to make light, in these dark times. But I shouldn't have—"

Her words trailed off as, in front of them on the path, Niko froze, and Alexei followed suit. "What's wrong?" Katerina said, straining to see, but her Shadow blocked her way.

"There's someone here," he said, his tone terse. "I can smell them. Someone who doesn't belong. Not Grigori, but...three strangers. And their mounts."

Katerina smelled nothing, heard nothing. But if Niko said there were strangers here, she trusted him. Her magic hummed beneath her skin, ready for battle.

"Alexei?" Ana said, the teasing cadence gone from her voice.

"I smell them, too," her Shadow said, running a hand through his auburn hair and revealing the star-shaped brand that had manifested after he bonded with Ana. "Human, like Niko said. Not Dimi or Shadow."

Without a word, Ana moved up to flank Alexei, and Katerina did the same for Niko. They made their way down the path, following the Shadows' unerring sense of smell. Twenty yards later, a man's arrogant voice split the air, demanding to speak to Baba Petrova. Then he barked Katerina's name, in a tone of clear command.

Next to her, Niko flinched. He turned and looked at her full-on, for the first time since that night in the woods. "Katya," he said, the word heavy with all she had been dreading.

Whoever had come to Kalach, they had come for her.

Ana was staring at her, dark eyes wide, and Katerina set her shoulders, refusing to show fear. "No point in dawdling. Wouldn't want to keep them waiting for me, after all."

She lengthened her stride, stepping in front of Ana and Alexei. Making a disapproving noise low in his throat, Niko nonetheless did the same, so that he stalked alongside her, one hand resting easily on the hilt of his favored blade. "Katya," he said quietly, so that Alexei and Ana wouldn't hear. "Whatever they want, state your terms in response. I'll not let them take you—or us—against your will."

Katerina gave a sharp nod. She'd hoped she would have more time before a summons came. But clearly she'd been deluding herself.

The path opened up into the village square, revealing three men clad in the gold-trimmed garments that marked them as the Kniaz's favored squires. They sat atop horses that were finer than any in Kalach—a golden palomino, an onyx stallion, a blue-speckled, muscled roan. The men were equally impressive: bearded and broad, with an unyielding set to their shoulders that indicated they were used to getting what they wanted. Before them stood Baba Petrova and the five village Elders.

A crowd of villagers gathered at the edge of the square, murmuring in confusion and alarm. And to their right, with the Vila not on child-minding duty this morning, stood Elena and her closest friend, Alyona.

The Vila's eyes went at once to Niko, as if to assure herself that he was all right. But Niko didn't notice. His attention was fixed on the men on horseback. A deep, subterranean growl rumbled in his chest.

"Where is the Dimi you call Katerina Ivanova?" the man on the palomino said, his tone imperious. He must be their leader, she thought, his beard woven with the red-and-purple ribbons that denoted his higher rank. "I won't ask again."

Next to Katerina, Niko snarled. "He cannot call you like a dog!"

Katerina refrained from remarking on the irony of this statement. She strode forward, shoulders back and head high. "I'm right here," she said, her voice ringing out in the cool spring air. "Cease harassing the citizens of Kalach and state your business."

She didn't dare look at Niko, but next to her, she could sense the amusement baking off of him. Well, let him be amused, then. She had no intention of bowing to these men's wishes, no matter how fine their garments or how demanding their tone.

Out of the corner of her eye, she saw Lara, a fellow Dimi, and Ilya, her Shadow, heading Katerina's way, closing ranks with her and Niko. Joining them were Svetlana and Luka, a Dimi and Shadow pair beside whom Katerina and Niko had fought many times. On their heels came the other seventeen Dimi and Shadow pairings that were of age to fight. The three unbonded Shadows who had lost their Dimis in battle— Valentin, Pyotr, and Mikhail—accompanied them.

Niko gave a low hum of approval in reaction to the welcome presence of his black dog's pack. But Katerina didn't feel soothed. If these men were here for her, then all the other Shadows and Dimis in the world would do her no good. Their gesture was symbolic, nothing more—for if Katerina intended to kill these men, she could do so easily, calling fire to her hand and unleashing it upon them. No, this was a matter of politics. She could not harm these men without bringing down the Kniaz's wrath upon Kalach.

"Our *business*," the leader said, imbuing the word with scorn. "Why, our business is you, Dimi Ivanova. I thought I made that clear."

The insolence in his voice was unmistakable, and Niko growled louder, a hair-raising, threatening sound. He bared his teeth at the man, and next to him, Alexei tensed in solidarity.

"Niko," Katerina said quietly. "Hold."

"He cannot speak that way to you!"

"No," she said, stepping forward, away from her Shadow and their friends. "He cannot."

Perhaps she would have restrained herself, had it not been for the expression on Elena's face: lovestruck, as if seeing Niko's protective Shadow nature rise to the surface was a gift just for her. As if she were imagining what it would be like for him to protect *her,* not Katerina. As if all her dreams were coming true at last.

She had no right to take her anger out on Elena; the Vila was betrothed to Niko, after all. But the arrogant man who had spoken to her as if she were his vassal was another story.

At the Trials, she'd had to hide what she was capable of. But after what had happened on the road to Drezna, there was no hiding anymore. And if she didn't have to conceal what she was, then by the Saints, she would use it to her advantage.

Letting an unpleasant smile lift her lips, she sent her magic out, heat curling through the space between her and the men on horseback. It gripped the leader by the back of the neck, scorching him, and his eyes went wide. "You—you dare...? Let me go!"

"I will," Katerina said calmly, the smile widening, "as soon as you address me with the respect I deserve."

Behind her, Ana snickered. Baba Petrova, far less amused, said, "Katerina! Think about what you're doing, for once in your life. Think about who these men are. Who they represent."

"I know well who they represent." Katerina tightened the grip of her magic, and had the satisfaction of watching the man squirm. His mouth fell open, and a gasp of pain escaped him. "But I don't bend the knee for vassals. Address me with respect, servant of the Kniaz. Or ride back the way you've come, empty-handed."

Baba Petrova raised her hands to her face, presumably to hide her dismay at Katerina's attitude. But before those gnarled hands hid her expression, Katerina could have sworn she detected the slightest glimpse of pride.

Next to her, Niko's growl had tempered into a deep-throated chuckle. "You heard the lady," he said. "What will it be?"

The man scowled, red-faced and furious. Sighing, Katerina

summoned the wind and commanded it to shake him, like a kitten in the grip of an angry beast. His horse shifted under him uneasily, and behind him, the two men who accompanied him looked as if they would like nothing more than to flee. Katerina couldn't blame them.

"Dimi Ivanova!" Elder Dykstrova snapped. "Leave off toying with him. You've made your point."

"Fine," Katerina said, and lifted a lazy hand. The wind died down immediately, and the heat retreated. "Feel better?" she said as the man's body stilled.

He shot her a furious glance, then opened and closed his mouth twice before he spoke. He looked, Katerina thought, like one of the giant goldfish she'd seen in the moat that surrounded the Kniaz's castle. "How dare you?" he snarled again when he got his breath.

She rolled her eyes. "You disrespected me. I showed you your place. You're not the Kniaz, to whom I owe fealty; you're merely one of his emissaries. So speak, already. This is growing tiresome."

"I had every intention of speaking, before you used your... your..." He flapped an ineffectual hand in her direction, and she fought the urge to laugh. Her amusement must have shown on her face, because the man's cheeks reddened. When he spoke, his voice was tight, each syllable clipped.

"I am Andrei Borodin, lieutenant of the Velikii Kniaz, nobleman of Iriska. These are my companions, also employed in His Grace's service." He gestured at the other two men.

"When the Dimi Nadia Dobrow and her Shadow paid a visit to Rivki on their way to the Magiya, to reveal what had transpired and to ask for aid, it was...quite revelatory. Imagine the Kniaz's surprise to discover that you and your Shadow were responsible for defeating an army of Grigori single-handedly."

He raised his bushy eyebrows at Katerina, his gaze flicking behind her to Niko.

"We had no choice," Katerina said, her voice flat. "They would have killed us."

"Be that as it may." He matched her tone. "Choice is one thing, Dimi Ivanova. Ability, another. When questioned, Dimi Dobrow informed us that your control of all four elements renders you capable of great things. The Kniaz is willing to forgive your deception, in this time of great need. He will pardon you and your Shadow, along with your Baba and your village."

His lip curled as he gestured at the citizens of Kalach, so humble in appearance compared to the finery of Rivki's denizens. But Katerina couldn't care less about his contempt. At the knowledge that the Kniaz wouldn't make them pay for keeping her secret, a weight lifted from her heart. Just as quickly, though, another took its place.

"If you're not here to exact punishment," she said slowly, "then what do you want?"

He folded his beefy arms across his chest. "Given the danger that is afoot, the Kniaz requires the best protection available. He demands that you and your Shadow ride back to Rivki with us at once."

Katerina's brain churned. Her stomach did the same, clenching until she feared she might eject the contents of last night's stew onto the stones of the square. "Leave with you now? But it's not—we still have a year until the second round of the Trials—"

Andrei smirked, the satisfaction on his face unmistakable. "Not so brave now, are you? Come, witchchild. Pack what pitiful possessions you own. Have no fear; the Kniaz will supply you with satins and silks soon enough. Perhaps"—his gaze raked over Katerina—"he'll want even more than that. He's fond of spitfires, after all."

Next to her, Niko snarled, the fury that emanated from him palpable. If he leapt to her defense now, it might trigger a violent altercation that could compromise Kalach. Worse still, it would show Andrei that she needed her Shadow to defend her honor. And Katerina was perfectly capable of speaking up for herself.

"Why is it," she said, giving Andrei her most charming smile, "that unimaginative, petty little men would rather envision a powerful woman on her back than on the battlefield? Because I assure you, should the Kniaz value me for my fire, I would rather it be for the flames I can call to my hand than the passion I might ignite with my body."

The villagers gasped, and Andrei's knuckles whitened on his palomino's reins. "You dare to call me unimaginative and petty?" he said, his lip curling. "You will pay for that, witchchild. As the Kniaz's right hand, there is nothing little about the power I wield." He drew himself up, one hand on his smallsword's hilt. "Call me names here, if you like, in the heart of your sanctuary. You'll leave this village soon enough. And when you do, I'll be waiting."

The growl in Niko's chest rose to a roar that filled the square. Before Katerina could stop him, he lunged for Andrei, throwing him from his horse. Then the two of them were wrestling on the stones, Niko in human form but so enraged that the growls rattling from him sounded as if they were ripped from the throat of his black dog.

Andrei's horse, unsettled by the commotion, reared again and again. Its hooves came down repeatedly on the stones, mere feet from Niko's head. The two other emissaries had drawn their smallswords, but their gazes flickered back and forth between the battle on the stones and Katerina's fellow

Dimis, who had come to stand behind her in solidarity. Their Shadows growled as one, the menacing sound ricocheting off the wood-fronted shops that surrounded the square.

Katerina threw Baba Petrova and the Elders a desperate glance, but they simply stood there, faces impassive. For them to call a halt to this would demean Niko, to suggest he couldn't defend himself, and by extension, Katerina. It would weaken her Shadow forever in the eyes of these men and the others that served the Kniaz. To keep his position as alpha—as a Shadow worthy of fighting by her side—he must triumph on his own.

But if Niko persisted—if he couldn't stomach the insinuation that the Kniaz wanted...

It was an insult, to be sure. But would a Shadow typically react with such vehemence, if he didn't have inappropriate feelings for his Dimi? If he hadn't bedded her the night of his betrothal, told her he had loved her all his life?

What had he said that night in the clearing? *When you told me that the Kniaz wanted you, it took every bit of my restraint not to hunt him down, nobleman or no.*

It felt as if every eye in the square had fallen upon her, as if they were all staring. As if they could tell. As if they *knew*—

Niko was on top of Andrei now, his blade at the man's throat. But the man was fighting viciously, struggling to draw his smallsword.

If this oaf damaged a hair on her Shadow's head, she would kill him. She wouldn't be able to help herself. And what would the villagers and the Kniaz's remaining minions think then?

Her magic rose, called by her rage and frustration, and she let it come. The wind bent the birch trees as it swept toward her, and she lifted one hand, shaping it, directing it. Concentrating hard, she wrapped its cold fingers around Andrei, immobilizing his legs, then his torso, then his arms. She left his head alone; it was worth it to see his stunned expression when he realized he couldn't move. His eyes darted back and forth, terrified, and his hand rose to his chest, struggling to make it rise and fall.

A satisfied smile lifted Katerina's lips. He deserved this and more, for insulting her and threatening Niko. Let him suffer. Let him wonder at what a Dimi and her Shadow could do.

"You're suffocating him," Ana whispered from behind her. "If he dies here, Katerina, there will be trouble."

With a sigh, Katerina lifted both hands and called the wind once more. It came, blasting Andrei through the air. He flew into the grove of birches, and she resisted the urge to slam him into a tree. Instead, she dropped him—very kindly, she thought, given the circumstances—into a clump of ferns next to the path. He fell with a thump and a crash, and didn't move.

"You've killed him!" one of Andrei's companions howled. "Make no mistake, you will pay for this, witch!"

Her magic settled back inside her, satisfied and sated, like a cat curling up in front of a roaring fire. Katerina smirked, and Baba Petrova shot her an exasperated look. She ignored it. If Baba didn't like how Katerina had solved the problem, then *she* should have intervened. This was what Baba got for standing there like a lump of coal while this moron threatened her and suggested that the Kniaz take Katerina as...what? His replacement courtesan? His plaything?

Dimis could choose their own mates, true—but if the Kniaz chose *her,* refusing wouldn't be so simple. Most would see it as a great honor, an act of service to the realm second only to serving in the Druzhina.

Well, Katerina did not. Besides which, Dimi Zakharova would poison her every meal or slit her throat in her sleep. Let the Kniaz try to make good on the way he'd undressed her with his eyes in the arena. No matter what Niko threatened, she didn't need him to protect her against a mere man, ruler of the realm though he might be. *Spitfire,* was she? If the Kniaz laid a finger on her, noble or no, she would show him what it meant to burn.

On the stones, Niko sat up, still looking furious. He stalked over to Andrei, blade in hand, and glowered down at him. "Not dead," he reported. "Just an idiot."

At this, Katerina laughed out loud. "You're all fools," she said to the man in the grove and the two on horseback. "The Kniaz wants me because of what I can do, yet you seek to insult me and suggest my place is in his bed rather than fighting by my Shadow's side to defend Iriska? Perhaps you've confused me with my softer sisters." She raised a hand and gestured at the Vila, who were clustered next to the Elders, as if seeking their protection. Elena's eyes were wide, pupils dilated with fear. Perhaps, Katerina thought, she had truly feared for Niko's life.

She shouldn't be uncharitable to Elena. The Vila had never done Katerina harm, no matter how differently they saw the world. Katerina was the one in the wrong. She had to keep reminding herself of that.

Forcing her shoulders back, she watched as the man in the grove struggled to get to his feet. She had to strike now, while she still had the advantage, before his wounded pride got the best of him. "I won't leave Kalach," she said. "Not undefended like this, without their strongest Dimi and their alpha Shadow." *State your terms,* Niko had said. Well, this was the best she could think of. "Let us hear back from the Magiya as to the nature of this threat. Then, once I'm assured Kalach can survive in my absence, my Shadow and I will go to the Kniaz."

"No." Brushing leaves and dirt from his clothes, Andrei strode toward her. The red-and-purple ribbons had come undone from his hair, and his face was scarlet with rage. "This is not a negotiation, witch. The Kniaz calls, and you come."

Niko had followed him, blade still out. Now he came to

stand by Katerina's side. "Do Katerina and I need to teach you another lesson?" he said, his voice mild. He turned his knife idly, so the sun reflected off its blade. "My Dimi heels for no one. She serves the Light, and I'm proud to fight by her side. Would you like another demonstration of our skills?"

Andrei's eyes narrowed. "You—"

Before he could say another word, the man on the roan spoke up for the first time. "Have patience, Andrei. The Kniaz suspected she would resist, did he not? Offer her an alternative. It'll all be the same, in the end."

Andrei scowled at Katerina. Then he turned to face Baba Petrova and the Elders. "You," he said, gesturing at Baba with one meaty hand. "Do you concur with the witch and her dog? You wish for her to defy the Kniaz's command and stay here, for such time as His Grace might see fit to allow?"

Baba stepped forward. The light glinted on her white hair and deepened the royal blue of the gown that marked her as what she was: ancient witch and keeper of the village's rituals. "Though I may disagree with Dimi Ivanova's tactics," she said in her cracked voice, "I agree with her opinion."

Katerina's eyebrows rose, relief washing over her. She had hoped Baba would speak on her behalf, but she hadn't been certain of it. Defying the Kniaz's wishes was no small thing.

Then again, neither was assaulting one of his emissaries and using witchwind to throw him fifty yards into a birch grove. Katerina couldn't imagine that she and Niko had made any friends today.

Well, if the Kniaz didn't care for her, so much the better. She would be his weapon, not his wench. Better she make that clear now, before she found herself having to bind him the same way she had this stupid oaf. And Saints forbid Niko got word of such a thing. She feared that if the Kniaz laid an unwanted finger on her, Niko would kill him. And then where would they be?

"I'm listening," Andrei said in a haughty tone that made Katerina snort. Across the square, Baba Petrova sighed.

"Dimi Ivanova and her Shadow are the strongest protection we have," she went on. "I apologize for her insolence, but you yourself have seen her strength, and believe me when I tell you she restrained herself."

"Indeed." Sarcasm clung to Andrei's every syllable. He looked pointedly down at his sullied clothes.

Next to Katerina, Ana rolled her eyes. "Maybe I shouldn't have stopped you," she whispered. Katerina smirked at her, biting back a sarcastic reply.

"All of us know that a terrible force is among us, something unlike anything I have ever seen," Baba went on, ignoring them both. "We have no answers, only questions. This is a dangerous time. I humbly request that the Kniaz give me the opportunity to train others as best I can to take Dimi Ivanova and her Shadow's place, and to appoint another alpha for the pack." She spared a warning glance for Katerina. "Though her attitude is regrettable, her abilities are...unprecedented. Should the threat that destroyed Drezna come our way, I fear that without Dimi Ivanova and her Shadow, we stand no chance against it."

Katerina steeled her spine. She feared little, but the crater that had eaten Drezna whole, the Darkness that had swirled at the bottom of it, calling to her...could she have defended Kalach against such a thing? What if she had tried, and failed?

Niko shot her a concerned look, and she mastered her expression, settling her features into a neutral mask a moment before Andrei said, "His Grace gave us permission to grant you a month, until the full Blood Moon, when the next tithe of grain will be due."

A murmur rose up from the villagers. Katerina was sure they were all thinking the same thing—that the harvest would likely not be nearly as fruitful as expected. Several times in the past week, waterwitches had had to take time away from training, summoning rain from the river to fall upon the fields, but it had yielded few results. The crop of wheat was failing, with little explanation as to why. There had been no invasion of locusts, no drought, no paucity of sun. But still, the fields weren't yielding as they should, and they had nearly exhausted the winter's stores. If this kept up, they would struggle to make their tithe.

Andrei barreled onward, with no concern for the villagers' distress. "The witch and her bastard Shadow"—he gazed at Niko with disgust that verged on hatred—"will bring the tithe, and they will stay. As for now, you will give us three additional Dimis and Shadows to take back to Rivki, to stand surety for Ivanova and her dog. We will release them to you when the witch and her Shadow deliver the tithe."

There was a collective gasp from behind Katerina, where the rest of the Dimis and Shadows stood. Baba Petrova spoke for all of them. "Three? But that would leave us with only seventeen Dimi and Shadow pairs to defend ourselves in the event of an attack. The Kniaz has thrice that. Surely he doesn't require three of our own—"

Andrei's features grew steely. "Either you send the witch Ivanova and her black dog now, or you give us three others. The choice is yours, Baba of Kalach."

Baba was a small woman, barely coming to Katerina's shoulder. But such was her authority in the village that she loomed much larger. She had the last word on which Dimis and Shadows bonded. Which Shadows and Vila married. Everyone, including Katerina, revered her. But now she looked smaller somehow, like the ancient crone she was. "Give me a few minutes, then," she said to Andrei. "I need to confer with the Council."

Andrei inclined his head. "I'll allow it," he said in an entitled tone of voice that made Katerina want to send him flying through the air all over again.

Baba stepped off the stones of the square, and the five members of the Elder Council followed. Katerina watched, her heart pounding, as they retreated down the path to Baba's cottage and disappeared inside.

20

KATERINA

Katerina didn't know what to wish for. If Baba and the Elders were to send her and Niko now, then that would mean leaving her village and everyone she loved behind. It would mean breaking her vow to defend Kalach. But perhaps it would also mean delaying Niko's marriage to Elena, for surely the Vila wouldn't travel with them based on a mere betrothal. In that case, would it be worth it?

Around her, the villagers muttered amongst themselves, and across the square, Elena was trying desperately to catch Niko's eye. Her Shadow wasn't looking at his betrothed, though, nor at Katerina. His gaze was fixed on the men on horseback, his blade sheathed but his hand resting on the hilt, his body poised for violence. And his fellow Shadows flanked him, taking his lead.

A sudden swell of pride filled Katerina. He was a prince among Shadows, not just because he was hers, but because of his strength and talent and force of will. Where he led, his pack would follow. It was no small thing to be the alpha of a pack of Shadows. His absence would leave a gaping hole.

Once again, she cursed the Kniaz. How could he not understand that Iriska was only as strong as the villages that protected the portals to the Underworld? If the Darkness devoured the rest of the Seven Villages, Rivki would fall, too. And when it did, the demons would pillage and devour, consuming human souls until there was nothing left.

The Kniaz, Katerina concluded, was a fool as well as a tyrant.

Next to Katerina, Ana said, low-voiced, "What do you think they'll do? If they don't send you and Niko, do you think..." She stole a look at Alexei, standing straight-backed by Niko's side, then fidgeted with a willow twig she'd scooped from the stones, shredding the leaves from the wood. "I never thought I would go to Rivki, Katerina. I always thought it would be you."

You and everyone else, Katerina thought but didn't say. "Even if you did go," she told Ana, trying desperately to lighten the mood, "it would only be for a month. You could think of it as an adventure. Drink oceans of kvass, bed all the women you like before you have to choose a mate to sire your Dimichild..."

Ana snorted. Her proclivity for beautiful women was well-known in Kalach, though she was fond of handsome men, as well. Every time she and Alexei brought the Kniaz his tithe, Ana had returned full of tales of the gorgeous, daring women at court who were only too happy to take a firewitch to their bed.

"Any man I marry will have to be happy to share me." Ana's smile looked forced, but it was better than no smile at all. "And the pickings are indeed slim here in Kalach. Perhaps you're right. I should pray to the Saints to send me to Rivki, before the Darkness eats us all and I haven't yet had a chance to sleep with the most beautiful woman in Iriska."

Katerina bit back her retort as Elena broke loose from Alyona's side and traipsed across the square, her flowing purple garments adorned with white charms for fertility, love, and domesticity. Her blond hair streamed behind her, stirred by the fresh spring breeze, as she crossed to where Niko and Katerina stood. Andrei's eyes lingered on her with an avidity that would've made Katerina want to carve them out of his head, but Elena just gave him a coy smile, accepting the tribute as her due.

"Katerina," she said breathlessly as she crossed the invisible line between the Kniaz's emissaries and the clump of Shadows and Dimis, "what do you think Baba will decide? Do you think we'll have to leave so soon?" She lowered her voice. "That horrid man—he could have hurt Niko. I don't blame you in the least for tossing him into the grove."

"Yet you smiled at him," Katerina said without heat. Her heart wasn't in needling Elena, as she usually did.

Elena spared Andrei a glance from beneath her lashes. "You have to learn how to manage men, Katerina. You can't always hurl them through the air, after all. And certainly you don't plan on lighting the Kniaz on fire should he show you favor."

Katerina rolled her eyes; it was as if the Vila had read her mind. "I would never," she said, loud enough for Andrei to hear. "Perhaps I'd toss him in the moat as a snack for the Vodyanoy. Less waste, you know."

Andrei glared at her. Elena gave a shocked gasp. And Ana, bless her kindred little heart, began to laugh.

"Worry not, Vila Lisova," she said. "Your betrothed will keep Katerina from doing anything too rash."

"Ha," Katerina said before she could stop herself, remembering how Niko had launched himself at Andrei. "Only because he'd be too busy doing it himself."

"He *was* glorious," Elena said dreamily. "But impulsive. I want him to live long enough to seed our Shadowchild, after all."

To the Saints with the Kniaz. Katerina wanted to light everyone in the square on fire, especially herself. "In the name of Sant Antoniya, what is taking so long?" she said to Lara, who had stepped up next to her.

Her fellow Dimi shrugged. "It's no small choice. But look. Here they come now."

Sure enough, Baba Petrova and the Elders were making their way down the path that led back to the village square. Katerina held her breath as they approached. The murmur of the villagers, of the Shadows and Dimis and Vila, faded into silence.

"Well?" Andrei said, his lip curling as Baba and the Elders took their places once more. "What say you, Baba of Kalach? Have you come to a decision?"

Niko's eyes were fixed on Katerina's face, boring into her, as Baba's voice filled the square. "We will grant you the three pairings you requested. Lara and Ilya, Svetlana and Luka, Natalya and Ivan—you will ride out with the Kniaz's party."

Lara sucked in her breath, and Katerina squeezed her hand. "You will do well," she whispered. "It's just for a little while."

Lara nodded, but her eyes shone with tears as Baba turned to the three men on horseback, her expression grim. "We grant you this, on the condition that they'll be returned to us at the Blood Moon, when Dimi Ivanova and her Shadow deliver the tithe."

"So shall it be," Andrei replied. "You have the word of the Kniaz, before witnesses."

Katerina schooled her expression to blankness. Relief blended with guilt, that her sisters would be forced to ride out from Kalach in her stead. And a burning sort of joy: she and Niko would doubtless go to Rivki on their own, giving her two months when she wouldn't have to endure the sappy, anticipatory way Elena regarded her Shadow—

"We are agreed," Baba Petrova said, interrupting her thoughts. "But allowances must be made. Vila Lisova"—she gestured at Elena—"is meant to wed Niko Alekhin three months hence. This changes things. When the tithe is delivered at the Blood Moon, she will ride out with them, as Shadow Alekhin's wife."

The ground dropped from beneath Katerina, the world fracturing to bits as it had during the Trials: Elena's delighted smile, the clench of Niko's jaw, the satisfied expression on Andrei's face at the notion that Elena would be within his reach —for clearly he cared not a fig for the bond of marriage.

All eyes were on the three of them—Dimi, Shadow, and Vila. She couldn't let her devastation show.

Katerina lifted her hands and summoned the wind. It came, bending the trees that lined the square low, as if in obedience. "As you speak, Baba Petrova," she said, "so shall it be. As for you, Andrei, servant of the Kniaz—I advise you to cease regarding my Shadow's betrothed with such avarice. If he pressed his blade to your throat for the mere implication that the Kniaz might like to bed me, I shudder to think what he might do if you laid a finger upon his wife."

Without waiting for his reply, she turned her back on the crowd in the village square and stalked off, leaving a shocked silence in her wake.

21

KATERINA

The three Shadow-and-Dimi pairs rode out that afternoon, at Andrei's back. The rest of them trained all the rest of that day and into the night. After that, Baba bade Niko and Elena to come to her cottage, to discuss details of their impending nuptials. Pretending like this didn't tear her apart, Katerina walked home with Ana and Alexei. They spoke of Niko's fight with Andrei, the way Katerina had thrown the man into the grove, whether Nadia and Oriel were well on their way to the Magiya and what they might learn there. By the time the three of them reached Katerina's doorstep, she ached with the effort of acting as if nothing was wrong.

She didn't do a very good job of it. But so much was *already* wrong that perhaps her glum demeanor aroused little suspicion, because Ana, usually quick to call Katerina out, didn't say a word.

Katerina had changed out of her leather training gear, swept the floor of the cottage, and taken a bath by the time Niko came home at last. She was sitting in front of the fire in a midnight-black gown that matched her mood, staring into the flames, when his step echoed on the walk. A moment later, he'd unlocked the door. It creaked on its hinges as it swung inward, the wind stirring Katerina's hair and making the flames flare higher.

She should have turned to greet him. It was petty to do otherwise. But she wasn't ready to see his face. She didn't trust what she might say, what she might do.

There was silence as he paused behind her, assessing her mood. Metal clinked as he set his blades down on the table. Then he came on, the floorboards protesting as they took his weight. He knelt in front of her, peering into her face.

"Katya," he said. "Forgive me."

She had to clear her throat before she spoke. When her voice came, it was harsh-edged. "There is nothing to forgive."

"No?" His lips quirked. "Then why are you glaring at me like you'd like nothing more than to burn me down to ashes?"

"I don't wish to incinerate you," Katerina said haughtily. "Who would fight by my side then?"

Niko gave a rough sound that, under other circumstances, might have been a laugh. "I had to go to her, my Dimi. Baba insisted."

She didn't bother to ask him to clarify who *her* was. They both knew. "She's your betrothed. Of course you did. I have no right to protest."

"And yet," he said wryly, scanning her—arms wrapped tightly around her bent knees, defiant gaze meeting his— "clearly you *do*."

Anger welled up in Katerina. "What do you want me to say, Niko? That I begrudge every word you speak to her, every second you spend by her side? That the thought of you touching her makes me wish to vomit? That I'd rather face a thousand Grigori than imagine the night when you take her to your bed?"

Her Shadow's eyes narrowed. The firelight played on the

long line of his throat as he swallowed. "That depends," he said slowly. "Is it true?"

Katerina looked away. "Does it *matter*?"

"Of course it matters. I thought you didn't want this." He gestured between them. "That it was to be once and once only. To satisfy your curiosity, as it were."

Katerina's eyes sprang wide. She shot to her feet, infuriated. "You think being with you was some sort of *experiment*? That I wanted to...to try you out and then cast you aside?"

He gave the one-shouldered shrug that meant something was truly troubling him. "What was I meant to think?"

"You were meant to think that you're betrothed to another! That there are demons afoot, and Iriska is crumbling! That there's a prophecy that forbids us to be together, lest we bring about the end of everything we hold dear and the death of everyone we know!"

A faint smile lifted Niko's lips before they fell back into a grim line. "I told you, Katerina. I believe the prophecy to be superstition. As for Elena, I'm not wed to her yet, am I?"

"But you *will* be." Katerina couldn't keep the distress from her voice. "And soon. What kind of people would that make us, if we..."

Her voice trailed off. She closed her eyes, not wanting to look at him anymore. He was too much—too immediate, too beautiful, with his black hair tumbling loose from its tie. Too wild, with the firelight streaking his body, dark as demon blood. But a small current of air caressed her face, and when she opened her eyes again, he'd moved closer. "You are my Dimi," he said, his voice husky. "I am your Shadow. Only claim me again, if that's what you want, and I will be yours."

"We *can't*," Katerina protested. "It doesn't matter what I want."

One of his dark eyebrows rose. "Come now, Katerina. When

have you not taken what you wished, and damn the consequences? Am I meant to believe that you don't truly want me, then? Is this a game for you?"

"A game?" Rage heated her cheeks. "I toppled a bridge for you, because I couldn't stand to watch you claim Elena's silly little boat for your own!"

Her Shadow's jaw dropped. "But you said—"

Katerina ignored him, barreling onward. "In a month, we'll leave for the Kniaz's estate. Sooner than that, you'll be married to a woman who idolizes you and has been waiting all her life for this moment. What is the point of starting something that can come to no good end?"

She glared at him. "Or is it that you fought with that fool Andrei today? Everyone knows Shadows seek solace in a bottle or a woman's bed after a fight. Are you simply using me, then, to get out your—"

Before she could finish her sentence, his mouth was on hers, hungry, devouring. His hands wound tight into her hair, the scent of him all around her, his tongue licking along hers. When he pulled back, they were both panting.

"I want *you*, Katerina," he growled. "Not some nameless, faceless woman. Not Elena. *You*, who challenge me at every turn. I nearly slaughtered that idiot in front of the entire village for speaking of the Kniaz taking you to his bed, yet you were the one who had to stand up for my betrothed. Soon to be my *wife*. I didn't even notice the way he was looking at her. Is that not proof enough for you?"

Katerina's hands shook. When she finally found her voice, it shook as well. "We can't, Niko. You know we can't."

His face darkened. "Tell me what you want, Katya."

This time, she was the one who reached for him. He came eagerly, the leather of his gear rough against the thin material of her gown, his body holding the heat of the fire and the leashed strength of a Shadow. She could feel him tremble with the effort it took to hold back when they kissed. To let her lead. But he did it, as he was sworn to do, and inside her, the wall she'd built between them began to crumble.

He pulled back once more, lips slightly parted, breath coming hard. Gently, he brushed the crimson waves from her face. "Perhaps you're wise to fear the prophecy," he said, his voice breaking. "To regret Elena. But for me, the damage has already been done. For wherever I go, whoever I wed, I will always belong to you."

Katerina stared at him, eyes wide. Was she dreaming, to have Niko say the words she'd only imagined for so long?

She was sure she hadn't spoken aloud. But perhaps she had, because Niko's raven-black brows rose. "No dream, Katerina," he said. "This is real, Saints help us both. I've wanted to say this to you for so long, and held back. But I fear this may be my last chance. If the Darkness takes us tomorrow, I don't want to die knowing I didn't have the courage to speak what's in my heart."

Katerina's mouth had gone bone-dry. She regarded Niko, and he looked back, his face calm, expectant. Braver than she could ever hope to be.

She should have backed away. Disentangled herself from his arms and fled the way she'd done the first night they kissed. He would have let her go.

But she didn't move.

Niko didn't, either. His arms around her, his lips an inch from hers...they were a question, asked over and over again. And Katerina had only one answer.

She stood on her tiptoes, giving him every chance to pull away. Her lips pressed against his, taking his breath for her own, giving it back again. Still he remained motionless, a statue above her. She traced his lips with her tongue, tasting him: blood and fire. A growl rose in his chest, but he stayed perfectly still, letting her use him as she would. Letting her decide.

When she pulled back, it was only to unbutton his shirt and toss it to the floor. His gaze grew darker, his eyelids sinking to half-mast.

"On your knees, my Shadow," she said softly, curious to see what he would do.

Niko obeyed at once, his hands falling open at his sides. It was a posture of supplication, of submission. But he did it, without hesitation or question.

I'm yours, it said. *And if you want me, then...*

"You kneel for no one," she said in wonder, gazing down at him.

His throat worked. "I think we both know, my Dimi, that I kneel for you."

Another time, Katerina would have teased him with the promise of pleasure, made him wait until neither of them could stand it, made him beg. But not now, when every cell of her body craved his. Instead she knelt in front of him, skating her teeth along his jawline. She nipped his collarbone, then pressed her palm against his Mark.

At that, Niko's control broke. His hands came up and he dug his fingers into her hips, yanking her hard against him. Somehow she was on the floor on the hearth rug, and he was looming over her, murmuring her name, his hands roving the length of her body. Her magic surged out to meet him, caressing his skin, and he moaned above her, his eyes darkening as he undid the ribbon at the neckline of her gown and tugged it over her head. He knelt before her and worshiped her and when they merged into one single, burning being, their shadows coupling on the wall beside them, there was no point in pretending that this would be the last time.

22

GADREEL

The Bone Moon sank, readying the Blood Moon to rise in its stead.

Backlit by the dim glow that blanched the forest, a cluster of Grigori crept through the trees. Masters of illusion, they didn't look like creatures of Darkness. Instead, they'd shifted their shapes to resemble the men and women of Kalach, the better to infiltrate and devour. But the denizens of the forest knew them for what they were, and hid as they passed.

"To me, warriors," Gadreel hissed as they came within sight of the rowan-fires that burned along the boundaries of Kalach. This was the home of the Dimi who had slaughtered his soldiers, the one who was stronger than any who had come before. He could feel her here, her power like a magnet drawing him onward.

But he could feel the Darkness, too. Swallowing Drezna whole had sustained it for a while, but now it was stirring again. There was no time to waste. Gadreel's army wasn't as massive as it would have been if the Dimi hadn't vanquished his minions, but that was all right. He couldn't bring too many soldiers to Kalach, lest he arouse suspicion. Even among his own ranks, there were spies. He had to lead his soldiers to believe this was nothing other than a typical raid, one he had decided to monitor personally after the disaster outside Drezna, lest word get back to Sammael that there was something special about Kalach.

It might be too late for that already. If he could feel the extraordinary Dimi's power, then chances were that Sammael could, too. Even if the other demon believed Gadreel was responsible for the devastation of Drezna, that didn't explain the cracks that had appeared in the barrier separating the Underworld and the world of humans. Gadreel could feel a yielding to the wards that protected Iriska. A sense of openness that hadn't been there before.

Normally, this would have been cause to rejoice. But anyplace that yielded to him would yield, as well, to the Darkness. It was only a matter of time until what happened at Drezna took place again. And what if it took place here, in Kalach? What if it took the talented Dimi with it?

He couldn't afford to wait. He needed her for his own—to leash her abilities, to bend her strength to his will before the Darkness destroyed them all.

His soldiers quickened their pace, and Gadreel gave a warning growl, holding them back. The assault on the village had been carefully plotted, every detail accounted for. It would not do for the greed and haste of his fellow Grigori to ruin it.

Grigori were not known for their obedience, nor for their patience. But they understood power and coveted it. What Gadreel demanded, they would fulfill, until it suited them to do otherwise. They fell in behind him, blurring the edges of their borrowed shapes until they blended with the trees and the dark.

Gadreel paused at the treeline, taking in the silent village. The fires burned high, reeking of the rowan smoke that scorched his lungs even in this form. They could not tarry here for long.

But even getting this close without being recognized by the wards was unheard of. The world was folding, breaking. Either he would slip through the cracks and back again, taking the Dimi with him, or everything would crumble and they would all be doomed.

The Dimi's Light called to him. Burning. Beckoning. And suddenly, Gadreel found that he had run out of patience, himself.

"Now," he said to Azazel, his second in command, and crossed the line that separated the village from the forest, without waiting to see if his company followed.

23

KATERINA

When the alarm sounded, Katerina was asleep, curled beneath her quilt. The cottage was otherwise empty; Niko was out on patrol with Alexei, pacing Kalach's borders.

She hadn't wanted to let him go. The forest had felt strange to her recently, its energies off-balance—as if when she drew power through her, something was drawing it back again. The more they flouted the prophecy, the more she feared the return of the Darkness. But Niko had only kissed her, his lips feather-light, and slipped out the door.

The gong sounded again, its ominous cries reverberating throughout the village, and Niko's amulet flared to life, pulsing against her skin. His voice came, agitated, inside her mind: *Wake up, Katerina. I need you.* It was the form of communication they used when they fought side by side, when he took the form of his guardian dog. Never had she known him to use it otherwise. She hadn't thought he could.

It was bad, then.

She shot to her feet, braiding back her long hair and yanking on the leather garb she wore for battle. The hide was no protection against the bite of a Grigori, but it was flexible and easy to move in. She shoved two syringes filled with antivenin into her pocket and laced on her boots just as Niko's voice came again. *Katerina!*

I'm here, she told him, touching the rowan cross that hung beside the mantel for luck and flinging the door open.

He was there, eyes wild, shirt and breeches splashed with someone else's blood. *Stay by me*, he said, though his lips didn't move.

Always, she said, and meant it.

Together, they ran toward the sound of carnage, feet pounding down the stone paths that led to the center of Kalach. The place was in tumult, families pouring from their houses to be met by a paired Shadow and Dimi, each of whom was assigned to guard a quadrant of the village. Katerina caught glimpses of the little ones' wide eyes and pale faces as she and Niko hurtled past them. She winged a prayer to the Saints that they would be safe. As the strongest Dimi in Kalach, her role was on the front lines. She couldn't stay behind to protect them.

"How many?" she asked Niko as they ran. "As many as on the road to Drezna?"

"No. But at least twenty. Maybe more. And there's something in their midst... Not the Darkness we encountered in Drezna, but a power unlike anything I've felt before." His voice was hard. "They stabbed Alexei. Took his father's form and sank a blade into him before I could stop it. I outran them, coming for you. He..." Niko's throat moved as he swallowed. "He's likely gone."

Katerina's heart ached for Alexei and Ana, but there was no time to reflect on what they might have lost. Surrounded by shops and gardens, the square was deserted, save for a demon in the shape of one of the schoolteachers, dragging a little Vila girl—Dominika—onto a path that led to the forest. Rage boiled beneath Katerina's skin as Niko seized a knife from his belt and threw it. The blade pierced the demon through the eye and it fell, writhing as it lost control of its form. Blue blood flowed from the wound, the scent sickly-sweet.

"Come," Niko said roughly, taking the little girl's hand. She clung to him, face streaked with dirt, as he spun, looking for the Shadow and Dimi sent to guard the other Vila.

"Give her to me." It was Elena's voice, breathless but determined.

She stood in the middle of the square, yellow hair tousled from sleep, clad in her shift. Her hands were steady as she reached for Dominika.

"Run," Katerina told her, pushing the little girl into her arms.

Elena held Dominika tight. "Saints be with you both. Bring him back to me." With a terrified glance at the writhing demon, she and Dominika fled toward the Shadow who stood at the outskirts of the square, waiting to see them to safety.

Clouds scudded across the waning moon, obscuring its light, as Katerina and Niko raced through the woods, heading for the source of the screams.

24

GADREEL

G adreel felt it when the Dimi who had slaughtered his soldiers spilled from the darkness of the village paths, her Shadow at her side. He tilted his head, examining her. They were a study in contrasts: her with her vivid red braid and pale skin, the Shadow with his hair the color of the night itself and his narrowed, storm-gray eyes.

He had seen this Dimi before, he was sure of it. But where? The memory nagged at him with the insistence of a fish caught on a line, slipping free when he sought to grasp it.

Gadreel stepped forward, beyond his demon soldiers. Some had already dragged Vila children from their beds, for a witch without her Shadow was greatly weakened, and without Vila, no Shadowchildren could be born. Others stood, awaiting his orders. The Shadow who had been patrolling alongside his packmate lay curled at Azazel's feet, choking on Grigori venom.

The red-haired witch stared at the fallen Shadow, mouth open in horror. She fell to her knees, pulling a metal syringe from her pocket and stabbing it into the Shadow's arm as she muttered an incantation. But the Shadow didn't stir.

The witch's head came up and she sought Gadreel's eyes.

Within them roiled a pure fury that resonated with his own. That look called to him, echoing in the vast chambers of his memory. And suddenly he knew, with a certainty that thrilled through his veins, where he had seen her before. She had been a fighter then, too; he remembered it well. Now she had come full circle, finding her way back to him once more.

Exaltation surged through Gadreel. He had waited so long, but it had been worth every century. This one was perfect.

"We meet again, little Dimi," he said, a smile lifting his lips. "Well met."

Her copper brows creased with confusion. She didn't remember him. No matter: it had been some time, and the circumstances had been unfortunate—for her, anyhow. Gadreel had enjoyed them quite a lot. Sometime soon, he would take pleasure in refreshing her memory.

The Dimi's contemptuous gaze raked over him from head to foot. "You walk in another's skin. But I see you for what you are. Demon filth. You shall do no more damage here tonight."

"That," he told her, "is your choice. For I am Gadreel, ruler of the Fallen realms, and I came for you."

By the witch's side, the Shadow stirred. When he spoke, his voice was rough with the beginnings of his Change. "You'll not touch her."

A harsh laugh tore from Gadreel's throat. "Shadow of the most powerful spellcaster to walk in centuries. How I will enjoy ripping out your heart."

The man's form blurred, just as Gadreel's soldiers' had in the woods. Then, in the fastest Change Gadreel had ever seen, he was on all fours, snarling, covered in fur as dark as his hair. The black dog lunged, teeth bared, as the Dimi closed her eyes and the wind began to rise.

25
KATERINA

Alexei lay crumpled in the dirt. Thank the Saints, he was still alive—his chest moved, air rasping in and out— but he wouldn't be for long, without more antivenin and Baba Petrova's magic. But Baba was with the other Dimis and their Shadows—scattered throughout the village, protecting the Vila and the elderly, the non-magical folk who had few defenses against the Grigori. And if Katerina used her remaining syringe of antivenin to save him, she would have none left for Niko.

Would she have to stand here and watch Alexei die?

The demon that had taken his father's form loomed over the fallen Shadow. Next to him stood Gadreel. Tall, slim, and clad in black, his face all sharp angles and his eyes a brilliant blue, he looked more like a well-bred nobleman than a threat. But Katerina knew well how dangerous he was.

He had lured them to the forest's edge, while their fellow warriors were occupied elsewhere. With such a large show of force, he could divide his soldiers, sending half into the village to wreak havoc while the rest remained with him. It was a trap, and the two of them had run right into it.

She didn't understand how so many Grigori had broken through their wards. Usually, the demons preyed on unfortunates who wandered off on their own, who traveled between villages selling wares or visiting relatives. For them to enter Kalach this way was unprecedented.

Was it her fault for burning so brightly, as Baba had insinuated? Or hers and Niko's, because of what they'd done?

Gadreel grinned at her, teeth gleaming in the moonlight, and rage surged through Katerina anew. This creature wanted her? Well, then, he could have her. She would show him how powerful a Dimi could be.

Eyes fixed on the Fallen Angel of War, she opened herself up to the power of the Light. It filled her, electrifying every synapse, and the demon's tongue slipped out, tasting her magic as it rode the air.

"Yes," he hissed. His lips rose, showing even more of his venom-coated teeth, as his form slid sideways, taking the shape of her Shadow.

"See, he can still be yours," he said, his smile widening in a parody of Niko's mischievous grin. "When you are mine."

In the form of his black dog, Niko stood between them, his outraged growl filling the air. He had his calling, what he was born to do: protect her from demonic attack when she opened herself up to her magic; defend them both from evil. And she had hers.

"I will never be yours," she said, and called on the power of the sky.

It broke open at her command, rain lashing the trees. The wind roared, sending huge branches hurtling downward. The Grigori shrieked, and she redoubled her efforts, harnessing the wind to drive a massive branch through the air like a battering ram.

Niko, she whispered, mind-to-mind. *Hold.*

He braced, pressed tight against her. Just as it had on the road to Drezna, a luminous glow encased his form, holding the demons at bay. *I am your Lightbringer*, he whispered back. *Nothing will harm you while I live.*

Katerina didn't have time to wonder about the evolution of her Shadow's gifts. If he was right, and they were a response to the growing demonic threat, then she had even more reason to fear. They all did. She gritted her teeth and drove the spear forward, impaling one demon after another as they closed ranks in front of Gadreel. They screamed in agony, and Niko echoed them, his howl triumphant.

Gadreel roared in rage as his soldiers fell. Niko growled back, advancing toward him—but the demon held his ground, his roar growing louder still. Her concentration shivered, shook. What if he made good on his threat, ripping out Niko's heart?

Their bond trembled as her resolution faltered. To hell with the Grigori soldiers. All she wanted was to put herself between Niko and the monster, to save him at any cost.

Katerina. His voice rose in her mind, tight with uncertainty. *What—*

Gadreel was laughing now, fury transmuted into a victorious, scornful barrage of sound that filled her ears and crawled over her skin, stinging like nettles. He charged Niko, and they met in midair, her Shadow's teeth grazing the demon's throat as Niko fought to bring the monster down.

The sight snapped Katerina out of her haze. If Niko were to perish because of her, she would never forgive herself.

Summoning all her strength, she reached for the spark of the rowan-fires, burning a half-mile away. The inferno rose to her call, flaming sticks flying through the night on the back of the wind. Fists clenched with the effort, she guided the missiles to fall amidst the Grigori, where they ignited in a blaze worthy of poisoning a thousand demons. The Grigori wailed in agony, and Niko howled again. *Victory, my Dimi,* he said.

For a single, burning instant, her eyes flickered shut. When she opened them again, Gadreel had vanished. And Niko flung himself forward, shifting from dog to man, grabbing his knives from the ground as he went. He cut through the remaining Grigori like a whirlwind, dodging their blades, giving a ululating battle cry as Katerina's storm raged higher, a maelstrom of hail and leaves and flame.

She stood where she was, wind and fire whipping into a frenzy around her, watching her Shadow paint the night with demon blood.

26

KATERINA

The Shadows and Dimi scattered throughout the village had slain half the pack of Grigori. Together, Katerina and Niko had killed the rest. Caught between forms, their misshapen, pitch-blackened bodies lay strewn on the ground, run through with her tree-spear or Niko's blade. Gadreel and the one that had injured Alexei were nowhere to be seen.

"Fled, most likely," Niko said with disgust as he stood over Alexei's unconscious body. Katerina had injected her second vial of antivenin as they raced back to Kalach, uttering every healing charm she knew. Niko had carried Alexei back to the surgery, then stood, hands white-knuckled on the counter, as a healer administered a third dose, overseen by Baba herself. Thank the Saints, his heart beat strongly now, though he hadn't woken up yet. Katerina didn't think she would have been able to face Ana, otherwise.

Once Baba had assured herself that Alexei would live, she'd left to attend to the other injured. Katerina and Niko had stayed to watch over him as his breath came easier and the color returned to his face. Ana sat on his other side, gripping her

205

Shadow's hand. Baba hadn't allowed her to fight, afraid that without Alexei to protect her, she'd be too vulnerable. Since Niko had carried Alexei back, though, she'd refused to leave him.

"You saved his life," Ana said to them both. "I won't forget."

"He's my brother," Niko said simply, and laid his hand on Alexei's shoulder before he and Katerina turned to go.

Outside, the sky had just begun to lighten. She wanted to touch Niko, to bare the skin beneath the gashes in his shirt and make sure he was unharmed. But though the stone courtyard in front of the surgery was empty, she didn't dare.

She should feel relieved. No one else had been badly wounded, and only one woman had been taken captive: Trinika, the baker who made the pies Niko loved.

It was a miracle they hadn't lost Alexei. A miracle the Grigori hadn't stolen the children or slaughtered the adult Vila.

All because Gadreel had wanted Katerina for his own. His hammer, his pet.

Katerina shuddered. She would die before she let a demon use her that way.

"Are you all right?" Niko said quietly. His eyes found hers.

She lifted one shoulder and let it fall.

"He wanted you." His voice was tight. "He said he *knew* you."

Katerina gave him a small, one-sided smile. "He's delusional. I'm hardly in the habit of fraternizing with demons." She let her smile grow into a knife-edged grin. "Perhaps he's confused me with another Dimi bent on eradicating him from the earth. It must be a familiar experience."

"You can joke all you want, but I was in your head when he said those things. I know it frightened you." His teeth sank deep into his lower lip, as if he imagined rending the demon limb from limb. "No matter how great our victory, I wish their leader had been one of the creatures we killed. For the Dark Angel of War will be back, and you know that as well as I."

"He will," Katerina agreed, "but not tonight. We destroyed his soldiers. Banished him to the Dark."

Niko bowed his head. "You were magnificent tonight. I'm honored to be your Shadow. To know that you hold such strength—that you can look evil in the face and burn it to ashes."

Katerina inhaled, taking in his familiar scent—overlaid now with the reek of rowan-smoke and the residue of demon blood. She opened her mouth to tell him that she was humbled by his courage and his faith in her. That with him by her side, she had the confidence to take risks she wouldn't otherwise, because she knew he would never fail her. That she'd almost failed *him*, and she was sorry for it.

But before she could speak, Elena appeared at the edge of the courtyard, a shawl wrapped around her shoulders. Her face lit at the sight of Niko, whole and unharmed, before her gaze flicked sideways, taking in Katerina next to him. Her smile widened—then dimmed.

Niko swore under his breath, stepping back even as he lifted a hand in greeting. "We were just discussing the battle," he called to Elena. "You're unhurt?"

Any of the other Shadows, Katerina thought, would have gone to their betrothed, murmuring words of reassurance, embracing them. But Niko didn't move.

The Vila shifted her weight in clear invitation, one hand on her hip. "I'm fine. Only frightened, for you as much as for myself. They told me you lived, that you had not suffered so much as a nick. But I wanted to see with my own eyes."

You saw, Katerina wanted to say. *So now you can go.* Instead she pasted a smile onto her own face in her best attempt at welcome. It must have looked as strained as it felt, because Elena's look of puzzlement deepened.

"Are you two all right?" she asked.

"We're fine. Just a little shaken," Niko said, moving so that he blocked Katerina from view—protecting her, she realized with dull amusement, even from herself. "I'll be right there."

"Take all the time you need. I'm going home, to help see to the children." Elena's voice shook, betraying how frightened she'd been. She forced one last brilliant smile for their benefit—that was Elena, always trying to put the best face on a situation—then went off down the path as silently as she'd come.

"Saints and demons," Niko muttered, watching her go.

Katerina was silent. She'd rather deal with a horde of Grigori than this.

"I don't want to leave you. But I need a moment," he said, the words coming hard. "I need to go check on her."

"Of course," she said, turning away.

"Katya, don't." She felt the movement of the air as he reached for her, then thought better of it and let his hand fall.

"I understand," she said, her back still turned. "You wouldn't be who you are—loyal and honorable—if you acted otherwise. Go."

But still he didn't move. "Look at me," he said, as he had that first night in the forest.

Katerina spun on her heel, prepared to tell him again to leave—but at the desolate expression on his face, she bit back the words. A muscle twitched in his jaw, and his eyes shone. She had never seen him cry, not even when he was twelve and broke his leg jumping from a haybarn, on a dare.

He shoved his hair back with a rough, impatient gesture. "This is tearing me apart. Understand that, if nothing else."

Even before they were bonded, she'd felt his pain as if it were her own. Now, it was a thousand times worse. "You should go to her," she said, struggling to keep the emotion from her voice. "She needs you."

His eyes searched her face. "That she does, Katerina. But I need *you*."

As I need you, she thought but did not say.

"I know what you think of her," Niko said. "Of all the Vila. But if no Vila lived, then I wouldn't be standing in front of you today. And you would have likely died when the Grigori attacked."

"I'm the hero of my own story." Her lip curled. "I save myself."

Conviction drove his voice deep. "We save each other, Katya. We're stronger—together. You're the one who told me so. Remember?"

His fingers closed, warm, on hers a moment before he strode away, toward the cluster of cottages where the Vila lived, the weight of his destiny heavy on his shoulders.

27

GADREEL

If there was one thing Gadreel disliked more than Sammael, it was being forced to attend a meeting. Being forced to attend a meeting *with Sammael* was truly the eleventh circle of Hell, where all the demons were inconsequential, the rain smelled of over-scorched sulfur, and the torture was unimaginative.

The meeting was about the Darkness, of course. Sammael had requested it, concerned about what he termed "Gadreel's overzealousness." He wanted to make sure that what happened in Drezna was not, as Sammael put it, "about to become a regular occurrence." And Gadreel couldn't put him off any longer. To do so would look suspicious.

Sammael had been so obnoxious about this meeting, too. It had to be today, even though Gadreel had just returned from his raid on Kalach hours before. It could only last for a specific amount of time, because Sammael had somewhere to be. Secretly, Gadreel suspected Sammael had nowhere to be at all. He just wanted to aggravate Gadreel as much as possible.

But the more he cooperated with his archenemy, the less suspicious Sammael was likely to become. If the other demons knew the truth of what Gadreel had set loose on the world, even the ones who had allied with him for millennia would turn on him. He had to buy time until he could get his hands on Katerina Ivanova, and that meant playing relatively nice with Sammael.

He couldn't very well meet with the other demon in his throne room, since it still bore the marks of Drezna's collapse. So he'd chosen the next best thing—his library. They would meet via Gadreel's mirror and Sammael's scrying pool, which were handy for such things. But before then, Gadreel wanted the lay of the land, so to speak.

He assumed Sammael spied on him, too, after all. It was only fair.

Gadreel lounged back in his favorite leather chair, wearing a blue velvet suit he'd stolen from an unsuspecting human some time ago, while the latter was insensible from drink. He could have conjured the suit, but where was the fun in invention when you could engage in acts of trickery? Not to mention, there was something softer, finer, about the real thing. As foolish and weak as humans might be, they did have a talent for beauty.

He peered into the mirror that stood across from him, admiring his reflection. Blue was an excellent color on him. It matched his eyes.

"Show me the Venom of God," he said. "Seducer, destroyer, and general inconvenience. Show me Sammael."

The mirror rippled in response to his command. It went foggy, mist drifting across its surface. And then it cleared.

There sat Sammael, in the guise he'd kept for the last hundred years: broad shoulders, short red hair, cheeks free of stubble. His wings were invisible, glamoured to lie flat beneath his loose-fitting shirt. The demon had never had a good sense of style, unlike Gadreel, who had dressed for their meeting. A shame, really, given the millennia he'd had to improve himself. Gadreel had tried to give him pointers, but alas, it had not gone over well. He was missing a few feathers from his own equally glamoured wings as proof.

Sammael was doing...absolutely nothing interesting. He was sitting at the desk in his scrying room, a book from one of his shelves in hand, paging through it and making notes on a piece of parchment.

Really, he was the most boring demon Gadreel had ever met. The most interesting things about him were his on-again, off-again relationship with Lilith and the doors to his palace, which were studded with the eyes of his favorite victims. Gadreel had tried to compliment him on his choice of décor, but again, it had not gone over well. He had protested that he wasn't being sarcastic, but Sammael's bird-headed guards had made a concerted effort to kill him, and, well...that was the last time Gadreel had been invited to pay Sammael a visit in person.

It wasn't Gadreel's fault, really. If Sammael didn't want blood all over his foyer, he needed to learn how to accept a compliment.

Gadreel narrowed his eyes at Sammael, who was oblivious to his presence. The demon didn't look suspicious, like he'd called their meeting to confront Gadreel about setting the Darkness free and bringing about the end of the human and demon realms. He looked like he almost always looked...like someone had inserted a stick into his posterior and run it straight up his spine. He looked like this even in battle, dispatching his enemies as efficiently as possible and with a minimum of fuss. The only time Gadreel had seen him look any different was when a woman was concerned. They were his weakness, especially fragile ones in need of aid. Gadreel suspected this was because Lilith had been the opposite of that, in every way.

As Gadreel watched, Sammael ran his fingers through his hair, which stood on end. He slammed the book down and glared at the parchment. At the ceiling. Heaved a sigh. Back at the parchment again. He looked...frustrated.

Was it possible, Gadreel wondered, that he was up to something?

Perhaps. Or perhaps his ink pot had run dry. It was hard to tell with Sammael, who was always scheming. Scheming Sammael, they should call him, rather than the Venom of God.

Gadreel snapped his fingers at the mirror, which clouded over again. He looked down at the woman kneeling at his feet, who looked back up at him with her big, dark eyes. Waiting for his command. His soldiers had taken her from Kalach, as the spoils of war, and Gadreel had demanded her obedience. It was everything he would usually enjoy. And yet he felt nothing. Worse than nothing...he felt empty. The ragged hole inside him nagged, a vacuum that couldn't be filled by deviltry or debauchery.

He thought of how Dimi Ivanova had faced him down in the forest, hurling curses and fire. She was a match for the void that pulled at Gadreel, sucking in pleasure and spitting out emptiness. If he hadn't already needed her to vanquish the Darkness, he would have coveted her for his own. When they had driven the Darkness back together, he would have her. Maybe Gadreel would bring her Shadow too, as a pet. He'd take joy in chaining the black dog to his throne and throwing it a bone every now and then. But first, he had to save the demon realms. And tonight, his means for doing so had slipped between his fingers.

Gadreel had been arrogant. Foolish. His foot soldiers were one thing; his own strength was another. He had assumed no Dimi, no matter how powerful, could stand against him, especially with the weakening wards. And sure enough, his soldiers had been able to invade Kalach in a way they never had before.

The wards had bent before them, giving way to the Dark and letting the Grigori through. But when it came time to confront the Dimi he'd come for, nothing had gone as planned.

She had called the rain, on a night as dry as any he'd seen. She had broken the very sky open and summoned a wind powerful enough to sever the trunks of ten oaks. She'd called rowan-fire from a half-mile away and lit her battering rams aflame, killing demon after demon while her Shadow fought by her side. Gadreel shuddered to admit it, but he had feared for his life. He'd made his intentions clear; she knew he wanted her. She would kill him, if she could. Or at least vanquish him to the Void, which was as close as he could come to dying.

He had never encountered a Dimi who was a match for him. Even as he'd retreated to the closest portal, near the ruined altar where the Dimi's accursed saints had worshiped centuries before, he'd been filled with a vicious exultation: She was stronger even than he had believed. She was the one who could stand with him against the Darkness, which hungered more with each passing second. Its craving echoed in the call of the wind, in the voices of the Void that whispered inside him.

In another place and time, Gadreel would have made a game of claiming this Dimi for his own. He would have tempted her and teased her, making her promises that he had no intention of keeping, before he tethered her to his side. But as he sprawled in his chair, counting down the minutes until his meeting with Sammael, he knew time was not a luxury he had. If he was going to save the Underworld and maintain his superiority within it, he needed a solution *now*. His direct attack on Kalach had failed. He needed to lure the Dimi out, to trick her. But how?

She was a twenty-one-year-old woman, barely more than a girl. And yet she had managed to stand against him. It was unsupportable. But here, in the heart of his realm, he was still king. And no matter how powerful she was, she could not resist him forever.

His mirror clouded over and cleared once again to reveal Sammael. Heaving a sigh, Gadreel braced himself. "In the name of Lucifer, Prince of the Power of the Air, King of the Bottomless Pit, and Father of Lies, I welcome you to this regrettable get-together," he drawled.

"Gadreel. Right on time," Sammael said in his usual fussy way. "What a surprise."

Gadreel leaned back in his chair, beckoning to the woman who knelt at his feet. "Would I disrespect the Venom of God by being late?"

His fellow Watcher glowered at him. "You can. And you do. Frequently. To what do I owe the honor of this unexpected punctuality?"

"You said you had somewhere to be." Gadreel rolled his eyes. "Besides, you know how I feel about meetings. 'If it were done when 'tis done, then 'twere well it were done quickly,' no?"

"You and your human scribes." Sammael smirked at him. "You do have a weakness for the creatures."

Gadreel bristled. Just because he'd kept Dante Alighieri's head as a door-knocker for a few centuries... What was more entertaining than a disembodied butler who announced, 'Abandon hope, all ye who enter here'? "And you have no sense of humor," he said. "Not to mention a disturbing fondness for paperwork. Of the two of us, I am far more popular at parties."

Sammael shoved his parchment hastily aside, as if he'd forgotten it was there and didn't want Gadreel to catch a glimpse of it. Very interesting, indeed. "How would you know? We hardly run in the same circles."

With an effort, Gadreel refrained from making a cutting remark about the boring nature of Sammael's realm. Instead he said, "In search of some new reading material? Perhaps there's something in my library I might be able to lend you. It is rather...extensive."

"My library is just as well-stocked as yours," Sammael huffed. He was so easy to rile. "If you must know, I'm looking for an ancient tome from the Seven Villages. It was lost some time ago, and lately I've found myself curious about it."

It was Gadreel's turn to smirk. "Now who has a weakness for the creatures? You must be hard up for entertainment indeed. The thing's probably crumbled to dust long ago."

"Most likely," Sammael said, but his expression was unmistakably cagy. "I see you're as obnoxious as ever. Now that we've dispensed with the pleasantries, let's get to business, shall we?"

"We shall," Gadreel agreed, heaving another sigh. "After you."

"Well, there's the matter of..."

The meeting was every bit as excruciating as Gadreel had imagined. The whole time, as the woman at his feet did his bidding, as he lied about the Darkness and pretended to be as concerned about its origins as Sammael, he strategized about next steps. But as their interminable conversation at last came to a close, he had reached just two conclusions.

Sammael was, indeed, up to something. He intended to find out what it was.

And the next time Gadreel came for Dimi Ivanova, she wouldn't be so lucky. He just needed to figure out a way.

28

ELENA

E lena stood, watching Niko walk down the path that led away from the Vila's cottages. The wind whipped his torn shirt against his body and swept his hair back from his face, baring his scar. She shivered, thinking of how vulnerable a Shadow could be.

"I'm so glad he's all right," Aly said from behind her.

Elena jumped, heart pounding. "Don't sneak up on me like that!"

"I wasn't sneaking." Her friend's voice held the hint of a smile. "You're so enamored with your Shadow, a horde of Grigori could attack all over again and you'd have no idea."

Elena shook her head, her heart still thumping a torrent of uneven beats. She'd tried to be strong for the Vila children—especially Dominika, poor thing—but the truth was, she'd barely held herself together. All she could think of was seeing Niko again, making sure he was safe...and the moment he'd fold her into his arms, like she'd seen the other Shadows do with their Vila.

But Niko hadn't come to her at first. Hadn't touched her when she'd sought him out in the square. She'd been

217

back at the cottages for a quarter-hour before he'd come striding up the path—and when he'd found her, he'd offered her only the same kindnesses he'd extended to the other unwed Vila, all of whom fluttered around him in a way that would have irritated Elena if he'd paid them any attention at all.

He hadn't gazed at Elena with the same intensity he'd reserved for Katerina when she'd come upon them in the courtyard. Hadn't acted nearly as eager to come to Elena as he'd been reluctant to leave his Dimi.

Why would such a thing be? Elena had done all that was expected of her, and more. She had always honored Sant Viktoriya. The other Vila revered her. So why did her Shadow not bless her with his regard? Did the fault lie with her?

"He's always walking away, isn't he," Aly murmured as Niko reached the end of the footpath and took a shortcut through the garden.

Elena took a step backward, under the grape arbor that shaded the entrance to the side yard of the cottage she and Aly shared. "What do you mean?"

Aly gave her a tremulous smile. "Shadows are so busy. Always somewhere to go. Someone to protect. Do you ever wish he would stay with you—just for a little while?"

Her words echoed Elena's thoughts so closely, she wondered if Aly's empathy had tipped over into the ability to read minds—which was, of course, ridiculous. "I do wish that, sometimes." She wrapped her arms across her body, holding herself close, the way she wished Niko had done. "It's selfish, I know, but sometimes I want him to myself."

It was a dangerous admission. For yes, she loved Niko—but her love for him was bigger than the two of them. It was about what their love could yield, how it could bear the fruit of the covenant and uphold the mission of the Saints. She regretted the words as soon as they left her lips, worried what her best friend would think.

"I don't think that's selfish at all." Aly twined one of her auburn curls around her finger. "He protects everyone else—his Dimi most of all. But he's vowed to swear his heart to you. Why shouldn't he put you first, when the fighting is done?"

The sentiment felt blasphemous to Elena—but it also called to her, resonating in the deepest, most secret part of her heart. "He's supposed to protect Katerina," she said, hating the doubtful note in her voice. "If he didn't, Kalach would fall."

Aly plucked a half-ripe grape from the vine entwined around the arbor and rolled it between her fingers. It was a wasteful gesture, and one that was unlike Aly, who always chastised the little ones for picking fruit before it ripened. The children used the fruit as ammunition, flinging tiny green apples or pellet-sized berries at each other; Aly just squeezed the grape until its juice dripped onto the ground, swallowed up by the thirsty soil. Watching her, Elena realized her friend must be unnerved too; huddling in the shelter the village maintained for such occasions, a Shadow and Dimi posted at every entrance and the little ones clutching each other to keep from crying, was an experience that left its mark.

"I know this is the last thing you want to hear, Lena," Aly said, dropping the empty skin into the grass. "And maybe I shouldn't say it—but I'd be less than a friend to you if I didn't speak my mind. There's something odd between the two of them. Even their magic, of late—a Shadow and Dimi alone shouldn't have been able to hold off so many Grigori."

"Katerina is the strongest Dimi to walk in three hundred years. Everyone says so." Elena's voice sounded brittle. "And Niko is alpha of his pack. He is worthy of her." *And of me.* "Else, Baba would never have made the match."

"Still," Aly said, "there is a time for fighting at your Dimi's side, and a time for softer things. Everyone knows Shadows seek release after they fight—be it in drink or the arms of a woman. I've never known Niko to find solace in a bottle. If he is not turning to you—then..."

She didn't finish her sentence, but her meaning was clear enough.

Elena's lower lip trembled. She turned away to hide it, but Aly had known her for too long. She swept Elena's hair back, her touch gentle. "Don't worry, Lena," she said, remorse clouding her face. "Please don't think of it any longer. Today's been dreadful, and my imagination's run away with me. I must be a lunatic, to say such things."

Wordless, Elena nodded. Squeezing her friend's hand, she went next door to check on the Vila children whose parents were clearing the debris left by the attack. The next time she saw Aly, her friend was all smiles, filled with relief they'd survived unscathed. She didn't say another word about Niko and Katerina, and Elena was only too happy to let the subject drop. But she couldn't stop thinking about it, and that night, after Aly had fallen asleep, Elena pulled her shawl off its hook, slipped on her shoes, and made her way through the silent village, determined to rid herself of her worries once and for all.

She tiptoed up the path to Niko and Katerina's cottage, expecting him to throw the door open and demand to know what she was doing there. A Shadow's job was to guard his Dimi, and Niko would be on edge now, after the demon attack. But the door remained stubbornly closed, and the seed of doubt Alyona had planted in Elena's heart bloomed larger still.

She crept up to the side of the house, where a loose shutter banged in the breeze, and stood on her tiptoes to look inside. Katerina's fire blazed high, casting shadows on the walls. The cottage was dark otherwise, but there was more than enough light for Elena to see the impossible.

Niko and Katerina lay on her bed. She wore her nighttime shift; he was bare from the waist up. Her hair was down, and one of his hands was twined in it. He leaned on his other elbow, looking down at Katerina, his gray eyes fixed on her face.

"It's harder than it used to be, fighting beside you." Niko's voice was husky, but the night was silent save for the chirp of crickets and Elena could hear every word. "Sometimes, I wish our fates lay along another path."

Katerina made a small sound of surprise, and he loosened his grip in her hair, his hand skimming over her body until it came to rest on her hip with the familiarity of long acquaintance. "I don't say it from cowardice, my Dimi. You know as long as I draw breath, I'll keep my vow. I just dream, sometimes, that there is a peaceful place where the two of us coexist, without bloodshed, or demons, or the Dark. Where I'm free to love you the way I wish."

Katerina curled her fingers around the back of his neck, pressing him down to her. Their lips met, until Niko broke the kiss with a growl.

"When I think of what could have happened—all the things that could have gone wrong—"

"Hush." Katerina sounded gentler than Elena had ever heard her. She traced Niko's bare back, following the lines of his scars. "We're both here. We're safe."

Niko trailed kisses along her throat, then lower still. "I could have lost you," he said against her skin.

"But you didn't."

"I could have. So easily. It would kill me, Katya."

Katerina propped herself on her elbows, glaring at him. Elena was sure what she must be thinking of: how his mother had died of heartbreak after his father had been sent away. "You're not allowed to say that. Don't ever say that again. If I died, you'd go on. You have to."

Niko groaned, pulling her tight against him. "I know we shouldn't. But I need to feel you. To know you're all right. Can I —please—"

Katerina didn't answer in words. Instead, she arched so Niko could pull her shift over her head, then moved so he could kick his breeches to the floor. Elena watched in shock and horror as their bodies merged into one by the light of the flickering fire, Niko murmuring all the while how gorgeous Katerina looked, how brave she'd been, how good she felt.

Elena lost her grip on the shutter. It banged against the house, but Niko and Katerina didn't notice a thing. She thumped onto her heels and ran, down the path that led to the village square and into the darkness beyond. Heedless of the danger, she fled through the woods, tears streaking her cheeks and brambles tearing her clothes. Her breath came in great sobbing gasps, and her head was filled with an incoherent buzzing, like the sound of a thousand angered bees.

How could Niko do this to her? She loved him. She'd trusted him. Soon, she was supposed to stand before the village and give him the gift of herself. As for Katerina—the Dimi was supposed to be her *friend*.

Niko was steadfast and loyal. No matter what Alyona had tried to tell her, Elena clung to that belief. Someone didn't change overnight, going from being kind and honest and true to betraying their betrothed in the worst manner imaginable.

It was Katerina's fault. It had to be. She was the Dimi, the witch who could bend an entire forest to her will. What was one man's heart, in the face of that kind of power?

She had stolen him. Had used her magic to cast some kind of spell, and woven a web around his heart. Had taken what was Elena's, disrespecting the time-honored traditions of their village. How could she do this? Didn't she know that violating the prophecy this way would bring them all down?

Swiping at her eyes, Elena blundered through the woods. The trees rose tall, choking the light of the moon from view, and she moved by touch alone, shoving branches out of her way to forge a path. Then her foot hit the corner of something hard—a stone?—and she tripped, falling headlong.

Hiccupping, she sat up, drew her bruised knees to her chest, and looked around. The waning moon shone down, bathing the place where she sat in light.

She'd tripped over the ruins of Kalach's old chapel, destroyed by a Grigori raid a century ago. Rose-briar vines encircled the half-broken columns; moss carpeted the cracked steps. It was a forsaken place, a forgotten place.

The forest had reclaimed the chapel, nibbling away at it. Still, this had once been a place of grace, of power. Surely some of that strength and magic remained, embedded in the stones, sunk deep into the earth. If Elena could find peace anywhere, it would be here.

She got to her feet, climbed the moss-covered steps to what remained of the cobblestone altar, and fell to her knees.

"Saints and angels, hear me." Her voice rose, still thick with tears, into the silent forest. "I am Vila Lisova, betrothed to a Shadow, bearer of Vila and Shadowchildren. I keep your promises; I honor your covenant. Sant Viktoriya, I am your most loyal child. Hear me now, for I call on you for aid."

Her eyes closed, Elena lifted her face toward the star-streaked sky. Hands folded in prayer, she drew a deep breath, inhaling the scent of roses and ruined things.

One breath. Two. Three.

There was a change in the air, a tempering of pressure. The pattern of the light gracing Elena's face altered, moonlight sliding sideways into shadow. Her breath hitched.

"Open your eyes, child." The voice came low, melodious.

Gathering bravery around her like a cloak, Elena obeyed. A

monstrous, dark-edged shape loomed in the shadows, and she bit back a scream. Then she blinked, and a man stood on the steps below her, red-haired and clean-shaven. The angles of his face were as sharp as those of the Saints etched into the new chapel's stained glass windows, as unforgiving as an angel's. But the scent that drifted from him, stronger than it had any right to be—rosemary and the intoxicating aroma of crushed cloves—could only mean one thing.

"Demon," Elena whispered, horror plain in her voice.

"Hello, Vila Lisova, mother of Shadowchildren," he said.

29

ELENA

"Don't be afraid."

Elena stared at the demon incredulously, her blue eyes wide. She had been a fool to think she had the right to summon anything—be it demon, angel, or saint. Even if Niko were here, could he defend her? His gift worked in concert with Katerina's. He was meant to aid a Dimi.

Elena was on her own.

"I won't hurt you," the demon said, opening his hands at his sides as if to show he meant her no harm. She had never been so close to a Grigori before, but she'd always imagined them as fearsome, ruthless beasts regardless of the circumstances. This one was smiling at her, a guileless grin that reached his eyes. "Really, you are far too pretty to harm."

Elena got to her feet and cocked her head. She was used to compliments of this kind.

"Indeed," she said, putting her fear and sadness aside with an effort. She would need her wits about her if she were to survive. "You mean to tell me all that was needed to stop the war between us was to place myself on the front lines? If only I'd known, I would have made the sacrifice long ago."

The demon laughed, and the sound caressed Elena's skin—a silken scarf, slipping over her body. "Beautiful *and* charming. How happy I am that it is you who summoned me."

"But how did I summon you?" Elena said, emboldened. "I called on saints and angels for help. Clearly, you are neither."

"Clearly," the demon said, brushing a fallen leaf from the shoulder of his linen shirt.

"Then how—"

His full lips pursed. "Would you believe me if I told you I am not certain? Something in the balance of your world has changed. There are—openings, shall we say, that did not exist before. Places where the veil between what you would call good and evil has thinned."

Something that's changed. Openings that didn't exist before. Elena would be willing to gamble that this disturbance was due to Katerina's bewitchment of Niko. To the prophecy coming true just as Baba Petrova always told them it would.

She hadn't thought it was possible for her to hate Katerina any more than she already did—but she'd been wrong. The Dimi was destroying the fabric of everything they depended on to survive.

Everyone knew that Dimi and Shadows weren't meant to be lovers. But had Katerina listened? Of course not. She thought she was better, stronger than everyone else around her. That she didn't answer to the same laws.

And now look what had happened. Elena, the disciple of a saint, was standing in the middle of a desecrated chapel, having a conversation with a demon.

The demon in question studied her, dark eyes flickering over her face. "You have thought of something troubling, I see. Would it be untoward of me to inquire what it might be?"

He sounded genuinely concerned, and Elena considered confiding in him. But as nice as he was being to her—and by *nice*, she meant he hadn't eaten her yet—he was still a demon. "You're a stranger," she said, erring on the side of politeness, "and I'm not in the habit of sharing my innermost thoughts with strangers. Also, we're sworn enemies."

"Not personally," the demon said, sounding affronted, "but I take your point. Let me introduce myself. My name is Sammael. It means 'Venom of God.' I've thought of changing it, but the company I usually keep doesn't seem to mind."

Despite her misery, a giggle escaped Elena, and she clapped a hand over her mouth, horrified. It had never occurred to her that demons had a sense of humor. But Sammael— "You're not just a Watcher," Elena said as the weight of his name sunk in. "You're...you were an Archangel."

The demon shrugged. "I was. But as you see, I didn't find the company of Heaven too much to my liking, either." He winked at her. "Now you," he went on, as if this were a perfectly normal conversation, "are a companion of an entirely different ilk. For you, I would consider a pseudonym, should you make such a request."

"Sammael is fine," Elena said between her fingers.

"If you prefer. And who might you be?"

"You know my name." The words scorched her throat. "I said it, when I called you."

"Ah. But then, you did not know I was the one who would answer. I would far prefer you gave it to me freely."

The damage had already been done; she'd laughed at the demon's joke, made a jest of her own, and accepted his compliments. Elena sighed and dropped her hand. "I am Elena Lisova, Vila of Kalach."

Sammael inclined his head. "It is a pleasure to meet you, Elena of Kalach. If you weren't summoning me, you were certainly summoning *someone*. I heard your call for aid. Perhaps if you share your troubles with me, it will be in my power to offer succor."

"You're a demon," Elena blurted, before she could stop herself. "Demons don't make things better; they destroy. Why would you want to help me?"

"If I may," Sammael said, gesturing in her direction. She nodded and he approached slowly, sitting down on the moss-covered steps that led to the altar. From this position, he looked non-threatening, like any of the village boys. Or men, rather—now that she had the chance to study him at close range, he appeared to be in his early twenties, without the lankiness that characterized so many of the boys who had not yet grown into their height. He had ginger eyebrows and an endearing freckle on the right side of his nose.

Of course, this was just the form Sammael had selected for the occasion. For all Elena knew, he was five hundred twenty-nine years old and more truly resembled a blacksnake.

"Well," he said, tracing a finger along the meandering line of moss, "perhaps I would like to correct the impression you have of my kind, which understandably is not all that positive."

Elena suppressed a snort. "You could say that."

"Perhaps I am intrigued that you may have the answer to the question that has been plaguing the Grigori: what has caused this mysterious shift that gives us greater strength, and weakens the wards between worlds? If I assist you, you might be kind enough to assist me as well. Perhaps you have merely caught me in a good mood. Or perhaps," he said, looking directly into her eyes, "I like you, Elena Lisova. It is not often I have the opportunity to have a conversation with a lovely, charming Vila."

"*Perhaps*," Elena retorted, "that's because you're too busy slitting our throats or carting us off to be ransomed like chattel."

This time Sammael threw his head back, giving a full-throated laugh that took Elena by surprise. She wasn't used to coming up with snappy, sarcastic retorts. That was Katerina's territory. But here she was, making a demon guffaw.

Maybe Elena had been so busy buying into everyone else's perception of who she was meant to be—kind, pliant, gentle—that she'd never figured out her true identity. She liked this new version of herself a great deal. But what did it say that it had taken the worst betrayal of her life and a conversation with a demon to bring it out in her? And was she dishonoring her vow to Sant Viktoriya by the very notion?

"Touché," Sammael said when he stopped laughing at last. "But I may be of use to you, just the same. Tell me, what are you doing out here alone, calling on forces we both know Vila are not in the habit of summoning?"

Elena bit her lip, undecided whether to speak. *My Shadow has committed the unthinkable with his Dimi. She has bewitched him, I know it. But I can fix it. I just need enough power, enough strength to set him free.*

"You have no reason to believe me." Sammael's voice was soft. "But I truly wish to help you—if such a thing is possible."

Elena had no magic except the blood gift that allowed her to give birth to Vila and Shadowchildren. But she'd called, and the Dark had answered. Perhaps she was wrong to fear it. What if the Saints had heard her prayer and pitied her? What if they'd sent Sammael to her to give her the strength she needed to make things right?

Maybe the Saints intended Sammael to gift her with magic, enough to become more powerful than Katerina. Maybe they meant her to rescue Niko from the spell the Dimi had cast upon him, and put Katerina in her place once and for all.

She couldn't go to Baba Petrova or the Elder Council for help. What if they held Niko responsible for the fulfillment of the prophecy, believing that he was acting of his own free will, and punished him terribly? What if they cast him out or even killed him? They would never listen to Elena if she protested; Vila's opinions weren't held in high regard, not like Dimis'. She had to find another way to save Niko's soul and make Katerina pay.

She'd called on Sant Viktoriya. This had been the answer to her prayer. To ignore or dismiss it would be to dishonor the saint she revered.

Elena looked into Sammael's dark eyes, fixed on hers with an expectant, sincere expression, then down at the moss that sprang up between the stones of the altar. *Katerina would know what it could do,* she thought. *If it could hurt or heal.*

She dug her fingers into the moss, ripping it free of its moorings, and told the demon everything. He listened as she poured out her heart, not interrupting once, treating her tale with the attention it deserved. When she finished, he said only, "That is a terrible story indeed, Elena Lisova. I wish I could be of service to you, for a lovely woman such as yourself deserves better than such a betrayal."

Elena sniffed, wiping away her tears. "My betrayal is the least of it," she said, looking up at him through clumped lashes. "This could mean the end of Iriska. I know you'd likely love nothing more than that, but I've dedicated my life to upholding the mission of the Saints. I have to do something. But what?" The tears flowed harder, streaking her cheeks.

She felt a gentle touch on her arm. When she looked up, the demon was extending a handkerchief to her. It was such an absurd sight, she almost laughed. "Thank you," she said, taking it and blowing her nose.

"You are most welcome. At least I could perform that small service for you." He smiled at her. "Tell me, Elena—this Dimi. What is her name?"

Perhaps Elena shouldn't tell him. Her instinct to protect Kalach ran deep. But surely the harm here had already been done. "Katerina Ivanova," she said.

The demon's red brows rose. "The name is familiar to me," he said. "Is that not the Dimi that vanquished the Grigori on the road to Drezna?"

Of course, he knew who Katerina was. "Yes," she admitted. "Along with the Shadow to whom I'm betrothed. It wouldn't have been possible without him."

The demon stroked a finger across his chin. "I see," was all he said. "It occurs to me—well, never mind."

Elena leaned forward, eyes on his face. "Never mind what?"

"It's nothing." He looked down at the moss between his feet.

"Have you thought of something that could help me?" She didn't bother to suppress the eagerness in her voice. "If you have, please tell me."

"Your Saints matter so much to you," he said, sounding reluctant. "Even on short acquaintance, I can tell that. And I hesitate to voice an idea that might add to your misery."

Elena gave a harsh laugh. It scraped at her throat, already sore from crying. "My misery is at a peak. I doubt there's anything you could say that would add to it."

He glanced sideways at her, his expression almost shy. "Did you not say that this Dimi commands all four elements? I have lived a long time, and rarely seen the like. And she was near Drezna when the Darkness devoured it. I only wonder...is it possible that the two events are connected?"

At first, Elena didn't understand what he meant. Then she did, and her eyes sprang wide. "Are...are you saying that Katerina is the cause of the Darkness? That she's possessed by it? That she is...an agent of the Dark?"

The demon shrugged, looking away from Elena, as if he

didn't want to see the effect that his revelation might have. And well he might; Elena's mind was racing.

It was true that Katerina had been close by when Drezna fell. That she had accomplished what no Dimi had ever done, slaying so many Grigori on her own, with only the aid of her Shadow. That she had seduced Niko. Her brazen attitude...her arrogance...it all fit. Maybe the events of recent weeks were due to more than her flagrant violation of the prophecy. Maybe Katerina was so powerful because her gifts came not from the Light, but from the Dark.

Maybe she'd been sent to Kalach by the Darkness from the start, to test them. And kind, pure Niko had fallen victim to her wiles.

Elena had been a fool not to see it before. But she saw it now, and just in time. She, a humble Vila, would defend Iriska against the corrupt Dimi who threatened to infect them all.

She'd always known that she was meant for something greater. Perhaps *this* was her destiny.

"I need to save him," she whispered. "To save all of them, before we ride out for Rivki. But what can I do?"

The demon cleared his throat. "If you would meet me here tomorrow," he said, gesturing to the ruins of the ancient chapel, "I might have an idea."

30

KATERINA

Katerina was exhausted.

They'd spent the day training with the other Dimi and Shadows under Baba Petrova's vigilant eye. Katerina had been terrified that with every glance she and Niko shared, they risked giving themselves away. She'd gone out of her way not to touch him, until Baba had snapped that if they didn't stand closer together, a demon could waltz right through the space between them, black dog and witchfire be damned.

There had been another Grigori attack on the village two days before. This one had been minor, squelched almost as soon as it began, but she couldn't remember a time when one attack had followed so closely on the heels of another. An ever-present sense of *wrongness*, as if the universe had spun off its axis, pressed heavy on her chest, making her breath come short.

She tried to tell herself this was normal—who wouldn't be anxious about the constant threat of demonic invasion, especially when your village was depending on you to save it, and Gadreel himself was out to get you? Not to mention that the man she loved was soon to wed another. But logical as these reasons might be, she knew them for the flimsy excuses they were.

Something was *off*. She felt it in her bones and sinew, the same way she felt the call of earth and flame.

The clock was ticking, the sand running through the hourglass. They had barely more than a week until Niko and Elena wed, and just over a fortnight until they had to deliver the tithe to Rivki. She dreaded going back there, especially now that the whole of the Druzhina knew why she'd performed so well in the Trials. After what she'd managed on the road to Drezna and Nadia's confession, there was no hiding anymore. They'd see her both as a traitor and the means to their salvation, triggering a potent mix of contempt, gratitude, and creeping envy. The Kniaz might not want her dead or banished, but his Guard was another story, even in terrible times like these. Katerina would spend every second watching her back.

Not to mention, now that Dimi Zakharova knew what she was capable of, the Kniaz's consort would see Katerina as more of a threat than ever. She'd have to sleep with one eye open and a knife under her pillow, since Niko would no longer be curled by her hearth. And Saints protect them all if Zakharova somehow made good on her suspicions, discovering the truth of what Katerina and her Shadow had been up to. Even if they never laid a finger on each other again after arriving in Rivki, what they'd already done was worthy of condemnation.

Perhaps, condemnation was the least of it. Quite possibly, it had doomed them all.

The fields were shriveling, struck by a blight like the one that had laid waste to Drezna: a terrible, blackening frost, suitable more to the dead of winter than to the burgeoning spring. There were murmurings about the prophecy, and even Ana, usually so practical, had turned to Katerina during dinner, the rations for which grew ever-smaller, asking if she imagined that such a thing could be coming true.

"Who would do that?" Ana had said. "Seek to cleave to their Shadow, knowing what devastation might follow? With so many men and women ripe for the picking, who would choose the only one they were never meant to have?"

Katerina had only shrugged, turning away from her Dimi sister for fear that her face would betray her guilt. "A fool," she'd said, filling her voice with the disgust she felt for her inability to let her Shadow go. "Someone who should know better."

She hated lying to her friend. She hated *this*.

Maybe Baba Petrova was right; she could only bring trouble to Kalach. Maybe it was for the best that she was leaving. But the blight that was devouring the fields—if she were truly responsible, would it leave when she did? Would it follow her, like a well-trained dog? Or was she merely the epicenter of destruction that was doomed to spread throughout Iriska?

And then there was Gadreel. What did he want her for? Did he simply want to harness her strength, to turn her Light to Darkness? Why did he believe he'd seen her before? Was he behind what had happened to Drezna—had his soldiers caused it? And if that was the case, did it mean that Katerina herself wasn't to blame? That, as Niko had always believed, the prophecy wasn't the source of their strife? Surely it couldn't be based on a romance between Dimi and Shadow that ran only the course of a single month—from Bone Moon to Blood.

She was desperate for answers. But none were forthcoming, and it was far too soon for Nadia and Oriel to return from the Magiya.

Restless, she puttered around the cottage, sweeping the floor, setting sweet herbs to burn atop the stove. Niko lay on the

235

bed watching her, eyes half-shut, one arm crooked behind his head. He looked so peaceful, she hated to break the silence. But she did, anyway, voicing one of the myriad worries that troubled her.

"Do you think Elena suspects anything?"

"Hmmm?" Niko said, his voice lazy.

Katerina plucked a drooping petal from the spray of daisies on the table. "Elena. Do you think she knows?"

"Of course not, Katya," he said, pushing himself up on one elbow. "It's been a long day. Come here. Let me hold you."

"I'm serious, Niko." She tugged another browning petal from its stem.

"I can tell." Sighing, he sat up and shoved his hair out of his eyes. "Leave that poor plant alone, would you? And stop cleaning, for Saints' sake. Sit down and talk to me."

Katerina hesitated to comply, for fear of where it might lead. Each time she kissed him, each time he laid her down on the rug before the hearth and covered her body with his, she vowed it would be the last. He would be married soon. This had to end.

She should have turned him away the night they'd fought Gadreel. But the fear in his eyes, the need in his touch, had been so blatant. She'd been as desperate as he was to feel his heart pounding against hers, to know that they'd survived.

"Katya," Niko coaxed. "Enough stewing. Come tell me what's on your mind."

"You're bossy tonight," she said, cutting her gaze at him.

"It's been known to happen. Why are you so worried about Elena all of a sudden?"

One of the shutters, as always, refused to latch. It banged against the house, filling the silence between them, as Katerina came to stand beside the bed. "I just...have a feeling."

"I'm listening." He rose to his knees and dug his thumbs into the column of her neck, massaging the tense muscles.

"She wouldn't be the only one. Before we left Rivki," she said, letting her head fall forward, "Dimi Zakharova suspected there was something between us."

Her Shadow's hands paused, then gripped her shoulders tight. "What are you talking about?"

"She saw how I looked at you." Katerina sighed. "She... threatened to betray me, as a means of getting rid of me once and for all."

"That's why you were so eager to leave." He shifted behind her, bewilderment pulsing through their bond. "Katya—why did you not say something?"

Katerina twisted, looking up at him through her lashes. "What should I have said? *I wish to do with you all manner of things a Dimi should never wish to do with her Shadow, and the Kniaz's consort sees right through me. Shall we go, before I bring ruination upon us all, or would you prefer I undress you on the hearth rug and prove her right?*"

Despite the gravity of their situation, a low chuckle moved through Niko's body. She felt as well as heard it, and the gust of his breath against her neck made her shiver. "All manner of things, hmmm? I don't know that my imagination is up to the challenge, my Dimi. Perhaps you should elaborate."

"This is *not* funny." How had they reversed roles this way?

"Of course not." His hands caressed her once more, but this time they moved more slowly, tracing an intricate pattern on her skin. It took her a moment to realize he was shaping a series of runes: love, promise, protection. And then, simply, her name.

"I'm waiting, Katya," he said aloud, the edge of menace in his voice at odds with the gentleness of his touch. "Tell me. When I answered the door and you looked at me like you couldn't decide whether to flee for your life or lick the water off my chest, what were you thinking?"

Katerina's jaw dropped. "You—you knew?"

237

"Not then." He took firm hold of her shoulders and turned her away from him, his hands taking up their slow, tortuous motion again. One of them slipped lower, his palm flattening on her belly. "Then," he said, his lips ghosting across her neck as his hand drifted lower still, "I thought you were simply distracted and impatient. But now..." His lips curved against her neck in a wicked smile. "Now, my Katya, I have you where I want you."

She squirmed against him in a halfhearted attempt to get away, but he held her captive, that low chuckle coursing through him again. His free hand gripped her hip, fitting the hot, hard lines of his body to her curves. A raw, hungry sound rumbled from his chest as his fingers found their target, brushing her shift aside and sinking into her.

"Tell me," he whispered. "What did you want to do to me that night?"

"N-nothing," she managed, but it took an effort. Already heat simmered along her nerve endings, igniting everywhere Niko touched her, as if of the two of them, he were the firewitch.

"Wrong answer," he said, scraping his teeth over the delicate skin of her neck. "Try again, my Dimi."

Her body fluttered in response, and his fingers thrust harder. Now Katerina wasn't just aflame; she was melting, clenching around him. How could something that had the potential to doom them all feel so right? Why, despite everything, could she not stop craving him this way?

"Again," he demanded, his free hand rising to cup her breasts, pinching first one nipple, then the other. The pain was exquisite, and she cried out, her head falling back against his shoulder. It was unfair how well he knew her body, after years of training by her side. And yet, when he was touching her the way he was right now—as if he were addicted to the feel of her, his mouth descending over hers to swallow her moans—she could hardly complain.

"Katerina," he coaxed, pulling away.

Damn him. "If I'd told you what I wanted to do to you," she said, breathless, "what I'd imagined doing for months—*years*—would you have gone along with it, my Shadow?"

Niko withdrew his fingers, drawing a whimper from Katerina, and turned her so that she sat astride him. Arms tight around her, he arched upward, rolling his hips. Even through the rough linen of his pants, she could feel every inch of him, and from the way he shuddered helplessly beneath her, she knew he felt the same.

"I think," he murmured, his lips brushing her ear, "that you know exactly what I would have done, Katerina. But in case you need proof of how well I take instruction, perhaps we should experiment with it now. Hmmm?"

Katerina would have loved nothing more. She ached to finish what they'd started, to tell him every filthy thought that had gone through her mind when she'd seen him framed in that doorway. But that would only end one way, and no matter how much she wanted to lose herself in Niko, they had important things to discuss. Kalach was crumbling around them, and Elena might know more than she should.

She opened her mouth to tell him so, but Niko stopped her with a kiss, his tongue sliding against hers and his teeth skating along her bottom lip, devouring her. "Since you're so uncooperative," he murmured, "maybe I should tell you what *I* wanted to do that night. I wanted to get on my knees and crawl to you, my Dimi. Peel off your fighting leathers and taste every inch of your skin, until you called out for me instead of for the Saints."

Katerina gasped, and her Shadow gave a sinful, knowing smile. He thrust against her, his hips arching in a punishing rhythm, and Katerina's core clenched, aching for him. "Niko—" she bit out, knotting her fingers in his hair.

She wasn't sure what she wanted—to tell him to stop, to tell him to never stop—but it didn't matter. She couldn't manage more than the two syllables of his name.

"I'm not done," he promised darkly. "Then and only then, when I had you pleading for more beneath me, as desperate for me as I've been for you, would I bury myself inside you."

Niko wasn't inside her now, but Katerina felt him everywhere, nonetheless. Her body pulsed, climbing higher and higher. It would be so easy to reach that peak and slip over it, to forget everything but how good this felt. And yet—

"If you had done that," she panted, drawing back to see his face, "then Dimi Zakharova could well have caught us. And where would we be then?"

"What do you take me for?" He tugged her close again, one hand twining in her curls. "As soon as you licked the first bead of water from my body, I would have locked the door."

"I mean it, Niko." Much as it pained her to do it, she caught his free hand as it threatened to slip between their bodies, driving them both to a fever pitch from which there could be no return. "Stop for a moment. We need to talk about this."

A groan escaped his throat. "Right now?"

Katerina ignored the way her body throbbed in protest. It had no interest in conversation, unless said conversation involved more descriptions of what Niko had planned for her. She closed her eyes, fighting for a shred of common sense amidst the frenzy that threatened to consume her.

"Yes," she said, nodding vigorously. "Because if we don't talk now, we won't talk at all."

Her Shadow gave a dissenting rumble, but he disentangled his hand from her hair, leaning back against his palms. She opened her eyes to find his fixed on her, dark with need. His pupils were dilated in the firelight, his lips swollen from their kisses. The sight almost undid her.

"Hell's *teeth*, Katerina. You're going to kill me. But all right," he said, blinking up at her. "A small percentage of blood remains in my head. By all means, proceed."

Katerina struggled to put it into words, especially because she wasn't finding it all that easy to concentrate herself. Not with Niko sprawled beneath her, looking at her like he'd far rather be following the agenda he'd had in mind in Rivki than talking. "Dimi Zakharova is one thing," she began. "But Elena... Normally there's an air about her—not diffidence, exactly, but a hesitation...a shyness, almost..."

She drummed her fingers against her thigh in frustration. "I'm not saying it properly. It's just—she won't look directly at me. She hasn't since she saw us together in the courtyard, after Alexei was hurt. I swear she disappears sometimes. And there's this sense I get from her—a smugness, as if she knows some-thing I don't..."

Niko pressed a kiss to the hollow of her throat. "You're imagining things, Katya. You feel guilty, and so do I. It makes you see things where there's nothing to be seen."

The nighttime breeze wound through the cottage, bringing with it the scent of rain. Katerina drew a deep breath, steadying herself, and made a low, skeptical sound.

Her bed creaked as Niko shifted her off his lap and got to his feet. Gone was the playful Shadow who'd doubted his imagina-tion was up to the privilege of determining what she had in mind for him, or the hungry one who'd crooked his fingers inside her and lowered his mouth to hers. His expression was set in harsh lines as he looked down at her, his body rigid.

"This is hurting you," he said, his face grave. "I hate it. You know I don't believe in the prophecy, but still. Maybe—maybe we should stop, even before I wed."

She stared at him, trying to hide the grief that ran through her. "Is that what you want?"

Niko shook his head, sending his black hair flying. "I want to be with you for as long as I can, in whatever way I can. But I know how selfish that is. If you want to end this now, I'll do it, even if it breaks me."

She regarded him in silence, interrupted only by the thunk of the broken shutter as it moved in the wind, trying to see him with her eyes, instead of how she usually did...with her heart. It didn't matter. His gray eyes, his scar, the pleading expression he was doing his best to disguise—all of it was Niko. She wanted what he wanted: to be together as long as they could. "No," she said at last. "I don't want to stop."

Relief lit his face. He reached to tuck a wayward curl behind her ear, the gesture tender. "I'm glad, Katya. Still, I'm sorrier than you know."

The guilt in his voice gutted her. "Don't be. After all, I'll be married one day too. It's the way of things."

His jaw set. "I have no right to object."

"And yet you do," she said, studying him.

"I hate the thought of you with another man." His hands clenched into fists at his sides. "All the more because I know he'll be someone you choose. At least, with us at Rivki, I won't have to watch you marry that fool Maksim, with his insipid smile. Or Konstantin, who looks at you like you're something to eat. And not in a good way," he added, lips rising in a bitter smile.

"I—" Katerina began, unsure what to say. She had never spoken to him of Maksim or Konstantin. But her Shadow, sworn to protect her, had missed nothing.

Niko rubbed his chest, as if it ached. "I can't stand the

thought of it, whoever you choose. But I want that freedom for you, my Dimi. I would never want you to be trapped as I am. Watching the Kniaz try to claim you—knowing you'd rather incinerate him than go to his bed—would ruin me. If he pressured you or touched you without your consent, I'd kill him, ruler of the realm or no."

"We could leave now," she whispered. "Before we're sent to Rivki."

"Leave?" he said, his voice cracking. "And go where?"

"Anywhere. We could follow Nadia and Oriel to the Magiya. Find a way to subvert the prophecy—if it *is* real," she said, holding up a hand to keep him from interrupting, "stop the Darkness from encroaching. And if we fail, then we'll be gone from here. What does it matter, as long as we have each other?"

"You mean desert the village." He stared at her like he'd never seen her before. "Abandon our obligations."

Katerina straightened to her full height. When she spoke, her voice was cold. "I'm suggesting the opposite, actually. I want to save Iriska, with you. And we can fight demons wherever we are. They're unfortunately quite portable, and there's no shortage of them. Unless you're referring to another obligation entirely."

"I promised myself to her," Niko said. He sounded miserable, but Katerina forced herself to press onward.

"You promised yourself to me as well. First, I might add."

"I love you." His voice was hollow. "More than is right. More than I should. But you cannot ask this of me, not as my Dimi or as my heart. You know the choice my father made—and what it cost him. You know I'm the last chance for my bloodline to survive."

Compassion softened her voice as she thought of the wounded, orphaned boy he'd been. "Your father failed Dimi

Sokolova. Abandoned her in battle. You would never do such a thing."

"I would never desert you in battle, true. But to renounce my duty, to break the covenant between Vila and Shadow...it's almost as shameful." He drew a deep, resigned breath. "And I care for Elena as a friend. I wouldn't humiliate her before the village. She's done nothing wrong, Katerina. She deserves better."

The truth of his words hit Katerina like blows. Instinctively, she deflected them. "You may love me, but Elena loves *you*. Do you not shame her by taking her as your wife when your heart is given elsewhere?"

His gaze dropped to the floor. "What can I do? I stood before Kalach and promised her faithfulness in heart and body. I can give her neither. But the promise of marriage—I can keep that, if in name only. I can give her the Vila or Shadowchildren duty demands."

Katerina's face burned. "And I suppose you'll hate every minute of it!"

Niko ran a hand through his hair in frustration. "I don't want her. I want *you*. My heart is yours. If there were any other way—any honorable choice left to me—I would seize it. And when one day you take another man to your bed, Kniaz or no, it will destroy me." His voice was hoarse. "The way I feel about you is the greatest gift I've ever been given. And the deepest curse."

For once, Katerina was speechless.

He wrapped his arms around her, holding her close. "Elena knows nothing about us." His lips trailed from behind her ear to her collarbone, nudging the material of her shift aside. "If she did, do you think she'd keep it to herself for a second? She'd go running to Baba Petrova and have the Elders on our doorstep a moment after she found out the truth."

"That does sound like Elena," Katerina admitted.

"I know." She felt him smile against her skin. "Can we stop talking about her now, please? And finish what we started?" His fingers traced a path down the front of her shift, loosening the ribbon.

Despite the uneasy feeling that still shifted like mercury low in her belly, Katerina couldn't help but laugh. "Really? You're not tired?" she teased.

"There's tired, Katya," he said, tugging the ribbon free, "and then there's dead. And I'd have to be the latter to give up a chance to be with you. That said, if I fall asleep in the middle, feel free to wake me up again."

She looked down at his dark hair, head bent as he pressed a kiss to the slope of her breast. When she spoke, her voice was soft. "I love you, Niko." She had never been brave enough to say the words before, though she had thought them often enough.

Niko froze. Then his head came up and his eyes fixed on hers. In their depths she saw all the lifetimes they might have had: A thousand nights spent together, a baby with his black hair and her black heart—for she had long thought that of the two of them, he was kinder and more forgiving, not to mention far more honorable. If he only said the word, Katerina would flee with him in an instant, responsibilities be damned.

"Say that again," he whispered.

"I love who I am when I'm with you. With you by my side, I believe I can do anything." A sob wrenched its way from her throat. "I don't know how to give you up."

"My Katya." He ran his thumb beneath her eyes, wiping away her tears. "I love how you burn in battle. How your magic fills me, welling beneath my skin until I can't tell where you end and I begin. How every time we kiss, you shatter me like ice and you scorch me like a flame and you never let me lie."

Katerina fisted her hand in his shirt and tugged him toward

her. He came, his eyes darkening as he bent to her and she took his mouth with hers. The kiss was greedy, filled with her fear that it might be their last. How many more times would she hold him this way?

His breath caught as she pushed his shirtsleeve up and found his Mark. It came alive under her touch, its pulse echoing through her body.

So many times, he had faced down a horde of demons at her side, wielding his body like the weapon it was. But here, in her arms, he was undone by nothing more than a touch. The power of it—of what they were together—overwhelmed her.

Her hands went to his face, fingers tracing the stubble that lined his jaw. "If I'm the fire," she whispered, "then you are the kindling that lights the flame. Mind yourself, Shadow. Fire wants nothing but to burn."

He gathered her hair in his hands, then let it fall. It cascaded onto her shoulders, sparking red and gold in the light of the hearth. "Burn away, Dimi Ivanova. I dare you."

Katerina drew on the hearthfire, tracing his Mark with her fingertips as a line of heat slid down his neck, his chest, the flat plane of his stomach—then lower still, touching him everywhere her hands did not. His eyes widened with surprise before they fluttered shut. "Saints," he muttered, reaching out to steady himself against the wall.

"Do I shatter you, my Shadow?" she said, lips curving against his skin.

Niko went to his knees. "Every time, Katya," he said, his voice hoarse.

"Break me, then," she said, a challenge. "Break me like your promises."

Pulling her down to him, he did as she asked. But even as he stroked her hair and whispered how beautiful she was, as she cried out and he echoed her, she couldn't put that ever-present sense of wrongness to rest.

A storm was coming. And this time, hers was not the hand that spurred the wind.

AFTERWARD, she lay with her head on his chest, listening to the reassuring thump of his heart. He brushed his lips across her hair, his thumb tracing a gentle path along her collarbone, coming to rest in the hollow of her throat. "Now," he said, his voice a rumble beneath her, "I'm tired."

Though she hated to do it, she sat up at once, one knee on either side of his body. "I'm sure you are. You should get up, then." They were careful not to risk him falling asleep in her bed, lest someone barge in and discover the two of them together.

"Hmmm," he said, quirking a brow. "In a minute. Let me appreciate this view for a bit."

She poked his shoulder. "Now, Niko."

"I see how you are." He wrapped his arms around her, rolling her beneath him. "Get what you want from me, and then just kick me out of bed. I'm not going anywhere, Katerina. Not unless you want to use your witchwind, in which case you'll probably extinguish the fire, and I'm not rebuilding it for you. I'm tired, like I said."

"Ugh. Get *off*, you oaf!" she protested, shoving him.

Both brows were at it now. "Make me."

Katerina pushed harder at his chest, with exactly as much impact as if she'd attempted to move a brick wall. He grinned down at her, a bright, beautiful smile that made her heart ache. "You've got to try harder than that, Katya."

They were wrestling, then, the way they used to do when

they were children, and Katerina was honest-to-Saints giggling, Niko mock-growling at her in response, and—

Someone was pounding on the door.

Her Shadow let go of her as if she'd scorched him. She leapt from the bed, scrambling for her shift, as he stood, eyes wide with panic, and yanked on his pants, which had somehow managed to land on Katerina's dresser.

"Dimi Ivanova!" It was Natalya, one of the younger Dimis that Baba had been training to take Katerina's place. "Shadow Alekhin! Wake up!"

Niko had managed to button his pants and was struggling into his shirt. "One moment," he yelled in the direction of the door, and then, under his breath to Katerina, "Stay here. Get dressed. I'll delay her." He ran a hasty hand through his hair in a futile attempt to tame it. Throwing Katerina a look that mingled desperation and regret, he strode out of the bedroom. The door clicked shut behind him.

Adrenaline shot through Katerina, as much from being summoned in the middle of the night as from the fear of discovery. She sank onto the bed, struggling to catch her breath. On the other side of the bedroom door, she could hear Niko questioning Natalya, the Dimi's voice rising in hysterical response and another, deeper voice following a beat behind. She spared a quick glance in the mirror atop her dresser: color burned high on her cheeks, and her eyes were bright, the pupils dilated. Perhaps Natalya wouldn't notice, or if she did, she would attribute it to the excitement of being awoken so suddenly.

What was she doing, thinking about this now? Something was horribly wrong. She needed to act like a Dimi, not a love-struck girl.

Katerina laced the ribbon of her shift and pulled a shawl from the hook on the back of her bedroom door. Then she drew a steadying breath and rushed into the main room of the cottage, rubbing her eyes as if to erase the sleep from them.

Natalya stood there, with Gregory, her Shadow, behind her. The younger Dimi's chest heaved with alarm, her brown hair coming loose from its usual bun. "Dimi Ivanova," she cried when she saw Katerina. "Baba sent me to find you. Something terrible has happened."

Katerina didn't dare look at Niko. "What?" she demanded, anxiety sharpening her voice.

Natalya hiccupped. Tears glossed her eyes. "Nadia—Nadia—"

A spike of fear jabbed Katerina in the belly. "Nadia what? Is she back? Is she all right?"

The young Dimi shook her head, sniffling. "Her...her horse came back. B-burnt. Just hers. Not Oriel's. Without a rider."

Niko's expression was grim as he turned to the cabinet where he kept his blades. "Gregory was just telling me that he was on patrol when the mare found its way home," he said, buckling his holster around his waist. "She's in the stables now, in terrible shape."

"I want to see her," Katerina said immediately. Maybe there was a clue she could glean, some kind of explanation. She slipped on her shoes and pushed past Natalya and Gregory, heading for the door.

Niko got there first, holding it open for her. She was sure they were thinking the same thing—how Mika had spooked on the road to Drezna. How the mare had returned, lathered and scratched, her normally calm disposition shattered. How Troitze had never come home.

Natalya followed them. "But—but Dimi Ivanova. That's not all. There...there was a note in the horse's saddlebags. In Nadia's writing. Except it was written...written in..."

Katerina grabbed the younger woman by both shoulders and shook her, hard. "Written in what?"

"Her blood," Natalya whispered. Tears tracked down her cheeks.

A chill ran through Katerina. Her mouth had gone bone dry. "What did it say?"

Natalya was an earthwitch, still gaining control of her magic. The ground beneath their feet trembled as the younger woman bit her lip, then found the courage to speak.

"It said... *Tell Katerina. The Darkness is loose. The village of Satvala is gone.*"

31

ELENA

E lena slowed her steps as she approached the clearing where the ruined chapel stood, wondering if she was making a terrible mistake.

For seven days, against her deepest instincts, she'd agreed to meet with the demon. He no longer seemed as terrifying as she had once imagined him to be. Over the past week, he had almost come to seem like a friend—even an ally.

Who would have ever thought that a demon would aid Elena in her battle against the Darkness? Yet here they were, with him giving her the very tools she needed to rescue her Shadow. The old ways had been shattered, and together, he and Elena were ushering in the dawn of a new age. A holy age, where she could command the power of a Dimi.

Still, each time she went to meet him, she fought with herself over the decision. And each time, she came to the same conclusion: this was meant to be, gifted to her by the Saints. For Sammael had revealed something wondrous to her. He had shown her what she was truly capable of. She would use this power to defeat Katerina and reclaim her Shadow. She would prove her love to Niko, and he would love her in return.

Surely, when Baba Petrova saw what Elena had achieved, when she learned the truth about Katerina, she would banish the Dimi and find a true disciple of the Light worthy of Niko. After Elena and Niko married, there would be a week left before they left for Rivki. Sammael had promised her that by then, she'd be strong enough to stand against the Dimi, and he, Sammael, would stand with her. Elena wouldn't allow Katerina to rob her of her destiny. She would ride out to Rivki with her Shadow by her side, joined to a new Dimi. All of Iriska would know Elena as the Vila who saved her Shadow's soul and delivered the realm from the Dark.

Decided, she strode the final steps into the clearing where the ruined chapel stood. Sammael was waiting for her, pacing in front of the stones. When he spotted her, his face lit with a smile. "I worried you weren't coming," he said.

"Me, too," Elena said, giving him a hesitant smile in return. "But here I am."

"And I'm glad of it. I brought you this." He extended a ripe peach to her, his eyes crinkling when hers widened. "You told me of the blight. That the villagers are hungry. Farther to the south, near the lava fields, no such blight exists. I thought you might enjoy this."

Mindful of her manners, Elena did her best not to snatch it from his hand. "Thank you," she murmured, accepting the peach. It was sun-warmed, its skin yielding tart sweetness as she took a bite. The rich juice ran down her chin in a sticky stream, and Sammael laughed.

"If I'd known it would make you this happy, I would have done this sooner," he said, his tone indulgent. "Here; I brought you this as well."

He bent, opening the lid of a small basket at his feet. Inside were three perfect rolls, a second peach, and a small flask. "For you," he invited.

And so Elena found herself doing the unthinkable: sitting in the grass under the spring sun, having a picnic with a demon. As her empty belly filled, she found it hard to believe he was as evil as everyone said. Maybe he was just...misunderstood.

When she'd finished eating and washed the food down with ale from the flask, Elena turned her face up to the sun, letting its rays bathe her skin. She felt him watching her, but his gaze wasn't threatening. Instead, it was appreciative, as if she were a fine work of art.

"Elena," he said at last.

"Yes?" Her breath caught in her throat; was he about to say something that would make her regret all of this? Something that would reveal his true, wicked nature?

But all Sammael said was, "Are you ready to continue our lessons from yesterday?" He gestured to the knives he'd laid in a line on the remains of the altar.

Elena's heart picked up speed as she nodded. "Yes. I'm ready."

"Then let us begin," the demon said, excitement clear in his voice.

Elena closed her eyes, concentrating. She focused so hard, her body shook. When she opened her eyes, the knives that Sammael had laid in a line on the ruined altar rose, one at a time, to hover in the air. They turned to point at the demon, a phalanx of airborne blades.

He gave a triumphant laugh. "Good. Very good indeed. Have you been practicing?"

One of the knives broke from its fellows and inched closer, wavering, until it hovered scant inches from Sammael's throat. He snatched it, and Elena's concentration broke.

"It doesn't do me much good to practice this sort of thing without you," she said as the rest of the knives clattered to the stones. "It only works when you're with me. It's like the relationship between Shadows and Dimis, except instead of shielding me from demons, you're lending me your gifts."

Sammael laid the knives in a straight line once again. "I don't think I'm lending you anything, Elena. I don't have the gift of manipulating the elements. No, I think whatever has altered the dynamic of your world has allowed us to tap into the magical aspect of your own nature, the gift in your blood that allows you to give birth to Shadows and Vila."

The thought gave Elena a strange turn, as if she were perverting her birthright. "I don't have magic," she protested.

He flicked his gaze at the knives. "I beg to differ."

"That's different," she said, tucking a strand of hair behind her ear. "I told you, it's only possible because you're here."

Sammael leaned back on his hands, tilting his head as if in thought. They'd been meeting for a week, and each time, he'd imparted a different bit of magical lore. Sometimes it was their shared history—the centuries-long war between Dimis, Shadows, and Grigori. Sometimes, if she was lucky, it was a bit of his personal story. He'd laughed when she'd asked him if he was over five hundred years old. "Try five thousand," he'd said, lounging back against one of the rose-wrapped columns that flanked the altar, and laughed harder when her mouth fell open in shock.

But what Elena liked best was how Sammael treated her— like an equal, not a fragile girl to be protected or a deluded Vila who didn't know her own worth. He was never the slightest bit inappropriate with her, never impatient or angry. "Are you sure you're a demon?" she'd asked him once, after he'd spent thirty minutes explaining the basic principles of magical energy exchange, without once losing his temper or scoffing at any of her questions.

An odd expression had crept over his face then—sadness, mixed with regret. "If there is one thing I am sure of," he'd said, toying with the frayed cuffs of his shirt, "it is that, Elena Lisova. I never forget it for an instant. And if you are wise, neither will you."

He always came to her in the guise of the red-haired man. Once, she'd found the courage to ask him what he really looked like. He'd shrugged, looking abashed. "I hardly know," he'd said. "I've spent the years wearing a thousand faces. Do you not like this one? I can offer you an infinite number of alternatives."

"This one is fine," Elena had said hastily. Having such an obvious demonstration of his alien nature would have been more than a little off-putting—an inescapable indication of what she'd gotten herself into, for the sake of Niko's salvation.

As petrified as Elena was that she was committing a horrible sin in the name of a holy pursuit, she had to admit that being with Sammael was thrilling. He'd taught her how to draw on his demonic essence, pulling his energy through her so that she could accomplish amazing things. By the end of their first real lesson, she'd been able to suck the life from a patch of clover and send the plants shriveling to the earth. By the end of the second, she'd loosened one of the ancient stones from the altar and propelled it end over end down the steps into the grass, using the power of her mind. Now, a week later, she could lift knives into the air and send them hurtling at her enemy—not with tremendous force, but still.

"Have you ever done this before?" she asked him now, sinking onto the steps below the altar. "Shared your power with a Vila like this?"

He blinked down at her in surprise. "Never once. If you'd asked me, I would have told you it wasn't possible. You are unique in all the world, Elena Lisova."

A hot blush suffused her cheeks, and she looked down at the steps to hide it. "I still don't understand why you'd help me this way. Surely you have better things to do."

"Like what?" His voice was gentle.

"Oh, I don't know." She gave him a small, flirtatious smile. "Stealing souls. Corrupting the innocent. Picking the world's bones clean, one vulnerable creature at a time."

A shadow passed across Sammael's face. "What makes you think," he murmured, "that I'm not?"

Elena sat up straight. "Maybe that's what you do every second you're not with me, Sammael-of-the-Void. But you've been nothing but kind to me, and I won't forget it."

"I keep telling you, Elena, that I am a demon." His eyes dropped, as if the effort of holding hers was too much. "And demons do nothing for free."

She was about to ask him what his price might be when his head rose and his nostrils flared. He leapt down the steps, arms outstretched to shield her.

"What—" she began, getting to her feet, but he hushed her as a tall, dark-haired man strolled from between the trees that bordered the ruined chapel.

"Gadreel," Sammael said, the word a warning.

Gadreel. An extraordinarily powerful demon, the fallen Angel of War. Her heart began to thunder, so hard she worried he could hear it.

The dark-haired demon's lips lifted in a smile. "Sammael. So this is where you've gone off to. I suspected you were up to something, and here you are."

"Congratulations," Sammael said, not moving an inch. "Now leave."

"So rude. What are you hiding, I wonder? Is it that book of yours?" He sidestepped Sammael and looked Elena over with a focused scrutiny that made her skin prickle—as if he were wondering how she might taste. "Ah," he said. "Not a book after all, I see."

"You most certainly do not." Sammael's voice vibrated with scorn.

"Come now, Sammael. Are you not even going to introduce us?"

Sammael toyed with the cuffs of his shirt, rolling his eyes in exasperation. "Elena, meet my oldest enemy, Gadreel. Five thousand years at each other's throats, and still he enjoys antagonizing me as if it is the first time."

"The pleasure is mine," the dark-haired demon said, as politely as if they sat in front of a fire, sharing cups of tea.

"I beg to differ," Sammael said. "And you are leaving."

"I don't think so." Gadreel strolled closer. "Really, Sammael, will you not even let her speak for herself? What dreadful company you must be."

A snarl rumbled up from Sammael's chest, making Elena shiver. "Step away."

"So protective." Gadreel's eyes focused on Elena's face where she peeked over Sammael's shoulder. They were the rich color of delphiniums, surprisingly beautiful in his cold face. "Now you have me intrigued. What makes her so special?"

He stepped closer still, and Sammael snarled again. "Never think it. This one is mine."

There was a ruthless tinge to Sammael's voice, a hungry, fierce note Elena had never heard from him before. Perhaps it should have frightened her, but instead all she could think was that she'd waited all her life for someone to speak of her that way—as if she were the most important thing in their world. As if she mattered more than all else.

Gadreel's lip curled. "*That one* is a Vila, in case you haven't noticed. You can have her, and welcome. What can she ever be but cannon fodder, or a warm place to stick your—"

It was clear enough what he meant to say, but he never got

the chance. Sammael launched himself at the other demon, baring his teeth. Gadreel's eyes widened in surprise, a moment before he hit the forest floor with a thud that shook the saplings.

This, Elena thought as they wrestled, was what it felt like to have a Shadow fight for you. A person who was always willing to stand between you and danger—not that Sammael was precisely a person, but the point remained the same.

"Apologize," Sammael growled, his teeth inches from Gadreel's throat.

Gadreel laughed, a mocking sound that would have offended Elena's pride if Sammael hadn't sunk his venom-coated teeth into the other demon's neck. Silver-blue blood flowed from the wound, dripping onto the leaves beneath them.

"Apologize," Sammael said again, his tone conversational—which, Elena thought, made it all the more frightening. He might as well have been sitting next to her on the chapel's moss-carpeted steps, discussing the finer points of magical manipulation.

A small, lazy smile lifted Gadreel's lips. "If you insist. Far be it from me to disparage your latest plaything. Vila, I apologize sincerely for impugning your talents and reputation."

"Her name," Sammael said, pinning Gadreel down with a forearm across his bloodied throat, "is Elena."

Gadreel coughed, prying the other demon's arm away. "My, my. How the mighty have fallen." He cut his eyes at Elena, still smiling. "Elena of the Vila, beloved of Sammael, may I offer you my most abject regrets."

The apology didn't sound particularly heartfelt, but Gadreel was a demon, after all. Aside from Sammael, they were all monsters. Perhaps Sammael was a monster as well—but he was *her* monster, and that made all the difference. "I accept," Elena said, inclining her head.

"I never thought I'd see the day," Gadreel said, pressing a handful of leaves to his neck to stanch the blood. "The Venom of God, felled by a Vila. What do you plan to do with this lovely acquisition, Sammael?"

It was one thing for Sammael to claim her, sounding like he was proud to do it, and quite another for this strange demon to imply that she was Sammael's property. "I'm standing right here," Elena said.

"It seems I must apologize yet again. But I am sure you understand my curiosity. This is quite an unusual—arrangement." Gadreel arched a dark eyebrow, gesturing at the two of them.

Sammael snorted in disgust. "I am not consorting with the Vila in the way you believe. Unlike some, my imagination extends beyond such pedestrian activities."

Gadreel's other eyebrow rose to join the first. "Do tell."

"She is betrothed to Niko Alekhin. The Shadow of the Dimi you covet. And before you ask, I've heard all about it. Everyone has. The Scourge of the Demon Realms, vanquished by a witch and her dog. Somehow you left that out the last time we chatted."

Both pitch-dark eyebrows came down at once, like night falling. Gadreel hissed, a vicious sound that sent the prickling sensation of a thousand needles over Elena's skin. "Your pet is betrothed to Dimi Ivanova's Shadow?"

Of course, this man had heard of Katerina. Everywhere Elena went, Katerina had gotten there first. Everywhere and everything she thought was hers had to be shared with Katerina, too.

Elena thought of protesting that she wasn't Sammael's pet, but this wasn't the time for argument. Gadreel's teeth were bared, the bright blue of his eyes giving way to a solid, piercing green that eclipsed pupils, irises, and whites. He looked terrifying, and only the knowledge that Sammael would defend her if he attacked kept Elena from cowering back against one of the columns and trying to blend in with the climbing roses that twined around them, thorns and all.

Then realization dawned, crashing over her with an impact that knocked the breath from her lungs. "You," she said when she could speak. "You led the raid on our village. The one that almost killed Alexei. That was *you*."

As if it took great effort to do it, Gadreel's head swiveled toward her. His unnaturally green eyes locked onto her face, holding her in his gaze the way a snake would hold a rabbit. It was all she could do not to flinch under their weight. "I know not who Alexei is," he said, his voice rougher, deeper. "But yes, I led the raid. It was the Dimi I wanted. That night, she showed me she will be worth any wait."

Rage welled in Elena, making her clench her fists. Was she to have no respite from Katerina, even here—in her safe place, the place where she was the one who shone? "Alexei is the Shadow your soldier *stabbed*," she said, gritting out each syllable. "He almost died."

Gadreel tilted his head, as if considering. "Ah, I remember now. Not this one—" His shape morphed, appallingly, into Niko's, then back again—"but this." Again his body slipped its confines, transforming into Alexei's shorter, stockier form before he shifted back into the shape of the dark-haired demon. "He was easy to damage. Not a loss. Now your Shadow, on the other hand—he would be an honor to kill."

The now-familiar fury consumed Elena again. "If it's Katerina you want, soon you'll have to travel farther to find her. Your kind has loosed a plague upon our land. First the village of Drezna fell. Then, just nights ago, Satvala. Which doubtless you know; perhaps you were responsible." *You and Katerina, in league with the Darkness.*

She shivered at the memory of waking up to the news that the village to the south of them had been destroyed, that Nadia and Oriel were likely dead. "The Kniaz demands her protection. He will Reap her at the next Blood Moon, and Niko is meant to travel with her to Rivki." There was no need to reveal Elena's additional plans to the demon, about how surely Baba would sever Katerina's bond with Niko when she knew the truth.

Gadreel's eyes narrowed. "Your pathetic excuse for a nobleman plans to remove her from Kalach?"

Too late, Elena realized that perhaps she'd given the demon information he was thirsty to acquire. She didn't care what befell Katerina, but the last thing she wanted was to put Niko in danger. Time was running out, and she had little of it left to free her beloved from the Dimi's clutches. She had no intention of traveling to Rivki Island married to a man who believed he loved another. Still less did she intend to free Niko, only to lose him.

"Good fortune to you reaching her—or harming my betrothed—in Rivki, Grigori snake," she said, and spat at the demon. "I wish Niko had ripped your head off and mounted it on a pike in the village square. I would celebrate as the crows picked the flesh from your skull, and rejoice in the passing of a coward."

Twin fires blazed up in Gadreel's eyes. Elena could see herself reflected in them, a tiny figure engulfed in flames. Though his shape didn't change, his humanity evaporated, peeling away to reveal the beast that lurked beneath his skin. "How dare you," he said, and lunged.

There was no time to run. Elena cringed back against the column, forgetting in her terror about the knives that lay on the altar or the newfound knowledge of magic at her command. Her vision filled with the demon barreling toward her, teeth bared to strike.

Then Sammael stepped between them, blocking Gadreel's way. He grabbed the other demon by the collar and shook him. "Get away from her," he said, the words reverberating through the ruins of the chapel.

Gadreel snapped at him, teeth gleaming, but Sammael didn't budge. "Leave," he said again.

A growl rumbled up from Gadreel's chest, low and threatening, before he pulled free, smoothing the wrinkles from his shirt. "Happy to," he said, pronouncing the words with perfect, furious diction. "She is not worth the effort." Giving Elena one last venomous glance, he spun and strode back into the trees.

Sammael turned at once to Elena. "Are you all right?"

She couldn't help but notice the difference between Sammael's concern for her welfare and the way Niko had treated her after the recent demon attacks. This, she thought, a warm feeling bubbling inside her, was how it felt to be someone's priority. "I'm fine. Thank you for not letting him hurt me."

"I would never. You are mine to protect." He drew himself up to his full height, nostrils flaring as if to be sure Gadreel had gone. Satisfied, he mounted the steps to the altar, stopping below the column where Elena stood.

"I should have tried to protect myself." Shame colored her voice. "I have magic now. I could have tried."

"Against Gadreel?" Sammael sounded incredulous. "Not and lived. Believe me when I tell you it is best he knows nothing about your gifts. Let him think what he wants about us; let him underestimate you. It is to your advantage you acted as you did."

Elena shivered. "Couldn't you have stopped him, if he wished to kill me?"

"Perhaps," Sammael said, coming to stand in front of her, "and perhaps not. He was not truly resisting me when I bit him, and again, when I stopped him from attacking you. It was a test, to see how much you meant to me—the lengths I would go to protect you. One which I failed miserably."

"How so?" Elena gave him a small, tentative smile. "Here I stand."

"From your perspective, it was a success. You are not dead, after all." He smiled back at her. "But from mine—he sees now that you matter to me. You have become a weapon in a war that has raged since before your kind walked the earth. He will use you against me, if he can."

Elena tried to keep the fear from her voice. She'd known she courted danger when she entered into this bargain. To save Niko, she had to be brave. "Why do you two hate each other so much?"

He shrugged, looking weary. "It is an old rivalry. Nothing with which you need to concern yourself."

From the closed look on his face, Elena knew he was unlikely to tell her anything else. She switched tactics, letting her smile widen. "Thank you for protecting me. And for keeping my secret."

"It is my secret as well," he said, gathering the knives from the altar floor. "As advantageous as it is for you to gain the power you need to free your Shadow, it is beneficial for me to have access to that power as well—as I am sure you must realize."

As soon as the words left his mouth, she felt foolish. She had never thought about what Sammael would gain from helping her—but of course, he was right. What she'd done was tantamount to delivering a Dimi into the hands of a demon. Of volunteering to become a Grigori's weapon. The blood drained from her face.

"Ah," he said, watching her. "You haven't. Sometimes I think you are the most innocent creature I have ever met."

"I'm not innocent!"

"Oh, but you are." He set down the knives, came down the altar steps, and took her hands in his—the first time he had ever touched her in such a fashion. His fingertips were rough, his skin cold. "I mean no insult, Elena. You are pure of heart. Even this—consorting with a demon—you do to protect the one you love. It is….a revelation to me."

Elena was more than pure of heart. She was a Vila with a singular mission, to restore balance to their way of life and reclaim the man she was destined to wed. She'd never felt anything like the icy sensation of Sammael's magic slipping through her veins, the surge of strength when she'd lifted those blades into the air and pointed one at his throat. It was a wonderful, dangerous thrill to feel so powerful, to hold magic in her hands that a Vila had never dreamed of commanding. All in the name of driving back the Darkness that threatened to devour both Niko and Iriska whole.

Elena closed her eyes, gripping his hands in hers, and concentrated on reaching outward with her mind, the way he'd taught her. She drew on the currents of air that rippled through the grass as energy flowed from Sammael's hands into hers. A breeze began to blow, sweeping small sticks with it. They lashed against her legs as the breeze grew into a wind. When she opened her eyes, the tall grass bent to the ground, the leaves shuddering in the trees. The birds called in alarm as a branch above them broke free, hurtling to the ground with a thump.

Sammael's mouth fell open in amazement, the most unguarded expression she had ever seen on his face. "That—" he said, sounding stunned. "Can you do it again?"

She focused, summoning the breeze to lift the branch. It flew end over end up the steps, falling amongst the knives as the wind picked up speed once more.

Sammael's hands clenched tight on hers, his eyes bright. "An effort worthy of a Dimi, my Vila," he said.

An idea began to form in Elena's mind, shimmering at the edges as it took shape, ripe with possibility. She dropped Sammael's hands, stepping away. "What Gadreel did, taking Niko's shape and then Alexei's...you can do that too, yes?"

The brightness in his dark eyes dulled, replaced with caution. "Yes. Although I would not offend you by assuming the forms of those you care about. Gadreel does not consider such actions might be offensive, or cause pain. Truly, before I met you, it would not have occurred to me either. I assure you that I—"

She waved a hand, dismissing his apologies. "Can you only assume human form, Sammael? Or could you—for instance—take the shape of a black dog?"

"You mean," he said, cocking his head, "could I truly impersonate a Shadow?"

Wordless, Elena nodded. And just as silently, never taking his eyes from hers, Sammael transformed. One moment, he was the red-haired, smooth-shaven man she had come to know; the next, he stood on all fours, covered in lush black fur, his tail waving back and forth in greeting.

He padded toward her and leaned against her, making a low, comforting sound deep in his chest. She twined her fingers into his fur; it was warm, and alive as any Shadow's.

An effort worthy of a Dimi, my Vila.

Elena began to smile.

32

GADREEL

Gadreel stood at the door to his throne room, staring at the newfound mound of wreckage. The Darkness gnawed at his belly, a starving beast that was never satisfied. It gathered in the corners and crawled up the walls, eating away at them, searching for a way out. Gadreel had tried his best to imprison it, but his wards wouldn't hold for long. It had already escaped once, with dire consequences.

He had just finished repairing the roof and ceiling. His minions had cleared away the detritus of Drezna until all that remained was an ash stain on the floor. And now this.

He'd made the mistake of thinking that just because a shard of Darkness lived within him, he could control the force that now threatened to destroy everything he valued. To destroy *him*. But the hint of Darkness that fed each demon was nothing compared to the virulent, hungering entity that was attempting to escape his throne room. Even now, it called to the tendril that lived within him, urging him to act. To set it free to roam and devour.

The foolish Vila had been wrong about so much, but she'd been right about one thing: Satvala had fallen, gobbled up by

266

the Darkness. Thank the Devil it hadn't been Kalach. Dimi Ivanova still lived. And Gadreel was desperate to get to her.

That's what he'd been doing in the woods: prowling around Kalach, without the distraction of his incompetent legions, in hopes that the red-headed Dimi would venture out of the confines of her village. He hadn't expected to find Sammael there, but it was hardly a surprise that his nemesis had gotten word of how the Dimi had decimated Gadreel's troops. Perhaps this was where Sammael had gone, the night of his meeting with Gadreel. He had doubtless heard about the disastrous raid, gone to see for himself what was what...and now here he was, consorting with a Vila, dangerously close to the Dimi Gadreel needed for his own.

Luckily for Gadreel, Sammael seemed distracted. He hadn't seen his fellow Watcher this besotted since the days of Lilith. But the Vila didn't appear enamored of him, the way Gadreel had seen a bevy of women fall at Sammael's feet over the centuries. She wanted something else from him—and, it seemed to Gadreel, he from her, as well.

It was a mystery, and Gadreel didn't care for mysteries, unless he was the one engineering them.

Turning away from the wreckage of Satvala, Gadreel stalked moodily down the hall toward his library. The portraits on the wall chittered at him as he passed. Normally he found this entertaining; he'd spelled the souls of his more amusing victims into the paint's pigment, and every time he walked past the portraits, it reminded him of his conquests. But now, their insults and complaints grated on his ears.

He couldn't even sit in his damned throne room. The Darkness was holding him hostage in his own home.

Try as he might, he couldn't understand what Sammael wanted from a Vila, much less one that belonged to Dimi Ivanova's Shadow. She was beautiful, as were so many of her kind—

but other women were beautiful. She was fragile, as had ever been Sammael's weakness—but that was hardly a rarity. Dimi Ivanova's strength was the rarity, the way she'd faced him without a hint of fear. She was a prize, an incomparable weapon. Let Sammael have the Vila, with her pleading blue eyes and the way she'd cringed back against the column of the ruined chapel. Gadreel would take Dimi Ivanova, that wondrous creature made of wind and witchfire, any day.

Besides, if Gadreel didn't get his hands on Dimi Ivanova, he would have no need to worry about Sammael and the Vila. They would all vanish into the Void soon enough.

Gadreel came to the gilded door of his library and shoved it open. He slammed it behind him and stood, scanning the books on his shelves for the thousandth time, as if their pages would suddenly yield the answers he sought.

Was that what Sammael had been doing when Gadreel had spied on him—making notes on approaching Kalach and meeting with his Vila? Or had his archenemy already been colluding with her then? And what of that lost book, the 'ancient tome' Sammael had been blathering on about? Did it exist, or was it a mere invention, meant to distract Gadreel from Sammael's true purpose?

The Vila had been useless, except for what she'd said about Dimi Ivanova and her Shadow being Reaped at the full Blood Moon, less than two weeks away. That meant the Dimi would leave the village. She would likely travel with an entourage, but she would be vulnerable then. If Gadreel could get to her—if he could take her—then there might still be enough time to vanquish the Darkness. It was possible, even if she were protected by rowan-fire on the way. As the wards between the worlds weakened, the smoke affected him less and less. Perhaps soon, it would not trouble him at all.

The Dimi would be reluctant to cooperate, true. But when

Gadreel told her the truth about why he required her assistance, she would want to comply. She would do it of her own free will, or watch the rest of Iriska fall.

But what if she fought him off again? Much as he hated to admit it, he needed a backup strategy. Something based on stealth rather than brute force.

Gadreel flung himself into his favorite chair and snapped his fingers. An illusion of Dimi Ivanova sprang up in the middle of the rug, flowing red hair, leather gear, fierce expression, and all. She revolved slowly, taking in his library, then turned to face him again. Just like the last time they'd seen each other, she didn't look impressed.

Even in his fantasies, the damnable woman refused to cooperate with him.

This was, Gadreel recognized, the time when a lesser demon would ask for help. He could talk to Sammael, tell the other demon everything. He could admit he'd set the Darkness loose, that the destruction of the two villages hadn't been his doing. That he was in over his head.

And Sammael might well help him. But afterward? Gadreel would lose everything.

He stood, pacing the floorboards. The illusion of Dimi Ivanova watched him, a smirk lifting her lips. He could command her to kneel, to do his bidding. She was an illusion; she would do it. But how pathetic would he be? The Dark Angel of War, reduced to commanding a false image because the real thing had defeated him in battle. He refused to stoop so low.

He paced some more. Back. Forth. Back. Forth. And then he froze.

The wards were weakening. He could likely follow Dimi Ivanova and her party all the way to Rivki Island, which his kind had never been able to get close to before. And then...what if he could get inside?

What if he could get inside *now?*

A world of possibility began to unfurl before him. He could see it. He could *taste* it.

His eyes on the illusion of the Dimi who had defied him, the Darkness growling and twisting within him, the fallen angel Gadreel smiled.

33
KATERINA

The day Elena Lisova married Niko Alekhin, it rained from dawn to dusk.

Katerina knew this was her fault. As Niko's Dimi, she was the one to give him away. He stood by her side, resplendent in the traditional white garments that every Shadow wore to the altar. His clothes were marked by silver-and-red-threaded runes representing his union with Elena: hearts for Rozhanytsi, the spirits of fate and goddesses of fertility, hearth, and home; oaks emblazoned with guelder roses, for the fusion of Niko's strength and Elena's beauty. Every time Katerina glanced at him, the sky opened up, crying the tears she wouldn't allow herself to shed.

A Vila's wedding to a Shadow was a glorious occasion, followed by hours of revelry. The whole village attended, crowded into the chapel that had been built after the original one burned in the aftermath of a Grigori attack. The woods had taken that chapel back, devoured it Saints and all. It was desecrated ground.

Was it too much, Katerina wondered as Baba Petrova's apprentices placed incense burners in a circle around the altar, to hope that a demon attack would interrupt the ceremony? She would gladly see the chapel destroyed, holy relics and all, if it meant she didn't have to take Niko's hand and place it in Elena's.

This was what he'd wanted, she reminded herself. She'd asked him to leave with her. Had begged him, in a way she'd never begged anyone for anything. And he'd refused, choosing obligation and duty over love. Even after Satvala had fallen to the Darkness, he'd refused to go. Perhaps he hoped that marrying Elena would put an end to whatever had possessed Iriska. Perhaps he'd come to believe in the prophecy, after all. The end result was the same.

She respected him and hated him for it, all at the same time. But if she loved him, she had to honor his wishes, even if it decimated her.

So she stood at the altar next to Niko, her face a mask, wearing the iridescent gold-and-red gown that marked her as his Dimi. She watched as Elena's Shadow father walked her down the aisle, between rows of villagers who exclaimed in awe as they passed. Katerina couldn't blame them: Elena was a vision in her wedding white embroidered with hearts and guelder roses, her platinum hair threaded with rosebuds and her wide blue eyes transfixed with bliss.

Katerina didn't dare glance at Niko to see if he were as mesmerized as the rest. Instead she stood, eyes fixed straight ahead, as Baba Petrova's apprentices lit the burners, sending the scent of white sage and lavender into the air. Sage, for purity; lavender, for peace.

If Katerina hadn't been so miserable, she would have laughed at the irony.

"Who stands witness for this Shadow?" Baba Petrova spoke from the front of the altar, white hair braided in a complicated twist, draped in her ceremonial blue robes. Her voice reverberated off the wooden walls of the chapel, resonant and full even over the sound of the rain that lashed the stained-glass windows. It looked, Katerina reflected, as if the Saints depicted on the windows were grieving too.

She took Niko's hand in hers. Despite the warmth of the chapel, his fingers were freezing. "I do," she said, and forced herself to look into his eyes.

What she saw there almost leveled her. He gazed down at her as if they were the only two people in all the world. As if they stood here on this altar to be joined to each other.

It made her want to hit him.

"Unto another each must cleave," Baba intoned. "Katerina Ivanova, do you give your Shadow to this woman? To have and to hold, to share his heart as you share his soul?"

Niko's fingers tightened on hers. Pain flickered across his face, and Katerina felt an answering pang.

You have to do this.

"I do," she said, and placed Niko's hand in Elena's.

Thunder boomed, drowning out the words of the ceremony. But there was nothing to keep Katerina from seeing Baba Petrova give the slim gold ring to Niko. Or from seeing him take it and slide it onto Elena's waiting finger.

Katerina closed her eyes and prayed for grace.

34

ELENA

"Y ou look beautiful," Alyona said, sounding wistful.

Elena twisted to look at her friend. Aly sat behind her, unbraiding the flowers from Elena's hair. It was a ritual—after a Vila's wedding revels, she spent time alone with her closest female friend, drawing strength from the sisterhood that had been her strongest bond before she wedded her Shadow. "Thank you, Aly. See, things turned out fine after all."

Aly's auburn brows lowered in confusion. "What do you mean? Why wouldn't they?"

Was Aly really going to make her say it, today of all days? "You know—because of what you said about Niko and Katerina." The last word came out as a whisper. Even saying the Dimi's name made Elena sick to her stomach—not to mention the look on Niko's face when he'd stood on the altar with Katerina's hands in his. Only the thought that their unnatural bond would be severed soon had made Elena strong enough to bear it.

Aly sat back, dropping her hands to her lap. "What about Niko and Katerina?" Her face was blank, innocent.

A horrible, sinking feeling seized hold of Elena's stomach, as if she had taken a step only to have the ground fall away beneath her, sending her plummeting into an abyss. "Nothing," she said, yanking the rest of the roses out of her hair herself. The thorns sliced her fingertips, sending rivulets of blood running down her palms. "I must have misunderstood."

"You're hurting yourself, Lena." Aly untangled the flowers from Elena's fingers, setting them aside and dabbing at the cuts with a piece of cloth. "Did someone say something cruel to you about the two of them? You know how close they've always been. It means nothing. For Saints' sake, Niko just stood in front of the whole village and swore his heart to you."

A sprig of roses had fallen to the floor. Elena stood and smashed it beneath her blue silk shoe. ("The exact color of your eyes!" Aly had exclaimed when they'd dyed the fabric together months ago. Elena had been so happy then.) The perfume of crushed roses filled the air, nauseating her. "Of course," she said, each syllable clipped. "I'm grateful for their bond."

Aly studied her face. "Are you all right, Lena?"

Elena had never been very good at hiding her thoughts, but now she was lying for her life. If anyone found out she'd been consorting with a demon, the consequences would be dire— and Niko would be tied to that witch forever. "I'm fine," she said, offering Aly a small smile. "Just nervous about tonight. It was so effortless for Niko and Katerina to become Shadow and Dimi. I suppose I'm hoping it'll be as easy for us, in our marriage bed."

Sympathy rippled across Aly's features, and she threw her arms around her friend. "Is that what you're worried about? Niko is a gentleman, Lena, and honorable. He'll treat you with care. And you've loved him forever. It may hurt at first, but in time I'm sure it will be wonderful. The two of you are meant to be."

Elena allowed herself to squeeze Aly tight before she

stepped away. "You're right," she said. "I'm lucky to have a friend like you." She smiled at Aly one more time before she lifted her skirts and turned to go, tears pricking her eyes.

NIKO WAS WAITING for her at the cottage Baba Petrova and the Elders had given them. It had belonged to an elderly couple who had passed away within days of each other, the husband following his wife into death. At the time, Elena thought it was the most romantic thing she'd ever heard. Now, she just thought they'd been doomed.

The cottage was small and white, with pink climbing roses that formed a trellis over the entryway. She'd imagined passing beneath them as a bride hand in hand with Niko, how their delicate scent would welcome her into her new life. But instead, he stood still and silent in the doorway, one hand on the jamb, watching her come toward him—and the smell of the roses nauseated her.

He didn't look like a man eagerly awaiting his bride. He looked, Elena thought as his hand clenched on the wood so hard his knuckles whitened, like a man bracing for the inevitable—and not liking it one bit.

She forced a smile onto her face. "Hello, husband."

"Welcome home, Elena," he said, and stepped aside so she could pass.

Elena had imagined many things about this night—how their first kiss might be awkward, fumbling; how they might discover the way of things together, and laugh about their inexperience for years to come, cradling their Vila or Shadowchildren in their arms. Before Katerina had bespelled Niko, she'd never imagined her wedding night would be awkward because her Shadow refused to touch her.

He shut the door behind her and stood with his back to it, as if hoping for the opportunity to flee. When she walked farther into the room, he followed, stopping at an appropriate distance. Then followed her farther still, into their bedroom, where he stood once more with a hand braced on the jamb, as if anticipating she might grab hold of him and drag him to her bed by force.

The sight of it pierced her heart. "It's late," she said, gesturing to the trousseau that she and Aly had laid out together—a shimmering ivory gown Elena had sewn herself, hemmed with satin and scalloped with lace. "Perhaps I should change."

A look of relief crossed his face. "Late. Yes. I'm sure you want to sleep."

"Maybe not quite yet." She regarded him from under her lashes, then glanced at the gown draped across the foot of the bed once more.

His eyes flicked toward the gown, then back to her, and his hand tightened so hard on the jamb, she was afraid he'd tear it from the wall. "You must want privacy," he said, his face a careful blank. "I'll go into the other room so you can change."

"But—" Her face burned, hot with mortification. "Don't you want to—I mean, it's customary for a groom to undress his bride on their wedding night—"

Looking as if it cost him to do it, he let go of the doorjamb and stepped closer, his head lowered. "Of course. Allow me." A hand on her shoulder, he spun her to face away from him. The warmth of his fingers seeped through the fabric of her dress as one by one, he worked the tiny hooks free. "There," he said at last, when the last hook was undone and the dress fell to the floor—but in the satisfied tones of a man who had accomplished a challenging task, not a husband who couldn't wait to see his new bride unclothed.

Elena gathered her courage and turned around. He was gazing over her shoulder, eyes fixed on the painting of Sant Viktoriya above the bed as if it were the most interesting thing he'd ever seen.

"Niko," she said, trying to keep the hurt from her voice, "you can look at me. We're married, after all."

His gaze dropped and fixed on her face. "Perhaps," he said, the word making her think of Sammael, "you are such a lovely sight that I'm afraid gazing upon you will be too much for me to bear." One side of his mouth curved upward in the crooked, teasing smile she'd always loved.

"Don't worry. If you fall," she said, daring to touch his hand, "I'll catch you."

The strangest look passed across his face then—sadness, regret, and frustration, all drifting through his eyes like a storm cloud before they resumed their usual inscrutability. "You're a good person, Elena. I know you would."

You're a good person wasn't exactly a passionate endearment, but Elena would take what she could get. She moved closer and shut her eyes, standing on tiptoes to press her lips to his.

Niko's lips grazed hers for an instant—and then he stepped back, away from her. "Truly, seeing you unclothed has undone me," he said as her eyes blinked open. "I don't feel quite myself."

Elena tried to hide her hurt as he snatched up her bridal night finery as if it were on fire and thrust it at her. "Please put this on," he said with a horrible attempt at a smile. "Should I regard you in the altogether for much longer, you'll find me prostrate at your feet."

She took the gown from him with shaking fingers and slipped it over her head. "If you feel ill," she said, "maybe you should lie down." Surely if he were in bed with her, his body next to hers as she'd imagined for so long, she would be able to banish Katerina from his mind. After all, Katerina was only his Dimi. Elena was his *wife*.

He followed her to the bed willingly enough, pulling back the covers for her. "Comfortable?" he asked, as solicitously as if she were a grandmother with the ague.

"I'd be more comfortable with you beside me." She patted the space next to her, dipping her head in invitation.

Niko sat down on the edge of the bed, eyes fixed on the lace that fringed the pillows. "You make a lovely bride, Elena," he said to the quilt. "I'm sure I was the envy of every Shadow in the village today."

"I don't care about any other Shadow." Her voice was weighted with frustration. Why wouldn't he at least look at her? "All I care about is you. If you think I'm lovely, that's all that matters to me."

Silence fell between them. Elena broke it, reaching out to trace the hem of his white tunic, embroidered with the silver-and-red runes that marked him as hers. "Are you going to sleep in this?"

"I'm not tired." He offered her another strained smile. "You rest. I'll be right here." He lay down beside her, his body stiff.

The few inches of space between them felt like a gigantic gulf. Elena wanted more than anything to bridge it, to show him she could be what he needed, but she didn't know how. In the end she settled for laying her head on the scratchy fabric that covered his chest. His heart beat beneath her ear, a steady rhythm that both enraged and saddened her. How could his heart go on beating as it always had, when hers was broken?

Slowly, his arm came up to hold her. Elena lay still, afraid to so much as fidget lest she scare him away. He pressed his lips to the crown of her head. "Sleep, Elena," he said.

She let her eyes fall shut, forced her breathing to become even. The minutes ticked by, the clock that had been Alyona's gift to them marking the time. After fifteen minutes, Niko loosened his grip. After thirty, he eased his way from beneath her body, pulling up the quilt to cover her and moving soundlessly off the bed.

He stood in silence, and she tried to convince herself he was looking down at her sleeping face, thinking how beautiful she was, how lucky he was to have her for his own. But instead his footsteps sounded on the wooden boards of the cottage, moving inexorably toward the door. It shut behind him with a click, leaving Elena alone.

Her eyes blinked open. Sure enough, he was gone.

He'd gone to meet *her*. Elena was sure of it. On their wedding night. Tears slipped down her cheeks.

In the silence of their empty cottage, a moth fluttered onto Elena's shoulder. She moved to brush it away, but it came back again, this time settling onto her hand. She blinked at it through her tears.

"Sammael?" she said at last.

The moth's wings flapped twice, as if in assent.

"He left me." Elena's voice broke. "I'd hoped once we were together—once I wore his ring—it would be different. But it isn't. It's just the same."

The moth lifted one tiny leg and stroked her knuckle, as if in sympathy.

"You're the only one who knows the whole truth." She ran a finger along the moth's velvet wing. "Of course, I might not know the truth either, if it hadn't been for you. You pretended to be Alyona, didn't you? Somehow, you got past the wards and masked your scent. You stole her shape, and told me about Niko and—*her*." If she had to say Katerina's name aloud, she thought she might break something.

One moment, a moth fluttered on her fingertip. The next, the air in the darkened cottage wavered, and Sammael sat on the side of her bed, smelling of rosemary and cloves. "The wards have weakened," he said. "And as for the rest—I can explain."

A shriek escaped her, and she slid backward until she hit the wall. "Saints," she said, pressing a hand to her pounding heart.

She could barely make him out in the darkness, but there was no mistaking the apology in his tone. "I thought you knew it was me, Elena. It was not my intention to frighten you."

Elena had never shared a bed with a man before, but in the past quarter-hour, her boudoir had hosted a Shadow and a demon. What was next—an entourage of sacred Saints? "I did know it was you," she said, trying to imbue her voice with courage. "It's just—I didn't expect you to materialize like that. As a man. In my bedroom. On my wedding night."

"I assure you I meant no impropriety."

She sat up, pulling the quilt around her. "I think we're beyond that, don't you?"

His harsh intake of breath shook the bed. "I think you are beautiful, Elena. As lovely as the fairest flower in the forest, as vibrant as the setting sun—but I swear I will never touch you if you do not want me to. Demons covet, it is true. But I have tried to be better than that with you, no matter what Gadreel might insinuate. I will never lay a finger on you in desire, save you ask me for the favor. I set my word on it."

It had not occurred to Elena that Sammael might want her as a man wanted a woman. He had attacked Gadreel when the other demon had even insinuated as much. The knowledge of it broke over her like a wave on a hot day: terrifying, but also exhilarating. Her own husband felt no desire for her. It was refreshing to find someone who did, even if that someone was a damned soul. "And what, pray tell, is a demon's word worth?" she said into the dark.

His laugh was a serrated blade, scraping along her skin. "Ah, there you have me, Elena Lisova. I swear it on my pride, then, on the yearning I have for power—to defeat Gadreel, who lusts after the Dimi you detest—on the depth of the Darkness that eats all things. For a demon such as myself, there is no greater bond. And if you wish me to transform back into a moth, I will do so without question."

Elena considered this. "No, thank you," she said. "Moths cannot talk, and I find myself very much in need of conversation."

He dipped his head; she could see that much. "Your wish is my command."

"You lied to me." She clenched the quilt in her fist. "You let me believe Alyona herself told me of Niko's infidelity."

Sammael sighed. "I could tell you it is my nature; demons lie. I could lead us into a discussion of semantics, and tell you it was more a matter of trickery than falsehood. Both are true. However, both are also less than you deserve. So I will tell you once again that I am sorry, and hope it will suffice."

"You did me a favor." Elena let go of the quilt and sat up straight, her back against the wall. "Why, though, could you not have told me the truth after we got to know each other? I would have understood."

"Perhaps. Or perhaps I thought you would not forgive me, Elena. Even a kind nature such as yours must have its limits."

She wiped the last of the tears from her cheeks. "It does indeed. And Katerina has breached them. Niko has gone to meet her, I'm sure of it. I'd hoped to spend my wedding night differently, but what greater glory can there be than wrenching him free of her grip at last? I'm strong enough. I know I am. With you by my side, I can rival her power. I can set him free."

Sammael took her hands in his, his aim unerring despite the dark. As he'd promised, there was nothing of desire in his touch —just the strength of a partner in arms, the finality of a contract sealed. When he spoke, she felt the weight of his words on her skin.

"I am, as always, at your service."

35

KATERINA

Weeks had passed since Niko's betrothal. So much had changed. And yet here Katerina was, gathering elderflower in the forest, a mile outside Kalach, like she'd been after the first time she and Niko had kissed.

She shouldn't be out here. But she hadn't been able to think of anyplace else to go.

If the Darkness came for her now, she might welcome it. The thought of sitting alone in the cottage she and Niko used to share while he undid Elena's wedding dress one hook at a time, pressing his lips to her skin, filled Katerina's vision with a red haze. She'd been afraid the sheer rage and misery of it would make her burn the house down. So she'd escaped the wedding revelry as soon as she could and come here, to the clearing, where she'd ignited a circle of rowan-fires to keep the demons away and bent to her work.

She would make a life without Niko in her bed, without his lips on hers and his arms wrapped around her. She would find a way to have him at her side as her Shadow, and nothing more. It was what he wanted. She had to honor it. Even if it shattered her.

Or maybe she would leave him behind and go to the Magiya on her own. If she couldn't have Niko, then at least she could try to reverse the prophecy and save Iriska.

And if she felt him near right now, if she imagined he was with her here as he'd been weeks before, then that was her weakness. She wouldn't think about what he was doing at this very moment, if he lay naked in bed beside Elena, her blond hair fanned across his chest and his head propped on his hand, looking at her the way he always used to look at Katerina—

"I leave you alone for one evening, and this is where I find you. Honestly, Katya. Have you no sense of self-preservation at all?"

Her head snapped up. There he was, standing at the tree-line just like he'd been weeks ago, still in the ceremonial white he'd worn to marry Elena. The silver guelder roses on his collar set off his eyes, making them gleam like the Kalchek coins the children tossed into the village fountain on Wishing Day. By the light of the moon, his irises were flat, impenetrable disks, giving nothing away. With his black hair and pale skin, he looked as if he'd been carved from the night itself.

Katerina's heart clenched. "What are you doing here?"

"I've something to say."

She dumped the flowers into the basket with such force that most of them flew out again, tumbling into the grass. "Doubtless Elena would have something to say as well, if she knew you were here. Perhaps it is you whose sense of self-preservation has gone for a short stroll off a high cliff. Can you not leave me in peace?"

"Maybe I missed you."

Katerina regarded him in his wedding white, leaning against one of the oak trees that guarded the clearing with his ankles crossed as if he hadn't a care in the world, and wanted to smack him. She settled for sending a spray of dirt up from the ground, sullying his clothes.

His lips quirked. "Missed me too, I see."

"That part of our lives is done." Spurring the flames of the rowan-fires higher, she blocked his passage. "You shouldn't be here."

"Let me by, Katya. Please."

"I see no reason why I should."

Niko made a low noise of frustration. "I need to talk to you."

"And I'm under the impression that everything has already been said." She let the fires ebb, the better to glare at him. "Don't make it worse."

"If you won't listen to me, then perhaps a visual demonstration will be more effective."

He brushed back his hair, deliberately baring the white streak above his ear.

"Stop it." The words came harsh, a Dimi's command to her Shadow, but Niko didn't obey. Instead he shoved his shirtsleeve up, revealing his tattoo.

"These are your marks. Both of them. And I'll never regret them. They say I'm yours. That I belong to you."

"You don't!" Pain tore at her, and she pressed her fingers to her chest, trying to contain it. "Those marks say you're my *Shadow*. As you will always be, more fool I. I should have known my feelings for you for what they were and sworn my gifts to another."

His face paled still further. "Don't say that."

She forced her hands to her sides. "Why not? At least then I wouldn't have to look at you every day, to fight alongside you. To have you closer to me than any living being and yet lost to me in the way that matters most. To have brought ruin upon Iriska."

"Katya—"

"Go away, Niko." She schooled her face to blankness. "Go home to your wife."

"I didn't lie with her."

The words fell like stones into the still pool of the night. Slowly, Katerina's head rose. "What do you mean?"

"I couldn't, Katya. I couldn't do it." His voice broke. "I tried. I know it's my duty. But Saints help me, to even get near her— to put my hands on her—I had to picture your face. To pretend she was you. But she isn't. And I-I couldn't touch her."

Katerina was speechless.

"She wants me," Niko said, each word precise, "but for the sake of the image she's created—not who I truly am. She wants the Shadow in me. But you see through my pretenses and love me anyway, for the boy I once was and the man that stands alongside my Shadow. I cannot settle for less."

The knife fell from Katerina's hand, settling among the flowers. "What are you saying?"

He stepped over her guttering fires, cleaving through the night to stand in front of her. The scent of the sage and lavender incense Baba's apprentices had burned at his wedding rose up around them like a cloud. "Once," he said, his voice soft, "I told you that with a single kiss, you shatter me like ice and you scorch me like a flame."

"I remember." Katerina's throat was so dry, the words came out as a croak.

His eyes were on hers, their expression no longer inscrutable. In them she saw desire, resentment, grief—and a raw emotion that threatened to undo her fragile control. "When I realized I couldn't lay a finger on Elena—much less do as I must to get a Shadowchild on her—I wanted to hate you. For you have ruined me forever for another. But I can't. I love you, Katerina. And all I want is to burn."

Katerina's breath caught, and she pulled him down to her.

287

Their mouths collided gracelessly, his teeth sinking into her bottom lip even as she dug her nails into the back of his neck deep enough to draw blood. The kiss was a battle, their tongues tangling, his hands sinking into her hair and tugging at the roots until she cried out. In the circle around them, the fires flared, sparks rising up into the night.

"I'm yours," he said, a vicious whisper. "Whether you wish it or no."

She pulled back, keeping her grip on his neck. "You are mine, Niko Alekhin. To do with as I will."

One dark eyebrow rose. "A threat, my Dimi? Or a promise?"

"Both," Katerina said, and Niko's mouth found hers again. His arms wrapped around her, their grip gentling until he simply held her, clutching her with tenderness and a desperation that pierced her heart.

"Excellent," he said into her hair, his lips tracing their way down her neck, finding the spot above her collarbone that always made her shiver.

She moved out of the circle of his arms so she could see his face. "You really didn't touch her?"

Niko shook his head. "Why do you think I'm still wearing these dreadful clothes? I assure you, it's not for the sake of ease and comfort. Have you any idea how much this fabric itches?"

Now it was Katerina's turn to raise an eyebrow. "If you're angling for me to ask you to take your clothes off, you're going to have to do better than that."

He took her hand in his. "For once, I'm not. I'm asking you to run away with me. To the Magiya. We'll figure this out once and for all. We'll save Iriska. And then we can be together."

Katerina couldn't have been more shocked if the trees around them had grown feet and begun filing out of the forest. "What?" she managed.

"You heard me." His gaze was on her face, gray and wary.

"But——" she said, puzzlement clear in her voice, "the last time I mentioned this, you told me it was impossible. I believe your exact words were, *You cannot ask this of me, not as my Dimi or as my heart.* What's changed?"

With his free hand, he traced her chin, her bottom lip, her cheekbones, as if memorizing her face. "I can't live like this, Katya. Not split in two this way. You're more important than any obligation. And my love for you outweighs the price of my family's honor. You are my blood, my blade, and my heart. My soul is bound to yours." He took her by the shoulders, drawing her close. "I thought I could set all that aside—that I had to, or lose what mattered most. But what matters most is you. If I don't have you, then I could populate our village with a legion of Shadowchildren and my life would hold no meaning. Not to mention," he added, lips quirking, "apparently I can't do what's necessary to produce so much as one."

Katerina drew back and punched him in the arm, but she might as well have been hitting stone for all the good it did. "Yes," she said, her heart lightening for the first time in months. "Yes, I'll run away with you. To the Magiya first, to find out how to put a stop to this. And after that, I don't care where we go. I told you before, as long as we're together, that's all that matters to me."

A wide grin broke across Niko's face, and he swept her up in his arms, spinning her. The forest whirled, green trees and midnight-blue sky—and a flash of yellow, the moon reflecting off Elena's spill of unbound hair as she stepped into the clearing, a black dog at her side.

36

KATERINA

"Not so ill as all that, I see," Elena said. Her jaw was set, her eyes fixed on the two of them. At some point, she'd changed out of her wedding dress and into the clothes she usually donned for childcare or working in the garden: a serviceable shift of rough beige cotton. With the part of Katerina's brain that panic hadn't swallowed, she realized this was the excuse Niko must have given his new wife: He didn't feel well. Then, of course, he'd slipped away to find Katerina—and Elena must have followed. How long had she been standing there?

Cold sweat broke over Katerina's body at the thought. Her mouth opened, but no words came out.

They were so close to escaping. He'd asked her to run away with him. She'd said yes. And now this.

Niko set Katerina on her feet and backed away from her, hands open at his sides. "Elena, I can explain—"

"Don't bother making excuses. I heard everything." She turned her accusatory gaze on Katerina. "*When I realized I couldn't lay a finger on Elena, I wanted to hate you. For you have ruined me forever for another.* You should hate her, Niko—for she *has* ruined you. She's cast a spell on you, and you can't even see it."

Silence fell. When Niko spoke, his voice was gentle. "It's not like that. I love her and I always have. I never meant to hurt you."

"You don't know what you're saying. You've been bewitched. But I can help you. I can set you free." The Vila reached down, burying one hand in the fur of the black dog at her side. For an instant, Katerina feared it was Elena's Shadow father, accompanying his daughter to the woods to avenge her honor—but no. Anatoly Lisov had a torn ear in dog form, the result of a Grigori attack from which he'd been lucky to escape with his life.

So then, who was it? Who had Elena told about the two of them—and how much time did they have before the wrath of the village came down upon their heads?

As if he had read her mind, Niko's eyes narrowed, his gaze darting to the dog. "Who is that, Elena?"

"A friend." The Vila's voice held a smug, self-satisfied note.

Most of the time, when her Shadow was in human form, it was easy to forget the black dog lurked inside him, biding its time until needed. Above all, Shadows were taught control, to erect a barrier between their human selves and the guardians their skin sheltered. But there were occasions, like this one, where the division between man and beast blurred. Niko raised his head, sniffing the air. Then his upper lip curled back, displaying his canines. Wariness trickled through their bond as he regarded the dog, a territorial growl rumbling low in his throat. The animal stared back, its gaze flat, challenging.

Alarm rippled through Katerina. Something was terribly wrong. She could feel it in every cell of her body, in the touch of the breeze against her skin. Inhaling to see if she could sense what had troubled Niko, she took in the scents of sage and elderflower, lavender and rowan-fire. The smells seemed painted on the night's surface, concealing the rotten, dank stench of loss—and something else beneath, something she couldn't quite catch.

She forced herself to think, assessing the situation with the cold detachment she usually reserved for battle. She didn't recognize the black dog who stood beside Elena, but it was dark, excusable to mistake one Shadow for another. Niko had no such impediment. Even in human form, he could identify all of his brethren by scent. As alpha of his pack, they knelt to him.

And he didn't know this Shadow.

Now that Drezna and Satvala had fallen, Kalach was the only village that was home to Shadows, Dimis, and Vila within thirty miles. There had been no strangers at Niko's wedding, no visitors to the village since the Kniaz's emissaries. There was no way Elena had managed to conjure one out of thin air.

Unless that dog was not a Shadow.

A terrible, unfathomable possibility began to take shape in Katerina's mind. As soon as it coalesced, she wanted to dismiss it. Elena was innocent, naïve. She could be petty; she could be vain. But she wasn't evil.

Winging a prayer to the Saints that she was wrong, Katerina inched closer to get a better look. "'A friend,' Elena?" she said, sarcasm clear in her voice. "There are nineteen Shadows in the village, not counting the children and the one standing next to me. Their identities are hardly a mystery. You'll have to do better than that."

The black dog moved at her approach, placing his body between the Vila and Katerina. He snarled, and Niko echoed the sound, menace vibrating from every wordless syllable.

"Call him off," her Shadow said, dark eyebrows lowering. "Or I will."

The wind shifted, blowing the smoke of the rowan-fires

toward Elena and her companion. The dog coughed, a stran-
gled, choking bark, and the fine hairs on Niko's arms lifted,
rising like his hackles did in beast form.

"Elena," he said again, his voice deeper now, threatening,
"who is that? What have you done?"

"What I had to," the Vila said, lifting her chin. "You'll thank
me for it, when you're yourself again."

The dreadful feeling that Katerina had had for weeks—that
a disaster was bearing down on them—settled on her chest like
a weight. "That's no Shadow," she said, spitting each word at
Elena. "That's a demon. And you—you are damned."

Fury filled Elena's pale face, congesting it with blood. "Sammael is my friend. He's been among us all this time, impersonating Alyona to guide me to the truth about the two of you, and
has never hurt a hair on anyone's head. He's loyal, which is
more than either of you can claim." She pointed an accusatory
finger at them. "I saw you together, after the demon attack that
injured Alexei. You're a servant of the Dark, Katerina. You've
witched Niko. And you've underestimated me. I have power
now, just like you. I'm strong. And I will win him back again."

Hearing Elena confirm her suspicions—and hearing that
the demon had been walking among them, no less—iced Katerina's blood. It made her even sicker to see that Elena had
conspired to have a demon shapeshift into a Shadow,
perverting a Dimi's most sacred bond.

"My gifts come from the Light," she said, her mouth dry.
"That creature may look like a black dog, but he's no more than
a soulless worm. He's using you, idiot. Is it possible you're really
this much of a fool?"

"I am not a fool!" Elena's fists clenched at her sides, one of
them knotting so tightly in the dog's fur that the animal
swiveled its head, giving her a reproachful look. "You're the
fool, Katerina Ivanova, to think you can subvert the ways of our

village, ways that have stood for centuries. Niko is my husband. He's meant for me. And Sammael is proof of my strength. You're blind if you can't see that. And your blindness will be your demise."

Katerina opened her mouth to reply—then shut it as another demon emerged from the trees, impeccable in a black suit, a smirk lifting his lips. She recognized him: This was Gadreel, the creature that had commanded the soldier who nearly killed Alexei. The demon that had threatened to tear out Niko's heart.

Behind her, Niko snarled again, his energy shimmering with the first hint of his Change. His voice sounded in her head, harsh with rage. *I owe this bastard, Katya, for Alexei and for you. Say the word, and I'll kill him.*

Hold, Katerina sent back.

Her Shadow's breath was ragged as he fought for control. "Elena," he said, "you don't want to do this. I'm here of my own free will. Stop it while you can. Call your demons off."

Elena laughed, a high girlish giggle, brushing her hair back from her face. "Don't be silly, Niko. Gadreel isn't mine. He's quite nasty, really."

The Vila was on a first-name basis with two demons— including one that had threatened Niko's life—and she thought she was on the side of the Light? There was only one explanation, as far as Katerina was concerned: Jealousy had driven her mad. Elena had lost her mind.

Gadreel leaned against a tree and crossed his legs at the ankles the way Niko had earlier, his arms folded across his chest. He looked Katerina up and down, his gaze assessing. "The Vila called me nasty. You once called me demon filth," he said to her and her alone, as if they were on their own in the clearing. "Should I be offended, or flattered?"

Was he *flirting* with her? "Be whatever you like," Katerina said through her teeth. "It's no concern of mine."

Don't talk to him, Niko sent, low and urgent. *It's a trick, a trap. We have to get Elena away from them, no matter what she's done. Let me Change, let me fight. You can get her away—*

Katerina shook her head. *She's not worth it. And no matter what, I won't leave you.*

So stubborn. Let's hope it doesn't get us killed. He stepped forward, pulling his charm around him like a cloak. "Elena," he tried again, his voice coaxing, "we can work this out. Come here, away from the demons. Come here to me."

"You come here." There was an odd, sly note in her voice that made Katerina's skin crawl. "Come here, away from *her*."

From his position against the tree, a respectable distance from the rowan-fires, Gadreel laughed, an unnerving, sharp-edged sound that ended in a cough. "This is all very amusing, Sammael," he said, directing his words to the dog. "Have you nothing to add to the conversation?"

The black dog's body morphed, sliding effortlessly into the form of a tall man with bright hair in a shade that resembled Katerina's own. The scent of cloves rose, lifted on the heat of the fires. It reminded her of the cider that the villagers made each fall, culled from the apples that graced the orchard. Then, the scent meant comfort and companionship; now, it made her think only of deception and death.

Sammael shot a possessive glance at Elena before his gaze settled on Gadreel. "For once," the demon said, his tone wry, "our goals are aligned. There stands the witch you covet, next to the Shadow who rightfully belongs to my Vila. Avail yourself of the one, and I will happily claim the other."

Niko's mind-voice was thick with disgust. *Grigori scum—*

"Oh, I intend to." Gadreel straightened, brushing invisible dirt from his hands. "But first—I admit to being most curious as to what you have in mind. You associate with this useless, weak creature. You debase yourself for her sake in the form of an animal. I cannot imagine what debauchery you are planning next, but whatever it is, kindly get it over with. The smoke is most irritating, and I have a Dimi to make my own." He winked at Katerina.

His arrogance pushed her over the edge. "You want me? Come and get me, then." She strode toward the boundary of the clearing, her magic spurring the fires higher. *Now, Niko,* she sent, and his satisfaction echoed through their bond.

With pleasure, my Dimi, he said.

"No!" Elena's voice was shrill. By the gleam of the Blood Moon, Katerina saw the Vila slip a hand inside the neckline of her shift. When she withdrew it, she clutched a knife. "Mine," she hissed at Katerina. "You are mine to kill."

Katerina almost laughed; Elena could no more wield a blade than she could summon fire. But then the Vila's lips pressed together in a pale line of concentration. The knife left her hand, spinning toward Katerina, borne onward, impossibly, by the force of Elena's will.

"What—" she managed, stunned.

Katerina! Niko's mind-voice reverberated with terror, a second before his body collided with hers, knocking her out of the way. Eyes fixed on the weapon, her Shadow flung himself in front of her, still in human form, a growl ripping from his throat. Elena cried out in horror as the blade sank deep into his chest and stuck there, handle trembling.

37

KATERINA

The forest howled, and Katerina howled with it. Above her, startled birds took flight in a cacophony of flapping wings.

Niko's eyes locked on Elena's, betrayal and fury clear in their depths before pain glazed them. Blood poured from his wound, black in the moonlight. His knees crumpled, legs giving way as he fell.

Katerina caught him, face bleached with shock. She knelt on a carpet of crushed elderflower, cradling Niko as he gazed up at her, trying to speak. Blood gushed down his chin, rivulets joining the stream that soaked his clothes and seeped into the earth.

Saints, so much blood.

Keening, Katerina ripped his shirt open, careful not to move the knife lest that make matters worse. But when she saw the wound beneath, she knew things were already as bad as they could be. This was a Grigori-poisoned blade, sunk deep into the heart of a Shadow in human form. Even were they in Baba Petrova's surgery, with all her potions and remedies at hand, it was doubtful Baba could save him.

297

"No," Elena whispered from where she stood between the rowan-fires. "Sammael—help me—*no*—"

The Vila's demon gripped her shoulders, anchoring her. "I am sorry, Elena. I cannot," he said in a smoke-roughened voice, sounding as if he actually regretted it—which was impossible. Everyone knew demons were incapable of empathy or remorse.

Katerina shuddered at the sight. How had Elena been so foolish as to fall for a Grigori's lies? She had been a tool, a pawn. What else could a Vila be in the hands of a demon? And now here Niko was, dying in Katerina's arms, a mile from the closest vial of antivenin.

She wouldn't let it happen. Somehow, she would heal him. Desperate, she pressed her hands to his chest, trying to stop the flow of blood. *"Prohibere sanguinis,"* she chanted again and again, a spell against blood loss, but the poison was too strong.

The dark-haired demon laughed. "What a tragedy this all is. Sammael, you've done my work for me yet again. I would have gone to a lot of trouble to kill Niko Alekhin. Yet here your plaything of a Vila is, doing it for me. Perhaps she isn't so useless after all."

Sammael hissed in response, launching himself at Gadreel. The two tumbled into the grass, a snapping, cursing heap of limbs. Branches crashed to the ground as they fought, snarling at each other in a guttural language she supposed must be their native tongue. Good. She hoped they murdered each other, and took Elena with them. It would spare Katerina the trouble—for if Niko died at Elena's hand, Katerina would spend the rest of her life avenging his death. It was her privilege as his Dimi; but as his lover, it was her right.

The Vila stepped forward, trying to move between the fires. Katerina bared her teeth and arched her body over Niko's, covering him. "Stay away." The flames flared higher still as she spoke, blocking Elena's path.

Elena froze, hatred and shock vying for position on her face as she stared at Niko, gasping in Katerina's lap.

His mouth moved, forming words Katerina couldn't decipher. One bloodstained hand floated up, searching, and she grasped it, pressing it to her lips. "Hold on," she begged. "You'll be all right. I'll get help. We'll leave together, like we planned."

Niko's head shook in negation. His mouth moved again, and this time Katerina could make out what he was trying to say: *I love you, Katya. I'm sorry.*

Tears filled her eyes and overflowed. They dripped from her face onto Niko's, mixing with the blood that bubbled from his lips.

Her gaze rose, finding Elena's. "I curse you," Katerina said, putting all her power into each syllable. The words bubbled up from a wellspring of agony, and though she had never been taught or trained to do such a thing, as she spoke them, she felt their truth. "Damned you are, and damned you will be for eternity. Cleaved to a demon, may your soul walk in chains. May your spirit rot, Vila Lisova, and may death bring you no peace."

38

ELENA

The curse hit Elena like a blow. It stole her breath and sunk its ink-dark teeth deep into her bones, digging into her marrow until she feared she might splinter apart.

Sammael howled her name. She wanted to turn to him for help, to ask him what was happening to her, but Katerina's curse held her in its grip, pain coursing through her until her head arched back and she shrieked.

How dare the Dimi curse her, when Elena was the one who had been wronged? She had been loyal. She had done everything right, and damnation was to be her reward?

She refused to accept this as her fate.

Righteous anger swelled inside Elena, bursting her skin. She called forth the power Sammael had taught her and felt a vital force rip free, following the path of her rage, flowing through every limb until her body could no longer contain it. It exploded from her fingertips in bolts of darkness blacker than the night itself.

She opened her mouth to scream in triumph. *Look at me*, she wanted to say. *Look at the magic I can wield, and dare to stand against me now.*

But instead of words, a black cloud spilled from her mouth, tasting of old blood and the hopelessness of despoiled souls, buzzing like a hive of angered wasps. As if magnetized, the cloud fused with the bolts from her fingertips. She willed it to devour Katerina, and it swarmed toward the Dimi, intent on revenge.

But it never reached her.

Elena's howl of victory died in her throat as the cloud hovered between the rowan-fires. She focused on it, forming it into a spear that could pierce Katerina's heart. But the cloud didn't hold its shape. No matter how hard Elena tried, it broke free from her control again and again. It stretched wider, thinning, and then, with a crack of silver-blue lightning, a rip emerged in the fabric of the night.

Aghast, Elena watched as the cloud became a man-sized doorway, a ragged mouth emitting faint, despairing wails. Demon-corrupted, silver-blue flames poured from it. They shot along the ground, ignoring Katerina, tongues of fire searching until they found what they were hungry for: A Shadow's blood. The tongues licked the earth where Niko lay, tasting, devouring. Then they licked *him.*

Elena shrieked.

"Stop this!" Katerina's voice echoed in the clearing, raw with grief.

"I can't." The words were Elena's, but the voice wasn't her own. It was layered, spoken in the timbre of a thousand others. With horror, she realized that the tear in the night was a portal into the Void itself—what Sammael called The Darkness that Eats All Things. Her voice had become one with the cries of damned souls, stolen by the Grigori and condemned to an eternity of servitude, their spirits powering the Underworld and the

Void. The very cries that fueled the Darkness that had devoured Drezna and Satvala.

Somehow, Elena's magic had called this portal into existence.

Her power wasn't like Katerina's at all. It came from the Dark, and she had been fooling herself to think otherwise. It had ripped a hole in the night, and set a terrible force loose upon the world.

Baba Petrova had always taught them *like calls to like.* Well, here was the proof. Elena had violated her vow to Sant Viktoriya. She had brought shame on everything she'd sworn to uphold. She had used a dark power, and now the Void itself had come to claim her.

Katerina's curse echoed in her ears: *Cleaved to a demon, may your soul walk in chains.*

The doorway sucked at Elena, tugging, as if the chains Katerina had cursed her with had sunk hooks into her flesh—and deeper still, into her very soul. She took a step toward it, then another. Obsidian smoke writhed in its depths, vicious as a nest of snakes. Terror shot through her as she fought to stay where she stood, but it was useless. The Void called, and the Dark inside her answered, pulling her forward. Claiming her.

"Help me," she tried to say, but the words stuck in her throat. Her legs moved without volition, taking her closer and closer to the rip in the night. She tried to turn her head, to look at Niko, but all she could see was blackness, pulsing, calling her home. The more she struggled, the harder it tugged. She screamed, thrashing in the Void's grip, and stepped closer still.

39

KATERINA

The silver-blue flames that spilled from the Void cared nothing for Katerina. They curled around Niko, knotting around ankles and wrists, binding him. By a miracle, he was still alive, but his breath came shallow and irregular, blood pumping from his wound with each sluggish beat of his heart. Desperate, Katerina tried to pry the flames loose, as if disentangling a plant from an invasive vine. They didn't burn her, but neither did they give way.

The circle of rowan-fires still burned, protecting Katerina from the demons' attack. But what did that matter, if she couldn't save her Shadow? If the rowan-smoke kept the demons out, but let their hell-flames in?

She cast spell after spell, sending wind whipping through the clearing, her hands pressed to Niko's chest to stop the flow of blood. When those failed, she pressed one hand to Niko's Mark, clutching the amulet around her neck with the other. Maybe she could force him to Change, to give his body a chance to heal itself in the form of his black dog, impervious to Grigori venom.

Her Shadow shuddered in her arms, a low growl escaping

303

his throat, trying his best to obey—but there could be no shifting with a Grigori-soaked blade in his heart. His Change stalled and stopped, the growl subsiding into uneven, soundless gasps. Blood ran from his eyes and nose, streaking his face.

Elena had done this, her and whatever unnatural bond she had formed with her demon. Maybe she could undo it. For that, Katerina would join her power with a Grigori's, no matter the cost. For that, she would give her life.

Katerina glanced upward, preparing to humble herself by begging Gadreel for help—and froze. Elena was staggering toward the doorway to the Void, compelled by Katerina's curse. She walked one uneven, drunken step at a time, all of her usual grace gone.

The Vila convulsed, her face contorted. A scream ripped from her throat, then another. Her demon lunged for her, only to have her slip through his grasp as she took another lurching step forward. Gadreel laughed, a low, rich sound that made Katerina's skin crawl.

And then, mere feet from the doorway to the Void, Elena's body stilled.

40

ELENA

*E**lena.* The voice sounded like Sammael's, but she was sure he hadn't spoken aloud. She could feel him inside her head—could feel him deeper, moving through her body, in places a human hand couldn't reach. His power surged within her, bringing a momentary respite from the gnawing lure of the Void. *Help me,* she begged. *Make it stop. Keep me here. With you.*

His mind-voice came low, hesitant. *I promised you I would never touch you in desire, save you asked it of me. But the Void demands a price, Elena. It is the absence of all things, the origin of the Darkness itself. Fueled by the witch's curse, it craves to claim you as its own.*

She could barely make out his words over the cacophony of the Void: the buzzing of wasps and the sound of desolate, abandoned voices. *Come, Elena,* they taunted. *Be with us. One of us. Forever with us, here, in the Dark.*

Elena couldn't imagine a more terrible fate.

"No," she begged aloud. "There must be something you can do."

There is one thing. His power coursed alongside hers, finding the source of her strength low in her belly, curling around it protectively. His touch was icy, the way his hands had felt in hers that day by the ruined chapel, a balm to the fire her rage had summoned. *I can claim you as my own, and then the Void will be sated, the terms of the curse satisfied. But if I take you that way, it will be forever. You will be bonded to me. You will be* mine.

There was a time when the idea of belonging to a demon would have decimated her. But anything would be better than eternity in the lightless hell of the Void. And Sammael cared for her. Once, he had been an Archangel, and the Light must surely burn somewhere within him still. She could rekindle his flame, and he hers, and together they would be the Saints of a new age.

"Yes, Sammael," she gasped, digging her feet into the ground in an effort to resist the Void's call. "Do it. Please."

My Vila. Sammael's whisper resonated through muscle and sinew, settling lower still, stroking her with gentle, invisible fingers, the way she'd always imagined Niko would. She staggered, trying to keep her feet, and felt his body behind her, solid, bracing hers. *I know you grieve your Shadow. But I can give you things he couldn't dream of. Together, we can make the world burn.*

Sammael's touch pushed the Darkness back, chased the voices away. She forgot they stood at the edge of a clearing where Niko lay dying, forgot she meant not to incinerate the world but to save it, forgot everything but the incomparable relief of feeling the lure of the Void abate and those awful hooks disengage from her flesh. The ragged hole still shimmered in the air, but she felt safe in her demon's arms. As long as he held her, the Void could not touch her.

"Yes," she said again, her head lolling back onto Sammael's shoulder. "Make it stop."

Dimly, she was aware of Gadreel shouting, of the other

demon's hands on her, trying to pry her from Sammael. "Fool," Gadreel was yelling, "don't you see you're feeding the Darkness, giving fuel to the Void?" But Sammael only swore, peeling Gadreel away. He held Elena tight, and she felt his invisible caress again, filling her, stroking faster still.

"Make it let me go," she begged.

Let me please you, her demon whispered back, *and it will.*

Nodding, Elena closed her eyes.

41

KATERINA

Stunned, Katerina stared. The look on the Vila's face, the blush that rose to stain her cheeks as her lips parted—it reminded her of Niko's expression when he was buried inside her, his hands roving over her body, lost in pleasure. Agony shot through Katerina at the thought that he might never hold her so again.

Somehow, though they stood before Katerina fully clothed, Elena was engaging in illicit congress with her demon. She had stood up before the village and pledged herself to Niko—then accused him of being unfaithful—when all along, she had been consorting with a Grigori. Niko lay *dying*, and Elena was despoiling herself with a damned, soulless creature.

Hatred and disgust welled up in Katerina's heart.

She fixed her eyes on Gadreel, who stood a respectful distance from the rowan-fires and the Void, blue eyes flicking from the doomed Vila to Niko and back again. "You, demon—I know you want me. For your paramour, for your slave, for your weapon...I don't care. You can have me. I'll stand at your side, if you save him." Tears choked her voice. "Please. I'll do anything."

"A rich offer," the demon said over the crackle of the flames and the unsettled murmur of the Void. "But a pointless one. Your Shadow is dead where he lies, Dimi Ivanova. Once hellfire takes a beast such as that, he is damned. He will die burning, and you will be mine, anyhow." His laughter rose, barbed and poisonous, stinging Katerina's skin. It devolved into coughs as the smoke from the rowan-fires polluted his lungs, and then the sound faded into the dark.

As if the demon's words had called them, the silver-blue flames crawled up Niko's limbs, one bloodstain at a time. He rolled feebly, trying to extinguish them, but the more of his blood they tasted, the brighter they blazed. Katerina clutched him, trying to beat the demon-flames back with her hands, to no avail.

In desperation, she closed her eyes and reached out for the river that fed the village. She had never tried to summon water at this distance, and her body trembled with the force of her concentration. Her mind filled with the image of the river's overarching willows and the rocks that lined its bed, making a slippery path that she and Niko used to chase each other across when they were children.

A roar rose in the forest, growing louder until a wall of water loomed above the trees and crashed into the clearing, extinguishing the rowan-fires but doing nothing to quench the demon-flames. Fish poured from the sky and into the Void, their silver bodies strewn across the dirt of the clearing. The forest reeked of iron, tidal mud, and rosemary, undergirded with the acrid scent of fear.

"Please," Katerina said over and over, her fingers pressed against Niko's Mark, tethering his soul to hers. "Please don't leave me. Niko, please—"

The water broke around his burning body, drenching Katerina but leaving him untouched. His teeth sank into his lower lip, back bowing as the silver-blue flames traced the blood that spilled from his mouth, then slipped inside when he gasped. He glowed with an unearthly light as the fire slid down his throat, illuminating him from within. It slid lower still, encasing his wounded heart, and Niko howled, his body arching out of Katerina's grip. His voice resounded in her head. *Let me go, Katya. I will always be with you, I swear it. My soul is yours. Set me free.*

His pain was hers, her body an inferno, her heart struggling to beat. It was selfish to keep him with her, to let him suffer this way. She fought to think, to find the strength to do as he wished. Breath coming short, she closed her eyes once more, picturing the bond that tied them together. As his Dimi, she had to be the one to sever it. Better she should grieve for the rest of her life than for him to linger in this brutal half-existence. He would never leave her if there was the slightest chance he might live. She knew that with every fiber of her being.

The bond shimmered in her mind's eye, frayed but holding. She dragged in a deep, scorching breath and braced herself to cut it.

42

ELENA

The voices murmured, troubled. The Darkness called. But as Sammael's power slid over her skin and moved deep within her, Elena couldn't bring herself to care. Dimly she knew something terrible had happened, was happening still—but the more she tried to grasp the knowledge, the more it receded, a tide drawn back to the sea.

I would be human for you if I could. His voice shivered over her body, and she shivered with it. *Alas, I cannot. But I can give you this.*

The darkness unleashed by her rage circled inside her, seeking to fulfill Katerina's curse. Sammael's power entwined with it, ink-black and silver-blue, twisting tighter and tighter. They fused, detonating outward in a spray of lightning that forked through Elena's veins, spreading through every inch of her body, into the air, the sky, the earth.

Elena shook, and the earth shook with her. Behind her, within her, Sammael cried out, a sound she heard with her ears and her mind, with the power that was remaking her into something new. She shattered, and was reborn.

Into the trembling silence came a voice. It was everyone's, and no one's at all.

"Hail, Elena-of-the-Void," it said.

43

KATERINA

Before Katerina could cut the bond that tied her to her Shadow, the very earth convulsed, ripping Niko from her arms. The murmur of the Void rose in a cacophony of clamoring voices; the air buzzed with the discordant power of it. Katerina forced her eyes open as silver-blue lightning flashed, splitting one of the huge oaks that guarded the clearing and catching it aflame. By the lightning's unearthly gleam, she could see its source: Elena, body curving backward in her demon's arms. Darkness and bolts of hellfire poured from her, merging with the night. The demon wailed, an awful sound of metal-on-metal, as the hellfire blazed again, silver-blue tongues of flames gobbling the trees and snaking toward where Niko lay. Clots of dirt flew through the air, hurtling into the Void. Elena was screaming, her demon was screaming, the Void was screaming—

Then, as suddenly as it had begun, everything fell silent—but for an awful, triumphant voice that issued from everywhere and nowhere: *Hail, Elena of the Void.*

On her hands and knees, wiping dirt and ash from her face, Katerina crawled to where Niko lay. He was motionless, face and body awash in blood, his open eyes reflecting the gleam of the night sky. She gathered him into her arms, brushed his hair from his face, pleaded with him to stay with her, but it made no difference.

She knew it from the hole in her heart where he should be, from the emptiness in her mind where she'd become accustomed to hearing his voice. From the ripped-apart feel of their bond, sheared fibers sparking in a hopeless attempt at reconnection. But she pressed her fingers to his neck nonetheless, praying to feel the thud of his pulse, however faint. More than anything, she wanted him not to have died alone.

It was too late for her to give him the end she'd wanted for him, the end he deserved—cradled in her lap, her lips against his as he breathed his last. Too late for so many things.

Her Shadow was gone.

44
ELENA

E lena was herself, still—but she was more than that. She was Elena-of-the-Void, beloved of Sammael. She was something that had never existed before in all the history of the world.

Black edges hemmed her vision as she stood, watching Katerina clutch Niko's lifeless body close. The Dimi shook all over, a tremor so consuming that the pool of river water in which she sat flowed in waves uphill toward the border of the clearing, defying the laws of gravity.

The rowan-fires had gone out, as had the silver-blue flames that had consumed Niko. But the flames ignited by Elena's lightning still smoldered in the trees, illuminating the doorway to the Void. It gaped, swirling with Darkness, but it no longer lured her onward. The bond with Sammael had worked—but at what cost?

Niko was gone. Dead. And it was Katerina's fault. She was the one for whom Elena had intended the knife. Out of bravery and misguided loyalty, Niko had stepped into the path of the blade. Katerina's hubris, her spellcraft, had taken more than Niko's fidelity and his honor—it had taken his life.

The unfairness of it filled Elena, spearing her chest as if the blade in Niko's heart had pierced hers as well. Why couldn't Katerina be the one whose life was over? Why should Niko pay the price?

She would not let him go, not like this. She would keep him with her, in whatever form. He would be hers, at last, and he would be grateful for it. If anyone could accomplish such a feat, it was she. Taking Sammael's hand in hers, Elena stepped forward, into the clearing.

"What have you done?" It was Gadreel's voice, grating with accusation. His fingers dug into Sammael's wrist, holding the other demon still. "Your foolish habit of rescuing damsels in distress has reached new heights. It wasn't enough to share your power with an unworthy vessel such as this." He flicked his fingers at Elena in disgust. "Now you've bonded with an unhinged lunatic for eternity and fed the Darkness into the bargain." Pointing into the depths of the Void, he snapped, "Why do you think *that* didn't vanish when you altered the terms of her curse? How do you imagine this will end? You are a fool, Sammael."

Elena turned on Gadreel, hissing. Dropping Sammael's hand, she ran for Niko—but Gadreel followed. He lunged for Katerina, who sent him stumbling backward with a gust of wind.

"Don't you touch me." The Dimi's eyes gleamed with grief and rage. "Don't you touch him!"

A sob caught in Elena's throat as she saw what Katerina's arrogance had done to her Shadow. His skin was as white as the face of the Bone Moon, his wrists and ankles marred by the flames. His beautiful clothes—their *wedding* clothes—were torn and drenched with blood.

It wasn't too late. She could feel him here, guarding Katerina in death as he had in life. Even with their bond severed and his body limp as a rag doll's, Katerina's spell held firm.

Elena could still save him. She could set him free of the Dimi's web, and keep him by her own side as he was meant to be.

Teeth gritted, she dropped to the earth beside him. Katerina was speaking, muttering curses and incantations, but Elena ignored her. *Sammael,* she said, and felt the demon stir in her mind. *Tell me what to do.*

This is Dark magic indeed. His voice was hesitant. *Death magic. If I help you, Elena, I cannot say the results will be what you dream of.*

Elena sent a bolt of impatience down their bond. *His soul lingers, I can feel it. Help me before it's too late.*

She felt him yield as the knowledge rippled through the cord that bound his mind to hers and the words rose to her lips. "With Darkness I bind you. With your sacrifice I bind you. With the dirt of your grave I bind you." She dug her fingers into a handful of the loam beneath his body, seeded with blood. "With my will I bind you, Niko Alekhin. May you rise, and rest no more."

As the words left her lips, Niko's form flickered into existence, a transparent figure with his hand resting on Katerina's shoulder. His eyes were huge and solemn, the accusation in them clear. He looked beyond her, at Sammael and Gadreel, into the Void—then back at his Dimi, whose arms were wrapped tight around the shell of his body. His mouth moved, saying Katerina's name, but it was useless; she couldn't hear.

Quick as it had been in life, the Change took him. One moment he was the ghost of a man; then he was the shade of a black dog, moving quick and soundless into the forest. He vanished between the trees, a Shadow amongst shadows.

It was done.

45

KATERINA

"**N**o!" Katerina's cry filled the air, resounding through the woods. Clouds gathered in the night sky, the trees bending before her will as the wind began to rise.

With my will I bind you, Niko Alekhin. May you rise, and rest no more.

Katerina had chained Elena to the Dark, and Elena had bound Niko's soul to hers.

Niko, a ghost. Niko, a prisoner.

Niko, a captive of the damned.

Katerina stood, fists at her sides, a gale whipping her hair back and plastering her blood-soaked shift to her skin. The earth cracked once more, this time at her command, the great oaks ripping free of their roots. Hail pelted the clearing, striking Elena and the demons. Gadreel tried once more to reach her, but a gust drove him backward, slamming him into the trunk of a fallen oak head-first. He fell and didn't move.

The doorway to nothingness drifted closer, hanging in midair, unaffected by her storm. Inky tendrils seeped from it, leaving blackened, withered grass in their wake when they reached the ground. The Void sucked at her, icy and demanding.

She remembered what Nadia had written in her own blood —*The Darkness is loose. The village of Satvala is gone*. As the cold crawled over her skin in deadly, inexorable invitation, Katerina knew her fellow Dimi had been right. The Darkness that fueled the Void and had given rise to the Underworld, a shard of which lived within each demon... It was here, in this clearing. As it had been in Satvala and Drezna, before it had swallowed them whole.

The Darkness had gotten free somehow. It had wanted Elena, and been denied. And it was hungry.

Without her Shadow's protection, Katerina was vulnerable. The Darkness could consume her. Own her, as it did Elena. And then it would take Kalach next.

That would never happen, as long as Katerina lived. Digging deeper than she ever had, praying to Niko's soul for strength, she summoned the wind. It rose to her call, lifting the demons and Elena into the air. The Vila struggled, and though Gadreel hung limp, Sammael shifted shape again and again, trying in vain to break free of Katerina's hold.

With a roar that shook the forest, she threw her power outward, forming a net around Elena and the demons. Every muscle clenched with effort, she imagined dragging the net closer and closer to the ragged hole, aided by the force of the wind.

Niko, she thought as the creature that had been Elena spat and fought, *if you're still here, if you're still with me like you promised, help me now.*

The wind screamed, its voice as eerie and plaintive as the cry of the snow leopards that roamed the woods north of Rivki. And then he came, melting out of the forest to stand before her: Niko's shade, in human form, his mournful gray eyes fixed on hers. The flames of the smoldering trees flickered through his transparent body, so that for an instant he shone with Light, as he had on the road to Drezna. She could feel his strength bolstering hers one last time. Protecting her from the onslaught of the Dark.

Tears streaming down her face, she reached out a hand to him. His voice echoed in her mind, maybe a memory or maybe the answer to her prayer: *I am your Lightbringer, Katya. Nothing will harm you while I live.*

But you're dead, she thought stupidly, even as she howled his name.

A terrible realization dawned on her: She could cast Elena into the Void, and the demons with her. She could save Kalach. But with Niko's soul chained to the Vila, then that meant—

She hesitated, her magic stuttering. But it was too late.

With a suddenness that sent Katerina reeling backward, the four figures—demons, corrupted Vila, and her beloved Shadow—flew toward the entrance to the Void, which yawned wider, as if in invitation. There was a dreadful sucking sound as the portal swallowed them whole...and then stillness, as the night knit itself back together. The hole was gone, like it had never been there at all.

Katerina dropped to the ground, gasping. The clearing and the forest that surrounded it were destroyed, awash in mud and blood, littered with rocks, tree limbs, and the corpses of fish. She crawled through the wreckage to where Niko lay, sobs ripping from her throat. As dawn broke over the treetops, she knelt, cradling the broken body of her Shadow. Beneath her knees, the delicate bones of tiny trout shattered, piercing her skin. She welcomed the pain; it was an echo of the serrated misery that gnawed at every inch of her body, perforating her heart.

She'd had to do it. If she hadn't sent Elena hurtling into the

Void, taking the Darkness with her, it would surely have consumed Kalach. But condemning Elena that way had done the same to Niko. In saving Kalach, she had cast her Shadow's soul into the Void.

It was unbearable.

Over and over again, she remembered Niko flinging himself in front of her, taking the knife meant to end her life. Over and over he fell, the Darkness swarming from Elena's mouth and the flames consuming him as he writhed in agony.

And then, as surely as if Baba Petrova stood beside her, the words of the prophecy echoed, uttered in Baba's cracked, kvass-roughened voice:

Vila to Shadows, as dawn slips to dusk. Never Shadow to Dimi, betrayal of trust. In the slow slide to hate, so come secrets to light. Fuel for the war, for the unnatural fight. So will they forfeit what they love the most: Lost demon. Witchfire. Wandering ghost. So shall she burn as she brings his demise: The Dark will fall. The shadow will rise.

46

KATERINA

Katerina stumbled back to Kalach, using her witchwind to guide Niko's body through the air with what strength remained to her. He was too heavy for her to carry, and it was unthinkable that she abandon him in the clearing. She arrived to a village in pandemonium, the Shadows at the gate demanding to know what had happened to their alpha and Ana clinging to Katerina's arm, saying everyone was searching for her, they'd heard and felt terrible things, Elena was missing and the river had burst its banks and there had been a sound that had eaten the world—

Ana had nothing but questions, but Katerina couldn't bring herself to answer. She crumpled to her knees, weeping, Niko cradled in her arms. The chaos around her faded into the background, a blur of *how can it be* and *did the Darkness come* and *Katerina, speak to us were you attacked was Elena taken where have you been.* She ignored them, clutching Niko tighter, burying her face in his hair. He still smelled like himself, beneath the ash and blood: mint and blade oil and the ineffable scent that just meant *home.*

Baba tried to pry her Shadow from her grip. But Katerina

wouldn't let him go. She pressed her lips to Niko's cold cheek, running her fingertips along his stubble. An ache sprang up in her chest at the memory of their last kiss in the clearing, at his rough whisper, *I'm yours, whether you wish it or no.* At the way he'd held her, the desperation in his grip, as if he'd somehow known it would be the last time. Sobs wracked her body, and when someone—Konstantin? —tried again to take Niko from her, she snarled at them and clung to him, peppering kisses to the sharp line of his jaw, whispering how much she loved him.

Some part of her, still capable of rational thought, knew that this was a terrible mistake. All of the effort they'd gone to conceal their relationship, and here she was, proclaiming in the village square that they'd flagrantly violated one of Kalach's most sacred covenants. But what difference did it make? Niko was dead, and nothing mattered anymore.

Around her, suspicious murmurs rose. Then more hands were on her, their touch gentle, familiar. "Come, Katerina. Let Alexei take him," Ana coaxed, her voice breaking. "You can't stay here."

Katerina lifted her head, blinking back tears, to see Ana and her Shadow kneeling on the cobblestones. Alexei's gaze was dark with grief, but his hands were steady as he reached for his alpha's broken body. And Katerina had to trust *someone.* Swiping her fingers beneath her eyes, she gave a sharp nod of acquiescence, and Alexei lifted Niko in his arms.

She walked next to Alexei, Ana, and her fallen Shadow, following Baba to the old woman's cottage—a silent funeral procession. The crowd parted for them, their accusatory, shocked gazes fixed on Katerina. Let them stare, then. She deserved every bit of their ire.

Niko had died saving her life. Because of her, he was dead.

Baba held the door for Alexei when they reached her cottage and he stepped through, careful of Niko's sprawling limbs. At the ancient Dimi's direction, he set his alpha on the hearth rug, and Katerina went to Niko at once, lifting his head into her lap. He wouldn't be alone for an instant, not if she could help it.

Baba tsked, her frail shoulders heaving in a massive sigh. "Katerina—"

"No!" She shook her head, her matted red curls sticking to her face. "I won't leave him."

"Sant Antoniya, help us," Baba muttered, touching the rowan cross that hung next to the door. "The two of you"—she gestured at Ana and Alexei—"out."

Casting Katerina a troubled glance, Ana lingered for an instant. Then she touched her Shadow's arm, and Alexei stepped away, bowing his head. The front door snicked shut behind them, and an instant later, Baba was in front of Katerina, kneeling on the hearth rug.

"What has happened?" she demanded, each syllable a razor blade. "Is this as bad as it looks?" When Katerina didn't answer, Baba gripped her shoulder. "Let *go* of him, Katerina. Sit up and speak to me."

Katerina folded herself over Niko protectively. "No. You can't have him. No."

Another massive sigh, and then Baba stood, her joints creaking. There was the clatter of china, the splash of water, and then the sensation of something warm against Katerina's chilled fingers, penetrating the awful numbness that had encased her. "Tea," Baba said simply. "Take it."

Katerina protested, but Baba forced the cup into her hand nonetheless. She clutched it, trembling so hard that the contents spilled all over Niko's bloodied face. The scent of ginger wafting from the mug reminded her of the first time her Shadow had kissed her. How had it come to this? How had everything gone so horribly wrong? It had to be a nightmare; it couldn't be real.

324

And yet it was. The hollow in her soul where her Shadow should be, the ache and stab of their severed bond—all of it meant this was no dream.

There was no fixing this. No turning back. Niko was gone, and now, Iriska would fall.

She sobbed until she couldn't catch her breath, her throat aching and the tea sloshing everywhere. Dimly she was aware that it was hot, burning her fingers, but so what? At least she could feel *something* other than this awful grief, a rabid animal that clawed at her insides, fighting to be set free. She spilled it again, this time deliberately, and reveled in the pain.

"Katerina!" Baba said, snatching the cup away. "Pull yourself together. And speak."

There was no point in lying. Baba had already seen too much. Struggling to stem her sobs, her voice a rasp, Katerina told the old witch everything.

The old woman listened without interruption, her expression growing increasingly grim. "Oh, Katerina," she said at last, knotting her gnarled fingers in her lap. "You have doomed us all."

"I—" Katerina tried, but Baba cut her off.

"You have spoken. Now it's my turn." She rose, slamming Katerina's cup down on the table with so much force, the china cracked in two. "It's bad enough that you've done this. Your blatant disregard for your duty, your violation of the prophecy and your thoughtlessness for Iriska, let alone Kalach—that is sin enough. But the display you made in the square...that is just stupidity. You are many things, but I never thought to call you brainless, Katerina."

Deep inside Katerina, where the capacity for indignation still lived, a spark flared. "You call me 'brainless,' because I grieve my Shadow?" she snapped, her voice still thick with tears. "Well, I would rather be bereft of a brain than a heart."

"You are a *fool!*" Baba glowered at her. "Had you not made such a public display of your illicit actions, we could have kept them secret from the villagers. Now, all those who were in the square when you returned will have spread the word that you lay with your Shadow, and brought disaster upon us all. They will see you not as their protector, but as their undoing—and they are likely right. There will be no hiding it. Instead, there will be chaos."

Katerina's nails dug into the ripped linen of Niko's shirt. "What do I care how it looks? This is the *truth*. I am to blame, and I take responsibility for what I've done. But I won't renounce my Shadow. My love for him is pure, prophecy or no prophecy."

The floorboards shook beneath Katerina as Baba's power rose, her cheeks purpling with fury. "This is not about you, Katerina! This is about our people. You have been unbelievably selfish. And now, not only you, your Shadow, and Elena, but all the rest of us, will pay the price."

She knelt once more, the ground trembling in warning. "Let him go now, Katerina. Say goodbye to your Shadow. And pray, if you still believe the Saints will listen, that the Kniaz will spare your life."

THEY BURIED Niko outside the small village cemetery late the next day, in unconsecrated ground. Normally, the entire village would turn out for the burial ceremony of a Shadow, to honor his commitment to Kalach. But even though he had died giving his life to save Katerina, his death wasn't considered an honorable one. And so only his Shadow brethren and their Dimis, a small group of Vila, and Baba Petrova had come to see his body lowered into the ground. If Katerina hadn't been so numb, it would have filled her with rage to see him being dishonored this way. Her Shadow, who deserved a hero's farewell. But there was nothing she could do, other than stand silent witness. Certainly no one was interested in hearing what she had to say.

She stood alone, not daring even to meet Ana's eyes. She hadn't spoken to her friend since the other Dimi had persuaded her to let Alexei carry Niko's body. And frankly, she was afraid to try. If even Ana wanted nothing to do with her, then Katerina truly had no one.

Alyona was bracketed by the other Vila, her face stark with shock and grief and her hands trembling with the nerves that had dogged her as long as Katerina could remember. Her companions all stared at Katerina with accusatory eyes. It made her want to scream. Did no one hold Elena responsible in the least for her actions? Yes, ultimately this devastation could be laid at Katerina's feet. But no one had made the Vila listen to what the demon Sammael had to say. No one had forced her to hatch the misguided plan that had led to Niko's death rather than going to Baba and confessing what she'd seen.

There had been a seed of Darkness inside Elena all along, hidden beneath the coy, charming surface she showed the world, like rot at the heart of a rose. But no one cared to acknowledge that Elena's corruption had begun with a choice. It was, Katerina reflected as she fought to keep her face expressionless and her spine straight, far easier for them to blame her: Niko was dead and Elena was gone. Here she stood, a convenient scapegoat who had brought ruination upon Iriska. It was far easier to blame Katerina than to admit the role Elena had played in her own undoing...and everything that followed.

Alyona sniffed loudly, and Oksana, the Vila standing next to her, wrapped a protective arm around her shoulders. She glared at Katerina as Baba intoned, "Niko Alekhin, Shadow of Kalach, I commend your body to the earth and pray to the Saints for the restoration of your soul."

A wind swept through the small clearing at her words, and Baba's eyes sharpened, her gaze intensifying on Katerina's face, as if to ensure Katerina wasn't about to make a scene. But Katerina hardly noticed. She was too busy scanning the empty spaces between the trees that hugged the gravesite, straining to see whether Baba's words had somehow summoned what remained of her Shadow. If he had not been sucked into the Void with Elena after all. But nothing stirred other than the sun-dappled leaves, bending to the will of the wind.

Katerina folded her arms across her chest, struggling to hold herself together, as, one after another, Niko's fellow Shadows came forward to pour shovelfuls of dirt atop his coffin, honoring their fallen alpha, no matter his end. Alyona was weeping openly, doubtless thinking of how there was no such grave for Elena. Nor would there be, for the Vila was not truly dead.

Baba and the Elders had called a Council meeting as soon as the sun rose, summoning Alyona to testify, as Elena's closest friend. She'd told Baba of waking to find herself in bed in her cottage time and again, with no memory of having gone there; that she had gaps of time she couldn't account for. Given Katerina's testimony about what had transpired in the clearing, Baba and the Elders had concluded that Sammael had needed to get Alyona out of the way, and so he had likely influenced her mind, to ensure she would remain unconscious while he worked his evil on Elena.

He shouldn't have been able to do such a thing, not within the boundaries of the village; but with the weakening of the wards, much was possible that had been unthinkable before. A demon had been walking among Kalach, undetected by the Shadow guard. A Vila had been corrupted by the Dark. These were unprecedented times, and the village blamed Katerina for everything. She saw it in the way no one would speak to her, how even her fellow Dimi shunned her, how no one would meet her eyes as they stood around Niko's grave. Even her magic had become unpredictable and furious over the past few hours, sometimes refusing to come when she called it, other times blasting through her with a ferocity that controlled her, rather than the other way around.

Katerina watched, head aching and sick with nausea, as Alexei poured a shovelful of dirt atop Niko's coffin and tamped it down. He had been Niko's second; Baba had promoted him to alpha now. The pack was his.

The other Shadows followed his lead. Then they stood, ringed around Niko's grave, paying their respects in silence, hands laced behind their back as Baba said the final, painful words of the eulogy that would send Niko on his way: "Though your soul has been stolen from the Light, we pray that you will not lend your strength to the Dark." Her gaze found Katerina, forbidding and grim, as she spoke. "May you not be cursed to wander; may the Darkness taste you and find you lacking; may you burn with the fervor of one who once held claim to the Light."

Katerina lingered long after everyone else had gone, hoping against hope to catch a glimpse of her Shadow's shade. She spoke to him when she was alone at his graveside, telling him how much she missed him, how she wouldn't rest until she made this right—but the only answer she got was the sound of the wind whistling through the trees.

She'd had no choice. The Darkness she'd felt outside Drezna had been with her in that clearing. It had howled through Elena's mouth and fought to crush Katerina beneath its weight. To take her with it. If she hadn't forced the two demons and whatever Elena had become into the Void, closing the portal, surely the Darkness would have devoured Katerina and then come for Kalach.

But Niko...

This was her fault. Maybe Baba had been right, weeks before, when she'd said that Katerina's power attracted Darkness in equal measure. But that didn't account for the events that had set Niko's death in motion. Katerina had told him she loved him. She'd urged him not to marry Elena, to flee with her to the Magiya instead. If she'd never opened her mouth, never acted on her feelings for him, all of this could have been prevented. The prophecy would never have come true.

She had to find a way to make this right, to free his soul and reunite him with the Saints, where he belonged. And she wanted, with an ache that bordered on the visceral, to wreak revenge on Elena—though how she would get her hands on the former Vila, she had no idea. Elena had gone where Katerina couldn't follow.

But there had to be a way.

Rising from her knees, she brushed dirt from her mourning gown and walked slowly back down the road that led away from the gravesite. Her body ached with every step. She trudged through the woods, making her way back into town, passing the blacksmith's shop and the bakery, where she used to buy Niko the pies he loved. Even after Trinika had been taken, her husband had kept the bakery going. But now, the shop was shuttered; flour was scarce these days, and few had money for treats.

As usual, people stared at her as she went by, but this time, they didn't look at her with awe and envy. No—their faces were fixed in expressions of horror and disgust. Some of them whispered to each other, not even bothering to conceal their contempt. One gray-haired, bearded man, his face gaunt from hunger, spat in the dirt at her feet.

Katerina held her head high, trying to pretend that none of this troubled her. But in truth, it broke her heart. She deserved every whispered word, every curse. She had failed in her mission to protect Kalach.

The first stone came from behind, hitting her hard in the back and stealing her breath. Then came another and another, pelting her between her shoulder blades, thudding against her legs with a sharp pain that made her gasp. "Traitor," a high voice called. And a man's deeper one echoed: "Shadow-killer!"

Katerina could have called her magic. She could have summoned a wind that would have knocked all of them off the path, turned their weapons back on them. But that would have been a terrible perversion of her gift. She couldn't imagine deliberately using it against the very people she was sworn to protect. Besides, she didn't trust herself to control her magic. So instead she kept walking, down the road that was now lined on either side by angry inhabitants of Kalach. She saw Konstantin, his lips pressed together in a grim line. And there was Maksim, his face pinched, his normally jovial green eyes as cold as chips of ice.

They didn't hurl projectiles or insults. But neither did they speak up for her. Neither did they lift a hand to save her.

Katerina concentrated on putting one foot in front of the other. She just had to make it back to her cottage, where she could seek solace. Where she could grieve in peace and plot her revenge. Tearing her gaze from Maksim, she fixed her eyes on the distance and kept walking.

The stones came faster now, hitting her cheek, her stomach, her forehead. The crowd's voices overlapped, each louder and more incensed than the last. "Shadow-killer!" "Betrayer of the prophecy!" "You have destroyed Kalach!" "You have doomed us all!"

A stone hit her temple, breaking the skin. Blood poured

down Katerina's face, blinding her. She gasped and tasted it on her tongue, copper-bright.

The other Dimis and Shadows had abandoned her. Baba was nowhere to be seen. She was alone and bleeding, a pariah. Her Shadow was dead. Kalach was starving. Maybe setting Niko's soul free was a fool's errand. Maybe she should just lie down and die on this road—

"Shadow-killer!" a high voice cried again. Others joined it, a chorus of shame and blame.

A fusillade of stones hit her in the backs of her knees, and her legs buckled, threatening to give out altogether. The crowd roared as someone grabbed her by the arm, yanking her to her feet.

"Enough!" a familiar voice said. "The damage has been done. No matter her actions, Katerina Ivanova is still the strongest Dimi in Kalach. What good will wounding her do? How will that protect you from the Darkness? You're only hurting yourselves."

Katerina scrubbed the blood from her eyes to find Ana standing beside her. A wave of gratitude washed over her, mingled with shame, as Ana stood tall, meeting the eyes of each of the villagers who lined the road. One by one, they dropped their stones and backed away. Ana didn't budge from Katerina's side until the last of them had turned, muttering, and made their way back home or into their places of business. Then she sighed, stepping away, and said, "I'll walk you home. Help you clean up."

Katerina wiped her face with the sleeve of her mourning-gown. It came away wet with blood. "You don't have to. I know you hate me."

"I don't," Ana protested.

She gave the other Dimi an incredulous look. "Right."

"I *don't*," Ana protested.

"Well, if you don't," Katerina said wearily, "then you're the only one." She shot Ana a wary look as the two of them began walking toward Katerina's cottage. Katerina was limping; her body hurt everywhere. She would be bruised tomorrow, and badly. "Why don't you hate me, exactly?"

Ana bit her lip. "You're my best friend. I could never hate you. Besides, you and Niko saved Alexei's life. I owe you everything."

She raised her hands, palms open. Two small flames flared within them, before she grimaced and they extinguished themselves. "I just wish you'd told me the truth, Katerina. Maybe I could have helped you somehow. My heart is cracked straight down the middle at Niko's loss, and whatever I'm feeling, I know it's only an echo of your pain. It hurts that you felt you couldn't trust me. I would have kept your secret."

Katerina's shoulders slumped. "I wanted to tell you. But how could I? Niko and I knew how wrong it was, prophecy or no prophecy." She hugged herself, wincing. "I kept telling him I thought Elena suspected, but he said I was imagining things. I told him she seemed different. Like she was hiding something. But Niko, he..." Her voice trailed off on a sob. "This is all my fault, Ana. And now everyone hates me—and Kalach...Kalach will..."

The tears were flowing now, streaming down her cheeks. She was crying too hard to speak, and Ana's harsh expression softened as she wrapped Katerina in her arms.

"It's not all your fault, Katya," Ana whispered, rocking her. "Don't do this to yourself."

At the sound of her nickname, the one only Niko ever used, Katerina cried harder. "It *is*," she insisted, forcing the words out between sobs. "When we came back from Drezna, Baba said my power was what had called the Darkness. That the world

333

needed balance, and my Light was so strong, the Dark sought to cancel it out."

She sniffed against Ana's shoulder, trying and failing to pull herself together as she ticked off all the reasons she was to blame. "If I didn't exist, Drezna and Satvala would still be here. Sofi and Damien wouldn't have lost everything—and everyone. Nadia and Oriel wouldn't be missing, or...or dead. Niko would have been bound to another Dimi, someone worthy of him. And he would still be alive."

"Katerina—"

It hurt to say these words aloud, to let Ana know the worst of her, but they had to be said. Ana had stood up for her when no one else had been willing. Had stood between her and an armed mob. "You need to know who you're defending," she said stiffly, straightening from Ana's embrace. "I don't deserve your kindness or even your pity. I'm the one who urged Niko to consider running away with me instead of marrying Elena. I'm the one whose existence weakened the wards, so Sammael could find his way into Kalach and corrupt Elena. I should never have been born, Ana. It would be better if I hadn't."

Ana shook her. "Don't you ever say that. You're my friend, Katerina, no matter what you've done. You'll never change my mind. Come on, let's get you home."

Sighing, Katerina pulled back from Ana's grip. She limped alongside her friend in the direction of her cottage, her temple throbbing. "Do you think the Kniaz will still want me?" she said, her voice dull. "Baba sent word of what happened; she could hardly hope to keep it a secret. The arrangement was for both of us to go to Rivki. Not for myself alone. Now...it matters not where I go. But Lara, Svetlana, and Natalya will expect to come home. I couldn't bear to think I was the reason that they're marooned in Rivki forever...that Lara would think I broke my word when I promised she'd just be there for a little while..."

Ana wrapped an arm around Katerina's shoulder. "If you'd run off to the Magiya, what would have happened to them then?"

"I don't know," Katerina admitted. "I wasn't thinking. I guess I hoped I would find answers. That together, Niko and I would discover a way to defeat the Darkness and thwart the prophecy. And then we would use that as leverage to set them free."

The words scraped at her throat. It was yet another way she'd failed. "There's less than a week until the Blood Moon is full and the tithe is due, Ana. If I leave here, I'll be deserting Niko. Who will watch for his shade then?"

"Niko's gone," Ana said, her voice gentle as she guided Katerina around a jagged rock that protruded from the path. "We have no way of retrieving him from the Void—or the Underworld, if that's where he's gone. You know that as well as I."

A spark of rage flared within Katerina, the first genuine emotion she could remember feeling since her Shadow lay dying in her arms. Her magic spiked, radiating heat outward. "You're saying there is no hope? That I should give up on him?"

Ana dropped her arm, giving Katerina an exasperated glance. "Watch yourself," she said. "I'm only trying to help. And as for Niko...what can you do, Katerina? We're creatures of the Light. We have no business trafficking in Darkness."

"But if I could get him back..." Katerina said. "If there were a way—"

"If there were truly a way to save him, then of course I'd help you. I'd do anything. But you have to accept it. He and Elena are both lost to us." She took Katerina's hands in hers, squeezing tight. "When you're gone to Rivki, I'll tend his grave each week, I swear it. I'll bring him flowers and keep his marker free of moss and ivy. If his shade is watching, I'll make sure he knows he's not forgotten."

When you're gone to Rivki. Katerina tipped her head back, staring at the blue expanse above them, fighting the urge to weep at the thought of Ana kneeling by the tiny cross that marked Niko's grave, abandoned in that unconsecrated clearing. Of his body moldering in the earth as his soul wandered through the Darkness. Of Katerina, miles away, unable to even care for him in death.

The thought sent fury and misery spiraling through her in equal measure. Her body trembled with the force of it, until it burst free, unable to be contained. Witchwind erupted from her, spiraling heavenward, sending clouds scudding across the sky. They darkened and swelled, then burst. Rain poured down, soaking the path, plastering Katerina's clothes to her skin. But despite that, her witchfire stirred within her, creeping outward until it encased her in flames. She stood there, shivering and burning, as Ana gaped at her.

Blood from the wound on Katerina's temple ran down her face in rivulets. She touched her fingers to it, then knelt on the path and drew the three interlocking circles of Niko's Mark on the stones.

Ana gasped. To do such a thing was sacrilege; the drawing of a Shadow's Mark was the right of Baba Petrova alone. But Katerina was far beyond caring about such things. And for just a moment, she could swear she felt her Shadow's presence. For just a moment, she felt the pulse of his blood in the amulet that still rested above her heart.

To feel that again, she would do anything.

"One for the fire," she said, tracing her index finger over the first circle, then the second. "Two for the storm."

Above them, lightning split the sky. Thunder rolled, and in it Katerina could swear she heard her Shadow's growl. She traced the third circle, whispering, "Three for the black dog that guards against harm."

"Katerina," Ana managed, her teeth chattering. "What are you doing?"

Katerina lifted her bloody hands to the streaming sky, calling on the power of the Saints. It thrummed in her words, in the circles that burned on the stones, in the thunder that rolled through her bones.

"You swear you will tend his grave," she told Ana. "But I swear revenge on the Vila who put him there. I swear release for his soul. On the Light I swear it. On my gifts I swear it. On the memory of Niko Alekhin, Alpha of his pack, prince among Shadows, I swear he will be no slave to the Dark."

She stood, still burning, and limped up the path to her cottage, leaving Ana alone in the rain.

47

GADREEL

The Watcher Gadreel strolled the corridors of his new home, scheming.

He didn't mind it here. It was novel, which was a rare thing. Gadreel had been alive for thousands of years, and there were few experiences he hadn't been able to claim. The past few months, though, had been a time of wonders. First the Darkness. Then the surprise of Dimi Ivanova. Then Sammael's foolishness, and the little drama in the clearing. Now this.

It was convenient that Sammael's harebrained Vila had done most of Gadreel's hard work for him. In one fell swoop, Dimi Ivanova had been robbed of her Shadow, and the Darkness had been temporarily sated by claiming both that ridiculous Vila and the black dog. It had tried to eat Dimi Ivanova as well, and Gadreel had resigned himself to intervene on her behalf. But, wondrous creature that she was, she'd saved herself. He'd known she had the strength to stand against the Dark. That had been the proof.

Of course, she'd also knocked Gadreel unconscious and sent him hurtling through that damned portal, which had been aggravating. But that was just more evidence of her strength.

She would have cast him into the Void, and his three companions with him, if he hadn't woken at the last moment and leveraged his bond with the Darkness to take control, steering the four of them to the wasteland between the demonic realms rather than into the Void's lightless pit. It was a real shame that rescuing himself had accidentally resulted in saving the Shadow, the Vila, and the ever-aggravating Sammael. But it had been fortunate, too. They had their uses, especially the Shadow.

So, into the wasteland the four of them had gone, and from there, it had been easy enough for Gadreel to snap his fingers and transport himself back to his own realm. He assumed Sammael had done the same, not that he'd stuck around to find out.

Yes, Gadreel had gone home, long enough to assure himself that the Darkness had oozed down into his throne room once more. But it wasn't as if he had *stayed* there. He had business elsewhere, and now that a new, unexpected portal had sprung into existence, he found himself traversing it with great frequency. After all, he had a prisoner to monitor, and he could hardly do that from such a great distance. So here he was, in this glorious place, which was rich with entertainment. Humans were weak and greedy, yes, but they did make such lovely playthings. And their little melodramas—who loved whom, who'd betrayed whom for the sake of power or money —amused him so.

A low moan sounded from the vicinity of his feet, and, annoyed at the distraction, Gadreel cast his gaze downward. His prisoner was huddled there, arms wrapped around his knees, awaiting Gadreel's command. The Mark on the prisoner's shoulder gleamed dully in the light from the torches. Gadreel was quite proud of it; it had been an inspired touch. He supposed he could thank Sammael for that. Watching his fellow demon bond with a creature of the Light had been...instructional. Also, boring; Gadreel preferred his infernal unions with a side of bacchanalia. But the little drama between Dimi Ivanova, her Shadow, and the Vila had been entertaining, after all. And it had given him this excellent idea, so he could hardly complain.

The prisoner moaned again, and Gadreel prodded the man with his foot. "Shut up, would you?" he said. "I'm thinking. Or I would be, if you'd cease that irritating sound."

The prisoner's eyes rolled up toward him at once, wide with terror. His moaning tapered off into a whine, then stopped altogether. It was amusing, watching him bend to Gadreel's every whim. And instrumental to what Gadreel had in mind. But, again, boring. Dimi Ivanova would never submit to him this easily. She would pose a challenge, he was sure of it.

Soon, he would have her in his hands. Together, they would right the balance and banish the hungry Darkness, and then he would secure his base of power with the Dimi at his side. She was undone right now, fragile; Gadreel had seen as much in the clearing. Perhaps she would even be grateful for what he could offer her. Look what the Venom of God had done with his weak Vila and her hapless Shadow. It was pathetic, the way Sammael had been felled by his desire for that woman. What Gadreel wanted from Dimi Ivanova was far greater. Noble, even.

And if, after that, he chose to do...other things...with her, then that was his prerogative, was it not?

Gadreel licked his lips at the thought, and the prisoner's eyes grew even wider than before. Which reminded him: there were places his prisoner needed to be. People who were expecting him. And it simply wouldn't do to be late. His guests might get...ideas.

Gadreel yanked the prisoner to his feet and surveyed him. The prisoner gazed back, chin high, his expression as prideful as the first time Gadreel had seen it. Waiting for instructions. The contrast made Gadreel gleeful. There was nothing quite like making a vainglorious creature submit to your will.

"Leave this room," Gadreel said quietly. "Do what you must. But remember: I can hear through your ears. See through your eyes. And should you deviate from my requests, I will damage you." Not too much, of course; Gadreel needed him. But enough.

He smiled at the prisoner. The prisoner, predictably, flinched. Then he scuttled from the room, walking backward as if by keeping his eyes on Gadreel, he could defend himself against an unfortunate end.

Watching him go, Gadreel sighed. Mortal beings were such fools, their every action easily anticipated. All except Dimi Ivanova, who managed to thwart all of his expectations. What fun they would have together, now that her troublesome Shadow was out of the way. She would see what it was like to stand by the side of a truly powerful entity. To fight for the Light alongside the Dark. To accomplish the unimaginable. How delicious it would be.

Oh, yes.

When next they met, he would surprise Dimi Ivanova as she had surprised him.

48

KATERINA

Katerina stood in Baba's cottage, waiting for the old
woman to arrive. Her stomach growled, but she
ignored it, her attention focused on scanning the
books that filled Baba's shelves. *Magick and Mysterious Herbs.*
Treating Demonic Wounds. The Ancient History of the Magiya. All
of it was useless to her—though what had she expected? A
volume entitled *How to Rescue Your Shadow from the Clutches of a
Dark Vila and Set His Soul Free?*

When Katerina was younger, her mother used to tell her
stories about a famous volume called the Book of the Lost. The
complement of the Book of the Light, it was said to have been
inscribed by the Saints themselves. No one alive had seen it, her
mother said. No one knew for sure that it really existed. Still,
tales of it had been passed down through the generations—the
secrets it held, the miracles it could conjure.

Katerina had joked that of course it was called the *Book of
the Lost*—if it was real, which she doubted, it had been
misplaced centuries before. What else would you call such a
thing? But as she perused Baba's shelves, paging through one
pointless book after another, she remembered how she and Ana

used to joke about the miraculous spells the book might contain: *How to produce an endless supply of sugared syrnyky. How to spell Baba Petrova so she'd sleep through training. How to give demons duck-heads and make them dance.*

That was what she needed right now—a book that contained miracles. Too bad such a thing didn't exist.

There were just five days left until the Reaping, and Katerina still had no idea how to make good on any of her promises—to save Niko's soul, to protect Kalach, to bring her friends in Rivki home. The fields were failing badly, the wheat withered. The fruit and vegetables were dying on the vine. And the hunters were afraid to go too far afield, lest they fall victim to an attack of Grigori or of the Darkness itself. There was an inky nothingness nibbling at the edges of Kalach, and the few times hunters had gone out, flanked by a Shadow and Dimi pair, they'd come back empty-handed. Even the animals in the woods acted spooked and anxious, as if they sensed the evil that was afoot.

Katerina had volunteered to go out with the hunters, including Konstantin. To protect them. But the hunters had shied from her offer, and Baba had flat-out refused to allow it. Part of it, she realized, was that she was a distraction; no one trusted her anymore, and they could ill afford errors with the Darkness on the loose. But part of it was that her powers were no longer under her control. Without her Shadow, she was ungrounded. And out in the woods, without a black dog, she was vulnerable to possession, should the Darkness come.

She was a liability as well as a pariah.

Moodily, Katerina prodded a loose floorboard with the toe of her boot. She was sure she knew what Baba wanted: to choose a new Shadow to whom to bind Katerina before the Kniaz's emissary arrived to take her away. It would be far too dangerous to allow her to travel all the way to Rivki without such a thing. The idea made her sick.

Marrying Maksim or Konstantin was out of the question now, thank the Saints; aside from the fact that she didn't want them, they regarded her with disgust and fear, and Katerina would never force herself upon anyone. This, at least, was her choice; if she chose to wed someone in Rivki for the sake of bearing a Dimichild, so be it. But being bonded to a new Shadow...that was Baba's prerogative.

The thought both infuriated and terrified Katerina. As long as she wasn't bound to another Shadow, the potential to rekindle her bond with Niko existed. How could she save him—call him back to her—if she were bonded to another?

But how could she travel to Rivki unprotected, her soul ripe for the picking? She owed it to Kalach, to Iriska, to Lara, Svetlana, and Natalya to stay strong. To be able to defend the realm against the Darkness.

It was a terrible conundrum, and one that Katerina had no idea how to solve.

But solve it she must. She couldn't stay here. Throughout Kalach, the villagers had begun to look pinched and starved. Spring was usually a time of rejuvenation, of berries that grew tart and ripe tomatoes that bloomed bright and bursting. Nothing went to waste; whatever didn't get eaten was canned, jarred, preserved, and stored. But now, little remained to eat, and the pitiful amount of grain left in the storehouses after the winter had been set aside for the Kniaz. There was barely enough left for Kalach to make its tithe, and if the village failed to do so, Katerina shuddered to think what the nobleman might do.

Worse still was what had become of the Blood Moon. With just five days left until its height, it ought to be growing fuller and redder each night, casting a crimson glow over Kalach. But instead, as it waxed, its color faded, blanching into a familiar pale shade that sent chills through Katerina.

The Bone Moon came but once a year. Yet here it was, rising again. Through the window of Baba's cottage, Katerina could see the rim of it, peeking above the trees.

Whatever this boded, it was nothing good.

Shuddering, she stepped back from her pointless perusal of the shelves as the front door slammed open and Baba Petrova stepped through, her white hair mussed by the wind and her lined face thinner than Katerina had ever seen it. "Dimi Ivanova," she said in greeting, taking off her shawl and hanging it on the hook by the door.

"You wanted to see me?" Katerina said. Her stomach growled again, and she pressed a palm against it, doing her best to suppress the sound.

Baba Petrova's eyes softened with sympathy, but all she said was, "Kalach needs you, Katerina. Iriska needs you. Normally, after the death of a Shadow, we would give you time to mourn. Time, at least, until the next Bone Moon, so your bonding ceremony could take place under its sacred eye. But as you see…"

She gestured through her window, at the rind of moon that had risen even higher above the trees. "The Kniaz's emissary arrives in less than a week. I hesitate to bond you beneath this waxing moon, as it has clearly been brought about by Dark forces. But what choice do I have?"

"Please don't," Katerina whispered. She thought she could bear this, had braced herself for it. But as she pictured the ceremony—Niko's amulet being torn from her neck, repeating the vows she had sworn to her beloved Shadow to another—her heart crumbled into dust.

"You will do it, Katerina," Baba said, drawing herself up to her full height. "Tonight. There is no time to waste."

Katerina's stomach dropped. "But…but who…?"

"You'll see," Baba said, her voice brusque. "I've chosen. Now go, and prepare yourself. When the moon is high, you will pledge yourself to another."

~

BONDING CEREMONIES WERE PRIVATE, sacred. Normally they took place in Baba's cottage, with the ancient Dimi their only witness. But this ceremony was different. Baba and the Elders had decided to make an example out of Katerina, to quell some of the village's anxiety by showing that she was, indeed, bonded to a new Shadow.

Dressed in her black mourning gown, runes of loss and sorrow embroidered into its fabric, Katerina stood opposite the man who was to become her Shadow: Valentin, who'd lost his Dimi in a Grigori attack eight months before. He was a good man, a kind man. But he might as well have been a houseplant for all the impression he made on Katerina.

Like her, Valentin was supposed to be allowed the traditional year of mourning for a Dimi or Shadow who had lost their match. He wore all black, and the expression on his lined face was one of resignation. Katerina could see he wanted to be bonded to her no more than she wanted to be bonded to him. Polina, his Dimi, had been quiet and dutiful, a waterwitch who was as unlike Katerina as a kitten and a snow leopard. Katerina was sure that, of the three unbonded, mature Shadows in the village, he had been chosen on purpose, to gentle her.

She would have laughed at the thought, if she wasn't on the verge of crying.

Please, she begged the Saints, the spirits, anyone who would listen. *Please don't make me do this.*

The villagers ringed the square. Inside their circle stood the Shadows, Dimis, and Vila, with the Elders beside them. And in the center stood Katerina and Valentin, with Baba Petrova by their sides. Next to her stood a pot beneath which a rowan-fire burned. The water in it bubbled high, waiting for Baba Petrova to spill the ink that would make a fresh Mark upon Valentin's arm. Waiting for Katerina's blood.

Her magic clamored inside her, desperate for escape. Grimly, Katerina clung to it, afraid of what would happen if it got loose with everyone watching. What if she hurt them? Killed them? What if she killed *Valentin?* What would happen to her then?

"Katerina Ivanova," Baba said, and silence fell over the square. "Valentin Kuzvim. We are gathered together today to witness the sacred joining of Dimi and Shadow. Both of you once cleaved to another; today we wash away the traces of that pairing. You will start afresh, and honor each other, and fight by each other's side. And by so doing, you will honor the vow you once made to your Shadow and Dimi, who have passed beyond the veil. Do you swear this oath to me, before witnesses, so that you may begin the bonding ceremony with clear hearts?"

Katerina tried to speak and couldn't. Her mouth was dry. When she opened it, all that came forth was a croak. The crowd murmured in disapproval, and Katerina could have sworn she heard a whispered *Shadow-killer* in its midst.

Giving her an alarmed glance, Valentin squared his broad shoulders. "I do," he said, his deep voice carrying across the stones of the square.

Katerina's teeth chattered. Her eyes roved the crowd and settled on Ana's face. The other Dimi's eyes were filled with tears, and she touched two fingers to her heart. But then she nodded, and Katerina knew what she was saying, as surely as if Ana had spoken. *This must be done. For your soul. For Kalach. Don't make it worse.*

Katerina dug deep, praying for courage. "I—" she began, and bit her tongue so hard, she tasted blood. "I d-d—"

She couldn't bring herself to finish the word. But apparently Baba decided that this was good enough, because she bent and lifted a knife from the stones, passing it once, twice, thrice through the flames. She reached for Katerina's arm, holding it above the cauldron as she had done eight years ago.

"One for the fire," she said, and raised the blade.

Katerina braced herself for the pain. *I'm sorry, Niko,* she thought desperately. *I'm so, so sorry.*

Down came the blade, glinting in the light of the false Bone Moon and the glow of the flames. It was three inches from Katerina's arm. Two. One.

"Stop!"

For a moment, Katerina thought the word had somehow issued from her own throat. She raised her free hand to it, disbelieving. But then, the crowd scattered like pigeons as a familiar palomino cantered through them. On its back was Andrei, the Kniaz's lieutenant, who Katerina had thrown into a grove of birch trees weeks before.

He reined up, his horse's sides heaving. "I see I'm just in time," he said. Behind him came his companions, but Katerina ignored them. She only had eyes for Andrei, and his pronouncement, which had saved her.

"What's the meaning of this?" Baba snapped. "You dare to interrupt our most sacred ritual?"

"You sent a rider to Rivki," Andrei said, his tone as dismissive as Katerina remembered it. "Informing us of what had happened here. The Kniaz dispatched me at once to ride with all haste. He'll come in person to Kalach on the night of the full moon, bringing a Shadow of his choosing for you to bind to her. Not just anyone is fit to join the hallowed ranks of the Druzhina, after all. So whatever this is"—he waved a contemptuous hand at the bubbling pot, the gathering of villagers, and Katerina and Valentin, standing in the center of it all—"you will disband it at once. For Dimi Ivanova, treacherous though she may be, has another future in store."

Katerina had never expected to be grateful to Andrei, of all people. But even as the Elders murmured in disapproval and the villagers whispered to each other in dismay, as Valentin stepped back with an expression of unmistakable relief, she felt a rush of gratitude so strong, it nearly brought her to her knees.

So what if she were to be bonded to a stranger? She would deal with that challenge when it came.

She had five days to save Niko, before she was tied to another. Five days, when his soul and hers might still be one. And standing there under the light of the rising Bone Moon, she vowed to make the most of them.

She didn't care what it took. She would find a way.

49
SAMMAEL

S ammael had done everything for his Vila, and still it was not enough.

He had recreated Kalach in his own realm, complete with the cobblestone village square, quaint shops, and rolling fields, which were not blighted here, but rather ripe with wheat. Even the accursed chapel in which his Vila had married her Shadow. Much to his minor demons' annoyance, he had commanded them to take the forms of Kalach's villagers, not pinched and starved as they had been since their crops had failed, but healthy and hale. He'd recreated every detail of Elena's small cottage, the one she'd shared with her friend Alyona, down to the runes that were meant to keep demons such as himself out.

Of course, no matter how they *looked*, the runes here spoke of different things: temptation and trickery, lust and craving, eternal hunger for power. But those were not such bad things, were they? After all, they had brought Elena and Sammael together. She had called out, there in the ruins of the abandoned chapel in the woods, and he had answered.

Not the Saints. Him.

He had given Elena everything she had asked for, and more. Had made of her a shining, burning thing that blazed up with infernal fire, sending his Grigori essence twining throughout her body, wedding his Dark gifts with her allegiance to the Light. She was meant to bear fruit, just as years ago, his congress with the demon Lilith had given rise to Asmodeus, prince among demons. Elena had been so beautiful, burning with their shared power as her hellfire licked at the form of the fallen Shadow. But there had been something else within her then, a power greater even than his own. He could sense it: the Darkness that had consumed Drezna and Satvala. It had poured from her, even as it fed on her. He had never felt anything like it.

He sat on a chair in the replica of Elena's cottage, listening as she cooed to the shade of her Shadow. What remained of Niko Alekhin lay curled at her feet, in the form of his black dog. Sammael watched as Elena reached down and ran a hand through its fur. "Change for me," she urged him. "Change, and then we can be together."

The black dog flinched from her touch, as it did every time. And as it did every time, Elena's lovely face contorted with rage. "You should be grateful," she hissed at the dog. "I saved you from *her*. But you still want her, don't you? Even now, when you lie at my feet, you think of her. Well, I will cure you of this ailment, if it's the last thing I do. You will worship me, as you should, for I am your *wife*."

She raised a hand and struck the dog across the muzzle once, then again. "Change," she shrieked. "Or, much as it pains me to do it, you will spend the night in chains. For your own good."

Sammael watched as the dog raised its head, defiance clear in the depths of its gray eyes, and bared its teeth. A low growl emanated from its chest, and Elena straightened. The hellfire that had consumed her in the clearing began to heat her once again, until she blazed with it.

"You dare to growl at me? Me, Elena-of-the-Void, beloved of Sammael?" She waved a hand at the black dog, clenching her fingers into a fist, and *tugged*. The dog let out a desperate yelp, but there was no resisting: Elena pulled his human form from within, like a butterfly being forcibly dragged from a chrysalis.

"Elena," Sammael warned, but she ignored him, her attention trained on the crumpled form at her feet.

Sammael was all for employing violence when necessary. He'd had his fun with the Shadow when the creature had first arrived; he made a most amusing plaything, what with his ability to withstand pain. Sammael had enjoyed testing his limits. But no such thing was required here. The Shadow was already at Elena's mercy. She gained nothing from this show of force. And after all, she belonged to Sammael now, did she not? They were each other's. It was infuriating that she still harbored...feelings...for this pathetic creature.

And pathetic he was. Sammael had seen Shadows shift before; it was a natural, seamless transformation. This was different; it was slow, and agonizing. The dog fought it, but his power belonged to the Light, and here in the Underworld, there was precious little of that. It was no match for Elena's Darkness. She pulled, and he growled, and when she was done, the Shadow lay naked, panting and bleeding on the wooden floor of her cottage, in his human form.

"You see," Elena said to him, her voice laden with satisfaction. "You are mine. You do as I say. And now you will serve me, as you should have done when you took me to wed."

The Shadow didn't speak. He just glared at her, and in his silver-gray eyes burned an unmistakable, burning hatred.

"You will do as I wish," Elena said, each word imbued with

the force of her power. "As I deserve. And you'll see. We belong together, Niko. You were always meant to be mine."

She stood, the skirts of the diaphanous, iridescent gown Sammael had had made for her swishing as she made her way toward the bedroom. Then she perched on the side of the bed, her legs coquettishly crossed at the ankles, and beckoned. "Crawl to me, my Shadow," she said, her voice soft and deceptively gentle. "Now."

The Shadow didn't want to do it; Sammael could see the resistance in every fiber of his body. But Elena beckoned again, and even he, the Venom of God, could feel the pull. "Crawl," she said, and now there was nothing gentle in her voice at all.

The Shadow crawled, his eyes straight ahead, looking not at Elena but into the distance, at whatever thoughts occupied a being such as him. One caught between worlds, chained to the Dark but sworn to the Light. And Elena watched him, her gaze hungry and avid, as if the man came to her of his own free will.

Perhaps, it occurred to Sammael dismally, she could no longer tell the difference.

He had thought, when he first encountered Elena Lisova in that abandoned chapel, that her gifts came from the union of her Vila heritage with his own power. It had been everything he had dreamed of, when the Watchers fell; that he would find a woman to lie with who was aligned with the Light. She would want him as he wanted her, and from their union would come a power to best all others. Not merely the minor demon spawn of Watchers and human women, but a queen among Grigori, a warrior who would fight at his side and defeat Gadreel once and for all. He, Sammael, would rule once again below as he had ruled above.

But he had been wrong. Elena had grown so powerful, so quickly. And he had come to believe that her gifts came not from her ability to give birth to Vila and Shadowchildren, but from the Darkness that had been unleashed upon their land. The very things he'd come to love most about her—her innocence, her supposedly open heart—had been compromised. She treated the Shadow's shade like a possession or a pet. And though she claimed to love him, how Sammael saw her treat him wasn't love.

This wasn't the woman the spark of humanity inside Sammael had fallen for. But his demonic nature still drew him to her, like a glossy, crisp, red apple full of poison. It was a terrible, addictive thing.

And yet it wasn't him she wanted. It was the shade of this broken, desperate man.

"Rise," Elena said to the Shadow at her feet. "Rise, and serve me."

Niko Alekhin rose at her command, all of his natural grace gone. It was as if his body was being yanked to its feet by a pair of uncoordinated puppeteers. But Elena didn't notice. She was too busy smiling up into his face, tucking a lock of hair coyly behind her ear.

"First, tell me you love me," she demanded. "Say it now, so Sammael and I can hear. In front of a witness, declare your love for me, Elena-of-the-Void, beautiful even among Vila, sworn Queen of Darkness."

Sammael cleared his throat. This was a terrible waste of time, especially now, with Darkness devouring two of the Seven Villages and showing no sign of slowing. He had a realm to attend to, and a mystery to solve, but truth be told, he didn't trust Elena alone with the shade of her Shadow. She had shown herself to be capable of dreadful things. And increasingly, Sammael was beginning to believe he would need Niko Alekhin as a bargaining chip. It wouldn't do to have Elena damage him.

"Elena, you've had your fun," he told her, getting to his feet.

"Let the Shadow be. We have more important things to attend to."

But she shook her head, eyes fixed on Niko's. "Tell me you love me," she said again. "I know you do. She corrupted you. Despoiled you. But here, with me, we'll make it right. I'll save you. You'll be pure again."

Not for the first time, Sammael began to wonder if Elena had lost her mind. After all, she had been the one to wield the knife that had brought the Shadow down. He had never seen a creature of the Light converted to the Dark, not since the Watchers and the Archangels fell. Maybe her soul had been unable to withstand the transformation.

"Say you love me!" Elena insisted. "Say it!"

But the Shadow remained stonily silent, his gaze fixed somewhere over Elena's shoulder and his face expressionless. Even when Elena's hand cracked across his cheek hard enough to leave an impression behind, still he did not speak.

"I'll make you tell me," she snarled at him. "You'll howl it when I've finished with you."

The Shadow curled his lip, his eyes refocusing squarely on Elena's. And then, at last, he spoke. "I'll never love you," he said, each word tipped with venom. "You can force me into the form of my black dog and back again, but I'll never protect you. No matter what you do to me, what lengths you drive me to, my heart will never be yours."

Fury overtook Elena's features. "Even still, you're under her spell! Even here, with me, she wields her power. But I'm stronger than she can imagine. And I have all of eternity to outlast her." She caressed Niko's cheek. The Shadow flinched from her touch, but Elena grabbed his chin and held him still. "Say you love me," she said again as the Darkness poured from her, curling around every syllable, rich with compulsion. "Speak."

The Shadow's jaw worked, the expression in his gray eyes furious. Then his mouth opened and his voice came, reluctant and low, as if ripped from his throat the way his human body had been torn from the form of his black dog. "Elena, I..." he began, choking on the words like it poisoned him to speak them.

Sammael could watch no more of this. He strode from the cottage, pulling the door open and stalking toward his palace, the place he'd called home before Elena had come to the Underworld. It was made entirely from black stone, with tiny silver chips that glinted in the light of the white-hot sun that lit his realm. On the way, he passed demons impersonating farmers, healers, artisans, butchers. He wanted to pulverize them all, and they shrank from him, turning nervously to their appointed tasks.

Sammael strode past them, past the administrative offices that dealt with the everyday responsibilities of running his realm—requisitioning of wayward souls for purgatorial labor, recruitment of minor demons into his armies—and down the road that led to his palace. He nodded at the bird-headed guards who flanked the entrance and stomped inside, letting the doors slam behind him. They were studded with the eyes of his vanquished enemies, which blinked balefully as he disappeared into the cool darkness of the place where he felt most at home.

He drew a deep breath, settling himself. And then he squared his shoulders and made his way down the hall, to his scrying room. Much as he hated to admit it, he needed to talk to Gadreel. As the two most powerful Grigori, they needed to discuss what was becoming of the world above ground, and why the veil between the Underworld and Iriska was thinning. The implications could be dire, and ultimately, the two of them were on the same side. It would do neither of them any good to see the realms they'd so carefully built sucked into the Void. Especially now that Sammael had Elena to look after, such a thing would be disastrous. It would take millennia to rebuild.

He made his way down the opulent hallway of his palace, past the room that he had hoped one day to make Elena's. It was befitting of a queen, with its canopied, four-poster bed, mosaic tile floor, and lush, sweeping murals. Perhaps, when she tired of her plaything of a Shadow, when she ceased grieving for her old life, he could bring her here. Together, they would start anew. He would rule with her at his side.

At last, Sammael came to his scrying room. He pressed his palm to the door, which swung wide, and stepped through, locking it behind him.

The room was just as he had left it. The floor was covered by a thick burgundy carpet, inlaid with an intricate pattern of vines. Bookshelves lined the walls. And in the middle of the room stood a fountain, the water flowing downward from a pitcher held by the nude statue of Lilith that stood in its midst. Lilith, Sammael's first love. He wondered what she would think if she could see him now.

Crossing to the fountain, which served as his scrying pool, Sammael lifted both hands. He passed them across the water, and it rippled in response. "Show me Gadreel, Dark Angel of War, Wall of God, Silent Sentinel, among the first of the Fallen Watchers," he said. It was quite a mouthful, but then that was Gadreel for you. Never one accolade when four would do. "Invite me into his sanctum, where I will come, bearing assurance that I mean him no harm."

Typically, this was like knocking on a locked door; Gadreel could choose whether or not to answer, and frequently ignored Sammael, just for sport. At the least, he often chose to keep Sammael waiting, like a peon relegated to lingering in His Majesty's antechamber. Sammael had resigned himself to this, and was examining his nails in an effort to manage his impending boredom when the water in the fountain flickered, rose in a wave, and then reformed, allowing him entry into Gadreel's tower.

Well, this was new. Perhaps Gadreel had, for once, realized that the threat that confronted them was more significant than their mutual enmity. Wonders, indeed, never ceased.

The water stilled, growing transparent, and Sammael cleared his throat. "Gadreel, I need to speak with you," he said. "There are pressing matters, and we need to put aside our differences for once and discuss them."

The Wall of God didn't deign to reply, and Sammael sniffed, irritated. "The least you could do is answer me," he said. "Why bother to let me in if you're not going to be polite enough to speak?"

But Gadreel still didn't say a word, and when Sammael peered into the water, he could see why: he wasn't there.

A prickle of unease ran along Sammael's spine, juddering along his shoulder blades, over the skin that concealed his wings. This wasn't the sort of trick Gadreel played. His pranks were usually far more intricate, and involved considerable amounts of bloodshed.

But if Gadreel wasn't here, then why had Sammael been granted access to his throne room?

Sammael gazed more deeply into the pool of water, his gaze sharpening. And then he froze. His dark eyes widened.

Gadreel's usually-impeccable throne room was *destroyed*. His throne of bones and velvet still had pride of place, but at the center of the room, where his statue of lesser demons kneeling at the Watchers' feet and his collection of torture implements usually stood, there was nothing but a massive pile of rubble, extending as far as Sammael could see. Human bones protruded from the wreckage, and the rotting carcasses of horses, and what looked like an entire village—

Wait a minute.

Sammael stepped closer, dropping to his knees by the side of the fountain. He peered as closely as he could. And then he saw what he could have sworn was impossible: the margin of a rune of protection, etched deep into the splintered bits of a windowsill. The harder he looked, the more of them he noticed.

This was all that remained of Drezna and Satvala. He would have sworn his wings on it.

By all the infernal fires, what was the wreckage of the two villages that had been devoured by the Darkness doing in his arch-enemy's throne room?

There was only one answer to this question: Because Gadreel had done something to make them materialize there. And whatever he had done, it hadn't gone as planned. Gadreel was many things—bloodthirsty, faithless, vain, power-hungry. But one thing he was *not* was careless. His throne room, with its chair made from the bones of his victims, was his pride and joy. He would never willingly have brought such devastation upon it. Nor would he have left it this way, if he had to look at it every day.

Which begged the question...where *was* Gadreel?

The abomination of a demon had followed Sammael, Elena, and the Shadow when Dimi Ivanova had nearly blasted them all back into the Void with the force of her magic. Somehow, they had landed in the wasteland between the realms, and Sammael had had to conjure a collar and chain to put around the Shadow's neck, because he'd leapt at Elena as soon as all four of his paws had touched the ground and made a concerted effort to tear out her throat.

Gadreel had laughed and laughed. And then he'd knelt by the Shadow and whispered something into the beast's ear before rising with a self-satisfied smirk, winking at Elena—*winking!*—and vanishing back to his own realm.

At least, that was where Sammael had assumed he'd gone. Now, he wasn't so sure.

He leaned closer still, almost pressing his eye against the water, scrying for all he was worth. And then he saw it, seeping ink-black and insidious through cracks in the walls, swarming like clouds of incensed bees around the edges of the massive hole that the collapse of the two villages had made in the ceiling.

The Darkness was reforming itself in Gadreel's throne room. It had made itself at home there, as if that was where it belonged.

A sickening feeling took hold of Sammael. Because there was only one answer to this unasked question, too.

The Angel of War had called upon the Darkness, and the Darkness had come.

All of this—everything that had happened—was Gadreel's fault. *He* had unleashed the Darkness, doubtless in an attempt to defeat Sammael once and for all, and he'd lost control of it. *He* had let loose the force that had razed the two villages, not because his gifts had grown so strong, but because he had lost his grip on a power greater than any fallen angel could ever hope to harness. *He* had threatened the survival of both their worlds. *He* had corrupted Sammael's beautiful, innocent Vila. He was responsible for all of it.

Sammael got to his feet, vibrating with rage. He tilted his head back and howled, the sound so filled with fury, it shook the foundations of his scrying room. Paintings fell from the walls. Books tumbled from the shelves. High above, the crystal chandelier shattered, its shards falling like rain. And Sammael's wings burst from his back, obsidian and massive, his body assuming its natural form.

He would make Gadreel pay for this, wherever the hapless Watcher might be. He would rid himself of that troublesome Shadow and gain control of the Darkness. And then he would have his Vila for himself, and together they would accomplish great things.

Staring down into the rippling image of Gadreel's decimated throne room, his bloodied wings beating against the glass-flecked air, the Venom of God began to formulate a plan.

50

KATERINA

Katerina rubbed her eyes, which burned with exhaustion. She had spent the past twenty-four hours reading everything she could think of. She'd gone through every book in Kalach's small library and Baba's cottage. No matter how she searched, she found nothing to indicate that a dilemma such as hers had ever existed. In all the tomes she had perused, there were no clues to breaking a Dark curse laid on a Shadow's soul. How to lay a Shadow to rest, once slain in battle, yes. There were blessings aplenty for that. But not for this.

She slumped in her chair in the library, suppressing a yawn. It didn't help that all she'd eaten was watery potato soup, flavored with the last of the herbs in her personal store. It had only been a few weeks since the beginning of the blight, but already her hipbones pressed outward beneath the thin material of her gown.

This couldn't go on. They would all starve.

According to Andrei, the failure of the crops had not yet spread to Rivki. But surely it would, and then what? No one would be safe.

There was a knock on the door of the library, and Ana stepped through, her smile widening at the sight of Katerina. "I thought I'd find you here," she said, taking the chair next to her fellow Dimi. "Look what I brought you."

Bringing a hand out from behind her back, she presented Katerina with a perfect, beautiful roll, sprinkled with seeds. It was still warm, and Ana unfolded her hand to show Katerina the tiny flame burning beneath it.

"A gift," Ana said.

Katerina's eyes prickled with tears. "Surely you're hungry, Ana. I can't take this."

"Nonsense." Ana pressed the roll into her palm. "As hard as you've been working, you need to eat, Katerina. I...I wish I could help. Maybe I could look through these books with you, or..."

She cast a doubtful glance at the teetering stack of volumes, and despite herself, Katerina bit back a smile. Reading had always been the bane of Ana's existence. For one thing, it required sitting still for way too long. And for another, she'd always complained that the letters danced, turning backward and upside down and blurring off the page. For her to make an offer like this meant a lot to Katerina...perhaps even more than the present in her hand.

Accepting the roll from Ana, Katerina tore it in two, then gave half back to her friend. "You've already helped," she said. "You're the only one who's stuck by me. The only one who dares besmirch their reputation by being seen in my company. And now this." She took a bite of the ambrosial roll, chewing as slowly as possible to savor it. "I'm more grateful than I can say."

Ana pressed her lips together. "I've been thinking, Katerina. I know I told you that I would stay here to tend Niko's grave. And...and I will. But what if Alexei and I rode to the Magiya? Not now, but maybe the night that the Kniaz arrives to Reap you. It'll be chaos, I'm sure of it. Already there's much talk in the village of making preparations. He and I could leave then. We could ask the scholars if there's a way to save Niko. To free his soul." She gestured at the pile of books. "I know that's what you're doing. What you're trying so desperately to find. But if there's an answer here, you would have discovered it by now. And I just—I can't stand to see you..."

Her voice trailed off, and Katerina patted her friend's hand. "No," she said around the lump in her throat. "I won't risk you that way. Look what happened to Nadia and Oriel. I did this, Ana. Fixing it is my responsibility. Not yours."

"You don't have to do everything by yourself!" Ana said, wiping furiously at her eyes. "I know how prideful you are, Katerina. How stubborn. But just...just let me help you. Please."

Numbly, Katerina shook her head. "I told you. You've already helped. I...I care for you like a sister, Ana. I can't drag you down with me. And besides," she said, managing a small smile, "Kalach needs all of its defenders. I can't ask you and Alexei to abandon your duty now, with three Shadow-Dimi pairs away at Rivki and me about to leave, too. The village has already lost one alpha Shadow; it can't lose another. Much as I appreciate your offer, I can't be that selfish. I've already done enough."

Ana heaved a sigh. "I thought you'd say that. At least let me help you put these books away. And then I'll walk you home. Again."

No doubt, her fellow Dimi was thinking of the mob that had attacked Katerina. Of the chant, *Shadow-killer,* the fusillade of stones. Katerina couldn't ask Ana to put herself in the way of that, either.

"I'll do it," she said, managing a small smile. "There are some I still haven't read all the way through, believe it or not. You go home. Rest. And thank you for the roll."

She crammed the rest of it into her mouth and made exaggerated moans of delight, which elicited a reluctant giggle from Ana. "You're welcome," her best friend said. "Don't stay here too late, Katerina. That fool who's wandering about, Andrei...I don't trust him."

"Nor do I," Katerina said softly, remembering how Andrei's eyes had lingered on Elena. How he'd insinuated Katerina's place was in Kniaz Sergey's bed. "Nor do I."

She watched as Ana walked from the library, closing the door behind her.

AFTER SHE'D FINISHED every delectable morsel of the roll, even dabbing the crumbs from the table with a moistened finger, and reshelved all of the books, Katerina sat alone in the library, head buried in her hands. She refused to believe her quest was at an end. There were four days left until the Reaping, and she needed to use every one of them to save her Shadow.

She wished she could talk with Sofi. Other than Ana—and Niko, of course—the other Dimi had been her closest friend. But Sofi had more reason to hate Katerina than almost anyone. Because of what she and Niko had done, Drezna had fallen. Sofi and her Shadow had lost friends, fellow warriors, parents, home. She probably detested Katerina now. Maybe Sofi, Trina Samarin, and Dimi Zakharova were sitting around a rowan-fire in Rivki at this very moment, listing all the ways that Katerina was a disgrace to the realm.

If so, then Katerina deserved every word. But was it uncharitable for her to think that, homeless or not, at least Sofi and Damien still had each other? What would she herself do, if faced with a choice between saving Niko or Kalach?

She hoped that, whatever befell her now, one would not

preclude the other. That Baba had been wrong when she'd said, *Katerina, you have doomed us all.*

She wouldn't give up. She couldn't. There had to be a way.

I told you I would stay here to tend Niko's grave, Ana had said. Well, Katerina hadn't left yet. Maybe that was something she could do, while she tried desperately to free her Shadow's soul.

She stood, drawing a deep breath, and slipped from the library, making her way through the darkened village. No one spoke to her as she crossed the square, where Maksim and his father were putting up the last of the tents for the celebration to welcome the Kniaz in the gathering dark. No one stopped her when she passed by the tavern where Andrei and his cronies sipped watered-down ale, served by a woman who had once asked Katerina if the Dimi would bless her first-born child. She wondered if she'd become invisible. Or if the villagers had come to hate her so much, they could no longer bear to acknowledge her existence. The few people who spared her a glance gazed at her with such disgust, she could hardly stand to meet their eyes.

In better times, having Kniaz Sergey visit Kalach would be a tremendous honor. But now, when the village had so few resources, putting together an event worthy of welcoming the nobleman was devastating. If they failed to supply the Kniaz with enough food and drink, he'd be insulted, and Saints knew what he would do to them. But if they offered him what little they had left, then the villagers would starve in earnest.

Once again, this had somehow become Katerina's fault, even though she hadn't asked for the Kniaz to come here. Even though the idea of becoming the man's plaything, bonding to a stranger, and leaving Niko behind was the last thing she wanted.

An undeniable sense of relief washed over her as she stepped from the lights of the village onto the path that led to

Niko's grave. Here, at least, there was no one to stare at her with accusing, hungry eyes. No one to judge or ignore her.

She knew she shouldn't do this. That being alone out here, with the Darkness gnawing at the edges of Kalach, was dangerous. But who knew how many more chances she'd have to pay her respects to her Shadow? When she left for Rivki, she might never come home again. Any number of disasters might befall her between now and the rise of the false Bone Moon. If this was her last chance to sit by her Shadow's grave, she would seize it, and damn the consequences.

She walked as silently as she could through the trees, along the path that led to Niko's grave. She didn't dare use her magic to light the way. With as out of control as it had been lately, she might well burn the woods down. So instead she carried a small lantern, and hoped its light wouldn't summon anything untoward.

If it did, she reflected, would that really be so bad? Perhaps then she could confront whoever it was and demand answers. Perhaps if the solution to her problem were not to be found within the walls of the village, she could discover it elsewhere.

The thought nibbled at her, oddly tempting. She set it aside as she hurried through the forest, brushing aside branches that snagged her clothes and vines that threatened to catch her ankles. Five minutes, ten, and then she was there, in the small clearing where Niko's grave lay.

It was the first time she had been back here since the funeral, and she noticed all the things she had been too distraught to observe then: the beauty of the white-skinned birches and rowan trees that ringed the clearing, the night-blooming jasmine that curled around their branches, forming an arch overhead. The elderflowers that carpeted the ground beneath her feet.

It was a desolate spot, true, and unconsecrated. Lonely, yes.

But there was a certain wild beauty to it. In the summer, provided everything bloomed as it ought, it would be peaceful and lovely, scented with the perfume of a thousand flowers.

If only she would be here to see it.

Swallowing the lump in her throat for the second time that night, she knelt beside Niko's grave. Her knees sank into the dirt, crushing the elderflowers beneath them. "Hello, my Shadow," she said, forcing a smile. "You wouldn't believe what's happened since you've been gone. How I wish we could talk about it, that you could give me your advice."

She paused, waiting, half-hopeful. But she had no sense that Niko was there with her, nor did she see a hint of his form, human or black dog, moving in the woods beyond. Sighing, she called the wind, breaking dead branches from the rowan trees and setting them down in a circle around where she knelt. Then, carefully, she called her witchfire and set them alight. When the fires held, threatening neither to gutter to nothingness nor to set the forest aflame, she began speaking, telling Niko everything that was in her heart.

By the time she'd finished, her cheeks were wet with tears and her mouth was dry. She glanced up at the sky; the moon had risen even higher. It was time to go.

Katerina rose, in search of a gift to leave atop Niko's grave. She considered commanding the wind to strip some of the white jasmine-flowers from their vines, but it didn't feel right, as if she were desecrating the beauty of Niko's resting place. So instead, scooping up her lantern and lighting the wick afresh from the still-burning rowan-fires, she tiptoed between the flames and ventured into the forest.

She'd followed the path to Niko's grave by instinct. But now, walking in the opposite direction from the village, she found herself in a part of the forest she didn't recognize. She brushed aside the bushes that blocked her way, lifting the lantern high to see what lay beyond.

And then her breath caught in her throat.

She was mere feet from the ruined chapel, the one where Sant Viktoriya, Sant Antoniya, and Sant Andrei had first made their pact to defend Iriska. The one that had been defiled by a Grigori attack and left to be swallowed by the woods years ago. And around the crumbling columns twined early-spring roses, so deep a red as to be black by torchlight.

The bushes bent, making way for her as she skirted them and walked up the steps that led to the altar, barely visible beneath a carpet of moss and a wreath of jasmine and honey-suckle. Her feet thudding on the cracked flagstones, she reached the columns and pulled a knife from her belt to cut the roses free.

On impulse, she paused. The Saints had allowed her Shadow to be taken from her, true. But perhaps they might still hear her prayer.

"Sant Antoniya," she whispered, each word falling like a weight into the night, "look after my Shadow. Guide me to find him again. Hold his soul in the Light." And then she pricked her finger with the knife and let the droplets fall onto the ruins of the chapel, sealing her prayer.

Her blood hissed as it hit the stones, as if they were white-hot. Beneath the vines that covered them, letters began to appear.

Breath catching in her throat, Katerina knelt and yanked the vines aside, heedless of the thorns. Holding the lantern close, she peered at the words that were revealed, each glowing with light, like the Mark she'd inscribed outside her cottage.

Call ye upon the Dark in need
In service to the Light
Speak ye the words that set us free

And thwart the demon's bite
We three, we Saints, we fight with you
Our battle becomes thine
Dimi blood, your heart beats true
Call four, call Light, child mine.

Katerina's jaw dropped. Her head jerked up, eyes narrowing, ensuring that she was, indeed, alone. That this was not some kind of trick.

But how could a demon have known she would come here? That she would seek these roses, that she would cut herself here, on these stones?

She looked left and right. Nothing but empty forest. Up, at the flat, gleaming disc of the Bone Moon, drifting in a formless, black sea pricked with stars. Down, at the words etched into the stones as if with fire.

She had come this far. She had nothing left to lose.

Call four, call Light, she thought, and closed her eyes. She summoned all four elements to her hand, and sent them tunneling straight down into the stones.

A jagged bolt of lightning illuminated the world behind her eyelids. There was a tremendous cracking sound, then a crumbling clatter, as the earth beneath her gave way. The altar shook, and Katerina fell forward, digging the pads of her fingers into the space between the stones. Rose petals swept past her, pelting her face; she could smell their musk, rich with fruit and spice. The world whirred and spun and blazed. And then...all fell still and silent.

Slowly, gingerly, Katerina opened her eyes. The altar had collapsed, and the columns had fallen to their knees. The stones were scattered with rose petals, and though her lantern lay beside her, its flame had gone out. But she didn't need its light. Because in front of her, the stones had opened wide, revealing a shallow crevasse that gleamed with an illuminated pool of bright, still water. And inside it floated a leather-bound tome, drifting just beneath the surface. On the cover were stamped the words *Book of the Lost.*

Could this truly be the legendary volume her mother had spoken of, buried beneath the stones of the old chapel for safe-keeping? Had Katerina's blood called it to her somehow?

Heart beating in her wrists and chest and throat, Katerina reached into the pool and drew the book out. Somehow, it was bone-dry to the touch. When she opened it, the pages glowed from within, lighting the words inked onto them.

Katerina gasped as she turned page after page. On one, instructions for calling a demon and confining it within a blessed circle. On another, a spell to call the Dark, while still honoring the Saints. On a third, runes for summoning and protection, for strength and fortitude, for containment.

Call ye upon the Dark in need, in service to the Light. Was it possible that, centuries ago, the Saints had concealed this volume here for just such an eventuality? Had they foreseen that the events of the prophecy would come to pass—that such desperate measures might be needed?

This felt too easy, somehow: She had yearned for a miraculous solution, and here it was. But maybe she was overthinking things. Maybe her definition of *easy* had warped, after what she'd been through. She had stood against the Darkness, after all—stood and won. Was it too much to believe that the Saints had truly heard her prayer?

She wanted revenge and salvation for Niko. This was her chance. In the name of the Light, she would summon Sammael and demand answers. For where he was, Elena would be, and where Elena was, her Shadow would be, also.

If she couldn't bring Niko to her, she would go to him. She would find him and bring him home and lay his spirit to rest.

Katerina dipped her fingers into the shallow pool. She

marked herself with the sacred water, on her forehead and cheeks, over her heart. "Thank you," she whispered to the Saints. "I will make you proud."

She slid the book into her bodice, where it rested, safe, beneath Niko's amulet. Then she relit her lantern, scattered rose petals on her Shadow's grave, and walked home through the star-studded night.

5I

KATERINA

This was how Katerina found herself doing the unthinkable: standing in her bedroom, about to summon a demon.

She'd drawn the shutters tight and pushed the bed against the wall to create a wide expanse where she could cast her circle. Slowly, meticulously, she bent, using the point of one of Niko's blades to etch the Klyuchi runes from the Book of the Lost into the wooden floorboards. She drew the symbols with care, each loop and angle precise. Who knew what she might summon instead, if she made the slightest mistake?

When she was finished, she stood back and regarded her handiwork. It looked perfect, as far as she could tell—but what did she know? It wasn't as if she had anyone to ask.

She sank to her knees outside the circle, praying to the Saints for aid. They had given her the precious book. Surely if they understood the nature of her mission, they wouldn't abandon her. Perhaps then she could open a portal to the demon realms without compromising her soul.

Katerina wanted to do something—anything—but this. But she had just three nights left before the Kniaz's arrival. Three nights before she would be forced to leave for Rivki, before she'd be bonded to another Shadow. Who knew if she'd be able to reach Niko then?

She could practically *hear* her Shadow's growl, hear him admonishing her to beware. That this wasn't worth the risk. But she had no intention of listening.

Wearily, she got to her feet and made her way to the cabinet where his remaining blades were still stored, wrapped in velvet, the way he'd left them when he went to the elderflower clearing to find her that horrible night. He hadn't taken them with him to the cottage he was meant to share with Elena, and in the aftermath of his death, Baba hadn't demanded their return. Perhaps she believed they were tainted, like Niko's soul. Katerina cared little for her own life, but if she died summoning this demon, who would save Niko...assuming he still existed to be saved? His blades weren't a certainty of protection, but they were insurance, should something go wrong—especially given how unstable her magic had become.

A second blessed blade in hand, Katerina turned to regard the rest of her preparations. The wood that blazed up in her fireplace had been cut from a rowan tree, for an extra layer of protection. She'd memorized the spells in the Book of the Lost and tucked it beneath a loose floorboard, to conceal it if she failed to survive. She'd scar the circle she made with witchfire afterward, to disguise the runes, and push her bed back over the evidence for good measure.

There was nothing left to do. It was time.

Her heart pounded so hard she could barely breathe as she made her way over to the protective circle. Her back against the wall, she dragged one deep breath into her lungs, then another. And then she spoke.

"Sant Antoniya. Sant Viktoriya. Sant Andrei. I am Katerina Ivanova. Servant of the Light. Though these runes may be Dark, my purpose is far from evil. I am a Dimi of Kalach, sworn to stand by my Shadow's side. Look into my soul and hear me, for I call on you for aid."

The flames in the fireplace flickered in a wavering current of air, though the shutters were closed and bolted. Shadows swarmed from the corners of the room, amassing outside the circle in a vaguely human form. Panic choked Katerina, but she pressed onward.

"Saints, be with me as I call upon the Darkness, as I look into the Void. Be with me as I seek to find what's rightly mine." Her voice trembled as she spoke the next words. But she could swear she felt a hand on her shoulder, offering support, and it gave her the courage to continue. "I call on Sammael, Venom of God, ruler among demons. From the Underworld or the Void I call him, from the Darkness that eats all things. Wherever he roams, whatever form he takes, I call him from it. I call him with the power of the Light, and demand he come to me."

The runes she'd inscribed in the floorboards began to glow. One by one, they lit with silver-blue hellfire. Katerina watched in horror and fascination as the circle completed itself. The last rune blazed up, and her bones ached with power as the spell snapped into place.

She staggered back, fighting to keep her feet. Inside the circle, something was happening. Particles of dust were coalescing, swirling, coming together—

"Saints be with me," she murmured again, clutching Niko's blade. "Give me the strength to do what must be done."

One second, there was a whirlwind of dust in the circle. The next, *he* stood there. The red-headed man from the clearing. The one that had impersonated a Shadow.

The demon Sammael. In her *cottage*.

Katerina had done it. She had summoned this demon from the depths. A prince of Hell, a ruler of the Underworld.

And he was not happy.

The demon spun, dark eyes wide with confusion and fury. His gaze roamed over the ceiling, the floor, the confines of Katerina's bedroom. And then he spun, his eyes fixing on her. In their depths burned a rage that would have brought a lesser Dimi to her knees.

"Where am I?" he snapped. "What have you done to me?"

Katerina advanced, fingers digging into the blade's handle. "I summoned you, demon. You are in my circle. An unwilling guest, if you will."

It was a pleasure to hear the arrogance in her own voice, the tone of command, after weeks of feeling like a victim, a grieving supplicant begging for the favor of those who used to revere her. She smiled, and the demon snarled at her, baring his teeth. "Dimi Ivanova. How dare you summon me? I am Sammael, ruler of the—"

"Oh, I know, I know." Katerina cocked an eyebrow at him. "You don't have to recite your many accomplishments. Eater of souls, devourer of the innocent, plague of the Seven Villages. What good will they do you, after all? Right now, you are my prisoner. And you'll answer my questions, or I'll cross that circle and put this blade through your heart."

"If you cross this circle," the demon hissed at her, "I will kill you."

"And how do you think that will go for you? Perhaps you should ask the army of demons that sought to take my life on the road to Drezna. Oh, that's right...you *can't.*"

The demon threw himself against the boundaries of the circle, struggling to escape. Katerina watched him, eyes narrowed, her magic pulsing at her fingertips. But the circle held.

He took a step back, regarding her warily. "Gadreel was right to covet you, Dimi Ivanova. Centuries have passed since your kind have cast this kind of spell. I thought the magic had been lost. What do you want? Why have you summoned me here?"

It was such a ridiculous question, Katerina gave a bitter laugh. "What do I *want?* I want answers. What has Elena done to my Shadow? Is she torturing him, even as we speak? And if he exists alongside her, in whatever form...what must be done to set him free?"

"And you think I possess these answers." He folded his arms across his chest.

It might be worth crossing the circle, simply to see the look on his face when she put Niko's blade through his heart and set him aflame. "I know you do. I know you're with her, wherever she is. You worked too hard to bond her to you, whatever your reason. To make her what she became."

She glared at the demon, challenging him to defy her. He glared back at her. And finally he said, "I have the answers you seek."

Triumph shot through Katerina. "Give them to me."

"Let me out of the circle," he countered, "and I will."

Katerina snorted. "You must think I'm an idiot. If I let you out, first you'll kill me, and then you'll go rampaging through Kalach, on a murder spree."

Sammael sighed, and Katerina realized he actually looked... tired. Could demons be fatigued? "I give you my word that I will not. The realm has souls aplenty right now, Katerina Ivanova. Maybe too many souls."

Her eyebrows knit. Was he talking about the demise of Drezna and Satvala? "Then why don't you stop taking them?" she challenged. "Why destroy our villages?"

"That wasn't me." He shook his head. "If you'd let me out of here, I can explain—"

"You can explain from inside the circle." She glared at him, jaw set. "Tell me what has befallen my Shadow. Tell me that, and I might not incinerate you where you stand."

The demon drew himself up to his full height. His red hair glinted in the light that emanated from the runes. "After Elena chained your Shadow's soul to hers, you tried to cast us both into the Void, but succeeded only in banishing us to the Underworld. So...there she stays. And your unfortunate inconvenience of a Shadow with her."

Hearing this, Katerina swallowed hard. Relief coursed through her at the knowledge that her actions hadn't cursed Niko to wander the limitless Darkness of the Void for all eternity, even if it meant that the demons and Elena still remained a threat. Still, it boiled her blood and broke her heart anew to envision her Shadow, a creature of the Light, trapped in Sammael's realm, enslaved to the woman who had taken his life.

"I have tried to make her comfortable there, to make a home for her," the demon went on. "To make her happy. But she is filled with rage. She blames you for the death of the Shadow and for your curse. She commands the Shadow to do her bidding. To love her. And when he refuses...her wrath is a terrible thing."

A knot of anguish formed in Katerina's throat, threatening to choke her. Aside from dooming Niko to the Void forever, this was what she had feared most.

"Dimi Ivanova." His voice was low, persuasive. "I know how you must miss him. Let us strike a bargain that will benefit us both."

Katerina bared her teeth. "I don't bargain with demons! Unless you plan to end Elena once and for all, and give my Shadow peace, then you have nothing I want."

"I think," the demon said, offering her a terrible smile, "that you'll find I have something better to offer you. It's good fortune, really, that you summoned me this way. For if you hadn't, I had planned to come to you. We are running out of time."

She regarded him, puzzled. "You mean because the Reaping—"

He shook his head impatiently. "I care nothing for your foolish human games. Surely you see that the duplicate Bone Moon is rising, thinning the veil between your realm and the Underworld once more. It is...a chance. An opportunity. Once, and once only, will this door be open to us. If you want to see your Shadow again, you will listen to what I have to say."

Torn, Katerina tilted her head, taking his measure. He stared back at her, motionless in her circle of runes.

She thought of everything she had already lost. Of the Reaping, just three days away. Of Niko, condemned to suffer at the hands of a woman who had been devoured by the Dark. And she knew if she didn't do everything in her power to save him, she would never forgive herself.

"Speak, then," she told the demon.

"First," Sammael began, sitting cross-legged inside the circle, "there is the matter of the Darkness that devoured Drezna and Satvala."

Katerina tilted her head, eyes intent on his face. "What about it?"

He ran a hand through his close-cropped hair. "At first, I thought it was a tool of Gadreel's. That his power had grown exponentially. But then I came to realize the truth. Gadreel did set the Darkness free, thinking he could use it to bolster his strength. But he got more than he had ever bargained for. It was...hungry. And he could not control it."

A shudder ran through Katerina. "You mean—it's acting independently of him? Of any of you?"

Sammael nodded gravely. "It is sentient, in some way. Although all it wants is to devour. I believe this is why Gadreel desires you so badly. He needs a powerful partner in the Light to drive it back into the Void. To chain it, once again."

Horror bubbled inside her, and she drew her knees up, gripping them. "If I don't help him, then what will happen?"

"We will all die," Sammael said simply. "Demon, Dimi, Shadow, Vila, and non-magical human alike. For the Underworld is fueled by souls, and if the Darkness takes them all..."

His voice trailed off, but he didn't need to finish speaking. Katerina understood.

"I won't be his puppet," she said, her voice tight. "Not as Elena is yours. If he had me that way, he would never let me go."

A strange look flashed across the demon's face, as if the notion of manipulating Elena that way was...offensive to him. Was that possible? Could demons want anything other than to possess and destroy?

But Katerina didn't have time to contemplate it, because the demon was speaking again. "I understand that. I also know how much stronger you are with your rightful Shadow by your side. Whoever your nobleman chooses to bind you to, it will never be as strong as the one you had with Niko Alekhin. And until you are bonded to another, the bond you have with Shadow Alekhin still remains, in some form."

Katerina's brows knitted. "You know a great deal about Shadows and Dimis, demon. Perhaps too much."

"I have lived for many years." He waved a hand, dismissing this. "You want your Shadow back. I want him gone from the Underworld. You want Gadreel to leave you alone. I want him punished for what he's done. And most importantly, we both want the Darkness banished, lest it take our lives and destroy everything we've sought to protect. Let us strike a bargain."

The idea that Katerina might somehow be able to get Niko *back* had never occurred to her. The most she'd dared to pray for was that she could set his soul free and help him be at peace. She leaned forward, trying not to let her hope show on her face. "Get him back, how? Alive, or just his shade? And why do you want him gone from the Underworld?"

That odd look flickered across the demon's face again. "I told you. If he is restored to you, in whatever form, then he can fight by your side. Together, you can defeat Gadreel and drive the Darkness back into the Void, where it belongs. I will help you, in secret, so your fellow witches and your nobleman never have to know you allied yourself with a demon. Your reputation will be safe, your Shadow will be returned to you, and the Darkness will be secured once more. And I will take my rightful place as ruler of all the demon realms, as I should have long ago."

Katerina couldn't have cared less about the rivalry between Gadreel and Sammael. What she *did* care about was this: if the demon wasn't lying, he was handing her the key to saving Iriska. To restoring her reputation. And, just maybe, to rescuing her Shadow. It was more than she'd dreamed was possible. But—

She dug her nails into her palms. "Are you saying that *Gadreel* is responsible for the Darkness that's devouring Iriska? The failure of the crops, Niko's death, Nadia and Oriel's disappearance, the fall of Satvala and Drezna...all of it is due to him and him alone?"

The demon's eyes widened the smallest bit, as if she had surprised him. "What else could be the cause of it?"

Katerina's heart found its way into her throat, choking her. She tried to speak, but all that came out was a croak.

If Gadreel was responsible—if his greedy, foolish actions

had summoned the Darkness—then was it possible that Katerina wasn't to blame? That the crushing weight she'd been carrying, the conviction that her very existence compromised everything she vowed to protect, wasn't hers to bear? She gasped for breath, struggling to find words.

Sammael approached the edge of the circle, peering at her curiously. "Are you quite well, Dimi Ivanova? If only you would release me, I might be able to lend assistance."

The demon was inches from her, separated only by the magical barrier that bound him. He looked, she realized, like her dark mirror: same red hair, same ink-black eyes. Had he chosen this form on purpose, to antagonize her?

It was that thought, more than anything else, that allowed her to find her voice. "I'm fine," she managed, lifting her chin. Again she felt that strange presence beside her, the sense of a hand on her shoulder, centering her. Sant Antoniya, perhaps? Could it be?

She had prayed for aid. Perhaps it had arrived.

"I beg to differ," the demon said, cocking his head. He looked...amused. "Tell me. What do you believe is responsible for this mayhem, if not Gadreel's regrettable, impulsive behavior?"

If there was one thing Katerina couldn't abide, it was mockery. "There is a prophecy," she said stiffly. "Well known among our kind. It says that if a Dimi and Shadow fall in love, it will bring about the end of Iriska. It will doom us all."

At this, the demon's smile began to widen. And then he was laughing, a cold sound that echoed off the walls of Katerina's cottage. He laughed so hard he doubled over, his hands on his knees.

Katerina fought the desire to cross the circle and plunge a knife into his chest. "Will you *shut up?*" she hissed at him. "If we're caught here, the Saints only know what they will do to me. And they will most definitely kill *you.*"

Sammael's laughter cut off, as if sliced through with the very blade with which Katerina had wanted to impale him. When he straightened, the mirth had vanished from his face. "They can try," he said, and bared his teeth at her.

She ignored him. "Explain yourself," she said, endeavoring to keep her voice level, not to reveal how much the answer mattered to her. "What's so funny?"

The demon waved a hand. "You humans and your foolish prophecies. Since the dawn of time, you have been fond of them," he said, amusement once again lurking in the depths of his black eyes. "As if anything you could say—anything you could *do*—could unleash something like this."

Katerina's mind raced. Baba Petrova believed Katerina to be so powerful that her gifts had summoned the Darkness from the depths as a counterbalance. Had her existence created the opportunity for Gadreel to attack? Had it somehow strengthened the demon, given him the edge he needed to free the Darkness—and then her secret desire for Niko, their illicit love for each other, had tipped the balance? But if she were to blame... why would the Saints be helping her now? Would they not wish to strike her down, instead?

"You are a powerful witch, Dimi Ivanova," the demon said, his voice smoke-rough, as if he had read her thoughts. "I mean no insult to your gifts. But what is happening now...it takes a prince of Darkness to bring it about. Much as I detest Gadreel, he is a formidable agent of the Dark. You and Niko Alekhin's dalliances, however much they might mean to you and your ways—they are not responsible for this."

Katerina tried to leash the joy that flooded her at his words, but she must have done a poor job, because the demon smiled. It was a terrible sight. "I see I have alleviated your worries.

Truly, your village blames you for all that has befallen the realm? They must believe you to be omnipotent indeed."

She stared at Sammael, assessing him. Everyone knew demons lied. But what would he gain from this falsehood? If he was telling the truth, though, what was the significance of the prophecy? Was it possible, as he implied, that it meant *nothing*? Was it just words in a dusty book, as Niko had often said? Or did it mean something else entirely? *The Dark will fall. The shadow will rise.* Could it be—

"You are pondering something," the demon said. He stood as close to the boundary of the circle as he could, his eyes fixed on her face. "Let me give you more to consider. As I've said, in three nights the false Bone Moon will rise. Brought about as it is by the growing strength of the Darkness, it will create...how would you think of it? A two-way portal, let us say. Then and only then will a Dimi of the Light be able to make her way to the Underworld. Then and only then will an enslaved spirit of the Dark be able to leave."

Ice shot through Katerina's veins, as deadly as the plague that had cursed their fields. It was all she'd wanted—to find Niko, to set him free. But her plan, such as it was, had depended on stealth. To descend into the depths of Hell with the full knowledge of a demon...to do so on his invitation...she could think of few things more dangerous. Or more terrifying.

"You would open the way for me?" Her magic gathered around her, a protective shroud, so heavy she could feel its weight on her skin. "What do you want in return?"

The demon staggered back a step, as if even through the circle, the press of the Light pained him. His lips set in a thin, disapproving line. "I am doing nothing to damage you, Dimi Ivanova. You have already trapped me in this damnable circle. Was there really a need for that?"

Her magic swelled, a storm cloud shot through with lightning. Sparks gathered at her fingertips. A wind of her own making blew, lifting her hair and flaring the flames in her hearth. "Answer my question."

"I told you," the demon said, examining his shirt cuffs as if nothing more fascinating existed in all the world. "You are stronger with your Shadow. Gadreel is shortsighted. He believes if he captures you and forces you to do his bidding, you will be strong enough to hold back the Dark. But I know better. I've heard tales of what you and Niko Alekhin can do. Gadreel fears that the two of you, together, would defeat him...and perhaps you would. But *I* fear that without your rightful Shadow, you do not stand a chance of driving the Darkness back into the Void." He tugged the bottom of his shirt straight, as if he were on his way to a fine affair rather than trapped in Katerina's circle. "Of course, then you can defeat Gadreel once and for all. It is a mutually beneficial arrangement."

The invisible presence beside her grew stronger. It was no longer comforting, no longer lending her strength. Now, it was filled with warning. If the Saints were trying to tell her something, Katerina would do her best to listen.

"You lie." Katerina held his dark eyes with her own. "I think you covet Elena Lisova, demon. You claimed her. You trained her. You cannot stand that she believes she loves another. You want him gone, so you can have her to yourself."

The demon's lips drew back from his teeth, and he hissed at her like the snake she knew him to be. "He is a dog. I can offer her everything, and yet she chooses to cavort with a beast. She was mine. She will be mine again."

In his eyes shone nothing but madness and greed. This was his true nature, the devil behind the carefully cultivated façade. But it didn't frighten Katerina. On the contrary, relief swept over her. They understood each other at last.

Elena was his vulnerability, as Niko was hers. For the sake of whatever twisted emotions Sammael felt for her, he would do anything—just as Katerina would do anything to save her Shadow. Yes, he was driven to defeat Gadreel and drive back the Darkness. But that was strategy; this was passion. It was a chink in his armor, and she intended to exploit it.

"Go on, then, demon," she said, and offered him a small, satisfied smile. "I'm listening."

52

KATERINA

"You did *what*?" Ana stared at Katerina, aghast. "How could you?"

"Keep your voice down!" They were in the bedroom of her cottage, with the windows and doors shut tight. Still, anyone could walk by, and with Katerina under so much suspicion, they frequently *did*. Last night, she'd been woken from a restless sleep by the thud of rocks against her bedroom's shutters, followed by a whispered, "Shadow-killer!" If the knowledge that she'd made a pact with a demon left this room, she was done for.

"Who do you think is going to hear me? The kikimora?" Ana stomped over to Katerina's dressing table and sank onto the stool in front of it, regarding the burnt outline of a Klyuchi rune that was just visible beneath the bed. "Why would you do this? How did you even know how? Surely there wasn't a book in the library, just lying around..."

"No," Katerina said, leaning back against her bed. "No library."

"Then what? Did one of those beasts force their way in here? Are you being coerced? Or possessed?" Ana's witchfire flared at her fingertips, prepared to incinerate anything demonic in its path.

"I summoned it. If you would listen for a moment, I'll explain."

"If I would *listen,* she says." Ana ran a hand through her dark hair. "As if my impatience is the issue here. By all means, Katerina, go ahead. I cannot *wait* to hear this."

Katerina could hardly blame Ana for her sarcasm. In her shoes, Katerina would doubtless sound the same. And at least her fellow Dimi was here, argumentative or not. She hadn't denounced Katerina, or threatened to tell Baba, or fled in horror. She didn't look happy, but she was still here.

Setting her shoulders, Katerina told Ana everything. How she'd gone to Niko's grave, how her search for flowers had led her to the ruined chapel, how she'd pricked her finger and her blood had fallen upon the stones.

"And then," she said, drawing a deep breath, "I found the Book of the Lost. Or maybe I should say...it found me."

"You *what?*" Ana gaped at her. "That book is a legend, Katerina. I didn't think it actually existed. No one's seen it—"

"As long as we've been alive," Katerina agreed. "Or *ever*. But it revealed itself to me. As if it was waiting for me, all this time."

Ana shot to her feet. "I want to see it."

"And you will. But first...let me finish. And then I'll answer all your questions."

Katerina told Ana how she'd called Sammael and he had come. What he'd confided about Gadreel and the Darkness. And then, bracing herself, she explained the plan she'd made with the demon.

"I am to go down to the Underworld," she told her friend. "Two nights from now, when the Bone Moon is full. There's a portal near the old chapel; that's where Sammael came through, the night he met Elena. The Darkness that Gadreel summoned...it's somehow frayed the boundaries between worlds. Sammael says on that night only, the portal will work both ways. He's given me a charm to guide me to his realm. When I arrive, I can confront Elena and fight for Niko." She set her jaw. "With luck, I can kill her."

Ana's jaw dropped. "I hardly know what to say, Katerina."

That was a first; much like Katerina, her closest friend usually had a comeback for every occasion. Katerina bit her lip. "Say you'll help me."

"Me?" Ana's chestnut-brown eyes widened. "You wouldn't allow me to ride to the Magiya in your service! Surely you don't want me to go down to the—"

"No, no," Katerina said hastily. "That's not what I intend at all. It's only—that night, I'll need someone to cover for me. You're right, it'll be chaos, what with the Kniaz and Shadow's arrival, and the ceremony. But with so much of the focus on me, it'll be hard to get away. If you say you're helping me with my hair and my dress...if you say I'm too nervous to meet Kniaz Sergey again, like this...then it could buy us some time."

Ana picked up a glass vial of rose-scented perfume from Katerina's dressing table, then set it down again. When her gaze met Katerina's, wry amusement was clear in its depths. "Sure. You're too anxious to look upon a nobleman's face. But going down to the Underworld, no problem."

"Obviously, no one will know where I've gone. Unless you tell them." Katerina narrowed her eyes at Ana. She'd been so sure she could trust her; Ana was her closest friend, had stood by her when everyone else had abandoned her. But if she'd been wrong—

"Quit with the threatening glare, Katerina." Ana flicked her hands; sparks flew in Katerina's direction, falling onto the woven green rug. "I'm not going to say anything."

Katerina stomped the sparks out with her boots. "I didn't think you would. I just...had to be sure."

"I owe you," Ana said. "For saving Alexei. Not to mention, you're my closest friend." She sighed. "Even if you don't make it easy sometimes."

"So you'll help me?" Hope surged in Katerina's chest.

"I didn't say that." Ana's mouth set in a grim line. "Show me the Book of the Lost. And the charm."

Katerina knelt, prying up the floorboard beneath the bed. When she stood, she held the Book in one hand and the charm that Sammael had given her in the other. Carved from onyx, it was round, heavier than it ought to be, and cold to the touch, engraved with intertwining serpents belching flame. When she'd cast the spell to send Sammael back to the Underworld, he'd left it behind. Katerina had been reluctant to touch it, and had handled it as little as possible, sliding it beneath the floorboard with the Book. She'd hoped that the Book's Light would cancel out its Darkness. But last night, when she slept with them both beneath her bed, atop the faded remains of the Klyuchi runes, her dreams had been terrible.

Of course, that could be because she was considering the unthinkable. But what choice did she have?

Ana stood, crossing the room to Katerina and taking the Book from her hands. She opened the leather cover carefully, her eyes widening further still as she turned the ancient pages. *"To summon a demon, in service of the Light,"* she read, her finger tracing beneath the words as it always did, to keep her place. "You truly believe the Saints gave this to you, Katerina? Tell me again what it said on the stones."

Dutifully, Katerina recited the words. She watched as Ana's teeth sank deep into her lip. "You'll show me what remains of the chapel?" she said.

It only made sense that Ana would want proof. "Of course."

The other Dimi held out her hand for the charm. "Let me see it, then," she said.

Katerina tilted it into Ana's palm, relief rising as the small weight left her. There was something *wrong* about it, something her very magic recoiled from.

The other Dimi's jaw tightened as her fingers closed around the piece of polished onyx. "It's cold," she said. "So cold, it almost burns."

"I know."

Ana opened her hand and peered down at the stone. "Serpents...it makes sense, I suppose. The Venom of God, and all that. So very charming."

"Is that a pun?" Katerina said, her lips quirking up at the corners. Only Ana could find humor in a situation like this.

"Just trying to lighten the mood."

"Very funny. Here." Katerina held her hand out for the Book and charm, and Ana surrendered them, watching as Katerina knelt and secured them beneath the bed once more.

The other Dimi sat back down on her stool. "Why can't Sammael simply release Niko? Give his soul back to you?"

"Because he's tethered to Elena," Katerina said. "Unfortunately."

"I see. And despite the fact that Elena was willing to invoke Dark magic and bond with a demon to chain Niko's soul to hers, he believes that you'll somehow be able to convince her to let him go. Or force her." Ana cocked her head. "Will your magic even work in the Underworld?"

"No," Katerina admitted. "Not according to Sammael. At least, not well. He said that with every step I took, my gifts would drain from me. Blessed blades won't work, either."

"I see. So, down you go, all but defenseless, to confront the Venom of God, a crazed Vila, and Saints knows what else. Alone." Ana put her head in her hands. "You plan to do this

EMILY COLIN

under the light of a moon that has never existed before, on the word of the worst of the Grigori, when the Kniaz himself is descending upon our village, all on the hopes of retrieving your Shadow's soul and reviving him so that the two of you can confront the Darkness itself and defeat the fallen Angel of War. And you want to make me complicit." Ana lifted her head, spreading her hands wide. "Do I have it right, Katerina? Is there something in this insane plan of yours that I've failed to comprehend?"

Katerina pressed her fingers against her lips, swallowing hard. "When you put it that way, it does sound...less than practical."

Ana snorted. "Less than practical, she says. How about risky beyond belief? Deranged? Mad as a March hare?"

"I understand," Katerina said, her heart sinking. "It was too much to ask. If...if you could just keep my secret...if you could promise me that..."

"If I could just keep your secret!" Ana sounded indignant. "What is it you think I am?"

"I can't tell Baba," Katerina said, desperate. "She'd never let me go. You know that. And I have to save Niko. I have to try to kill Elena, and not just for revenge. You didn't see her in that clearing. She...she'll never stop. Even Sammael thinks there's something wrong with her, and I imagine his standards are low."

"Still joking, even now." There was an odd note in Ana's voice. "Only you would travel into the heart of the Venom of God's power, with the aim of double-crossing him. You didn't tell him you were going to try to kill Elena, I'm sure."

"I know how it sounds. But this is my only chance to rescue Niko, Ana. To save Iriska. If I don't succeed, the Darkness will devour what remains of the Seven Villages, and then break through the wards to the rest of the world. And I would rather

392

die trying to save my Shadow than fighting a battle I cannot win, in service to the Fallen Angel of War."

Ana said nothing, and Katerina dropped her head, staring at the floorboards between her feet. Was she doing this for the right reasons, or was her motivation ultimately selfish...to save Niko, regardless of if the world burned? Did she *really* think she had a chance of making this plan work, or was her vision clouded by her love for him?

She didn't care. She wanted Niko back more than she craved honor or power. And yes, she wanted to reclaim her reputation, save Kalach, and restore balance to the world. If she could take Elena down too, so much the better.

"You might never come back," Ana said softly. "Or you might come back corrupted, broken. I might have to...to kill you, Katerina. You're asking me to aid in sending you to your death."

"Don't you think I know that?" Katerina gritted her teeth. "But I have to try, Ana. I do. Maybe between all the Dimis and Shadows, you stand a chance against the Darkness. But Niko only has me. If I don't save him, no one will."

"Because no one else is crazy enough to try," Ana muttered.

Maybe Katerina *was* crazy, because some part of her harbored the slim hope that she would survive the Underworld unscathed, vanquish Elena and the Darkness, and still manage to reunite with Niko in the Light. But that seemed too grandiose to voice.

She remembered how her magic had faltered in the clearing, how she had prayed for Niko to help her drive the demons and Elena into the Void. Even dead, his shade had lent her the strength she needed. They were still stronger, together. If she could bring him back, in whatever form—maybe he could fight beside her one last time before his soul ascended to the Saints.

Anything else was unthinkable. She refused to believe that she could fail.

Suppressing the terrifying image of herself chained alongside Niko, subject to Elena's will while the Darkness rampaged through Iriska, she focused on the argument that was most likely to win Ana over to her side.

"You're always telling me to ask for help. That I can't do everything on my own. And you're the only person left I trust." She sniffed, fighting to hold back tears. "I know I've asked too much of you. So now I just ask that you keep this to yourself, and that...if I don't come back...you tell Baba the truth. Tell her that I died trying to make things right."

One tear fell from her eyes, splashing onto the floorboards between her feet, then another. She felt the current of the air as Ana moved, heard the creak of boards as Ana came to her. But she didn't look up, not even when Ana knelt at her feet, taking Katerina's cold hands in hers.

"You're a fool, Katerina Ivanova," Ana said.

Katerina wanted to wipe her mortifying tears away, but Ana had hold of both her hands. "Yes, I know. You've made what you think of this whole endeavor quite clear."

She tried to yank her hands back, but Ana held tight. "No, little idiot. You're a fool if you think I wouldn't help you."

Katerina lifted her head. Through her brimming eyes, she regarded Ana. "What did you say?"

The other woman's eyes were bright with tears, too, but her voice was steady and her grip firm on Katerina's hands when she spoke. "You saved Alexei. You're my best friend. And if I don't help you, we'll all die anyway, so..." She lifted one shoulder, then let it fall. "I'll lend you all the aid in my power, Katerina. Tell me what you need me to do."

53

KATERINA

The Bone Moon had not yet risen as Katerina stood in the doorway of her cottage, wearing her leather fighting gear beneath a long, flowing embroidered gown. She'd strapped two of Niko's blessed blades in her thigh holsters, and braided her red hair back, the way she always did when she fought. The Book of the Lost was safe beneath the floorboard, but she'd tucked the onyx charm into her pocket. It stung, cold against her skin, even through the thick leather.

Taking one last look at her cottage—for who knew if she would see it again—she turned and strode down the walkway. Ana waited for her, alone. "Are you ready?" she said.

Katerina nodded. "Yes," she said, willing it to be the truth. "Let's go."

They had agreed that Ana would accompany her as far as the edge of town, to avoid unnecessary attention. It was a tossup whether people ignored Katerina or swore at her, and today, she wasn't taking any chances. With Ana by her side, they'd be less likely to make trouble.

"You look like a stuffed sausage," Ana commented, giving

her the once-over as they made their way toward the square. "How can you even move?"

"Such compliments," Katerina said, smiling despite herself. "Watch out, or my ego will wind up as swollen as my—"

"Dimi Ivanova!" The shout came from a side street. It was Baba Petrova, dressed in her best navy-blue robes and red-heeled shoes, and looking less than pleased. "Why are you out and about? Ought you not to be at home, preparing for the ceremony? And what in the name of all the Saints are you wearing?"

Her keen eyes scanned Katerina's body, and the smile drained from Katerina's face. "I was just—" What could she say? What would she do if Baba stopped them now?

"We were taking one last stroll together," Ana said, coming to her rescue. "It's my fault, really." She ducked her head, somehow managing to look demure. "Everyone's so angry with her, Baba. So cruel. But she's still my friend"—she clasped Katerina's hand—"and I care for her. I'll miss her so. I promised Katerina that I'd help her with her clothes and makeup for the ceremony, if she came for a walk with me first. Katerina didn't want to go; you know they stoned her, after Niko's funeral. But I begged. And you know how persuasive I can be."

She squeezed Katerina's hand, her message clear: *Look pathetic.* Katerina did her best. It wasn't hard.

Baba's suspicious gaze darted between the two of them. "I do," she said, her tone dry.

"It's all right, isn't it?" Ana wheedled, her eyes big and brown and shiny. "Just a walk, Baba. And then I promise I'll deliver her safely home. She'll look like a princess for the Kniaz and her new Shadow."

Katerina worried this was gilding the lily. But when she glanced at Baba Petrova's face, the old woman looked as if she, too, were about to weep. "Ach, the two of you," she said. "Inseparable since the cradle. I know well what it's like to be parted from those you love. Fine, then. A brief walk. But no more than that." She wagged her finger in Ana's face, then Katerina's. "I have a meeting with the Elders, and when it's over, I must speak with you, Katerina. I expect to find you ready for me."

"Thank you, Baba," Katerina began, but before she could finish, Baba turned on her red-painted heel and walked back the way she'd come.

Ana let go of Katerina's hand, and they stood next to each other until Baba's small figure disappeared, hardly daring to breathe. "Such a good liar you are," Katerina managed at last.

Ana snorted. "You should hope so. Because when she comes back after her meeting and you've gone missing, I'll be lying for your life. And mine."

A pang struck Katerina's heart. "Ana," she began, but the other woman shook her head, lips tight.

"Let's go," she said.

Wordlessly, they made their way down the path to the village square, which they would have to cross to reach the road that led to the boundary of Kalach and the ruined chapel. The Kniaz had not arrived yet, but the village had been abuzz with preparation for days. The town square was filled with brightly-colored tents, musicians and dancers, and such food as the villagers could manage. People had gone without several days, in order to create a welcome worthy of the nobleman.

Katerina and Ana crossed the square, dodging vendors' tents and workers who were hammering nails into the makeshift stage's supports. No one spoke to them, though a few people shot hostile looks over their shoulders at Katerina. She hardly noticed. If that was the worst that happened, then she would accept it, and gladly.

"All right," Ana said when they cleared the square. "Now we

just need to make it to the edge of town without someone harassing you. All in all, I think this is going rather well."

But she'd spoken too soon, because of all people, Konstantin stepped from between the trees, a shovel resting on his shoulder and a look of pursed disgust on his face. His dark gaze settled on Katerina. "Where are you going, Shadow-killer?" he said.

Katerina opened her mouth, then shut it again. Under normal circumstances, Konstantin would never dare speak to her in such a disrespectful fashion. In fact, he'd never dare speak to her at all, unless she'd spoken to him first. But these circumstances were far from normal, and Katerina could hardly threaten to incinerate him where he stood—not if she hoped to avoid drawing attention.

She'd hoped Konstantin was, at least, alone. But the branches behind him rustled, and out stepped three men. They had apparently spent the day hammering, digging, and pruning in preparation for the Kniaz's arrival, because they were filthy, covered in sawdust and mud. Dark circles underscored their eyes and their cheeks were drawn, as so many of the citizens of Kalach's were, from lack of food. None of them looked very happy to see Katerina.

"Where she's going is none of your business," Ana said, stepping in front of Katerina. "Don't you have work to do?"

Konstantin's dismissive gaze flicked over Ana. "Where is your Shadow, Dimi Rozanova? Have you done away with him too?"

Fire trembled at the tips of Ana's fingers, and, alarmed, Katerina stepped from behind her friend. "It's one thing to insult me," she said. "It's quite another to impugn Ana's good name. She and Alexei are loyal and honorable. They fight for you—for all of us. Now stand aside and let us pass."

"I don't think I will," Konstantin mused, gripping the

shovel more tightly. "You know, Katerina, once I dreamed you might be my wife. I escaped that fate, thank the Saints for small mercies. But before Kniaz Sergey claims you as his own, I can't help but want a little taste." His tongue darted out, licking his lips, and his olive skin flushed. "You won't hurt me. After all, your reputation can't stand much more damage."

He took one threatening step toward Katerina, then another, the shovel cocked over his shoulder and a smug smile on his face. Katerina braced, readying herself for a fight. There was no way she was going to let Konstantin touch her. And certainly no way she was going to let him prevent her from doing what must be done tonight. But he was right on one count; she didn't want to bludgeon him or light him aflame. That would send his companions running for help, and then her scheme would go right out the window. Her tongue, though, was as good a weapon as any other. It had stood her in good stead against Andrei, all those weeks ago.

"My reputation may be ruined, true," she said, tossing her head. "But that only means it can't get any worse. Of the two of us, you're the one with something to lose. I belong to the Kniaz now, and I hardly think he would tolerate laying a hand on what's his. Not to mention," she said, deliberately closing the space between them with small, stalking steps, "my magic's unpredictable right now. Surely you know that; it's been the talk of Kalach. It would be unwise for me to damage you on purpose. But antagonize me enough, and..." She extended a finger, running the point of her nail down his cheek. "Someone might...get...hurt."

Konstantin's black eyes widened. "You wouldn't."

Katerina summoned the smallest gust of wind, praying it didn't turn into a tornado. She used it to push Konstantin back, one step at a time, until he stood in front of the men who'd followed him out of the woods. "Go," she said, her voice soft. "And trouble me no more."

Konstantin glared at her. "Kniaz Sergey wants you for your power," he said. "To protect him, along with his precious Druzhina. But I see you for what you truly are. Evil. You will bring shame upon his house, just as you've brought it on Kalach."

Flames flared in Ana's hands again, and the burly man next to Konstantin shifted uneasily at the sight. "Come, now, Konstantin. You've said your piece. It's treason to speak against the Kniaz, and the witch isn't worth it. Let us go."

Konstantin shook his head. He tried to move forward again, to get to her, but Katerina's magic held him still. His black eyes burned with indignation, and his knuckles went white on the shovel, as if he'd like nothing more than to beat her to death with it. But finally, blessedly, he turned without another word and disappeared into the trees. The other men followed, until at last, Katerina and Ana were alone again.

Ana drew a shuddering breath. "I'm glad you didn't marry that one, Katerina, Niko or no. He's dangerous. A man who would speak to you that way is a man who would beat his wife."

"A man who would speak to me that way is a man who would lie about what happened between us," Katerina said. "Who would be threatened that, even compromised, I got the best of him. He'll be telling everyone that I threatened him unprovoked, and next thing I know, there'll be a mob on my heels. I have to go, and quickly."

Nodding in resignation, Ana threw her arms around her friend. Her embrace was tight and fierce. "Be brave," she whispered in Katerina's ear. "Know that I stand with you always, in the Light."

She dropped her arms, and Katerina fled.

FIFTEEN MINUTES LATER, the embroidered gown concealed beneath a pile of leaves, she stood at the foot of the abandoned chapel, girding her courage. No matter how much she wanted —*needed*—to do this, she was still terrified. She touched the blades in her thigh sheaths to make sure they were still there, then the charm in her pocket. *Sant Antoniya,* she prayed, *watch over me. Keep me safe.*

She peered through the thicket, toward the clearing where Niko's grave lay. If she succeeded, what would happen to his body? Would he rise from the grave, spirit and shell reunited once more? Or...

Katerina didn't want to think about it. It was too disturbing, and at any rate, she didn't have time. Any moment now, Kniaz Sergey could arrive in Kalach, with her potential Shadow in tow. Konstantin could send people after her, determined to enact revenge for his humiliation. Or Baba Petrova could wrap up the meeting with the Elders and come to look for Katerina, as she'd promised. She had to go.

Pulling the charm from her pocket, she braced herself against the unnaturally cold weight of it in her palm. And then she said the words that Sammael had given her, before she'd banished him from her circle.

"Show me the path to the deep and Dark, the underbelly where the fallen thrive. Show me the door through the veil and beyond, forbidden to those who are alive. I call not on the Saints but the demons below, hungering in the gloam and the Grey. With this charm I possess, I call on a Watcher, and command him to open the Way."

She fell silent, the charm clutched in her fist, and waited. At first nothing happened, and her heart skipped a beat, fearing that the demon had tricked her. That Grigori would come boiling out of the woods, prepared to drag her away. But then she saw a shimmering in the air, at the base of an oak that over-hung the ruined chapel. It looked...stained, flecked with wavering bits of Darkness.

Gathering every bit of courage she possessed, she walked toward it and stepped through, onto the Shadow Path.

54

KATERINA

I t was dim on the other side of the portal, the earthen ceiling of the tunnel low. Roots dangled from it, brushing Katerina's face with eerie caresses. She slid the stone back into her pocket, where it rested, heavy as a warning.

"Lux," she whispered, afraid to speak too loudly lest she summon who-knew-what. Her voice echoed off the walls of the tunnel, resounding back to her as a hiss: *Luxxxxx luxxxxx luxxxxx.* And though the light came, hovering over the palm of her hand, it was with an effort, as if the roots that drooped from the ceiling had found their way inside her and were holding her magic fast.

Well, she'd known her gift would be affected. As disturbing as the feeling was, it was no excuse to turn back.

Sammael had told her that as long as she possessed his charm, the tunnel would lead her to his realm. It would fork and turn, but she would always know which way to go. The tiny light cupped in her hand, she crept through the narrow passage, which grew colder and damper as it descended into the earth. The light in her hand flickered, though there was no wind, and Katerina suppressed a shudder. What would she do if it went out entirely, leaving her alone in the dark?

The ground was uneven beneath her feet, the small roots trembling with an energy that threatened to break through the soil. Her back throbbed from the hunched position the low ceiling forced her to maintain. More than once, she felt a small, wicked hand caress her feet, but when she looked down, nothing stirred.

Her magic shifted restlessly, and Katerina reached for it, seeking to soothe. But it slipped through her grasp, seeping away. Shivering, she glanced at the light above her palm. Was it her imagination, or had it grown weaker? She drew a deep breath, trying to steady herself, but it didn't help: the air was dank, redolent of rot.

The stone in her pocket flared cold, and she blinked at the dim corridor. A fork lay ahead, as the demon had told her. She prowled into the left-hand tunnel, and the stone flared colder still, as if in confirmation of her choice. Excellent; one step closer to escaping this dismal place.

This tunnel was larger, the ceiling higher. Katerina straightened, but before she could take another step, a whisper echoed in her ears.

"Katerina." Her name drifted on the still air of the tunnel. "I tried to ride to the Magiya. To get the answers you needed. But the Darkness took me and Oriel both. It devoured us and spit us out and left us here. We've been waiting so long...finally you've come..."

Katerina froze, peering into the depths of the tunnel. "Nadia? Is that you?"

"I know what they've said of you." Oriel's voice floated toward her, from the same direction as Nadia's. "Prove you are no Shadow-killer. You never meant for me to die, Katerina. This is no place for my soul. For Nadia's. Bring us back to the Light."

Katerina held up her palm, where the tiny light winked. But try as she might, she could see nothing in the gloom. She called her witchfire, and it came reluctantly, as if dragged forth from the depths. Drawing back her arm, she hurled the ball of flames down the tunnel. For an instant, she could have sworn Nadia and Oriel's silhouettes flickered there. But then her fireball dissolved into blackness, and the figures vanished.

Could Nadia and Oriel really be trapped here? Or were these the voices of demons who walked the Shadow Path, hungry to bind their souls to Katerina's?

"Nadia?" she called again, but no one answered. The shades of Nadia and Oriel had disappeared into the gloom, if they had ever been here at all.

An icy finger traced its way down Katerina's spine. She walked faster, taking one fork, then another, guided by the stone in her pocket. But the faster she walked, the more voices filled her ears, an unearthly clamor that reverberated inside her skull.

I died because of you, Baba Volkova's voice whispered, rising above the rest. *We all died, because you could not stand against the Dark.*

"No." The word trembled in Katerina's throat. "No...I would have saved you if I could..."

The voices rose until they filled the air. *Drezna and Satvala fell because of you, because you weren't strong enough. Because of you, we are dead, lost to the Light. You rose, and the Darkness followed. Save us. You owe us that. You owe us everything.*

"It's not my fault," Katerina cried, turning in a circle, peering into the darkness. But no one was there. Just the voices, echoing from everywhere and nowhere at once. "I never meant to hurt any of you. Stop it. Stop!"

Flame burst from her, along with a gust of wind. It drove the voices back, like they were indeed a physical thing. The tunnel flared brightly, and the faces of the friends she had lost in Drezna and Satvala emerged from the gloom. Then her witchfire faded, extinguished as if doused by a giant hand. The ghostly figures that surrounded her sank back into the dark.

Girding herself, she began to walk again. In the distance gleamed the outline of a door.

Almost there, she told herself. *Just a little more.*

And then yet another whisper came from the shadows.

"Katerina." It was her mother's voice, gentle, shaping each syllable of her name.

Katerina sucked in a sharp breath. "Mama?"

"Don't leave us here," her mother begged. "We're so lonely. Take us with you, so we may fight at your back."

That is not your mother, Katerina told herself grimly. *Any more than those voices belonged to Nadia or Oriel or Baba Volkova. That is a demon, and demons lie.*

She stuffed her fingers in her ears, but it didn't matter; now the voices emanated from inside her head. "My little Firebird," her father crooned. "Even here, you shine so brightly. If you bear us with you down the Shadow Path, then we'll fight by your side. Only invite us in, so we need not linger here in the Dark."

"No," Katerina said, shaking her head as if to shake the voices out of it. "You're not real. Not here. You've passed on into the Light."

"I died defending you." There were tears in her mother's voice now. "The demon *took* me, Katerina. Dragged my soul weeping and shrieking into the Dark. And here I stay, on the Shadow Path. All this time, I've been waiting for you. Now my prayers have been answered. My girl, you've come for me at last."

As if summoned, the image of the last time she'd seen her mother alive sprang into Katerina's mind, clarified in every detail. She saw a demon charging toward her small self, saw her mother throw herself between them. Witchfire exploded from her mother's fingertips, a ball of flame barreling inexorably through the air. It found its target, but as it did, another demon lunged for Katerina's mother.

She hadn't relived this moment in years, had deliberately shoved it down into the deepest recesses of herself. Whenever it had come to her, usually in nightmares, the demon who attacked her mother had been a blur. She could have sworn she had never seen its face. But now she watched her memory unspool as the demon reared back and sank its teeth into the juncture between her mother's neck and shoulder, each detail of the image crystal-clear. With a shock, Katerina recognized the diamond-sharp angle of the jaw, the lithe build and dark fall of hair.

Gadreel.

Her mother's Shadow roared, breaking away from his own battle and charging toward Gadreel, but it was too late. Blood sprayed from Katerina's mother's torn throat. The fire at her fingertips flickered and went out.

"No," small Katerina shrieked as she watched her mother fall. "Mama! Mama!"

"No," Katerina whispered now, dropping to her knees before the door that led out of the tunnels. Tiny roots bit into her knees, digging in. She could *feel* the hot blood splatter her cheeks as it had when she was a child, fighting to reach her fallen mother. The howl of Tima, her mother's Shadow, reverberated in her bones once more as she fought to escape the Vila who held her fast. She tried to call her own magic, to vanquish the demon, but she was too small and her fear too great and nothing came.

"Katerina," her mother whispered, the word rasping from her torn throat, just as it had that day. "Run..."

EMILY COLIN

The Vila lifted small Katerina, still kicking and fighting, and fled. Over the woman's shoulder, Katerina saw Tima fall beneath the onslaught of another Grigori's blade. Gadreel stood there, head tipped back toward the darkened sky, her mother's blood pouring from his mouth as he gave an inhuman howl of triumph.

"He took my life," said her mother's voice inside her head. "And left me here. Don't you want to avenge me, Katerina? Together, we will have such strength. Let me in...let me in...let me in..."

There on her knees, she could swear her mother's hands held her tight. She had longed to feel her touch again. Had Gadreel really murdered her mother, then left her soul in this purgatory rather than using it to power the Dark? Had she been here all this time, waiting for Katerina to find her?

Guilt consumed Katerina, just as it had the day she had tried to save her mother, to destroy the demon that had taken her life. Every time she faced the Grigori, every time she vanquished one to the Void, it was a victory over what she had failed to do before, a drop of water in a bucket that could never be filled. And all this time, *Gadreel* had been the faceless enemy she'd sought to defeat.

We meet again, little Dimi, he'd said to her in the woods. Finally, she understood.

If that part of the memory were true—if the demon that coveted her was the same one who had killed her mother—then what about the rest of it?

"Please, Katerina," her mother coaxed, her fingers encircling Katerina's upper arms. "Your father and I miss you so much. All we want is to be with you. We can be together again. Only open your heart."

Katerina tried to summon the Light, but it flickered weakly, refusing to flare into a flame. In desperation, she thrust her

408

hand into her pocket. Her fingers closed around the charm. It was icy as ever, the engraved snakes slithering against her palm. But as her grip tightened around it, her head cleared.

Her mother's touch turned cold and grasping. She blinked, and found the roots had burst through the tunnel's earthen walls and floor, twining around her, seeking to bind her. *They* held her fast, not her mother's shade.

With her free hand, she scrabbled for the knife in her thigh sheath as a root wrapped around her fingers. Blessed or no, the blade was still sharp, and she sliced at it, freeing her arms first, then her legs.

The invisible demon impersonating her mother shrieked, the sound piercing. It echoed off the tunnel's walls and floor and arrowed through Katerina's head, nearly making her lose her grip on the knife. "Why would you hurt me, my Firebird?" it wept. "Stay with me...if you loved me, you would stay..."

"You lie!" With the last bit of her strength, Katerina wrenched her way free. The door loomed in front of her, arched and shimmering with the same flecks of Darkness that had marked the portal outside Kalach. She grasped the handle and shoved with all her might, and it gave easily, hungrily, beneath her touch. Fear metallic in her mouth, heart thrashing in her chest, she fell across the threshold and into the unknown world beyond.

55

KATERINA

S omehow, impossibly, Katerina was standing in Kalach. Had things gone horribly wrong? Had she traveled through a portal to the Underworld only to arrive home again?

She was at the edge of the village square, watching as Maksim passed by her without so much as a nod of acknowledgment. Behind him came Alyona, and Katerina braced herself for the Vila's invective. But Aly merely waved at her, batting her lashes coquettishly in Katerina's direction. Her green eyes were devoid of any kind of resentment or suspicion. And her cheeks were plump and full, unlike the last time Katerina had seen her, at Niko's funeral.

That sense of *wrongness* intensified as Katerina turned, taking in her surroundings. There was the blacksmith's shop. The apothecary. The marketplace. All where they should be. Except...the marketplace's stalls were overflowing with lush, ripe fruit and vegetables, fresh-baked bread, cookies, and cakes. The air bloomed with the earthy scent of borscht and the tempting aroma of vareniki, sizzling in oil. Hungry as she was, her mouth watered at the sight.

As Katerina watched, the ruddy-cheeked villagers lined up for helpings, Konstantin and Ana among them. They chattered amongst themselves, looking healthy and fit and *cheerful*. There wasn't a sallow-faced, malnourished one in the bunch. Mid-square, fiddlers and tambourine musicians played a jolly tune as dancers held hands and twirled. In the center stood a khorovodnitsa, directing the festivities.

Katerina stared, speechless. Kalach had been planning a celebration for the Kniaz's arrival, but this was more than the village could usually manage for the fall Harvest Festival. What was happening? Where *was* she? And how long had she been underground?

"You, girl!" an elderly woman in a bright yellow apron called, motioning at Katerina. "What are you waiting for? Get the finest cheese vareniki in Kalach right here!"

Katerina loved vareniki; the fried, stuffed dumplings were her favorites. Every cook in town knew it, and had vied for the honor to have Dimi Ivanova sample their goods. In conse-quence, Katerina knew every vareniki-maker in Kalach by name. And this woman was a stranger. Odder still, how had she gotten the flour for the dough, when the fields were barren and the storehouses had been emptied for the Kniaz's tithe?

Everyone's happy expressions and well-fed bodies. The way Alyona hadn't recognized her. The profusion of food. None of it made any sense.

"Would you prefer mushroom?" The woman smiled, showing unusually sharp, white teeth. "I picked them myself, just this morn. Tender as a baby's flesh, they are."

A fruit vendor, her hair tied back with a patterned kerchief and her cheeks unnaturally rosy, rummaged among her wares. She came up with a pomegranate, sliced in two. The seeds glis-tened in the harsh sunlight, ruby-bright and slick with juice. "Fruit of the damned," she called cheerfully. "Beautiful fruit!"

"Or perhaps you would prefer borscht," the man in the next stall over suggested, leering at Katerina. He gestured to a steaming cauldron, perched over a crackling fire. "Red as blood, and twice as sweet. See?"

Dipping a ladle into the cauldron, he lifted it for Katerina's inspection. As fat, gleaming drops fell from the spoon, Katerina smelled not the tangy-sour aroma of the soup she loved but the coppery scent of blood. She gasped, and the man cackled, a horned, blue-skinned beast shimmering beneath the surface of his wrinkled skin.

"Come and get it!" he cried happily. "Come and eat...and eat...and eat..."

He bared his teeth, stepping toward her. And then he stopped, his nostrils flaring.

"What *are* you?" he said, his voice deep and threatening. "From whence have you come? You smell of Light, little one. You smell...tasty."

The square fell silent, the fiddlers lifting their bows and the tambourines ceasing to jingle. The dancers, still clutching each other's hands, turned as one to face Katerina. And then, as if attuned to a signal only they could hear, they all began to advance upon her, their eyes alight with hunger.

Normally, Katerina would have stood her ground and fought. But here and now, her magic wavered inside her, a candle flame whose wick was guttering. If she called, she couldn't trust it to come.

So instead she turned and fled like a hunted rabbit, past the abandoned stalls of fresh-cut flowers and iced cakes and simmering stroganoff, past the fiddlers and the beribboned dancers who reached out taloned hands to grasp her. She ran and ran, her breath rasping in her throat, until she finally arrived at a familiar place.

Elena's cottage.

The yellow siding, the white trim, the bright blue door...all of it was the same. Only the runes that twined along the window frames and beneath the eaves were different. They spoke of demonic influence, not goodness and Light.

Katerina stood, silently, and listened. She could no longer hear the crowd chasing her. The crowd, she realized now, that had been comprised of Grigori who had likely been ordered to take on the forms of the villagers of Kalach. Sammael had constructed a replica of their village for Elena. As she had left her home behind, he had brought her home to her.

It would have been sweet, if it hadn't been a fallen angel's gift to a deluded murderer.

She could see Elena through one of the windows of the cottage, sitting at her table, in front of a samovar and tea set that had been her Shadow father's wedding gift. She was wearing the gown in which she'd married Niko, her platinum hair threaded with thorned greenbriar vines, in an eerie, sinister echo of her wedding's roses. She looked remote, and lovely, and...untouchable.

Katerina pulled one of her blades from its sheath. Breath hissing through her teeth and witchfire licking her ankles, she crept toward the house. Through the wavy glass of the window, she saw Elena raise a cup to her lips, one hand resting casually on the head of a black dog that leaned against her side.

Katerina's breath caught. But the dog was not Niko, with the white streak above his ear that marked him as hers and the wit that blazed in his gray eyes, even in dog form. It was the beast that had accompanied Elena to the clearing.

Where, then, was her Shadow?

Katerina scanned the front room of the cottage, all that she could see from where she stood. Niko was nowhere in sight. There was just Elena, sipping tea from her wedding china like a demented bride, and the black dog, her obedient companion.

The demon Sammael did not need to take a Shadow's shape. It could have resembled anything: A man, a monster. Yet there it was, impersonating a Shadow, perpetuating Elena's delusion that she was anything other than an abomination.

Rage swelled in Katerina, and her magic flared, escaping her. One of the windows blew inward, shattering. The shards of glass whipped around Elena, a tornado painting her white skin in blood, slashing her wedding dress, tearing the lace from its hem.

The Vila's gaze fixed on Katerina. For a moment, her wide blue eyes reflected shock and horror. And then she started to laugh.

"Katerina?" she said, her voice unconcerned, as if she weren't bleeding from a thousand tiny cuts. "What are you doing here? Come to join me for tea?" She gestured at the table before her. "There's plenty, after all."

Perhaps she had gone mad, altogether. "I've come—" Katerina began, but Elena wasn't listening. Instead, she turned to the black dog at her side.

"Did you ask someone to impersonate her, for my entertainment? You are too good to me, my beloved. Let us spend the evening torturing her, and imagine that it's truly Katerina who stands before us. It will be such fun."

But the black dog was no more. Sammael stood there, in the guise of the redheaded man. "No," he said. "I did not conjure her, Elena, nor yet did I command a minor demon to impersonate her likeness. I called her here, in hopes that the two of you could come to terms."

Elena's mouth fell open. "What?" she croaked. "Is this a joke?"

The demon shook his head, his expression grave, and a rageful flush suffused Elena's features. "I don't understand. Why would you betray me this way?"

"Think of it as a favor, rather than a betrayal." Sammael's gaze lingered on the empty air by the Vila's side. "You are not yourself. And like it or not, we share a common enemy."

"Katerina *is* my enemy." Elena stood, advancing toward the window frame, studded with shards of glass. Her cuts were already healing; were it not for the bloodied dress that swirled around her ankles, Katerina might believe they had never been there at all.

The Vila peered curiously at Katerina, as if she were looking through her. And then she shook her head so hard, one of the greenbriar vines came loose from her intricate braids. "That is truly her, and not an illusion or charm? How is that possible?" Her upper lip rose in a snarl more befitting a rabid beast than the demure Vila she had once been.

Katerina's heart fluttered: a desperate sensation, as if it were trying to break free and flee back above ground where it—and she—belonged. Her magic faltered, the witchfire around her ankles winking out. She forced a smirk onto her face. "Surprise," she said.

Elena let out an infuriated squeak. It would almost have been amusing, if it hadn't been accompanied by a burst of the silver-blue flames that had surged from the portal in the clearing, devouring Niko alive. "I will have vengeance on you for this," she said, turning on Sammael. "You brought the corrupt witch herself to our threshold!"

That was rich. "If one of us is a corrupt witch," Katerina retorted, "I don't think it's me."

The Vila didn't spare her a glance, as if Katerina hadn't spoken at all. "She's interrupted tea-time," she said, her fury transmuting to sulkiness with alarming ease and her lower lip protruding in a pout. "Now I'll have to get rid of her. And I was having *such* fun."

What was Elena capable of? Could the Vila vanquish Katerina, send her hurtling back aboveground, before she'd even laid eyes on her Shadow? Fear gnawed at Katerina's stomach with vicious, razor-sharp teeth, and she fought to keep her voice level. "If you're so keen to torture me, then invite me in, Elena. Before the demons who chased me through the square and into the streets do it for you."

Sammael looked contrite. "Sorry about them," he said. "In truth, I expected you to emerge here, rather than in the square. The portals right now aren't..." He made a seesawing motion with his hand, as if to indicate everything the portals were not. "But have no fear. My minions know not to approach Elena's cottage without permission."

So that explained the demons' sudden disappearance. She supposed she should be grateful for small favors. "Where is my Shadow?" she demanded.

Elena's pink-tinted lips rose in a sneer. "He's right here, of course," she said, gesturing to the empty space on her left. "Right beside me, where he belongs. What, can you not see him, Katerina?"

Katerina stared at the spot Elena indicated. There was a shimmer to the air, a vaguely man-sized shape that wavered, flickering in the breeze from the open window. "But—how—"

"He's mine now," Elena said, gloating. "I see his true form. If you cannot, then perhaps you should accept what you should have known all along. He was never meant for you."

Katerina strained, trying to will the shimmer into being. And then she saw it, fractured by the shards of glass that clung to the edge of the window frame behind him: her Shadow's transparent shape. For an instant, she caught an unmistakable glimpse of Niko's face, his eyes wide with shock and misery. His lips moved, trying desperately to say something, but there was no sound. A moment later, he winked out of existence again.

What had Elena *done* to him?

The Vila was laughing now, a self-satisfied sound that Katerina wanted to smack right out of her throat. "I will kill you," she told Elena, her voice cold. "I'll take what remains of your cursed existence, and free my Shadow from your clutches."

"This is not why I brought you here—" Sammael began, just as Elena's laughter cut off. She glared at Katerina.

"You can't hurt me," the Vila said. "You've already done your worst, and I'm invulnerable now. It's too bad the same can't be said for you." A chilling, self-satisfied smile lifted her lips. "I wanted nothing more than to hunt you down and end you like the murderer you are. Yet here you are, coming to me, sparing me the trouble. Make no mistake: I'll be the one to take your life."

To the Saints with whatever agreement Katerina had made with Sammael. Seizing the fading remnants of her power, she harnessed the wind. The front door flew open and she lunged at Elena, her witchfire surging up to devour the cottage and the Vila with it. She would vanquish Elena and her demon, save her Shadow, and flee.

Her blade was inches from Elena's throat when the Vila snapped her fingers. Again in dog form, Sammael growled and leapt through the fire, knocking the blade aside and pinning Katerina to the ground. She fought and thrashed, but couldn't move him: He was no ordinary dog, and had no ordinary mistress. And even fueled by rage, Katerina was half of what she'd been. Her magic slipped through her fingers, draining away.

The dog bared his teeth, crushing Katerina into the floorboards. Her lungs heaved, straining for breath, as rain called by her power blew through the empty window frame, drenching both of them. Above her, the demon beast growled in warning.

Elena's voice came toward her, drifting on the rain-soaked breeze. "On second thought, I don't think I'll kill you so quickly.

You should suffer, the way my Niko did, and pay for your crimes. I'll chain you here, next to him. Every day, I'll take another piece of you. You'll weep while I watch and take pleasure in your pain. For I am Elena-of-the-Void, beloved of Sammael, Queen of Darkness, and you are at my mercy."

There was a flash of light above Katerina, and then the weight of the black dog was gone. Sammael was himself again, standing and brushing bits of glass from his clothes. "Come now, my Vila," he said, his tone cajoling. "Is there really a need for this? Here, the Dimi is as helpless as a babe. You are the one with all of the advantages. What could it hurt to hear her out?"

"I want," Elena said, her tone glacial, "nothing to do with anything she has to say, unless it's to beg me for clemency. I think I'd like hearing that, quite a lot."

Katerina sat up, struggling to catch her breath. The storm outside had died down, and no wonder. When she felt for her magic, all that stirred was a weak echo of her usual power. She had been foolish to use so much of it attacking a creature that could heal whatever wounds she made, in a place where such a creature had, as Sammael pointed out, the high ground.

Think, Katerina. Baba Petrova's voice sounded in her head. *You cannot use your magic. You cannot use force. What is left to you?*

She got to her feet, surveying the room. Elena stood by the table, fastidiously righting the teacups that Katerina's assault had knocked over. Next to her, Niko's transparent form glimmered and guttered, his eyes fixed on the Vila in fury and his lips moving in silent protest. Sammael drummed his fingers on the back of the settee, Katerina's blade in his free hand. The clock above the mantel ticked.

Think, Katerina.

The duplicate of Kalach. The wedding dress. The china.

"You cannot walk above ground," Katerina blurted.

418

Elena's eyes flashed to hers, a hint of vulnerability in their depths. "What?"

"Bonding with Sammael prevented you from being devoured by the Void," Katerina said, certainty thrumming through every word. "But it didn't eradicate my curse completely. You're not just here"—she waved at the cottage—"because Niko is dead and you sold your soul to a demon. You're here because you can't leave. That's why Sammael recreated Kalach for you...because you can never go home again."

The Vila flinched. "That is none of your business," she said.

"Niko is my business." Katerina took one step closer to her Shadow's trembling image, then another. "The Darkness that threatens us all is my business. As it should be yours."

"The Darkness is no longer my problem," Elena said, but her gaze fixed on Sammael, and Katerina could hear an inkling of doubt in her voice.

"Elena," Sammael said, sounding tired, "I have told you and told you that it is."

Elena smoothed her bloodied wedding dress, the gesture both fastidious and petulant. "She wishes to steal my Shadow from me. She must die, as she should have died in the clearing."

"Is that all you have to say?" Katerina heaved an exasperated sigh. "*She must die. She should suffer. She will weep while I watch.* Wake up, Elena! We're all in danger of extinction, demons and humans alike. You'll kill me, and then what? Take away the best chance of vanquishing the Darkness? You'll have a few glorious days of satisfaction, before you get sucked into the Void, just like you would've been if Sammael hadn't rescued you."

Elena glared at her. "What do you propose, then, Katerina?" She spat the name, as if it tasted rotten in her mouth. "I can hardly wait to hear."

Katerina drew a sharp, shuddering breath. She had always

been a gambler, and never thought much of it. But now she was gambling for Niko's life.

"Give me my Shadow," she said. "Let him fight by my side. And when the Darkness has been defeated, let him decide where he belongs."

Katerina hardly dared to breathe. She watched Niko's mouth move as he tried again and again to speak, watched Sammael watch Elena, watched the Vila consider her proposal.

Elena inclined her head, and Katerina's heart leapt.

And then she answered, "No."

56
KATERINA

"I propose," Sammael said, "a compromise."

Katerina's eyes slid to the demon, her expression wary. "Excuse me?" she said, just as Elena snapped, "I think not. No proposal that includes the word *compromise* is worth my time."

For once, Katerina found herself in perfect agreement with the Vila. "Well, you do have so much of it," she said. "Time, that is. Perhaps you ought to at least listen to your beloved. After all, he's gone to so much trouble to bring me here."

The demon shot Katerina a look that suggested she wasn't helping matters. Katerina glared back at him. She wasn't in the demon-helping business.

"I propose," the demon said again, leaning back against the stone hearth and crossing his legs at the ankle, "that the Shadow spend six months above ground, roaming the earth as he chooses, and six months below, with you, my Vila. During that time, you will have him to yourself, to do with him as you will."

The words chilled Katerina to the bone. What, exactly, had

Elena been doing with her Shadow? What more would she do, if given the chance?

Beside Elena, Niko's shade bared his teeth, and Katerina could well imagine the growl that rumbled from his chest. The Vila cocked her head, eyes bright as a magpie spying a sparkling bit of metal. "And when he's above ground..."

"Demand that the Dimi lift the curse she placed upon you." Sammael shrugged one elegant shoulder. "And then you will move between the Underworld and the world above at your will. You need never be without your Shadow, if that is what you desire."

Elena considered this. And then a vicious smile lit her face. Deep in her ocean-blue eyes, obsidian flames blazed. "Hmmm," she said. "That is a compromise only for Katerina, is it not? For I would have all that I desire. Perhaps I can forgive your betrayal, Sammael. After all, you had my best interests at heart."

Sammael raised a single red brow in acquiescence, and Katerina clenched her fists. "This is what you intended all along," she accused him. "You tricked me. You never meant to set Niko free."

"What did you expect?" The demon's voice was almost... kind. "You made a deal with the devil. Well, *a* devil, anyhow."

"You basta—"

"If you're going to call me names," Sammael said, plucking a shard of glass from his sleeve and tossing it from one hand to the other, "you might as well know the truth. I followed you to your Shadow's grave. *I* enchanted the stones of the desecrated chapel and planted the Book of the Lost beneath them, so that you would find it and summon me. I feigned surprise when I found myself in your circle. Luring you here was always my intention. And it worked just as I planned. Humans..." He dropped the shard of glass onto the ground and crushed it to bits beneath his shoe. "So easy to manipulate. Not even a challenge."

"You...?" Katerina's stomach plummeted as Elena's lips rose in a smug, satisfied smile. Not the Saints, then. A demon. And she'd played into his hands from the start.

You know a great deal about Shadows and Dimis, demon, she'd told him. *Perhaps too much.* And how had he replied? *I have lived for many years.* But that wasn't the whole truth, was it? All along, he'd had the Book. He'd seen her visit Niko's grave, heard her pour out her heart to her fallen Shadow. And then he'd hidden the Book beneath the stones, and spelled them to respond to a drop of her blood.

Katerina had been a fool.

"I accept the compromise!" Elena said cheerily, gesturing to the table, set with the Vila's wedding china. "Will you have a drink on it, Katerina? To seal our bargain?"

Niko's transparent fists were clenched at his sides now, every muscle in his lean body tensed and his expression tight with rage. His gaze fixed on Katerina, and his lips formed a single, silent word over and over: *No. No. No.*

Though it pained her to do it, Katerina glanced away. "Like I would drink anything you gave me," she said, the sarcasm reflexive. Beneath it, her mind was churning.

Of course, Sammael had never intended to let Niko go. If Katerina had been thinking clearly, she would've realized that from the start. Freeing him would hurt Elena, and in his twisted way, he cared for the Vila. Besides, Elena would never agree to being parted from Niko. That much was clear.

But perhaps this bargain was the best Katerina was going to get. Lifting the curse was troublesome, to be sure, a blow to Katerina's pride as well as to justice. It was the punishment Elena deserved, to be banished forever from her home and from the Light for murdering Niko and aligning herself with the Dark. For nearly bringing the Darkness down upon Kalach.

But Katerina wasn't strong enough to kill Elena here. If she could get the Vila above ground, though, where they were on equal footing... There, Katerina and Niko would be together again. With her Shadow at her side, the two of them would be formidable enough to defeat the Vila and drive the Darkness back. Katerina would tell Baba what she had done, explain Gadreel's folly, send word to the Magiya, and together they would fix everything.

She cleared her throat. "I accept," she said.

Triumph glimmered in Elena's fire-shot eyes. "Then lift the curse, Dimi Ivanova. Do it now." She stamped her foot, like a child having a tantrum.

Katerina had never cursed anyone before, much less tried to undo such a binding. But she had given her word. And for Niko's life, she had to try.

Praying she wasn't making a terrible mistake, Katerina reached for the fraying tendrils of her power, drawing them up and through her soul, spilling Light into her fingertips. She forced herself to truly see Elena—not the damned woman who stood before her, but the aura that surrounded her, desecrated and stained. A hint of Light glimmered at its center, near where Elena's heart might still beat. But the rest...it was a cold, cold thing, dark with gossamer threads of corruption, clouded with shadows. Through it, like chains of gilded iron, wound the silvery bindings of Katerina's curse. They wrapped Elena from head to toe, passing through the floorboards and anchoring her to the earth beneath the cottage. They were a fearsome sight.

"Once, I cursed you, Elena-of-the-Void, now beloved of Sammael, vessel of the Darkness," she said, imbuing each word with her diminishing power, praying it would be enough. "*Cleaved to a demon, may your soul walk in chains. You bound* yourself to Sammael, Venom of God, of your own free will. I can't undo such a thing. But now I retract the curse I placed upon you. May the ties that bind you loosen; may your spirit be set free. May you rise from the Underworld as you please, and walk among the living once more."

Niko's shade glanced desperately between Katerina and the Vila, shaking his head. He was speaking, a silent spill of words from which Katerina could only make out *Stop* and *Katerina* and *Don't*. His hands rose, clutching his throat, as if to force the sound from it, but nothing came. Gritting his teeth, he tried to take a step toward Katerina. But his leg froze in midair, and then, as if an invisible chain reeled him backward, his foot sank down and he stood by Elena's side once more. Frustration washed over his features, and his lips moved again, forming what Katerina was sure was a plea.

I'm so sorry, my Shadow, she thought, and wished he could hear.

Drawing a deep breath, Katerina focused not on Niko but on the cursed woman who stood beside him. The air in the cottage trembled and the floorboards strained beneath the Vila's feet, as if the chains Katerina had visualized were real. She concentrated her waning strength, trying to break them, but the links held, as if soldered by Sant Antoniya herself.

Elena howled as the chains sank deeper into her ankles, wrapped tighter around her body in its iridescent, shimmering gown. She pressed one hand to her heart, where the tiny Light still burned. "What have you done? Make it stop!" she shrieked.

Grimly, Katerina fought to keep her promise, to unwind the chains of her curse from the Vila's aura. But they were tangled too firmly, and the more Katerina struggled to loosen them, the more stubbornly they clung. It was as if a force beyond Katerina's own will had placed them there. No matter what she did, she couldn't set the Vila free.

She fell back at last, panting, exhausted. The world ran before her eyes in streamers of gray, and she had to grab for the back of the settee to keep from falling. As she watched, steadying herself, the chains loosened until they were as they had been before.

Elena ceased whimpering and turned accusatory eyes on her. "Nothing's changed," she said, pointing a finger at Katerina. "You didn't keep our bargain!"

Katerina opened her mouth to tell the Vila that she'd done the best she could. But to her surprise, the demon got there first. "Dimi Ivanova did, indeed, try to lift the curse," he said, and Katerina could've sworn she heard regret in his tone. "Alas, my Vila, the Darkness grips you too tightly to let you go."

"Grips me too tightly?" Elena tugged at the lace that hemmed her wrists, as if it, rather than the Darkness, restrained her. "What do you mean?"

"He means," Katerina said, "that your soul is far too corrupt, Elena. The Darkness has claimed you, and my curse merely adds to its power. This is where you belong. Perhaps the Saints themselves could free you; I cannot." Her lips rose in a fierce smile. "Here you are, and here you'll stay, in this foolish, pathetic replica of your cottage. Give me my Shadow, and say goodbye until six months hence. For you shall never go home again."

Rage distorted Elena's fine features. Her blue eyes glimmered, coal-black flames gleaming in their depths. "I'll do no such thing! This is all your fault," she snarled at Katerina. "You did this to me."

"You did it to yourself," Katerina retorted. "*You* allied yourself with a demon. *You* made a devil's bargain for the soul of my Shadow. *You* took my Shadow's life and forced me to curse you to eternal Darkness, lest the corruption that claimed your soul devour all of Kalach."

"He is not your Shadow!" Elena shrieked, so loudly that the glass of the remaining windowpanes shuddered. "He is mine! Now, always, and forever mine! And I'll prove it to you."

She stalked closer to Katerina, stopping a foot away. Darkness stirred in the depths of her eyes, a storm brewing beneath the surface of the sea.

"I may have made a pact with you," Elena said, fitting one long-fingered hand around Niko's neck like a collar. Katerina wanted to rip it from her wrist. "But you didn't uphold your side of the bargain. I offer you one more chance, for I am a merciful Queen."

Queen of what? Katerina wanted to say. *Queen of this cottage? Long may you reign, broken wedding china, frayed wedding dress, and all.* But by a miracle, she managed to hold her tongue.

"I bound my Shadow to me in death, as Baba Petrova bound him to you in life," Elena said, greed coursing beneath the surface of her high, musical voice. "If you believe you still have a claim on him—that you can call him from my side—then I dare you to try, here in my realm where you have no power. Here, where I rule."

Katerina's breath caught. Could she do such a thing? Niko's soul was, indeed, bound to Elena's; the fact that he had disappeared with her into the portal when Katerina had banished Elena and the demons was irrefutable proof. Here, Elena shone and Katerina was the weak one. What if she couldn't do what Elena demanded?

The Vila was scrutinizing Katerina, triumph burning bright in those infernal eyes. Steeling herself, she forced the familiar arrogance into her voice. "*Rule* seems a bit of an exaggeration. This is Sammael's realm, not yours. You're merely a guest; you exist at his pleasure." She regarded the Vila, nostrils flaring with scorn. "Remember, Elena, Niko chose me, above and beyond Baba's bond. He'll choose me again."

The Vila hissed, an inhuman, serpent-like sound. The flames that flickered in her eyes flared higher, her irises swallowing the sclera, until they were nothing but blue fire. The walls of her cottage shuddered and wavered. "We'll see about that."

She tightened her grip on Niko's throat, yanking his head down until the Shadow had no choice but to meet her eyes. "You are *mine*, Niko Alekhin. If you love me—if our love is true—then you will stay by my side. Show Katerina that your bond with her is broken. That you care more for me than you ever did for her."

Niko's image blinked out of existence once more. When it materialized again, Katerina could see the tendrils of corruption winding through it, the veins of Darkness threaded through his Light, as if Elena's command had summoned them. Her stomach roiled at the sight.

"A fair fight, then," Katerina said, forcing her voice not to betray the terror she felt. "If I win, you must agree to uphold the terms of our bargain. And if *you* win, I'll leave the Underworld, and Niko's soul will be forfeit to the Dark."

Elena's eyes slid to Sammael, who hadn't moved from the hearth. "It is a true bargain, my Vila," he said, his voice devoid of expression, as if he too was trying to conceal the true nature of his feelings. "It is not the Dimi's fault she could not free you from your bond with the Darkness. She acted in good faith."

Elena scoffed, as if the very idea were ludicrous, then stepped forward and traced a rune in the air. Katerina recognized it from her bonding ceremony with Niko: the sigil for a promise made. Only here, it burned with the silver-blue flames of the damned. "I give my word," she said. "If you win, then for six months of the year, Niko will walk above ground. If you lose, then he will stay here, with me, for eternity. I place my mark on it."

Her word. Now Katerina was the one to scoff, for what was the word of such a creature worth? But she reached out and traced Elena's rune with what remained of her own magic. Her hand trembled with the energy it took to pull the Light from the depths of her being. "I, too, give my word and place my mark."

The runes flared together, one silver-blue with the flames of the inferno, the other red-gold with Light. For an instant, they blazed so brightly, Katerina was nearly blinded. And then, with a sucking sound that threatened to steal all the air from the room, they winked out, leaving the Vila and the Dimi facing each other. The transparent image of Niko's shade stood by Elena's side, laced with that ghastly Darkness.

"It is done," Sammael said into the silence.

The Vila began to laugh, an unhinged cackle that echoed off the walls of the cottage. "Excellent," she said. "Call my Shadow from my side if you can, Dimi Ivanova. Call him not with the shreds of your weakening magic, nor with your severed bond. Call him with the force of what he feels for you, and watch as he moves not from my side."

Digging deep, deep down inside herself, Katerina mustered what remained of her gift and called it to her hand. It came, but reluctantly, like a creature that had been beaten too many times and hesitated to return to its master. Her power was *afraid* here, she realized. And without her power, what was she capable of? What could she do? She was a Dimi, born to wield the Light. In its absence, she was nothing more than a woman who had lost the man she loved and taken a foolish risk, sacrificing everything to get him back again. She was nothing more than Elena, who had made a dangerous bargain with a demon and would have to pay the price.

Katerina channeled all of her strength, as she had when she incinerated the Grigori army on the road to Drezna. The roots of her power strained in the soil of her soul, threatening to rip free as she fought to imbue Niko's soul with Light.

Her Shadow's image solidified, brightening. He took one strained step away from Elena, then another, his jaw set and his muscles trembling, as if every inch were agony. With a growl, Elena reached for him—*through* him—to pull him back. But there was no need; the Light dimmed and he stumbled backward once again. His eyes met Katerina's, deep with sorrow. Then his lips moved, and with a pang that took her through the heart, Katerina made out what he was trying to say: *I'm sorry.*

Her Shadow, who had sacrificed himself to save her, who was the bravest person Katerina had ever known, was apologizing to *her.*

She held his gaze, trying to tell him this wasn't over, that she had no intention of giving up. Beside him, Elena was laughing, telling Katerina she had won, Niko was hers, the pact was made—

She lunged for the Vila's throat, drawing on the dregs of her power. Hands around Elena's neck, she called on what remained of her Light, determined to set the Vila aflame.

Elena shrieked as they fell to the floor, witchfire blazing up around them, overturning the table. The shards of the broken tea set bit into Katerina's leather gear as she sought to strangle the Vila—if indeed she could be killed. But as she tightened her grip on Elena's throat, the Vila's skin illuminated with those silver-blue flames. They scorched Katerina's fingertips with a cold so intense it stole her breath, and she fell away from the Vila with a gasp as the last of her power drained from her.

She felt so strange. Empty. Hollow. As if she were a shell of herself, the insides scooped out, and if she shattered, there would be nothing left but bones.

Elena lay on the floor in her wedding gown, the silk torn at the shoulder and the lace ripped away from the bodice's hem. She laughed and laughed and laughed.

"I told you, Dimi Ivanova," she said between jagged peals of mirth. "This is my place of power. You cannot touch me here." Her gaze shifted to Sammael, standing in the middle of the floor, then to Niko's insubstantial form beside her. "Are we done, then? Do you yield, and admit I've won?"

The words stuck in Katerina's throat. She refused to say them, to consign Niko to an eternity in the Dark. But what could she do? How could she save him now?

Her gaze traveled between the corrupt Vila, the inscrutable demon, and the shade of her Shadow, then back again, as her mind churned, desperate for a solution. And then, as her eyes fell on her Shadow's transparent face once more, revelation dawned.

Niko had not come to her aid as she and Elena fought. But neither had he defended the Vila.

He was a guardian, a black dog. Defending those who he was bound to was bred into his very nature. If he hadn't fought for Elena, then that had to mean he wasn't truly hers.

It was a thin thread of hope, true. But it was all she had. And if there was even a chance she could save her Shadow, Katerina would take it, or die trying.

Summoning the last of her strength, she rose to her feet. "No," she said. "I will not yield."

57

KATERINA

Elena sat up, eyes narrowed. She looked, Katerina thought, like an elegant doll that a child had played with too harshly and tossed to the floor, if that doll had been possessed by demonic influences. "Admit you've lost," she said, her chiming voice at odds with the infernal flames that lit her eyes. "There is no power left in you; I can feel it. Leave now, and I will let you live."

Katerina ignored her. Instead, she focused on the Light that still gleamed within Niko's shade, stronger than the infusion of Darkness. She thought of his loyalty, his compassion, the way he made her laugh. Remembered him saying, *I love you. More than is right. More than I should.*

Katerina drew a deep, shaky breath. Never had she tried to fight a battle this way, without access to her gifts. Never had she made herself so vulnerable, while risking so much.

Sant Antoniya, she prayed, *if I've ever been worthy of your blessings, help me now. Sant Andrei, the soul of your child hangs in the balance. Help me reunite him with the Light.*

As if in response to her prayer, a vision blazed up behind Katerina's eyes. Whereas before, she'd thought of herself as one with her gifts, the trunk of a strong tree that grew into a thousand branches of Light, she saw now that that wasn't the case. *She* was the tree, and her gifts were vines of Light that wrapped around the trunk and branches. They had grown with Katerina, thriving and powerful, but her *self*, her essence, was independent of the Light. And even if her Light couldn't shine brightly here, she, Katerina, could still fight. She could survive, even if her Light was doused by Darkness.

The realization broke over her with the force of the tidal wave she'd brought to bear in the clearing, the horrible night Niko had died. It squared her shoulders and straightened her spine and lifted her lips in a terrible, shining smile.

"Niko, if you can hear me, I'll always fight for you." She swallowed hard. "One for the fire, my love. Two for the storm."

Next to Elena, her Shadow cocked his head, listening. Encouraging Katerina to go on. And so she did, speaking the next lines of their bonding vow, the one that had first tied her to Niko. It had only been a formality, bonding them as Dimi and Shadow. They had always, always been meant for each other, prophecy be damned. The bond only recognized what the two of them had known all along: they were meant to be.

She pictured herself and Niko in their meadow as children, playing at Shadows and Watchers. Pictured them leaping from stone to stone in the river that ran alongside Kalach. Pictured him bending to kiss her, his dark hair falling into her eyes and his scent all around her. "Three for the black dog that guards against harm," she said.

Eyes on her face, Niko's shade took one tentative step toward Katerina, then another. The movements were slow, as if he fought for every inch, but steady. Watching him, Elena snarled.

Her heart in her throat, Katerina went on. "Four for the

silence that follows the dark. Five for the cold one whose path is stark."

As she said the words, she thought of the explosion that had filled the air before the Darkness swallowed Drezna. Of the deadly quiet that followed. And then of the animals that lay, frozen, on the road. An uneasy realization stirred within her.

"Six for the dream that brings secrets to light," she said, her eyes on Niko's transparent form as it advanced. "Seven for the curse that spreads blight through the night."

Gadreel's dream of harnessing the Darkness. The blight that had destroyed Drezna's orchards and drained the life from Kalach's fields. How had she never seen this before? How had she failed to put the pieces together?

The Shadow and Dimi vow...it was as if it had been written for them. As if it had been their story, all along.

It didn't matter now. All that mattered was that Niko was still walking toward her, even as Elena tried and failed to call him back again. Katerina was winning. She just had to keep going.

"Eight for the loss that cuts beyond price." Her voice shook, thinking of how it had broken her to see Niko die in that clearing. "Nine for the heart carved wholly from ice."

She thought of Elena's heart, of that tiny red-gold flicker beating within the frozen wasteland that her aura had become. And knew that the Vila was destroyed beyond repair.

"What are you doing?" Elena cried as Niko's shade stepped even closer to where Katerina stood. "Niko, no!" Lurching after him, she threw her arms around his neck. But he moved onward, and Elena tumbled to the floor.

"Ten for his tears," Katerina went on inexorably, her eyes fixed on Niko's face. "The rest for her fears."

She had feared so much, even though she was loath to let it show. And though she had never seen her Shadow cry, she knew that whether or not he had let the tears fall, he had wept for what had become of him and Katerina, in his heart. She remembered him standing with her after the battle, watching Elena walk away with glistening eyes, saying, *This is tearing me apart. Understand that, if nothing else.*

I'm not afraid now, Niko, she thought. *Nothing could be worse than losing you.*

She would give up anything—her destiny as a Dimi, her power, even her life—if it meant she could hold him in her arms again.

"Eleven for the blood that has tasted the blade." She choked out the words, thinking of Elena's blade sinking deep into Niko's chest. "Twelve for the one who breaks yet is bold."

Well, she was breaking now.

Niko's shade had come to a halt right in front of her, close enough to touch. She lifted one shaking hand toward it, just as Elena roared, the Darkness swarming from her throat as it had in the clearing. It came for Katerina, and in its wake came Elena herself, encased in silver-blue flames and bent on vengeance.

"Change for me, my Shadow!" the Vila shrieked, so loudly that the rest of the window-glass shattered. "Fight for me in the form of your black dog. Defend me against *her,* who sought to use and corrupt you. Prove you belong to me."

Niko froze, and for a dreadful moment, Katerina was afraid he would do exactly that. His shade flickered once, then again. But then it solidified, and his jaw set, as if he held his human form through sheer force of will.

Above Elena's howls, Sammael yelled for her to stop, that he and Katerina had had a bargain. Lunging for the Vila and trying to drag her back, he shouted that breaking her word would do worse than curse her: It would send her spiraling into the Void once and for all. That this wasn't her; it was the Darkness acting through her. That they needed Katerina, that Elena needed to control herself.

None of it mattered. Elena kept coming, dragging Sammael across the floor with her. Now she and the Darkness that poured from her were only inches away.

Niko's shade turned, placing his back to Katerina. Shielding her. He spread his arms wide, a translucent defense against the demonic onslaught. It would never be enough.

Katerina commended both their souls to the Light. "Thirteen for the story that remains untold," she whispered, and took her Shadow's insubstantial hand.

Niko's image blurred, shimmered, trembled, *shifted*. And then he was in the form of his guardian dog, his body between Katerina and the Vila. His teeth bared, he pressed against Katerina, urging her backward, away from the threat. Light radiated from the shade of his dog, the tendrils of corruption within it barely visible.

She hadn't asked him for this. Certainly hadn't demanded it, as Elena had. But Niko had Changed for her, even though their bond had been severed by death. He had done this of his own volition, to keep her safe.

Even in death, he was still hers.

She had won.

The Light that shone from her Shadow had driven Elena back. The Darkness hovered around her in a buzzing cloud. In the midst of it, Sammael still held the Vila, who was sobbing with incredulity and fury. "No!" she wailed in between sobs. "Witchery. Trickery. He is mine!"

Sammael spoke before Katerina could say a word. "You made a bargain, Elena. An unfair one, some might argue. You had power and might on your side; the Dimi had naught but her own determination. The Shadow made his choice; now you must honor your word."

Elena hissed and spat, a mad thing. His expression grim, Sammael spoke to Katerina over her head, struggling to hold her still. "Leave now, Katerina Ivanova. Trust that your Shadow will follow you of his own free will. You will not look back nor will you use your magic on your Shadow, for if you do, the deal is null, and his soul is forfeit once more."

Katerina nodded, accepting the bargain—for what choice did she have? With one final glance at the thrashing, debauched creature who had once been Elena Lisova, she fled the cottage, leaving the Darkness and its captive behind.

58

KATERINA

The portal shimmered outside the cottage, as if waiting for her. Katerina yanked the door open and stepped into the dank tunnel, her pulse thundering in chest and wrists and throat. She heard nothing behind her, not the thud of a footfall or the rush of another's breath. But Niko was a Shadow. He had ever been silent when he chose, so that meant nothing. And who knew what form he'd taken to follow her toward the Light...if he was there at all.

Taking one step, then another, was the hardest thing she'd ever done. With each one, she feared she was leaving him behind forever. Demons were not to be trusted; it had been drilled into her since the cradle. And Elena might as well be a demon herself.

She had lost Niko once. She couldn't lose him again.

"*Lux*," Katerina murmured. Sammael hadn't said she couldn't use her magic in the tunnels, just that she couldn't use it to search for Niko or bind him to her. She kept her eyes fixed on the tiny patch of light that hovered above her palm, so she wouldn't be tempted to turn around.

If it had all been for nothing—betraying her village, parlaying with demons and Elena—she didn't know what she would do. Baba would never take her back. Even the Kniaz might not want her. She'd be an outcast, prowling the woods without a Shadow, prey for demons. Maybe this was what Sammael had had in mind, from the moment he hid the Book beneath the stones.

But why would Sammael set her up to be easy pickings for Gadreel? They were at war, after all. The last thing he wanted was for his archenemy to get hold of Katerina. Still, what did she know of demons' twisted ways? Perhaps Sammael and Gadreel were in league, and their rivalry was simply a front, in order to accomplish a larger, more nefarious goal.

The notion nagged at her as she placed one booted foot after another on the path that led upward, out of the Underworld. It was troublesome, but not nearly as troublesome as the hook snagged in her heart. With every step, she worried that she was alone. That Sammael and Elena sat in their cottage, laughing at her, Niko hovering at Elena's side, a helpless, hopeless Shadow.

Her hand rose to the amulet around her throat. It hung there, a shell of its former self, cold and empty. Nothing beat within.

Had she been tricked again? Used?

She wanted so desperately to turn around. To see for herself. But Sammael had told her that if she did, the magic that cemented their bargain would be forfeit. And little as she trusted him, she wasn't willing to gamble with Niko's existence. With anything else, yes. But not him.

Katerina plodded onward. The voices that had plagued her on her first trip through the tunnels were blessedly silent, and the stone flared cold in her pocket, guiding her. Finally, the end of the tunnel came into view. It slanted upward, thin beams of light filtering down through the trees, falling in a weak spray on the walls and the floor.

She quickened her pace. Beneath her boots, life flowed within the small roots that supplied the world above the surface. They fed her magic, strengthening her. The tunnel narrowed, and she should have been able to hear Niko's steps behind her, echoing off the walls and the ceiling, but there was nothing. Only the rasp of her own breath and the pad of her boots and the pull of the Light drawing her upward, the terrible sense of wrongness that had swept over her when she descended to the Underworld retreating one unwilling inch at a time.

It didn't want to let her go, and it had no claim on her, other than its grip on her Shadow. If it was so reluctant to release her, then why would it ever let go of the man she loved?

The ceiling dropped now, lower even than it had been when she'd entered. Katerina dropped to her knees and crawled, gasping as the walls closed around her. A root broke free, twining around her ankle, and she hacked at it, afraid to use her magic, lest the spell backfire and collapse the tunnel, crushing her and the ghost of her Shadow beneath its weight.

The root dug in, wrapping tighter. It felt like a snake, all scales and greedy coils. Above her, the ceiling pressed down and down. The walls inched closer, and the light at the end of the tunnel receded, growing smaller and smaller, a pinprick in darkness.

Katerina fought. She struggled. But the roots had her now, drawing her toward them, claiming her, holding her fast. Her power narrowed to a trickle, the voices of the Underworld—*Mine* and *Yes* and *Fool Dimi, weak witch, slave to the Light*—echoing ever-louder in her ears.

Something tore the knife from her hand, casting down the

length of the darkened tunnel, in the direction where Niko would be. Though surely he wasn't there at all; her Shadow would never have stood for Katerina being tortured like this. He would have snatched up her blade and made short work of the roots that had her in their grip, whirling through them the way he used to dispatch hordes of demons, a blur and a blaze.

Her knife clanked to the earth behind her, though she didn't dare try to peer through the dark to see where it had fallen. No one lifted it again in her service. There was only chilling laughter, filling the tunnels, echoing in her ears and her head. *We have you now, Katerina Ivanova, Dimi of Kalach. You are ours. Serve here, with your Shadow, in chains. Serve the glory of the Dark.*

She felt herself diminishing. Felt the Dark trying to bloom within her, though the Light struggled to force it back into the corners of her soul. The earth pressed in on her on all sides, and her chest heaved, her lungs struggling for breath.

It would be so easy to give in. Without Niko, what was the point?

But no. Even if Niko were gone from her forever, she had a duty to honor his memory. And he would be so ashamed of her if she gave up now. She would not be a Dimi worthy of her Shadow.

She would honor Niko Alekhin, even if he had passed forever beyond the veil. She would be the Dimi she had been born to be. She was no one's slave. And she would rather die than be a handmaiden of the Dark.

Light burst from Katerina, seeping through her skin the way it had from Niko's on the road to Drezna. She glowed, the intricate tracing of her blood vessels visible, a mockery of the roots that fought to hold her fast. A scream tore loose from her throat, filled with rage and strength and power.

Scorched by the Light, the roots recoiled. The earth itself retreated, driven back, inch by grudging inch. Katerina's lungs filled with stale but welcome air as she clawed her way forward, crawling as fast as she could, gravel scraping beneath her fingernails. The square of light at the surface widened and she leapt for it, leaving the howl of the tunnel's voices behind as she flung herself through and landed on the forest floor at last.

59

KATERINA

K aterina lay on the ground underneath the eye of the false Bone Moon, struggling to catch her breath. Every part of her ached. Her knees, from crawling. Her chest, from struggling to breathe. Her fingers, the nails torn and ragged. And her heart.

The last vestiges of hope stirred within her as she turned her head, praying with all her strength that she'd find Niko standing there. But the clearing was empty.

The place where she'd clawed her way out of the earth had sealed over, an innocuous seam at the foot of an oak. If it weren't for her shredded clothes and aching body, she would have almost thought she'd imagined it.

But she hadn't. And what if Niko was still in the tunnels, what if he was trapped—

A moan escaped Katerina's throat. On hands and knees, she crawled to the oak and dug frantically at the spot where the portal had been, but all she managed to do was slice her finger on a jagged rock. Any magic that had once lived here had long since gone.

In desperation, she plunged her bleeding hand into her

pocket, grasping at the stone Sammael had given her. It lay inert in her palm, a dead thing. She loosened her grip, and it tumbled to the ground, as useless as Katerina herself. Above, the cold eye of the moon shone down, judging her. Well, let it. She was judging herself far more harshly for believing the word of a demon who had already tricked her once before.

Katerina drew one deep breath, then another. The air pressed in on her, heavy with the scent of the roses whose vines still clung to the crumbled columns of the desecrated chapel. As much as it shattered her, she had to accept it: Niko had not followed her, after all.

A wail trembled in her throat, and she clapped a hand over her mouth, refusing to set it free. If she started screaming now, she might never stop.

She had wanted so badly to believe Sammael when he'd said the troubles that plagued Iriska, the encroaching Darkness, could be laid at Gadreel's feet—that the prophecy had naught to do with it, and she wasn't to blame. But she had been a fool twice over. Niko was still trapped, still shackled to Elena—and now that he'd chosen Katerina once again, the Vila's wrath would be terrible. How might she punish or torture him? Had Katerina only made things worse?

Katerina scrubbed at her watering eyes, struggling to hold back tears. She hadn't thought beyond this moment, hadn't allowed herself to believe that she might fail. What was she supposed to do now? Creep back to Kalach and let the Kniaz carry her off over his saddle like a bag of grain? Take her place at his side, lashed to a lesser Shadow, and pretend Niko wasn't suffering every second because of her failures and mistakes?

She wouldn't. She couldn't. There had to be another way.

Steadying herself against the trunk of the oak, Katerina managed to get to her feet. Slowly, she made her way over to the half-buried stones that were all that remained of the altar.

This might be a desecrated chapel, but it was still a chapel, the place where Sant Andrei, Sant Viktoriya, and Sant Antoniya had been blessed by the Light. She had to believe that some of the Saints' magic lingered here still. That if she spoke, something might hear her other than the Dark.

Katerina squared her shoulders and lifted her chin. "Sant Antoniya," she said, her voice thick with the tears she wouldn't allow herself to shed. "Patron saint of Dimis. Mother of us all. I come to you as a humble penitent, a servant of the Light. Forgive me the sin of loving my Shadow more than I cared for keeping the covenant. I beg you now to guide my hand. For I cannot abandon Niko. Nor can I turn my back on my vows."

She cupped her hands; within them, a small flame sprang to life. Eyes on the Bone Moon, she raised her hands high. "See my offering, Sant Antoniya. I honor you with my flame and the gifts in my blood. Hear me, I beg of you. For I have sinned, and fallen, and made terrible mistakes. But I swear on the vows I made to Kalach, on my word as a Dimi of Iriska, I'll never be a tool of the Dark. I beg of you, show me a way to thwart the prophecy. Show me a way to save my village and my Shadow. For I refuse to believe this is the end."

Dropping her eyes to the stones, she waited—for what, she wasn't sure. Perhaps a vision, like the one the Saints had had so long ago, or a miracle. Perhaps the voice of Sant Antoniya herself, telling Katerina she hadn't doomed them all. Giving her a way to make this right. But nothing came. The night was still, only the smallest of breezes stirring the trees.

She was truly alone.

Katerina let her hands fall, the flame they cupped winking out. Tears burned in her eyes. They overspilled, tracing hot lines down her cheeks, and she didn't bother to wipe them away. What would be the point? There was no one here to see.

"Niko," she said, though she knew he couldn't hear. "I'm so

EMILY COLIN

sorry. This is my fault, all of it. If I had tried harder—if I had made you believe me, when I told you Elena knew—" She shook her head, the memory of that conversation piercing her like a venom-soaked blade. It was the first time she'd told him she loved him, and she would never forget the look on his face—joy and wonder and fierce desire. *Burn away*, he'd commanded her. And she had. Now there was nothing left of him but ash and shadows.

A sob tore its way loose from Katerina's throat, followed by another. She knew she shouldn't stay here; alone, she was fair game for Gadreel. But Saints help her, she couldn't bear to walk away, knowing Elena still held Niko prisoner. How could she desert him?

She fell to her knees on the stones. It hurt; her knees were bruised already, from her fight to escape the tunnels. But Katerina didn't mind the pain. It was a small thing, a welcome distraction from the agony of her broken heart. "I failed you, my Shadow," she whispered into the night. "I tried to save you. I swear I did. But I...I failed."

The last word emerged in a shattered croak. Bowing her head, alone in the darkness except for the glare of the moon, Katerina gave herself to her grief, not caring who—or what—might hear. The sharp edges of the cobblestones dug into her knees as she wept, hollow, empty of everything. She had tried all she could, and still it was not enough. *She* was not enough.

She would never be whole again.

And then, behind her, a voice spoke. Low and familiar, achingly beloved.

"Don't cry, my Dimi," it said.

60

KATERINA

Katerina choked mid-sob. Slowly, disbelievingly, she turned.

Beneath the unforgiving light of the Bone Moon stood Niko. The moonlight shone full on his face, illuminating the scar that ran from chin to hairline and the streak of white in his hair. He wore unfamiliar clothes: a loose gray shirt that matched his eyes and black pants of a material Katerina had never seen before. And he was smiling.

Katerina stared at him, there on her knees. Here he was, the answer to her prayers. And yet she couldn't think of a single thing to say.

"Don't cry," he said again, taking a step toward her.

The way he moved—like a piece of the night that had detached itself from the whole—was so familiar, it hurt her heart all over again. But—

"Don't come any closer," she said, holding up a hand. Around them, the wind began to stir, bending the saplings. "How do I know this isn't a trick? A trap?"

Niko froze. When he spoke, his voice was gentle. "I'm not a demon, Katya. I'm not Gadreel. I'm yours."

Was it possible that Elena and Sammael had kept their promise? That Niko had followed her out of the tunnel somehow? Or was this just another lie? Because if it was, Katerina thought she might not survive it.

"How do I know?" she said, her voice quaking. "How do I know it's you?"

Niko gave her a sad, small smile. "Because you fought for me," he said. "Because you saved me. Because, Katya mine, you shatter me like ice and you scorch me like a flame and you never let me lie."

His hand went to his waist, and Katerina flinched. She sent her power down into the earth, preparing to crack the ground where he stood if need be. But when he lifted it again, he held her blade, the one that had been stolen from her in the tunnels.

"You lost something," he said.

Before Katerina could reply, he drew the blade across his forearm. A rust-rich scent, nothing like the icy, sweet aroma of Grigori blood, filled the air between them as the first drops fell onto the leaves at his feet. They seeped through the leaves and into the earth beneath, meeting her waiting magic.

Katerina felt the unmistakable impact of recognition in her bones an instant before a shockwave swept the clearing, the earth buckling and the trees bending low, as if in homage. The altar crumbled to dust with a thud, leaving the vines grasping at nothing. And around Katerina's neck, the amulet came alive, the blood within it pulsing to the beat of Niko's heart.

Her own heart leapt. Heedless of the destruction, she ran for him, the call of his blood and her magic urging her ever closer. She threw her arms around him, holding him close. He smelled of rust and sweat and *home*.

Niko grasped her tight, so tight she could scarcely breathe. He lowered his head into her hair. "Katerina." The words were a whisper against her skin. "You came for me."

She was laughing and crying all at once, tears cascading down her cheeks. "Of course I did. How could I not?"

He grasped her by the shoulders and held her away from him, peering into her eyes. "You shouldn't have done it. You could have been killed. Or worse, chained beside me. Do you know what torture it was, to watch as you confronted them and be unable to help? To protect you?"

She sniffed, swiping the back of her hand across her cheek. "You told me once we were stronger together. That we protected each other. I was just keeping my end of the bargain. Next time, it can be your turn."

Her eyes ran over him from head to toe, taking in the man she had thought she would never see again: storm-gray eyes, darker than usual with emotion; rumpled hair; mouth set in the stubborn line she loved. She wanted—*needed*—to see the proof that he still belonged to her. And to believe he was really here, alive and hers, at least for the months he had been promised to her.

"Take it off," she said, gesturing at his shirt. "Please."

Niko's mouth quirked, but he did as she asked. His deft fingers moved to the buttons, undoing them one by one. And then he shrugged the shirt off and let it fall.

Katerina's breath caught. He was as beautiful to her as he had always been. But he was different, too.

There, on his chest, was the evidence of the wound that had taken him from her, but it was healed now, only a silvered scar left behind. She remembered pressing desperately against it, trying to keep his lifeblood from soaking the elderflowers beneath them, as Elena shrieked and Gadreel laughed. It seemed impossible that such a wound could be reduced to a mere silver seam against the pale glow of his flesh in the moonlight. But yet it was.

Niko stood stock-still, letting her examine him. It was an

unnatural stillness, like the coiled strength of his black dog before he shifted and leapt into battle. He was waiting, she realized. But for what?

Her gaze skimmed over his chest, finding the Mark on his upper arm that branded him as hers. She was afraid it would be faded or destroyed altogether, but there it was—the blue-black interlocking circles, representing the blood and magic that bound him.

Her Shadow. Her promise, made and broken and kept again.

Niko followed her gaze, and when he spoke, his voice was hoarse. "I never left you, Katya. All the time they kept me captive, no matter what they did to me, I thought of you."

No matter what they did to me. How had he been tortured, abused? How had the demon and Elena debased him? The thought of it made her tremble with rage.

Once, Niko would have understood everything she was thinking before she'd spoken a word. But now, watching her shake, his shoulders hunched. His gaze dropped, as if he feared what he might see in her eyes. "Don't be afraid of me, Katya, please," he said, his voice breaking. "I would never hurt you."

Katerina wanted to tell him she knew that. That the very thought of it was absurd. But at the sight of her proud Shadow standing before her, unable to meet her eyes, words left her. Instead, she did the only thing she could: she stepped closer, so close she could feel the heat of his skin. *Alive,* she rejoiced. Alive, and hers.

"Look at me, Niko," she said.

Eyes on the ground, he shook his head.

"Please," she said again. It was a word she rarely used, much less twice in the span of five minutes, and Niko knew it. His head came up, and the desolation in his eyes almost destroyed her.

Slow as if she was moving through water, she lifted her hand, closing the space between them. And then she pressed her palm full against his brand.

Lightning forked through Katerina, electrifying every vein and sinew, as the bond between them snapped into place. She gasped, and Niko's head went back, a growl escaping his throat. He bucked against her, his Mark searing red-hot beneath her palm.

"One for the fire," she whispered, refusing to let go.

"Two for the storm," he whispered back, and then his mouth was on hers.

If their first kiss had been a blaze, this was an inferno. Niko's hands roved over her, desperate and grasping, her hair tangling in his fists. He nipped at her mouth, growling louder, and she nipped back, reveling in the taste of him: mint and night and Niko. Her fingers traced his brand again and again, and he shook beneath her touch. His face grew wet against hers, their tears mingling as their bond rejoiced, its severed edges sizzling with light as it knitted together.

With each thread that wove into place, she felt the echo of it deep within herself. A moan escaped her lips, and Niko echoed it, his body shifting restlessly as his mouth devoured hers. Power poured between them, from her to him and back again.

"Mine," she vowed against his lips, and a rough sob escaped him.

"Yours," he whispered. "Always."

The final threads of the bond wove themselves together, forged in fire. There was something different to it now, a dark thread woven amidst the rest, and that scared her. But it was here, it was whole. And for the first time in weeks, so was she.

She drew back from Niko, raising her face to his. She had never seen him cry, but now, his cheeks were wet with both of their tears. "My Shadow," she said, and felt the rightness of the words in heart and soul and body. "For I have not promised myself to another."

The line of his throat moved as he swallowed. "You still want me, then? You would honor me by letting me fight by your side?"

The question floored Katerina. She tugged him down to sit by her, on the ruined stones of the altar. "Where else would you be?"

In his eyes glimmered a devastation that mirrored her own. "I feared you wouldn't want me anymore. That you'd think me sullied, after...what she did to me."

A wave of fury crested within Katerina. She wanted to ask what, exactly, Elena had done. And then she wanted to go back to the Underworld and hurt Elena Lisova in exactly the same ways, and worse. But she couldn't bear to frame the question. If Niko wanted to tell her, he would.

Instead, she took his face in her hands, her fingers tangling in the silken waves at the nape of his neck. "Whatever happened to you when we were apart," she said, her voice fierce, "whatever she did to you...it was not your fault, Niko. Do you hear me? You died with honor, giving your life to save mine. You are a prince among Shadows."

He shook his head again, his gaze falling to the stones at his feet. "You say that, Katerina, but you don't know. She...she made me kneel to her. The things she made me say and do... how she made me..."

His voice trailed off, and Katerina could feel the self-hatred baking off of him. The shame. She couldn't stand it. "Look at me," she said again, filling her voice with the command she used to employ when they fought side by side.

Niko's gaze met hers, filled with defiance and regret...and

the brokenness that made her want to tear what remained of Elena from limb to limb.

"*You* look," he said. "And tell me you still want me now."

Katerina straightened her spine. "I *know* you, Niko Alekhin, Shadow of Kalach. You're the other half of my heart. The other half of my soul. Whatever she did to you, whatever she made you vow, however she sought to use you"—her voice cracked on the last two words—"you're still beautiful. You're still mine." She took his hands, squeezing them tight. "I descended to the Underworld and dealt with demons for you, and I would do so again. You are worthy of the Light."

Niko bit his lip, swollen from her kisses. "How can you be sure?" His eyes searched hers, fear warring with hope in his gaze.

"You can trust me." She leaned forward to kiss him, feather-light.

A tear traced a line down his face, following the uneven path of his scar. "I swore to fight for you. To have you see me like that—helpless, her slave—to put you in danger..."

"You didn't put me anywhere." Katerina's voice was fierce. "I went of my own free will. Think about it. Since when have you been able to make me do anything?"

Niko gave a rough laugh. It was bitter, but better than nothing. "That much is true, more's the pity. When you confronted Elena—when the windows exploded and I knew it was you standing outside, really you and not one of their damnable illusions..." He scrubbed a hand through his hair. "I never thought I would see you again. To see you standing there—it was like my dreams and my worst fears had materialized, all at once."

"I know what you mean," Katerina muttered.

Her Shadow's jaw set in a grim line. "To go down to the Underworld, knowing you couldn't count on your magic...to confront whatever Elena's become and the Venom of God in his own realm, all on the slim hope that you could rescue me..." He shook his head. "What if you'd failed, Katya? What if they'd killed you, right in front of me?"

Katerina didn't want to think about Niko suffering the same way she had when she'd watched him die in the clearing. She sniffed, holding back tears. "How did you know it was really me?" she said instead. "Just because Sammael said so?"

The tears that glossed her eyes blurred Niko's face. When she blinked to clear her vision, he was smiling at her again—a sad smile, but a smile nonetheless. "I didn't need Sammael to tell me anything," he said. "Bond or no, alive or no, I know you, Katya, just as you know me. I would know you anywhere. You're beautiful and stubborn and *mine*. And as soon as I saw you standing on that infernal street, witchfire licking at your ankles and one of my blades in your hand, I knew you'd come for me."

The tears broke free, streaking her cheeks. "I'll always come for you," she promised. "No matter when, no matter where. The bargain I struck—it's less than what I wanted, but it's *something,* Niko. I'll figure out a way to break her hold on you. I promise."

He wrapped his arms around her then, holding her tight. She held him back with all of her strength, keeping him with her, keeping him *safe,* as she had not been able to keep him then. "You're everything to me," she whispered against his shoulder. "No matter what happens to either of us, dead or alive, I will always belong to you. And you will always, always be mine."

"My Katya," he whispered back, and this time when they kissed, she felt all of him: grief, love, regret, rage, and desire, an intoxicating brew that made her want to lay him down on the chapel's shattered stones and prove to him they still belonged together. To stake her claim, once and for all.

Niko's hands were all over her, tracing her shape as if trying to memorize it, his lips hot on her neck, her collarbone, the hollow of her throat. As if reading her thoughts, he drew back shakily to focus on her face. His gray eyes were wide and dark, their pupils blown wide. Moonlight gleamed in their depths. "I want you," he said simply. "But not here."

"Not here," she agreed, sparing a rueful glance for the ruined altar. "And not now, either, alas. But when we have time —" The word caught in her throat, thinking of the six months he was doomed to spend below ground. How, half a year from now, she would be forced to lose him once more.

She willed herself not to dwell on it. After all, she'd worked a miracle once. Surely, with him by her side and the Darkness defeated, with the knowledge of the Magiya at their fingertips, she would be able to do it again.

Niko was staring at her, his gaze quizzical. She cleared her throat. "When we have time, my Shadow," she vowed, "I'll show you what you mean to me. And you'll know you're exactly where you belong. By my side, no matter what threatens to come between us."

He smiled at her then, a genuine, wicked grin laced with hard-won happiness. "I look forward to it," he said, tucking a wayward lock of hair behind her ear.

She reached for him, and he took both of her hands in his. They sat, facing each other, cheeks wet with tears yet unable to stop smiling, and Katerina wished she could stay here in this moment, with him, forever.

But then Niko tensed, his hands gripping hers. "Speaking of time, how long was I in the Underworld, Katya? Because Gadreel...he has a plan."

The moment was effectively shattered. "Must we speak of him and his machinations? I've only just gotten you back. Can't we have two minutes of peace?"

Her Shadow shook his head. "I wish we could. But we have to talk about this. To stop him, before it's too late."

Katerina heaved a resigned sigh. "I know his plan." She lifted her shoulder in a shrug. "He wishes to use me to power his realm and defeat Sammael once and for all. To become the ruler of the Underworld. That's one of the reasons Sammael struck our deal; with you by my side, he knows I'll be better able to fight. Well, that and the fact that he wants you gone. As much as a demon can, I think he loves Elena." Katerina shuddered. "He wants her for himself. You're a...what did he say? *An unfortunate inconvenience.*"

"Oh, he wants her, all right," Niko muttered. "But—"

She interrupted him, not wanting to hear more about the demon's lust for the woman who had betrayed them all so terribly. Who had condemned Katerina for loving Niko even as she fled into the arms of a damned creature, killing her Shadow and forging an alliance that had nearly destroyed Kalach.

"Gadreel hasn't caught me yet, even though I never took another Shadow. Baba wanted me to, but the Kniaz sent word he wanted to bond me to one of the unattached Shadows in Rivki. I hated the idea, but it bought me time." She offered Niko a tentative smile. "Kniaz Sergey is meant to arrive tonight, actually, with the Shadow in tow. I would have come to you earlier, but Sammael told me that if Elena agreed to let you go at all, the magic would only work if it took place on the night of the false Bone Moon—"

Niko had been listening to her with an expression of dawning horror. He yanked his hands free and leapt to his feet. "Katerina, are you saying the Kniaz is coming to Kalach now? Tonight?"

"Well, yes," she said, "which is why we should leave this horrible place. I don't know if we can make it all the way to the

Magiya, given the unrest, but once, you agreed to run with me, so..."

He shook his head. "No, Katerina, you don't understand. All this time, Gadreel's had Kniaz Sergey chained in the dungeon of his estate. It's a trick, don't you see? He knew the Kniaz would want you to join the Druzhina, even without me. He's been holding the man captive."

Katerina stared at him, bewildered. "No, I...that can't be. Andrei came to Kalach a few days ago, to tell us Kniaz Sergey would be arriving tonight. Why would he say such a thing, if the Kniaz had been imprisoned? And how could Gadreel breach Rivki? How could he cross the moat, much less get past the Druzhina and the Vodyanoy?"

Niko paced the stones of the altar, running his hands through his hair. "The wards are badly weakened. That night in the clearing, when I...when Elena..." His throat worked. "When you banished us to the Underworld, Gadreel told me that he... marked the Kniaz somehow. He can control him, like a puppet. Kniaz Sergey speaks, but it's the demon's words he utters."

A shiver ran through Katerina's body. "Are you saying that the Kniaz is...is ..."

"He's controlled by Gadreel." Niko snatched his shirt from the ground, buttoning it with hasty fingers. "If Kniaz Sergey is coming to Kalach, then Gadreel will be nearby to make sure the nobleman does his bidding. You saw how Sammael breached the wards without the Shadows smelling him. Now that Gadreel knows it's possible, I'm sure he'll do the same. If he arrives at the village to find you gone..."

"He'll do his best to raze it to the ground." Katerina stood, panic making her heart race. "He should be there any minute, if he isn't already. They...they were making preparations when I left. It's how I was able to get away." She wrapped her arms around herself, glancing upward. "The moon has fully risen. If he was biding his time, waiting to attack..."

"He and his minions will be at their strongest now, with the veil between the worlds at its thinnest." Niko shook his head. "No wonder he chose tonight to arrive."

Terror choked Katerina's voice. "He's the one who killed my mother, Niko. I remember that now. And I—I abandoned Kalach to his wrath—"

"Not yet. We would know if he'd arrived, Katya. His anger will be something terrible."

Katerina shuddered at the thought. "Maybe we can get there before he does. To stop this. But Niko...if we don't..." She swallowed hard. "If he takes me, it won't only be Kalach that falls. Perhaps I'll be able to drive back the Darkness, with your aid. But after that, if he gets his hands on my powers...the world will burn."

Niko's gaze was steady. "We can't think about that," he said. "Katya, we can't desert them."

As terrified as she felt, Katerina knew he was right. Better for Baba and the Elders to rage at her, to condemn her for dealing with a demon and bringing Niko back, than to be responsible for the deaths of everyone in the village. Not if she could save them. "Let's go," she said.

Niko gave a short, sharp nod. And then they were running, shoving through the bushes that led away from the clearing and Niko's now-empty grave, sprinting down the tree-lined path that led back to Kalach. Katerina prayed desperately that they would be in time. That they wouldn't arrive to see their friends slaughtered or the village decimated by the Darkness. That she wouldn't have to look at Ana's bloodied face—Ana who had risked everything for her...

They were a quarter-mile from the village when a roar split the air: the embodiment of pure rage, bending the trees in its wake. Above the treetops, orange-red flames bloomed. Katerina prayed these were the rowan-fires, somehow stoked to a fever blaze. But then her lungs filled with the cloying, unmistakable scent of human flesh aflame. Even this far away, shrieks filled the air, borne toward them on the wind.

"No," she whispered. "*No!*"

"Katerina," Niko growled, and in that single word she heard the doom of everything she had ever loved and valued—except the man who stood beside her. The man for whom she'd been willing to sacrifice everything.

She had saved Niko, but at what cost? Gadreel was killing the villagers, because Katerina had left them. He had barreled through the Shadows and Dimis of Kalach, because Katerina had weakened them. This—everything that was happening—was her fault.

She was too late.

Eyes wide with horror, she watched the smoke drift over the treetops, toward the path where she and Niko stood. They had two choices now: run and pray to the Saints Gadreel didn't find them. Or charge into the village, and risk everything she'd fought to prevent.

A demon, with her power at his disposal. Her Shadow, dragged down again into the Dark.

"I don't know what to do," she said desperately, her gaze searching the horizon. "Saints, tell me what to do!"

"Listen to me, Katya." Niko took hold of her, his grip tight on her upper arms. "Remember the prophecy."

Her eyes found his. "How could I forget? He's killing them because of me, Niko. He's burning Kalach—"

"No. *The Dark will fall,*" he said, his gray eyes intent on her face. "*The Shadow will rise.* I've risen. I'll fight with you. That's our destiny: to go back, to stand against him. Not to run."

All this time, they'd thought the prophecy meant a shadow

would rise from the Darkness and devour Kalach. But instead it had meant her Shadow would rise from the dead.

What had Sammael said, when she'd summoned him into her circle? *You humans and your foolish prophecies.* He had always known that the prophecy was, as Niko had once called it, nothing but words in a dusty book. The Saints had been oral storytellers; they'd dictated the prophecies to their scribes. And from that simple error—the lowercase 's' in Shadow—had come a belief system that had governed generations.

For this, they had stoned Katerina and buried Niko in unconsecrated ground. For this, Dimi Zakharova had threatened to ruin her.

All for a misunderstanding and a misinterpretation. And now, it might be too late.

She refused to believe that. *The Dark will fall. The Shadow will rise.* Well, her Shadow was here, beside her once again. That part of the prophecy had been fulfilled. Now it lay to the two of them to defeat Gadreel, and all he stood for. To save Ana, and whoever else they could.

"We'll fight him, then," Katerina said, squaring her shoulders. "Together. It's as you always said...if we die, we die together."

"We won't die," Niko said. "I'm not sure I can. And I have no intention of letting him take you, alive or otherwise."

He bared his teeth, and a growl reverberated up from his chest. The air around him vibrated and flickered, shot through with Light. When it cleared, the man was gone and a black dog stood in his place, strong and solid.

Katerina placed her hand on his back, his fur rough and warm against her palm. Inside her mind, he spoke. *To the fight then, Dimi mine.*

"To the fight," Katerina echoed. Her magic rose, coming easily to her call, the way it hadn't since she'd lost him. I bubbled like lava inside the volcanoes far to the south, hungry to burst forth, eager to be used.

Together, she and Niko would destroy Gadreel and save their village. Together, they would put things right.

Katerina raced toward the tumult of Kalach under the unforgiving light of the Bone Moon, her magic cresting within her and her Shadow once more by her side.

PLEASE KEEP IN TOUCH!

Thank you so much for reading Katerina and Niko's story! They are truly the characters of my heart, and I hope you love them as much as I do.

Fate and Fury is book one in The Bone Moon duology. The second book, *Revenge and Ruin,* will be coming in fall 2025.

Want to be the first to know about new releases, in-person appearances, bonus stories, and more? Subscribe to my newsetter at emilycolinnews.com and join my Facebook group, The Shelf-Care Queens.

I would love for you to keep in touch!

Also by Emily Colin

FICTION

The Bone Moon Duology
    Fate and Fury: Book One
    Revenge and Ruin: Book Two (Coming Fall 2025)

The Seven Sins Series
    (Suggested Reading Order)

Sword of the Seven Sins: Book One
Sacrifice of the Seven Sins: A Novella
Siege of the Seven Sins: Book Two
Shadows of the Seven Sins: A Story Collection
Storm of the Seven Sins: Book Three

The Memory Thief
The Dream Keeper's Daughter

Unbound: Stories of Transformation, Love, and Monsters

NONFICTION

The Long Way Around: How 34 Women Found the Lives they Love
The Secret to Our Success: How 33 Women Made their Dreams Come True
The Changing Face of Justice: A Look at the First 100 Women Attorneys in North Carolina

GLOSSARY AND PRONUNCIATION GUIDE

Amulet: The silver locket that hangs around each bonded Dimi's neck, holding a drop of their Shadow's blood. Bestowed by the village's Baba during the Dimi/Shadow bonding ceremony, this is the complement to the Shadow's ink-and-blood Mark.

Antivenin: The agent that counteracts a Grigori demon's venom, enabling Shadows that suffer a blade wound or bite while in human form to heal. Without antivenin, the bite of a Grigori demon or a wound made with a blade soaked in Grigori venom is fatal to a Shadow.

Apprentices, Baba's: Non-magical girls that train with a village Baba, learning the art of healing and assisting with ceremonies such as betrothals and marriages.

Azazel (uh-ZAH-zel): The demon Gadreel's second-in-command.

Baba: An elder, powerful Dimi, leader of all the Dimis within her village. The position is appointed by the village's Elder Council and is for life. Babas are responsible for making romantic matches between Shadows and Vila; Dimis choose their own mates.

Black Dog: The animal form of a Shadow, black dogs are guardians of their villages and of Iriska. Shadows can shift into the form of their black dogs at will, and their bite is fatal to Grigori. If stabbed by a Grigori's blade while in the form of their black dog, Shadows can heal (though a vial of antivenin wouldn't come amiss!).

Blood Moon: A red-tinged moon that comes once a year in early spring, one month after the full Bone Moon.

Bobrov *(BAHB-ruv)*: One of the Seven Villages, located near the Brebenskul Mountains, which border the eastern edge of Iriska. Their primary export is buckthorn oil, for cooking, tea, jam, and healing.

Binding Ceremony, The: An ancient ceremony, conducted only by the Babas of each village, to bind a Dimi's power. Used only in the event of emergency or dire need.

Blessed blades: The silver weapons that Shadows employ when battling demons, forged by village blacksmiths and possessing rune-engraved, onyx hilts. Blessed by each village's Baba and consecrated to Sant Andrei, the patron saint of Shadows.

Blini *(BLEE-nee)*: Thin pancakes made from wheat, often topped with sour cream.

Bonding Vow, The: Lifetime blood vow made between a Shadow and Dimi, always held during a full Bone Moon in the Dimi's thirteenth year. Beginning "One for the fire, two for the storm," the vow's full text appears in the front matter of this book.

Bone Moon: Occurring once annually, the full Bone Moon is the time when the veil between the living and the dead grows thinnest, as well as the time that demonic activity is at its peak and Iriska is under the greatest threat of attack. It is also a sacred time for Iriska, when many important ceremonies are performed.

Bone Trials, The: Held every other year in Iriska's capital, Rivki Island, The Bone Trials is a competition between the Seven Villages' most powerful Shadow/Dimi pairings. Following a rigorous training period, two victorious pairs compete against each other twelve months after the Trials for the opportunity to join the elite Druzhina Guard (see *Reaping, The*).

Occasionally, the Kniaz chooses a third pair of Shadow/Dimi victors at the Trials. If they perform well at the following year's competition, they will be Reaped to take the place of an existing Druzhina pairing (rather than simply augmenting the Guard's existing ranks). This is the Kniaz's way of keeping his Guard from becoming complacent and resting on their laurels.

Book of the Light, The: Iriska's sacred text, dictated to scribes by the Saints.

Book of the Lost, The: A legendary text, considered the complement of the Book of the Light and believed to have been transcribed by the Saints themselves. As its name suggests, this tome has been lost to the sands of time—if it ever existed at all.

Borscht *(borsht)*: A beetroot soup, often made with cabbage, vinegar, and some type of meat.

Change, The: The shapeshifting process during which a Shadow shifts from human form to the form of his black dog and/or back again.

Cherkasy *(CHUR-kasy)* **Forest:** The forest that lies between Rivki Island and Drezna.

Dark, The: The opposite of the Light to which Dimis, Shadows, and Vila are consecrated, the Dark represents evil, demonic intent. Just as Dimis are sworn to the Light, Grigori serve the Dark.

Darkness, The: The force that fuels the Void and gave rise to the Underworld. Ever-hungry, it thrives on the consumption of souls—nonmagical human, Dimi, Shadow, and Vila alike. A shard of it lives within each Grigori, and is the source of both their power and demonic intent.

Dimi: A woman who possesses the ability to command one (or more) of the four elements. Consecrated to the Light, Dimis battle Grigori demons alongside their bonded Shadows and are descended from Sant Antoniya. They may choose who they marry; the Dimi gift is passed on through the matrilineal line.

Drezna *(DRIZ-na)*: One of the Seven Villages, located southwest of Rivki. Bordered to the north and west by Cherkasy

Forest and to the east by Krasa Lake. Their primary export is potatoes.

Druzhina *(druh-ZEE-na)* Guard: The elite warrior guard that protects Rivki Island, made up of the most powerful Shadow/Dimi pairings in Iriska.

Elder Council, The: The five-person council that governs each of the Seven Villages, alongside that village's Baba. Elders are chosen by the existing members of the Council for their wisdom, political savvy, and ability to keep the peace.

Firebird: A nighttime constellation. Also, a mythical bird with bright, fiery plumage, usually the object of a heroic quest.

Gadreel *(gah-dree-EL)*: A fallen Archangel turned Grigori demon (see also: *Watcher*), Gadreel is one of the two primary rulers of the demon realms (see *Underworld*). Once the Helper of God, Gadreel is the Dark Angel of War who, according to legend, instructed humanity in the art of weaponry.

In constant battle with the demon Sammael for dominance of the Underworld, Gadreel is also known as Scourge of the Demon Realms, Wall of God, and Silent Sentinel. He adores a good party and a well-cut suit.

Guelder roses *(GEL-der, with a hard 'g')*: Also known as *kalyna,* guelder roses symbolize beauty, love, and passion. They are white, with red berries.

Grigori: Fallen angels, now demons, who inhabit the Underworld and feed on human souls. They enter the protected, aboveground realm of Iriska through portals, with the goal of devouring as many souls as possible and breaking through Iriska's wards to the world beyond. Grigori are also known as Watchers, due to their tendency to observe humanity while plotting the best form of attack. They cannot cross water; hence, the moat around Rivki Island, seeded with Vodyanoy spirits for extra protection.

Iriska *(ih-REESK-ah)*: Made up of Seven Villages as well as its capital, Rivki Island, Iriska is a warded realm that protects the rest of humanity from demonic onslaught. Those who live beyond Iriska's wards are unaware that it exists. Should Iriska fall, the Grigori will penetrate and pillage the world beyond its wards, devouring human souls until naught remains.

Kalach *(kal-ACH)*: One of the Seven Villages, located in the heart of Iriska, southeast of the village of Drezna. Notable for being the place that Iriska's three Saints, from whom all Shadows, Dimis, and Vila are descended, first prayed to the Light for aid—and received it. Their primary export is wheat.

Kalchek *(kal-CHEK)*: Silver coins that Kalach's children toss into the village square's fountain on Wishing Day, praying that the Saints will grant their deepest desires.

Kikimora *(KEEki-mora)*: A feminine house spirit that hails either from the forest or the swamp. Kikimora who hail from the forest are more often helpful and kind, whereas those who hail from the swamp tend to be malevolent, kidnapping the innocent and sneaking into houses to cause trouble.

Kikimora have very strong opinions about how a house must be maintained, and even a kindly one will show her displeasure if she doesn't care for your housekeeping skills. Note: Once a kikimora claims your house as her own, it is very difficult to convince her to depart.

Rivki Island *(RIV-ki)*: The capital of Iriska, protected by Vodyanoy water spirits as well as the Druzhina Guard. This is where the Kniaz, Iriska's ruler, resides, as well as where the Bone Trials are held. Considered to be the wealthiest and safest place in Iriska, Rivki is more sophisticated than the outlying villages.

Klyuchi rune *(klee-OOCH-ee)*: Runes contained in the Book of the Lost, designated for powerful, potentially dangerous spells.

Kniaz, The Velikii *(KNEE-iz; VEL-iki)*: The ruler of the realm of Iriska and commander of the Druzhina Guard. Passed down from father to son, each Kniaz is believed to have inherited his power through divine right, anointed by the Saints.

Kohannya *(ko-HAN-ya)*: An annual ceremony held in all Seven Villages. Unmarried Vila set handcrafted paper boats afloat in a body of water, and unmarried Shadows stand downstream to collect the boats of the Vila they fancy. Considered a rite of courtship, the kohannya ceremony is an opportunity for Shadows and Vila to declare their romantic interest in each other, which the village's Baba will take into account when arranging marriages.

Khorovodnitsa *(core-ROW-vahd-knit-sah)*: Female leader of a ritual form of circular dance symbolizing movement around the sun. Often accompanied by choral singing.

Kvass *(kih-VASS)*: A fermented alcoholic drink, made from grain and often flavored with fruit or honey.

Light, The: A formidable force to which Dimis, Shadows, and

Vila are consecrated, and in whose name they battle Grigori demons. The counter-force to the Dark.

Liski *(LIZ-ski)*: One of the Seven Villages, located in the west of Iriska, bordered to the west by the Trolitza River, which also borders Kalach. Their primary export is firewood, especially rowan trees, which are a powerful protective resource against Grigori.

Magiya *(MAHG-ya)* **Library, The:** Iriska's largest repository of magical knowledge. Located in the northeast corner of Iriska, bordered on the east, south, and north by the Brebeneskul Mountains and surrounded by the Volshetska Fortress.

Members of the Druzhina ousted at the Reaping are sent to join the Guard contingent at Volshetska's outpost. This is considered a punishment, as Volshetska and the Magiya are extremely isolated. The scribes living at the Magiya often go years without seeing another living soul, and have dedicated their lives to scholarship.

Mark: Given by a village Baba at the bonding ceremony between a Shadow and Dimi, the Mark is a tattoo made from ink infused with the Dimi's blood. Resembling three interlocking black circles, it is inked on a Shadow's left bicep, and is a sacred bond between Shadow and Dimi. Only a Dimi can touch her Shadow's Mark, and even then, only in the case of emergency, to magnify their bond through the proximity of shared blood.

After a Shadow and Dimi have bonded, a second Mark of varying, individualized nature appears somewhere on the Shadow's body, indicating that he is sworn to a Dimi. In Niko's case, this is a streak of white in his hair.

Portals: Places where Grigori demons can enter Iriska from the Underworld. They are typically static in location (hence, the placement of the Seven Villages throughout Iriska), though weakening of the wards and the rise of the Bone Moon can cause new portals to appear without warning.

Povorino *(pah-VOR-ih-nah)***:** The most southeastern of the Seven Villages, bordered to the east by lava fields and active volcanoes, and to the southwest by the Strashno Mountains. Their primary export is red stones forged in the lava fields, highly resistant to the elements and prized for their unique, beautiful appearance.

Homes crafted from Povorino-forged stones are considered the height of wealth, sophistication, and protection, and primarily exist in Rivki, as the Kniaz demands the export of most of Povorino's production.

Preteska *(preh-TES-ka)***:** Yellow flowers that bloom in early spring, native to Drezna.

Prophecy, The: Drilled into every resident of Iriska from the cradle, the most famous prophecy in the Book of the Light dictates that if a Shadow and Dimi become romantically involved, they will bring a terrible Darkness upon the land, and Iriska will fall.

Reaping, The: Conducted a year after the Bone Trials, when the Shadow/Dimi pairings that were victorious at the Trials compete to join the Druzhina, this ceremony marks the Reaping of Shadows and Dimis from their villages.

A Reaped Shadow/Dimi pairing will reside in Rivki permanently, as a member of the Druzhina Guard (pending incapacity or banishment to Volshetska).

Rhomb *(rahm)*: Diamond-shaped symbol indicative of fertility, often embroidered on Vila's wedding dresses.

Rozhanytsi *(rose-ah-NEET-zi)*: Spirits of fate and goddesses of fertility, often embroidered on Shadows' and Vila's wedding finery in the shape of hearts.

Rowan-fire: Rowan fires repel Grigori, who are allergic to their smoke and will die if stabbed through the heart with a stake of rowan-wood (or a blessed blade, which is far less likely to give one splinters).

Saints, The: These are the three saints from whom Shadows, Dimis, and Vila are descended: Sant Andrei, Sant Antoniya, and Sant Viktoriya.

When the Grigori first fell from grace, the demons swarmed aboveground, devouring human souls with abandon. Terrified, Andrei, Antoniya, and Viktoriya fled across the realm until they could run no more. They ceased their flight in Kalach and prayed to the Light for aid. And the Light answered, transforming them into the first Shadows, Dimis, and Vila. Thus, the realm of Iriska and its Seven Villages was formed as a bulwark against the Darkness.

Sammael *(sam-AYE-el)*: A Fallen Archangel and powerful Grigori, also known as the Venom of God, Sammael is in constant competition with Gadreel for dominion and control of the Underworld. He has a weakness for fragile women, though his first love, Lilith, was arguably anything but. Also, he possesses a disproportionate love of paperwork and rule following (at least, if you ask Gadreel. Sammael would tell you he's just being practical, and Gadreel is an impulsive fool).

Samovar *(SAM-ovar)*: An urn or vessel used to boil water, typically for tea.

Sant Andrei *(ahn-DRAY)*: The patron saint of Shadows; all Shadows are descended from him.

Sant Antoniya *(anne-TONE-ia)*: The patron saint of Dimis; all Dimis are descended from her.

Sant Viktoriya *(Vik-TOHR-ia)*: The patron saint of Vila; all Vila are descended from her.

Satvala-by-the-Sea *(SAHT-vala)*: The most southwestern of the Seven Villages, bordered to the west and south by the Vohdanya Sea (the natural habitat of the Vodyanoy, some of whom have been relocated to the moat that surrounds Rivki). Satvala's primary export is sea salt.

Seven Villages: Located strategically near known portals to the Underworld, the Seven Villages are scattered throughout the realm of Iriska, but all must tithe to the Kniaz on a monthly basis. All are also expected to provide a Shadow/Dimi pairing to compete in the biennial Bone Trials. In return, the Kniaz supposedly offers the superior protection of Rivki and its Druzhina.

In reality, due to Rivki's geography, should a true threat arise, the more remote villages are on their own. Since the Kniaz is believed to hold his position by divine right, this impractical (and, some might say, unfair) arrangement has been allowed to stand.

Shadow: Sworn to protect their village and Iriska, and consecrated to the Light, Shadows are highly skilled warriors that can shapeshift into the form of a black dog. In the form of their guardian dog, their bite is fatal to a Grigori; but when a Shadow is in human form, a Grigori's venom is fatal to them. Unless their romantic preference is for men, Shadows are expected to marry Vila in order to continue the Vila and Shadow lines. They are bonded to Dimis for life via a blood vow, and fight the Grigori in tandem with them, protecting their Dimis from demonic possession and lending their blades to the Dimis' command of the elements.

Shadow Path: The path between Iriska and the Underworld, accessible via portals. This is the path most Grigori travel to walk aboveground and return to the Underworld once more. It is not typically accessible to humans, magical or otherwise.

Syrnyky *(SIR-na-kee)***:** Small cheese pancakes, often served with sour cream or jam.

Tithe: The monthly offering that each of the Seven Villages must make to the Kniaz at Rivki Island. Each village's tithe depends on their primary export.

Treshchotka *(TREE-shoat-ka)***:** A percussion instrument crafted from small boards that are strung together, designed to imitate the sound of clapping hands.

Underworld: The demonic realms that the Grigori occupy, separated by the wastelands between the realms and powered by devoured human souls (the spillover of which is used to feed the Darkness and fuel the Void). Both Gadreel and Sammael operate substantial realms here, while other, minor Grigori have insignificant holdings.

Iriska is accessible from the Underworld via portals. These

are most effective during the full Bone Moon, when the veil between the worlds grows thinnest and new portals can spring into existence (only to dissolve when the Moon wanes once more).

Vareniki *(vah-reh-NYE-ki)*: Fried, half-moon dumplings stuffed with potato, cheese, or other delicious fillings. Frequently served with sour cream, fried onions, and a dollop of butter, these are Katerina's favorite food.

Vila *(VEE-luh)*: Descended from Sant Viktoriya, Vila are the only ones who can give birth to Shadows and Vilas. Considered nurturers rather than warriors, they work as childminders for young Vila, Shadows, and Dimis.

Unless their romantic preference is for women, Vila are expected to marry Shadows and continue the Shadow/Vila line. They have a close sisterhood forged around their shared purpose, and most view it as a holy calling. Vila have no active magical powers of their own; their gift is a latent one, passed on genetically through their bloodline.

Village Elder: See *Elder Council.*

Vodyanoy *(VAHD-ya-noy)*: Vicious water spirits, native to the Vohdanya Sea that borders Iriska to the southwest.

By seeding the moat around Rivki with Vodyanoy, the Kniaz's intent is to provide a dual layer of protection from demonic attack (since Grigori can't cross water). Young residents of Rivki often dare each other to leap off the bridge that spans the moat and swim to shore before a Vodyanoy finds (and eats) them.

Void, The: The shapeless, lightless space from which new demons originate and into which demons go when slaughtered. Also known as The Darkness That Eats All Things, but this is a bit of a misnomer; the Darkness lives within the Void, and fuels it through the consumption of souls—the spillover of which powers the Underworld, only to be recycled and used to fuel the Void once more.

As the Darkness doesn't get out much—before a certain demon's Big Mistake, that is—the two are often used synonymously. To be clear, though: the Darkness is a force and entity. The Void is a place: the Darkness' rightful home, other than the shard of it that lives within each of the Grigori.

Volshetska *(vohl-SHET-ska)*: The fortress that protects the Magiya Library, guarded by select members of the Druzhina Guard. Assignment to Volshetska is considered a punishment for most.

Voronezh *(vah-ROAN-esh)*: One of Iriska's Seven Villages, bordered to the south by the Strashno Mountains. Their primary export is corn.

Vynohrad *(VI-nuh-rahd)*: A pattern of vines and fruit, often embroidered on a Vila's wedding gown, signifying domestic happiness.

Watcher: See *Grigori*.

ACKNOWLEDGMENTS

I first began working on *Fate and Fury* in 2018, and back then, the book looked very different indeed. For one thing, it had two timelines—past and present-day, where I'd set up a parallel storyline featuring Niko and Katerina's descendants. For another, it started in a very different place: the scene where Katerina fled through the apple orchard. And for a third, the story as a whole bore only a passing resemblance to its current form. There were no Trials, the demons went by another name, Ana didn't exist...I could go on. The one element that's always remained the same is the heart of the story—Niko and Katerina's love for each other—but beyond that, it's gone through some major metamorphoses!

Without the input of my incredible critique partners, this book might never have seen the light of day. I owe a massive debt of thanks to Lisa "The Plot Fairy" Amowitz, Ángela "The Book Bruja" Álvarez Vélez, Christy "The Story Jedi" Swift, and Sarah Anderson Vivien, an honest-to-Saints astrophysicist, author, and designer who brought her genius to bear on these pages. Without Lisa's dramatic interpretation of Broadway ballads (a certain cup of poison comes to mind), Ángela's willingness to delve so deeply into F&F's world that it's a wonder she emerged unscathed (or did she?), and Christy's patience as she read one revised beginning after another (and another), you'd be holding a very different book in your hands. Many thanks, too, to Marie "The Serial Darling Killer" LeStrange, for your brilliance and boundless creativity, and to Madeline Dyer for offering feedback on *Fate and Fury*'s pages! And to Michelle Hazen, who read an early version of this book and whose suggestions proved invaluable.

A thousand-and-one thanks go out to The Furious Fates, my kickass street team, especially Sandy Wheeldon Auld, Jen Barnes, Audrey "Needs Her Own Shadow" Costruba, Belinda Clemons , Amanda "Gadreel's My Shadow Daddy" Curry, Dani D.P., Tiffany Ewald, Aspen "Would Totally Jump Niko's Bones" Kelchen, Heather Flores, Kara "Goddess of Hype" French, Melanie "I'm With Ana" Guarente, Thea Hamilton, Ashlyn Kennedy (who makes a mean paper flower), Nancy Mendoza Smith, Momma T's Books, Kimberly Morgan, Jessica Landberg, Shelby Latter, Gabby Sadoine, Kasey "Hot for the Villains" Seal, Liliana Silva, Macey Tissot, and Savannah Thornton. I'm also bend-the-knee grateful to The Shelf-Care Queens, who make our little corner of the Internet the coziest bookish place to be.

Extra-special thanks go to Kara French, Amanda Curry, and Nancy Mendoza Smith. Kara burst into my world with the launch of *Storm of the Seven Sins,* and immediately made it a better place to be. She is the Maker of Reels, the Planner of Discords, and the All-Around Goddess of Hype. Everyone needs a Kara in their corner! Amanda is the all-around empress of the Shelf Queens, creating awesome graphics, entertaining my bizarre notions, and coming up with the best ideas to engage readers. I would be lost without her! And Nancy Mendoza Smith—street team guru, Discord organizer, planner of paper flower-making adventures, mistress of the ILM Silent Book Club, and all-around Spreader of the Fate and Fury Word—is a powerhouse beyond compare. These three fabulous folks make all the difference!

And to my readers, of course. Without you, there would be no audience for my stories. I am, as always, absurdly grateful.

About the Author

Emily Colin wrote her first romance novel in the fourth grade and never looked back. Today, she is the New York Times and USA Today bestselling author of books with kissing, ghosts, magic, swordplay, and lots of snark. If it's got romance in it, she writes it! When she doesn't have her nose in a book, you can find her making comfort food, chasing her badly behaved puppy, or drinking mochas by the sea.

For more books and updates
www.emilycolin.com

instagram.com/emilycolinbooks
facebook.com/emilycolinbooks
tiktok.com/emilycolinbooks

Printed in Great Britain
by Amazon

55022587R00283